THE IMMORTAL

A Novel of the Breedline Series

by SHANA CONGROVE

Novels of the Breedline Series by Shana Congrove

Sweet Chaos

Total Chaos

Unleashed Chaos

Sins of Chaos

THE IMMORTAL

THE CURSE... *coming next!*

Available wherever books are sold online

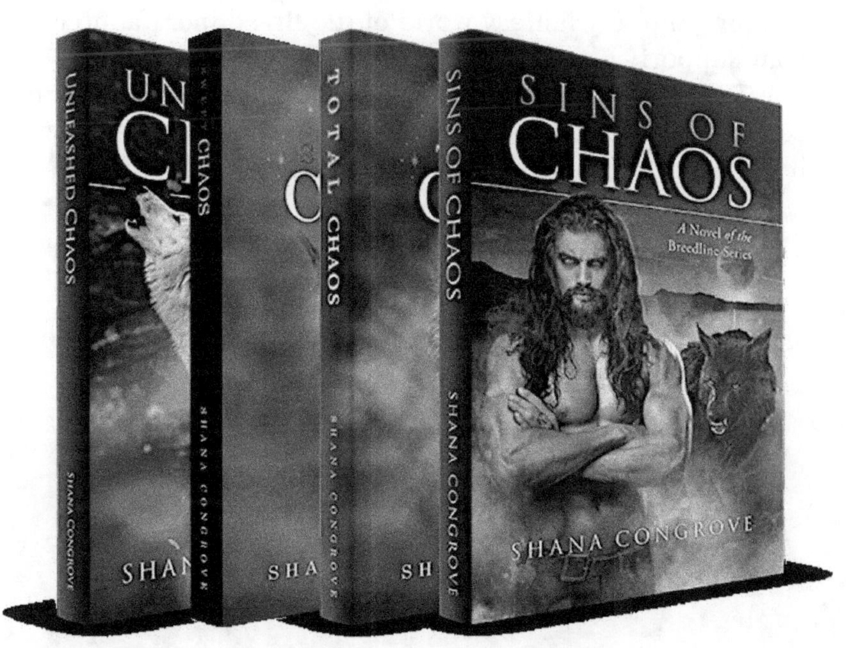

Author's Acknowledgments

In memory of my beloved Baby. Saying goodbye is hard to do. My heart feels lost without you, my sweet darling. You gave me a purpose, a healing comfort, and unconditional love. Rest in peace with your Sissy.

With love, Mommy, XOXO

Dedicated to all my talented friends on FanStory.com, my dear friends Angie Hawkridge Moore and Neal Owens, author of *Mirrors of Life*. Without your helpful advice and continuing support, none of this would exist. Good friends are hard to find. Thank you for being mine.

As always, immense gratitude to God's loving grace. Thank you for giving me guidance and courage with everything I do.

To all the readers, family and friends: Thank you for stepping into my fantasy world of the Breedline. I appreciate your support!

To the new little addition to my family: You brought me companionship and unconditional love when I least expected it but needed it the most. I love you, Chocco boy!

The Legend of the Breedline

Imagine all the myths, legends, and folktales that both captivated and terrified you as a child—*the monsters under your bed, the boogeyman in the closet, werewolves, vampires, witches, demons, ghosts, and so on*—really existed.

The story I'm about to tell you goes beyond unbelievable. This is the legend of the Breedline.

The story goes that a secret species of humans born with an identical twin had the power to shift into wolves. Some say it is an old tall tale, ancient lore derived from Native American legends, known mainly as stories of shapeshifting creatures.

For the Navajo and other tribes of the Southwest, each has their own version of supernatural creatures called skin-walkers, but each boils down to the same thing: a majestic being capable of transforming itself into a wolf, coyote, bear, bird, or any other animal. When the transformation is complete, the human inherits the speed, strength, and cunning of the animal whose shape it has taken.

So the question remains...

Do supernatural beings really exist among our mundane, humdrum existence?

The thing about myths, legends, and folktales is sometimes they're true.

How do I know, you ask? Because... I'm their queen, and this is our story.

Chapter One

Salem Cemetery, located in San Francisco, California

As Jena, Todd, and Sophie made their way through a small opening of the cemetery's wrought-iron gate, they hadn't expected it to look so eerie at this hour of the morning.

A mist of thick fog hovered among the nineteenth-century gravestones as the dead slept deep and undisturbed. Feeling a chill work its way up his spine, Todd quickly dug his hands into the front pocket of his pullover hoodie.

If zombies were real, Todd thought, *this would definitely be the perfect night and place for them.*

All around them, headstones stood in stiletto silence like guardians of the dead. Some of the stones were simple rectangles, others had rounded shoulders, and a few had angel statues perched over the tops. Most of the marble grave markers remained dark in the subdued light, but several shone under the full light of the moon.

Hidden in the shadows among the despair of so many wasted lives rotting in the graves around him, *he* heard voices from a distance. As he lay there, weakened and consumed with hunger, they moved dangerously close to where he rested. He listened with excitement, a renewed sense of power surging within his beast.

Can it be, he pondered, *that they were human?*

Thirst gripped his insides and his mouth felt as dry as ashes. It had been too long since he last fed. His eyes widened as an explosive rush of skin and muscle began to shift, changing and converging in an instant. He clenched his jaws as tightly as he could, stifling the anguished howl building at the back of his throat. His veins bulged, and his features twisted and rearranged into the face of a beast—half-man, half-wolf—with a muzzle, long curving fangs, and thick black fur. He could feel his ageless strength awakening from years of peaceful slumber. Now, it was suffocating. He had to *release* it.

Buried underground and desperate for air, he clawed and dug until a few faint beams of moonlight entered the underground, giving him just enough light to see by. Thick fog tumbled through the dark and murky pit. He exhaled a ragged breath as he crawled through the opening of the dark, confined space. The pungent scent of human flesh polluted the fresh air and ignited his appetite. For several years he had bided his time. *Kill.* He was ready to *kill* for life again.

Todd flinched at the sound of twigs snapping. With a gasp, he whirled around, his eyes probing the mist and the graves, his heart stuck in his throat. For one brief second, he could have sworn he saw two glowing eyes in the distance, staring in their direction. It vanished into the shadows as soon as he turned to get a closer look. *Something* was there. He was sure of it.

Todd choked down a taste of fear and blurted, "What the hell was that?"

As Jena and Sophie paused to listen, a muffled moan blew through the cemetery.

"It's just the wind, scaredy-cat," Sophie giggled.

He turned to Sophie with an aggravated expression. "No, it wasn't the wind, dammit. I swore I saw something."

Sophie shined a flashlight, aimlessly searching through the foggy graveyard and said, "Where?"

Todd directed her to a certain area of the cemetery and said, "Over there, somewhere."

Sophie looked to where Todd pointed. "I don't see any-thing," she said, holding the flashlight steady. "It's probably just your imagination."

"Yeah, well, what if you're wrong?" he said. "What if someone is here? They could call the police on us."

"Quit worrying, Todd," Jena said as she rearranged the leather satchel strapped over her shoulder. "There's no one here."

"Guys, I think this is a bad idea," he said in a hushed voice. "I mean, what if we get caught? You do realize we are all breaking the law. I could lose my job at the hospital, or worse... go to jail. Hell, is all this really worth it?"

Jena—with her perfectly flowing waves of blonde hair and tall, willowy model's figure—rolled her eyes. "Good grief," she grumbled. "Don't be such a wimp. We're not going to get caught. Besides, we have plenty of time. The security guards don't come in until six. That gives us two hours. Once we get inside the mausoleum, all we have to do is locate Carla Rosi's burial chamber. The rest is a piece of cake."

Todd snorted. "Yeah, whatever," he snidely remarked. "Don't forget about the creepy part."

"What's a matter, Todd?" Jena's tone was mocking. "You're not afraid of a little séance, are you?"

"Why do you always have to poke fun at me, Jena? You know I hate this kind of stuff. I only agreed to do this because I don't want you two here alone, especially at this hour. Besides, don't you think I deal with enough death at work?"

"Honey, where's your sense of adventure? For Pete's sake, pull that stick out of your butt."

"Yeah," Sophie chimed in as she glanced in Todd's direction—huge, dark eyes ringed with even darker layers of mascara. "Don't be so uptight, Todd. You've been driving an ambulance for way too long. I think it's starting to get to you."

"Whatever," he groaned, throwing his hands up in defeat. "This whole thing is stupid, anyway. Carla's body wasn't ever found. Her parents put an empty casket in the mausoleum."

"Her body may not be there," Jena said, cocking a brow, "but her spirit might be."

"Jesus, woman." Todd sighed, disgusted with Jena's idea that she could somehow connect with the dead girl's spirit. "You're a whole new definition of bat-shit crazy."

"But you still love me, right?"

He glared at Jena in silent menace. Then a hint of a smile drifted over his mouth.

"Come on, you two lovebirds," Sophie said, jogging ahead of them. "Stop arguing. Let's just do this already."

Todd took off through the cemetery in a trot, his senses on high alert for the slightest sound or movement, leaving Jena following close behind.

With little effort, they caught up to Sophie. When they neared the mausoleum, Todd paused in midstride. Without warning, a cold prickly feeling of someone watching took hold, and goosebumps crawled over his skin. For a split second, reality threatened to crush him. Was someone waiting close by, hiding in the shadows? Closing his lids, he forced himself to stay calm. He was probably working himself up over nothing. Most likely, it was just the wind playing tricks on him.

You're only imagining things, he tried to convince himself. *It's just the branches swaying in the wind. That's all it is.*

Todd opened his eyes and breathed a sigh of relief as his mind finally accepted this explanation. The rancid odor of stagnant earth and rotting leaves invaded his nostrils, instantly producing a nauseous reaction deep down in his gut.

Slowly, he approached the old, stone structure that reminded him of something straight from a horror movie like *Bram Stoker's Dracula*. Vines of ivy draped the dreary and ghoulish structure, covering the roof and the weathered stained-glass windows. A cracked and worn statue of an angel guarded the gated doorway. At last, he mustered the courage to move forward. With a trembling hand, he reached for the latch that was flaked with rust. Suppressing a shiver, he opened it and pushed his way through.

A rumble of thunder snaked its way through the cemetery.

Sophie looked up. "You've got to be kidding," she moaned. "We better hurry. It looks like rain."

Todd's heart hammered wildly in his chest as he climbed the steps that led to the miniature house for the dead. At the top, a creepy feeling gnawed at the pit of his soul. Then he turned to face Jena and Sophie, who still stood outside the gate. "Well, are you coming, or not?" he said, trying to keep his voice even.

As Jena reached up to adjust the ball cap on her head, a bone-chilling shudder went through her. *Carla Rosi?* she silently asked. *Is that you?* She waited for a sign and prayed that she'd pick up on something... anything. Then she felt a presence closing in around her. Felt a breath on her face.

"Jena... it's not safe... turn back now."

"What is it?" Sophie whispered, noticing Jena's blank stare as if she had seen a ghost.

Oblivious to Sophie's question, Jena turned slowly in all directions. "Sophie, did you hear that?"

"Hear what?"

"Come on, girls," Todd called out to them in frustration. "What the hell are you waiting for? If you're going to do this thing, let's get on with it before the storm rolls in."

"Never mind," Jena told her, ignoring the voice in her head. "It's nothing. Let's go."

As she went to take a step, Jena heard the voice again, but it seemed like some strange faraway echo.

"It's here! Run, Jena!"

Jena's body suddenly went rigid with fear. Oh God, was Carla Rosi's spirit trying to warn her? Seconds crept by, but she couldn't move. *Damn it!* Why had she ever come here? How could she be so stupid? What could she possibly have been thinking? Had she risked her fiancé and her friend's safety just to connect with a dead girl?

"Jena, are you okay?" Sophie asked.

Maybe she really had imagined the voice. Maybe it had just been her nerves. *I can do this,* she told herself. *I have to do this. I want to know what happened to Carla.* Waving it off like it was nothing Jena moved forward, and then stopped again, almost immediately.

As the creature moved in behind some bushes to watch its prey more closely, it fought a desire to spring out and kill them immediately. The urge to feed fueled its rage and gave it direction. It was exquisite torture holding in its lust for flesh and blood. After all these years, he'd been so careful, so cunning... concealing the ageless secrets of his kind.

Quickly, its crouching form slipped from the blanket of undergrowth and sprang to the decrepit structure that housed the dead. Then, he waited.

Jena's heart ricocheted into her throat as she caught a glimpse of a dark silhouette vanish behind the mausoleum. What she saw threatened her sanity. *Was it a dog?* Yet it seemed too fast. The unsettling size was something far too big to be a dog.

"Get out of here, Jena! Run!"

In sheer panic, Jena stood there, too stunned to breathe, much less move. She clung desperately to the voice warning her. The satchel slipped from her shoulder, and finally, she found her own voice, barely choking out the words, "We need to get out of here *now*."

"What?" Sophie said, looking at Jena strangely. "What are you talking about?"

A terrible howling cut through the darkness, and like a statue of stone, Todd froze with his mouth agape.

For a moment, Jena's head began to spin. She put a trembling hand over her mouth to keep from screaming. She tried to think, to calm her frantic breathing and her rapid pulse. In less than a heartbeat, she saw something stir from the shadows. A rush of terror surged through her, flooding her with cold and cruel certainty.

Startled, Jena heard the voice again.

"Run!"

Before Jena could get a word out, Sophie screamed.

Out of the corner of his eye, Todd saw something move from out of the shadows. His eyes widened in disbelief as a beam of light from the moon exposed a creature that looked like something he'd thought to be only a foolish myth. The sight of it nearly brought him to his knees. It looked so like a man, but it was huge and hairy like a beast. All of its hair was black, and its ears had a hideous peaked lupine appearance. It was moving toward Jena and Sophie, who appeared too frightened to move.

Todd held steady and drew in his breath, reaching for an inner strength he knew he possessed. *You have to save them,* he thought.

Sophie was already backing away from the creature's luminous eyes that continued to follow her as though she was its main target.

Todd waved his arms and shouted, "Get away from them!"

The creature quickly averted its eyes from Jena and Sophie and twisted fiercely in Todd's direction. Its pupils were vertical slits, like a cat's.

Jena saw Todd turn toward her. He opened his mouth and started to say her name, but he never got the chance.

For one brief second, Jena wavered between hysteria and total collapse as she helplessly watched the creature attack the man she was engaged to marry.

She hadn't even realized that she'd screamed his name. But there was no time. It happened too fast. At first, Todd struggled, choking violently, but the creature was merciless as its ivory fangs tore into his jugular.

"Please," Todd croaked painfully, but the words turned to bubbled, liquid sounds as the creature ripped at his body.

Jena's heart ached with grief and regret. *Oh God, this is my fault.*

She felt as though time had stopped, and this was someone else's nightmare. *It's not too late. I can still help him.*

Without a word, she began moving painfully in the direction the creature had vanished with Todd's body. Before she managed to get too far, Sophie grabbed her from behind and jerked her back.

"We need to go, Jena," she said quietly. "It's too late. We can't save him."

"It's *not* too late!" Jena cried. "We can't just leave him here."

Then, Jena heard the voice again.

"Run, Jena! It's coming back!"

An icy shudder worked its way up Jena's spine. She looked at Sophie with haunted eyes and uttered a small gasp.

"Run, Sophie!" Jena finally cried out. "It's coming back!"

Frantically, Sophie quickly peered behind Jena. Her eyes rounded in fear when she caught sight of two yellow eyes. They were like the color and brightness of the moon, glowing across the cemetery at her. Her mouth locked in open terror, and her eyes blinked in disbelief. The man-wolf was standing on its hind legs, glaring at her as though it wanted to kill everything in its path. Black hair covered its hideous face, and the smell of blood and flesh wafted up to her, making her gag.

Sophie felt weak and suddenly dizzy, falling on her hands and knees.

The ground shook with the weight of the creature as it set off after Sophie and Jena on all fours, letting out an ear-shattering roar.

"Get up, Sophie!" Jena screamed.

Sophie looked up at Jena. "I can't *move.*"

Jena quickly reached for Sophie's arm and pulled with all her strength. "Please, Sophie," she pleaded. "You've got to get up!"

In horror, Jena watched as the man-wolf got closer, looking hungrily at Sophie. Of all the terrors Jena felt, the greatest one, as she stared into that evil face, was that she was going to have to leave her friend behind. Torn between the decision to stay with Sophie or to run away, she had to make a choice.

"I'm sorry, Sophie," Jena said. Her voice was pain-stricken and full of regret. Then she released Sophie's arm and forced herself to run.

As she ran, it started to rain, but she could still hear Sophie's violent screams. Jena's heart clenched in her chest, and her eyes misted with tears. She felt guilty about abandoning her. *My God, please,* she painfully thought. *Someone help us.*

Jena tugged at the brim of her ball cap to help shield her face against the rain as it began to downpour. She ran blindly, stumbling across uneven ground, weaving between headstones, barely able to see where she was going. All she could think of was an escape, but there were no exit signs posted in the cemetery, just rows and rows of graves. Suddenly, she heard heavy footsteps coming from behind. At first, she thought it was only the sound of rain pounding against her eardrums, until suddenly they seemed to have a dreadful purpose, and she realized they were getting closer. Releasing a heavy gasp, she struggled forward as fast as she could.

A new fear began to rise in Jena when she heard long, guttural breaths all around her. As she plunged on through the rain, dark clawed hands appeared from the mists. It grabbed the long strands of her ponytail and detached the ball cap from her head. She cried out in pain but managed to pull free and resumed her endeavor to get away.

Without warning, Jena felt a searing pain slice through her shoulder, pain so intense she couldn't even scream. It was as if waves of fire burned through every nerve and muscle in her body. Jena tried to brace herself, but she slid on wet leaves and pitched forward. It seemed as though she fell for a suspended time until she finally landed on a floor, cushioned with mushy, saturated dirt. For a second she kept still, too shocked to move, then slowly she reached forward to push herself up. Gasping, she lifted her head and stared in horror. Even in the darkness, she realized where she had fallen. It was an open grave. That's when she heard the voice again.

"It's okay, Jena. You're safe now."

As Jena paused to listen, she felt a sudden chill crawl up her spine. She watched in fear as a girl's arm lifted slowly and reached out to her.

"Listen," the girl whispered, but her lips did not move, yet Jena could hear her as though she was speaking aloud. *"You must listen to what I tell you. You've been bitten."*

Jena could hardly see anything in the darkness, only brief flashes of the girl's features as the lightning flickered over her ghostly white face and the gaping wound to her throat. It was so deep you could see the raw, gruesome flesh and a glimmer of bone. She could feel the girl's eyes upon her, sensing her death, and the death tonight, drowning in it, drowning in all the death. Jena wanted to close her eyes, but she found she could not look away.

"Who are you?"

"Carla," the girl said, but her lips did not move. *"I'm the girl you came here for."*

"But how?" Jena whimpered. "Carla Rosi is dead."

"Please listen to me, Jena. You've been cursed," Carla murmured. *"And I'm here to help you."*

Confused, Jena shook her head, her thoughts spinning in all directions. "What are you talking about? What curse?"

"The curse of the Rougarou," Carla told her. *"If you give in to human blood—and I promise you will crave it with a burning desire—you will shift into the creature."*

Tears ran down Jena's cheeks and mixed with the raindrops that fell from the sky. "Are you saying I'm going to turn into that... *thing?*"

"Only if you consume the blood or flesh of a human," Carla continued to explain. *"Not only does the curse bring forth the beast, it gives its victim the power to transform into*

various nocturnal animals and also assume a cloud of misty smoke, or fog. It possesses the power of superior strength, and imperviousness to disease, and the ability to heal instantaneously from any bodily wound of any severity. Jena, you only have one hundred and one days to control your hunger. Do you understand what I'm saying? If you resist the urge within that time frame, the curse will be lifted."

"This is insane. This can't be happening," Jena sobbed. "Why are you saying these things?"

"Because, Jena, it's real."

"No, no, no," Jena babbled. "It's not real. This is all a nightmare."

"Please, Jena." Carla grabbed Jena's wrist and lightly squeezed. It felt cold and clammy against her skin. *"I don't have much time. You must believe what I'm telling you. All this is real. Promise me, you will take my warning seriously."*

Jena nodded. "Okay, I promise."

"What happened tonight is not your fault, Jena. You could not have saved your friends. Nobody could. But you gave me peace."

"Who did this to you, Carla?" at last her words choked out, consumed with sadness.

"The creature," she said in a voice barely above a whisper. Seconds later, Carla's glassy eyes shifted away to something far beyond, something Jena couldn't see. As her eyelids slowly closed, Jena could have sworn she smiled.

Dazed and weak, Jena took a deep breath and shut her eyes, but she couldn't shut out Carla's words that echoed over and over in her mind.

You've been bitten... the curse of the Rougarou... human blood and flesh...

She didn't want to believe it. But she had to, because to accept what she'd just seen in the cemetery was too horrifying to deal with. And there was a young, dead girl, lying beside her that had been missing for years. Jena prayed that someone would find her. She wasn't going to die in this muddy grave next to Carla's body.

Todd's and Sophie's deaths hung over her like a recurring nightmare. No matter how hard Jena tried to erase those horrific images, her mind kept trudging up thoughts of things she didn't want to think about. *Had she caused their death? Was that creature coming back for her?* Jena wrapped her arms around herself and shivered violently. Exhausted, she managed to shut out everything around her. Yet despite the urgency of the situation, she choked down the taste of fear and let herself drift into a hazy slumber.

That's when *he'd* come back. One last time. After he had done what he had to do, he could not get her out of his mind. He stood over the lip of the pitch-black opening and stared down at her with keen eyesight. He waited to see if her eyes would open. He wanted her to look up at him, but she did not move.

An overwhelming feeling crept into his dark heart and completely consumed him. It burned from deep within, filling him with a strange uneasiness and a craving he could not understand, a craving so intense he could almost taste it. *She should never have come here,* he thought. With a burning desire, he lowered himself into the muddy grave and knelt down beside her. As he wiped the mud from her face, he studied her features, all the while wondering how long she would resist the gift he had given her. Then, he glanced down at his strong hands... hands that could wield the power of life and death. Something had changed inside him since he first saw her. It was like looking into the mirror of the past at someone he once loved long ago. At that moment, he chose to give her life, instead of death.

Footsteps from a distance alerted his attention. They were coming closer. Now he realized he had to act quickly. He was in desperate agony, yet he could not help himself as his human transformation suddenly took over. His amber eyes glided smoothly down her body, then up again to her face. He bent lower, parted his lips, and squeezed his eyes shut. Oh so gently, he put his mouth upon hers and kissed her.

As Jena struggled to wake, she felt something warm and feather-soft press against her lips, sending wave after wave of delicious sensations all the way through her.

His mouth moved down the length of her neck. "I am your destiny, Jena." His whisper created a tingle over her skin.

She gasped and tried to pull away from the coppery smell of blood on his breath.

"Do you deny it?" he asked, kissing the pulse at her throat.

Jena was sobbing now, trying to choke out the word, *"No..."*

He drew back from her as she lay weak and helpless, lost in guilt and regret. Little by little, he would remove those emotions until they existed no more. Soon, thoughts of him would consume her.

Not far away, she could hear muffled voices. As Jena's eyes flew open, she found herself surrounded by a veil of fog. Then a feeling of relief invaded her senses as she caught a glimpse of colored lights that flashed above. She tried to scream out for help, but all that came out was a frightened whimper.

"It's okay, miss," a male voice said. "You're safe now."

Chapter Two

By one o'clock in the morning, Manuel Sanchez finally made it back to his apartment. After what he recently experienced, he had the sense that nothing was what it seemed. The rules as he knew them were completely off, and reality was slowly shifting into a bizarre realm. And the only thing on his mind at the moment was a bottle of Jim Beam. There was no way he was going to stay sober for the next twenty-four hours. Although he knew it was going to take more than a few shots of Kentucky bourbon to deal with what he had witnessed in the last few days.

Manuel never imagined in a million years that all the myths of vampire-like creatures and werewolves actually existed. *God, I feel like I'm losing my ever-loving mind,* he thought as he poured himself a shot. There was no doubt he'd seen his share of monsters—*the human kind*—during his years as a detective in San Francisco, California. Not to mention the fact that there was a secret species of humans born with the ability to shift into wolves the size of horses. *Shit!* And it was brought to his attention—in no uncertain terms—something that would've sounded insane only a few days before.

He was born one of them.

Manuel wasn't gifted with the wolf thing. According to the Breedline Covenant, you had to be born an identical twin for that. He didn't have a twin, but he carried the gene. He'd inherited it from his father, who had abandoned his mother, leaving her to raise Manuel and his older sister Lailah alone and on a waitress's salary. *Bastard.*

It was nearly three o'clock when he decided to call it quits after four shots. As he staggered to his bedroom, his sister came to mind. *Christ,* he thought, smoothing a hand across his brow. He wouldn't believe it if he hadn't seen it with his own two eyes. Lailah was an angel. Not in the virtue meaning, but an actual angel with wings. And a badass battle angel at that. It gave him comfort knowing she was in a better place.

Forty-one years ago, Lailah was brutally murdered. He'd never forget that dreadful day. If only he could go back in time.

At age thirteen, Manuel watched his sister climb in the backseat of her killer's car. That damn green Camaro tormented him for years. Little did he know, that particular day would be the last time he'd see her. As the car drove off, his instincts screamed danger. Instead of listening to his gut feeling, he let her go. He'd never forgive himself.

As hard as he tried to prevent them, more memories flooded in. The gloomy day of his sister's funeral, he remembered the weeping crowd of mourners, the priest in black, and the flowers arranged upon Lailah's coffin. Shortly after, the police became closemouthed about her death, which didn't surprise Manuel. Evidently, the investigation went tight-lipped to prevent an outbreak of hysteria in the community, not to mention his sister's best friend Carla Rosi. Her body remained missing. While his sister's case eventually went cold, Manuel started going to the shooting range three or four times a week. His instinct had been to find the monsters that had murdered his sister and blow their brains out. He didn't know their names, but if it took the rest of his life, he'd find out. So far, the only thing he had to go on was the car they drove. It would've been easier if only he'd gotten a look at one of the bastards' damned faces, or maybe gotten the ID off the tags.

Years later, Manuel joined the California PD. Lailah's death had been the reason he chose a career in law enforcement. Although her case remained unsolved, Manuel determined himself to reopen her file, which meant digging up old wounds. But that didn't matter to him. He took an oath to protect the innocent, and he'd keep that promise until he took his last breath.

Meanwhile, her killer remained at large, and Manuel swore he'd never rest in peace until he brought justice to the bastard that took his sister's life. When promoted to homicide, he all but exhausted himself, searching for the SOB responsible for her death. When he first saw those forensic photos...

God, he'd never get those images out of his head. By the condition of her body, it appeared a wild animal had attacked her... or a *vampire*—every bit of her blood reported to be drained from her body, and her throat torn open. Her skin was a lifeless pale gray. She also had bite marks on her chest, wrists, and her inner thighs. Lailah's homicide baffled the medical examiner and the detectives assigned to her case. Without any evidence or witnesses at the crime scene, and according to the type of injuries she suffered, they assumed it was some kind of satanic cult. They had no other good explanation. Besides, what kind of normal human being could be capable of such brutality, especially to an innocent, beautiful girl at the young age of seventeen? *Savages!*

Although Manuel now knew the world was not as it seemed, he was damn determined to keep his promise. That was to protect and serve. Obsessed with his sister's case, he set aside his personal life—no loving wife or kids, no white picket anything, just dead bodies—and vowed to do everything in his power to keep this from happening to another innocent victim.

Few people knew anything about Manuel's private life, except his partner, Detective Frank Perkins. At the station, he was nothing but serious, and sometimes he was all business while off work. Everyone on the police force knew him to be a true bachelor. If one of the detectives' wives tried to set him up on a date, he refused to have anything to do with a relationship. It wasn't that Manuel didn't attract women. He was definitely easy on the eyes, and resembling the handsome Spanish actor, Antonio Banderas didn't hurt. Sure, he visited the gym on a regular basis, stayed in shape boxing practically his whole life. Without a doubt, Manuel could give a young man a run for his money, but he was only one man, and the world was full of monsters. Whatever killed his sister wasn't human.

He stripped out of his clothes and practically collapsed onto the mattress. Man, he was so freakin' tired. Closing his eyes, he let go of everything. It wasn't long before he slipped into a dream. More like a nightmare.

Manuel was himself at the awkward age of thirteen, sitting on the steps of the old rundown house he grew up in, located in the San Francisco Bay Area. Then, the noise of a revving engine caught his attention. As he looked toward the obnoxious sound, he spotted a green Camaro parked in the drive. It had two black racing stripes over the hood. Through dark, tinted windows, he saw the silhouette of a man behind the wheel and someone in the passenger seat.

Manuel flinched when the horn blared. Shortly after, the front door slammed from behind. He glanced over his shoulder at his sister.

"I'll be right back, Manuel," Lailah said, ruffling his hair playfully.

Manuel looked up at her, his expression tense. "Lailah, please don't go. You know Mama said we're not supposed to leave without her permission."

She gave him a rueful smile. "Oh, Manuel, don't worry. I'm just going for a quick ride."

Manuel looked away from his sister and to the car waiting in the drive. He glared at the man behind the wheel and said, "I've never seen that car before. Who are they?"

"They're from out of town, visiting relatives," she told him. "Quit worrying." She rolled her eyes. "Carla introduced them to me yesterday at Quincy's café."

"But Lailah—"

"Give me a break, Manuel," she groaned, shaking her head. "It's fine. They're nice guys."

"Where's your friend Carla?" Manuel asked, his tone demanding. "How come she's not with them?"

"She's staying at her cousin's house. We're picking her up."

"And then where are you going? How long will you be gone?" he continued to grill her.

The horn blared again.

Lailah made a low grumbling sound. "Jeez, Manuel, quit being so nosy. I gotta go."

As Lailah turned away and jogged toward the green sports car, her long red hair streamed out behind her. She glanced over her shoulder and smiled at Manuel one last time. "I'll be back before Mama gets home from work. And don't be a tattletale."

With an uneasy feeling, Manuel helplessly watched her pile into the back seat of the stranger's car. She waved goodbye as it tore out of the paved drive, squealing the tires.

Manuel waved back as the Camaro sped away. *Please God,* he prayed. *Please keep my sister safe.*

That's when the dream shifted into a nightmare and Manuel begged his eyes to open. Instead, his lids remained closed, and he couldn't stop the horror show.

He'd never forget the pain burning in his mother's eyes when the police arrived with the bad news. She'd fallen to her knees when they told her they'd found Lailah's body lying in a ditch on the side of the road.

Manuel remembered the cops questioning him because he'd been the last person to see his sister alive. He told them he didn't recognize the guys in the car and that he'd begged his sister not to go. But when Manuel recalled Lailah mentioning her friend Carla Rosi had introduced her to the suspects, he immediately relayed the information, praying it would help in the investigation. Manuel wanted justice. He wanted vengeance. He wanted the bastards to pay for what they'd done to his sister. A life-term sentence behind bars would be too easy. He wanted the persons responsible to suffer a long and agonizing death.

Later, when the police made a visit to Carla's house for questioning, her parents told them their daughter was staying with her cousin for the weekend. Unfortunately, she never showed. Soon after, Miss Rosi became a missing person. To this day, they never found her body. Years later, Carla's parents finally accepted that their daughter wasn't coming home and placed an empty coffin in the mausoleum of the Salem Cemetery. Manuel would never forget the look of despair on her father's face, no doubt grief-stricken over his daughter's missing body.

Now that the door to Manuel's nightmare was open, it took him to a different place... to the place where dead bodies were stored. There was no way he would allow his mother to identify Lailah's body all alone.

As he entered the San Francisco Memorial Hospital, his hands went clammy and a cold sweat bloomed on his forehead. Swallowing the knot in his throat, Manuel reached for his mother's hand and lightly squeezed.

Manuel stiffened as a doctor walked out of a revolving door and said, "Ms. Sanchez, please follow me. The viewing room is this way." The physician gestured toward a long hallway. Above the pocket of her white coat it read JANICE KRAMER, MD, Chief of Surgery.

When they came to a stretch of whitewashed concrete walls, Manuel figured they were getting close, and he was right. Dr. Kramer stopped at a pair of double stainless-steel doors marked with the words MORGUE and AUTHORIZED STAFF.

"Wait here, please," said the physician. "I'll tell them you're here."

A few minutes later, the doctor opened the door. "The coroner is ready," she spoke softly. "If you need more time..."

Manuel's mother inhaled a deep breath. On a quick exhale, she said, "Please, I'd like to see my daughter."

The doctor nodded and looked to Manuel, her expression troubling. Then she shifted her eyes back to Manuel's mother. "Ms. Sanchez, are you sure you want your son to go?" Her tone seemed doubtful. "The body is—"

"It's okay," Manuel interjected. "I need to see my sister."

The physician nodded.

As they walked inside, the smell of formaldehyde filled Manuel's nostrils. It reminded him of his science classroom and dissecting frogs. His gut churned, and he took a deep breath.

Then he saw a white curtain hanging on the far side of the room. It blocked the view of Lailah.

"Are you okay, Manuel?" his mother asked.

He nodded in silence.

A man wearing green scrubs stood by the white curtain. When the doctor gave him a slight nod, he parted the drapes down the middle in a slow swish, revealing a body lying on a metal table, covered by a white sheet.

As Manuel fought to wake, to open his eyes, his heart went into overdrive.

Oh God, no... Please, not this memory.

With his hand clasped to his mother's, Manuel blinked tears as the medical examiner reached forward and folded the shroud back, unveiling his sister's face.

Manuel stared down and took his first look at Lailah since he'd last seen her alive. Her eyes appeared stitched shut.

Aside from the bright red hair and freckled cheeks, she no longer looked like the sister he once knew. Her mouth was blue and her bottom lip split from what might have been someone's hand or fist. The bandages on Lailah's throat mostly hid the wounds, but it was obvious she had suffered severe trauma.

"Oh, my poor baby," Manuel's mother sobbed into her hands. "Who would do such a thing?"

Emotion overcame Manuel. His throat swelled and tears streamed down his cheeks. In a moment of silence, he simply wrapped his arm around his mother and held on to her as tightly as he could. Finally, he whispered the only comforting words he could come up with, "I promise, Mama. Someday, I'll find the person who did this."

Dr. Kramer nodded at the examiner, who re-covered Lailah's face.

That same dreadful night, a sinister chill crept through Manuel as he huddled beneath the blankets in his bed like a child afraid of the dark. He wondered who—*what*—could have done something this brutal to his sister? It couldn't be human itself, he rationalized. Even an animal couldn't drain a body of that much blood. But what if it could? Maybe the killers could transform into *vampires*.

Manuel was letting his imagination take over now. Suddenly, he was afraid to peer from out of the covers, afraid even to move. Ice-cold terror coursed through his veins, and his heart pounded inside his chest. For one brief moment, he thought he heard a voice calling out to him, whispering his name.

In the midst of Manuel's horrific nightmare, images of his sister's corpse were so vivid they swirled together with the young woman he'd found in a dumpster, murdered a few weeks ago. Bits and pieces of the memories mixed until he could only see flashes of bright red hair, pale bare skin, blue lifeless lips, bruises, and teeth marks. It appeared that some kind of mythical creature attacked them.

"Lailah..." he whispered her name in his sleep, trying to bring back the image in his mind of her alive and happy, although he could not. The memories of her death stabbed through his heart, and all Manuel could see was her pale, lifeless face.

BANG! BANG! BANG!

The pounding on Manuel's apartment door and his French bulldog's barking instantly brought his eyes open, the abrupt sounds kick-starting his heart. As he looked at the clock on the nightstand, he saw it was already twelve o'clock in the afternoon. *Shit!* "Who the—"

BANG! BANG! BANG!

With its fur ruffled, the dog went into full-blown bark mode.

"Cool your jets, Ira," Manuel told his furry companion. "It's probably just the landlord."

Ignoring the throbbing in his head, he swung his legs off the bed and pushed himself to his feet. Then he sat back down, slowly. "Christ," he grumbled, rubbing his aching temple. *Coffee,* he thought. *I need coffee.*

The pounding started again.

"Damn it," he groaned, maneuvering back into the upright position. *Who in the hell is banging on my door at this time of the day?* He cursed to himself. *It's Sunday for crying-out-loud, and where in the hell are my damn pants?*

Finally, he managed to locate the pants he'd previously worn the day before. On shaky legs, Manuel stumbled with his trousers but caught his footing before he fell forward and pulled them up over his hips. *Shit!* If only he could get a little more sleep. Then he might feel like a human again.

BANG! BANG! BANG!

Ira rushed out of the bedroom barking, her nails clipping across the hardwood floor.

"Keep your damn pants on!" he called out as he zipped up, pulled on a T-shirt, and then headed for the living room. "I'm coming for Pete's sake!"

Manuel walked over to the door and put his eye to the peephole. When he saw the face of the person standing outside his door, he rolled over and pressed his back against the wall. *Shit!*

"I know you're in there," Captain Hodge said. "Come on, Detective Sanchez. Open the damn door."

Releasing an aggravated sigh, Manuel flipped the locks and threw open the door. Before he could say a word, Hodge barged past him.

Ira bared her teeth at Captain Hodge and growled.

"Nice to see you too, Ira." Hodge's voice suddenly became familiar to the dog as she came running with her tail wagging.

"Detective, don't you ever answer your damn phone?" Hodge asked as he bent down to pet Ira. "I've been trying to reach you all morning."

"Sorry, Captain. I've been a little *detained*," he said with his best, "*I don't give a shit*" snarl while shutting the door.

Hodge looked up with his brows furrowed. "You mean... *drunk*."

Manuel shrugged and plopped down in a tattered chair that faced the television. "Hell, Captain, you're the one that gave me the time off."

"Okay, okay," Hodge said as he sat down in the chair across from Manuel. "I get it. What you do in your free time is none of my business."

"Look, Captain, I'm exhausted," he said around a yawn. "Was there any particular reason you stopped by?"

"Yeah, well..." Hodge said, swallowing hard. "I thought it would be best if I came here and told you in person."

Manuel frowned. "Tell me what?"

Hodge leaned forward, his face dead serious. "I've got a lead on an old cold case. And it has to do with your sister."

Manuel's eyes snapped wide. "What—"

Chapter Three

Roman Kincaid stood outside the parking lot of Nate's bar where he'd last seen the beautiful redheaded angel, a hopeless expression marring his face. The Wolf's Lair was completely empty, closed down for repairs due to the extensive damage from what humans thought to be an earthquake, but in truth, they'd fought the most dangerous supernatural beings the Breedline and his kind had ever encountered. When all hope appeared to be lost, from out of nowhere five magnificent black-winged battle angels crashed through the bar's roof in the nick of time. Without haste, the angels—who towered at least ten feet or more—rendered the Fury powerless.

As he watched them take flight and disappear into the night sky with the defeated trio in their custody, he felt an unfamiliar ache in the center of his chest—the pain brought on by the angel named Lailah. When Roman first laid eyes on her, he knew she was the one. He could feel it deep down in his soul. Her long red hair that tumbled around her delicate and flawless shoulders would forever haunt his dreams. Her eyes were like the finest emeralds surrounded by thick, dark lashes that accentuated the color. And the freckles on her cheeks beckoned him. Why did she continue to affect him so strongly? His heart sped into a wild beat just thinking about her, but she was gone. Now he understood fully for the first time what it was to have a broken heart.

He dragged a hand through his hair and let out a frustrated sigh, wondering whether she felt the same, or was this emotion one-sided only. In the long run, did it really matter? Hell, she was an angel for crying out loud, and he was just a man. Besides, it wasn't likely he'd ever see her again.

The exasperating question plaguing him was whether he should let it go and move on. Should he forget that he'd ever laid eyes on her? Roman wasn't the kind of man to ever give up. All his life, he pursued what he wanted. And Lailah was all he could think about. Deep down, Roman knew the answer to the question he'd posed to himself. He would turn over heaven and hell if that's what it took to find her.

"What are you doing here?" Lawrence asked as he came up behind Roman and placed his hand on his shoulder.

Roman flinched at the contact, and his pulse leaped in alarm. "Shit." He snapped his head around. "You 'bout gave me a damn heart attack, you sneaky bastard."

Lawrence stepped back. "Sorry, man," he said with a chuckle, his white teeth flashing against his dark skin. "I didn't mean to startle you. Is there something you want to talk about? You seem to have a lot on your mind lately."

"Nah, I'm good." Roman waved it off like it was nothing.

Lawrence cocked a brow and his gaze flickered in question. "Roman, I've known you for years, and this is the first time I've seen you so..." he paused as if he was mentally searching for the right word, "...quiet."

Roman sucked in a breath, and his chest rose and fell harshly as if he was swallowing away his pride. Then he scrubbed both hands over his face and looked at Lawrence pointedly. "I can't keep a damn thing from you, can I?"

"Nope," Lawrence said shortly. "Spill it, buddy."

"So, why are you here?" Roman queried, trying to change the subject.

Lawrence snorted. "Are you trying to avoid the question? I'll make you a deal. You tell me what's going on, and I'll give you my reason for being here. Capeesh?"

"Okay, here goes nothing." Roman nervously rubbed his palms together, a look of anxiety simmering in his dark eyes. He didn't like how vulnerable he felt, how uncertain and uneasy with what he was about to tell his friend he'd practically known his whole life. Lawrence was the type of man that would take a bullet for a complete stranger. That kind of selflessness was hard to find. Not many men, no matter what, were willing to sacrifice their lives for someone else.

"I don't really know how to say what I'm feeling because I don't truly understand it myself," Roman continued. "But first, I need you to promise me something."

"What?" Lawrence asked, his eyes never leaving Roman's face.

"You can't tell a soul." His voice took on a serious tone. The very last thing Roman wanted was his vulnerability broadcast far and wide. "Everyone will think I'm a nut job."

"You have my word," Lawrence said. "Whatever you share stays between us."

"Remember the redheaded angel?" Roman asked.

"How could I possibly forget?" Lawrence said, exhaling a deep breath. "She towered at least ten feet tall with wings that turned to fire, and literally saved our asses."

In the silence that followed, Lawrence looked at Roman in inquiry and said, "What about her?"

Roman placed his hand against his forehead, trying to collect his jumbled thoughts. It felt as though a ton of bricks was pressing down on him. "Damn it," he cursed in a low voice. "I feel like I'm losing my damn mind."

Lawrence placed his palm back on Roman's shoulder. "Okay, calm down and collect your thoughts. Then tell me exactly what's going on."

The soothing note to Lawrence's voice was like a warm blanket surrounding him, easing some of the tension. Roman slumped and looked down.

"I... bonded with her," Roman finally managed to choke out. The words came out as scrambled as his thoughts were. "I know it sounds crazy, but I swear it happened. And I can't get her out of my head." Roman looked up at Lawrence as if he was pleading for help. "What the *hell* am I going to do?"

"Everything will be all right," Lawrence said with a calmness Roman sure as hell didn't feel. "We'll figure this thing out."

Roman shook his head. "But how?" he said, panic fluttering deep in his gut. "It's not like I can just go looking for her. She's a freakin' angel."

"Roman, listen to me. You have to pull yourself together. Losing your shit won't solve anything. You hear me?"

Roman nodded numbly. "Yeah, you're right."

"Okay, here's what I'm going to do, buddy. I know someone that can help us. She has..." Lawrence briefly paused and let out a long sigh, "...special talents."

"What kind of *special* talents?"

"She can speak to angels."

Roman rolled his eyes. "Are you talking about a psychic medium?"

"No. This person is something entirely different. In another life, she was a guardian angel."

"Oh, come on, Lawrence," Roman groaned. "You really believe that?"

"Why not?" Lawrence shrugged his shoulders. "Look at us. We're not exactly human, now are we?"

"I guess you've got a point there."

"I'm sure she'll do everything she can to help you," Lawrence said.

"How do you know? This *person* doesn't even know me."

"Because," Lawrence patted Roman's shoulder and smiled reassuringly, "she's my sister."

"Melanie?" Roman said in bewilderment.

"Yep," Lawrence said shortly.

He stared at Lawrence as if afraid to believe the unbelievable. "I can't believe it." His eyes rounded. "So, how come you never told me about this before?"

"What would you have me say?" Lawrence shook his head. "Oh, by the way, my sister used to be an angel," he said mockingly. "It's not exactly something you bring up in ordinary conversation. Besides, it's not something she's supposed to talk about."

Roman squared his shoulders resolutely and then nodded. "Yeah, I get it. You do trust me, right?" he asked. "You know I would never give her secret away."

"I trust you, Roman."

As Roman heaved a deep breath, a flicker of hope lightened the stormy gray of his dark eyes. "Then what are we waiting for? I'm ready to go find my angel."

"Then let's do this," Lawrence said. "You can follow me to Melanie's place. I'll give her a call on the way."

As Lawrence turned toward his SUV, Roman called out, "Hey, wait. What was the reason you stopped by Nate's bar?"

Lawrence looked at Roman and grinned. "Oh, yeah," he said with a slight chuckle. "No particular reason. I figured something was bothering you, so I followed you here."

"Thanks, man."

Lawrence nodded once. "Don't mention it, buddy."

"One more question before we leave," Roman said with a look of curiosity. "So, how did all this go about? I mean... the angel thing with your sister."

"Sorry, buddy." Lawrence's forehead crinkled. "That's something she cannot share."

Roman cocked a brow. "Ah, I get it."

Chapter Four

The intensive care unit Sebastian was in, located in the In-Between—the outer space surrounding heaven—had curtained glass walls, and even from the outside, you could hear the hum of the medical equipment that was keeping him sedated.

Now, for the second time, he'd given his life to save another. But were his good deeds deserving of another chance at life? Growing up, Sebastian had suffered a tortured childhood that darkened his heart, replacing the goodness with evil intent and revenge. In the eyes of the Creator, all life deserved a second chance. Like all of his beloved creations, Sebastian was, too, born with a purpose.

After the Creator had summoned his battle angels with the task of rendering the Fury powerless and bringing the trio back to the heavens in their custody, he asked them to bring Sebastian's body along with them.

Lailah stood beside the hospital bed, peering down at Sebastian as he lay in a state of deep unconsciousness. Her long crimson hair fell forward and brushed against his face as she leaned over him. "It's not your time to go," she whispered close to his ear. "The Creator needs you."

She winced at the sound of the door sliding open. As she stood straight and turned around, one of her comrades in arms barged his way in. Frigg was not your ordinary angel. Not only did he resemble the singer, musician, and actor Billy Idol of the '80s punk rock band—sporting the same trademark bleached spiked hair—he had served as a battle angel for more than a century. With a personality bigger than life, he still had his share of human weaknesses: a love for rock-n-roll, cheeseburgers, and classic black-and-white movies. The Creator presented Frigg with an extraordinary gift. He had the unique ability to shapeshift. He could transform and reshape himself into any living thing.

When he caught sight of Sebastian's pale face, he curled his upper lip. There were tubes going in and out of every orifice he had, and the wires attached to his chest made him look as if he were one of Dr. Frankenstein's lab experiments.

"He looks like hell," Frigg said, the words coming out in a sarcastic tone heavily laced with an English accent.

Lailah rolled her eyes. "He'll be fine in a few days," she said. "So, what are *you* doing here?"

"Cronus sent me. He wants to see you, and it sounded urgent."

"I'm not supposed to leave him alone," she said, glancing down at Sebastian with a worried expression on her face. She looked back at Frigg and shrugged. "Someone should be here in case he comes around."

"I guess I can stay," he grumbled. "But no more than an hour, tops. I don't want to miss my show." Frigg brought his wrist to his face and glanced at the shimmering gold watch. "One of Alfred Hitchcock's old classics will be on in an hour."

Lailah let out an aggravated sigh. "Ya know, it wouldn't kill you to put others before yourself, Fitzgerald Rochester," she said addressing Frigg with his real name. "It's just a movie for heaven's sake."

He shrugged off her statement as though it was nothing and crossed his arms over his chest. "Just make sure you're back in an hour and don't ever call me by that name again."

Lailah groaned. "Okay, fine, but when I get back, we're having a serious talk. Your selfish needs are starting to get out of hand."

"Whatever," he said with an arched brow and plopped down in the chair next to Sebastian's bed, no doubt counting down the minutes.

Before Lailah left the room, she placed her hand against the side of Sebastian's face and blanketed him with a healing power that traveled to every pore in his body. Then she closed her eyes and spoke to him telepathically.

"Get rest." Her voice was soft in his mind. *"I will return, and soon you will awake."*

Sebastian tried to nod, but his body would not obey what his mind commanded. He was going to make it, however.

As Lailah exited the glass room, she nodded at the two guards standing outside and then strode down a long corridor, passing the door to the confined space that held the Fury. Here, their powers were useless. Still, she wondered what the Creator had in store for the savage, supernatural trio. Were they to join forces with her kind? If so, could they be trusted? Although, the last thing she needed was to worry about their fate. She had other issues to deal with. Healing Sebastian was her main goal. And currently, all she could think about was the Adalwolf she'd momentarily encountered on earth. Lailah was confused with the feelings she had for him. *Was it possible to fall in love at first sight?* she thought. Although she did not understand why, she could not get Roman's handsome face off her mind. His striking features created an unfamiliar yearning within her. The alluring color of his eyes reminded her of two stunning, dark onyx gemstones.

The unbearable ache inside her chest brought back memories of the human life she'd lost at the young age of seventeen. Forty-one years ago, she'd been brutally murdered at the hands of a monster. Then she remembered things she could not get out of her head... the bugs that crawled over her naked body as her soul looked down at her corpse that had been discarded in that filthy ditch. Lailah frowned as she struggled with the horrific and dark recollection of her death. Tears gathered in her eyes, and she wiped one away as it trickled down her cheek.

Lailah felt cheated. Dreams of her falling in love and a family completely stripped away. Now, she had a reason to go back to earth. To be with Roman.

Lailah's sharp-edged wings soared across the heavens with ease, carrying her to her destination. The closer she got, the tenser she became, wondering why Cronus had summoned her. *Does this have anything to do with the Adalwolf back on earth?* She worried silently, her mind in a whirlwind. *Is Roman in some kind of danger?*

Moments later, she set aside her fears, floated to the ground, and stood outside the main headquarters of the training center. The wind had come up, and the long strands of her hair lifted and tousled around her youthful face. Before she went inside, she prayed for a miracle. If somehow granted one wish, it would be for her to see Roman once again.

When Lailah walked inside, she tilted her head up and gazed at the miles of spectacular, shiny gold walls that rose up from the pristine stone floor.

"Lailah," said a familiar male voice.

She quickly looked forward as Cronus moved in her direction. He was commander in chief of all the battle angels, and stunningly handsome. His dark hair hung in thick waves past his shoulders, and his eyes sparkled a pale gray. Similar to all the other battle angels, Cronus's muscular arms were marked with unique tattoos. With the sword of truth at his side and his glorious, black wings tucked behind his back, he dipped his head in her presence and said, "You have been summoned by the Creator."

Lailah dropped to one knee, bowed her head, and said, "Yes, commander."

As she rose back to her feet and stood tall, she focused on the seriousness of his face. Her mouth went dry, and finally, she managed to say, "Do you know why?"

"He has a task for you," Cronus told her and then pointed to a long corridor that led to a giant set of double doors. "Your assistance is required. There has been an incident down below." He felt compelled to tack on, "There is healing to be done and you're the only one capable for this particular task."

She looked away from him, her eyes wide with anticipation. Then she nodded in silence and hesitantly stepped forward, her heart racing like the wings of a hummingbird. *Does the task involve earth?* she wondered and prayed it was so.

As Lailah got to the massive entrance, she suddenly felt weak in the knees, not knowing what to expect on the other side. She had never actually seen the Creator. She had only heard his voice. When he had whispered into her mind, it was as if the most beautiful symphony magically transformed itself into vocal cords. Words alone could not express the euphonious sound. According to her commander, only a few chosen angels, including himself, had witnessed his glory. It was an honor and a privilege to meet him in person.

Her hand trembled as she turned the knob. Instead of rushing inside, she leaned in a little so she could peek past the door.

"Come in, my sweet child," said a deep but gentle voice that she instantly recognized, soothing her anxiety.

Lailah was awestruck when she pushed inside. With her mouth agape, she stood frozen in place, gazing into the most brilliant and glorious light. Life, as it existed, didn't get any better than this moment. Tears gathered in the corners of her eyes, and slowly trickled down her face. Overwhelmed by his presence, she dropped to her knees. "My Lord," she gasped, lowering her head.

"Look upon me, my child," he softly commanded.

"My eyes are not worthy of your grace," she said in a tear-laced voice.

"Of all my precious angels, *you* are most worthy."

Slowly, Lailah looked up and stared into the magnificent and wondrous sight with wide green eyes. She smiled and took in every word as he explained the task that involved the special powers she'd been given. Gifted with holy fire, Lailah not only possessed the ability to shape and manipulate holy flames—which were inextinguishable by normal means and were used to trap or immobilize their enemies, rather than killing them outright—she could also summon spirits of the deceased back to the world of the living, but only with the Creator's permission. This was going to be the most difficult task God assigned her to do, but she was determined to succeed.

As she headed back to tend to Sebastian, her heart gave a pinch, and she mentally scolded herself for allowing fear to fill her head with doubts. She forced the darkness out of her mind and replaced it with light. God had answered her prayers. She was going back to *earth* and taking Sebastian and the Fury with her.

Chapter Five

After a tense pause, Captain Hodge said, "We've located Carla Rosi's body."

"What? Where?" Manuel's heart plummeted.

"At the Salem Cemetery, in an open grave," Hodge said grimly. "And that's not all."

Manuel fixed Hodge with a level stare, shifting uneasily in his chair. Whatever this was, it couldn't possibly be good, he thought.

Before Hodge continued, an uncomfortable silence settled heavily on Manuel's shoulders. His mind flashed an image of his sister's pale face. It reminded him of how responsible he felt for her death. *He wished she had listened to his warning. Wished he had done more to stop her.*

"Early this morning," Hodge continued, "a call came through dispatch from one of the cemetery's security guards. Outside the gated mausoleum, they discovered two bodies identified as Sophie Turner and Todd Blackmon. Both victims were in their mid-twenties."

"What the hell does this have to do with Carla Rosi's body?"

Hodge lifted a restraining hand. "Hold on, Detective. I'm getting to that part."

The living room walls seemed to tilt and sway as Manuel struggled to keep his composure. Even his dog's patience had temporarily faltered, as she began to whimper.

Manuel snapped his fingers. "Ira, go lay down." His firm tone demanded the dog's attention.

As Ira obeyed Manuel and left the room, Captain Hodge said, "Detective Ratcliff and I were the first to arrive at the crime scene. Before we got to the victims, we spotted an open grave. It was so foggy, we damn near fell into the thing," he said, shaking his head. "As we flashed a light down into the dark hole, we saw someone inside, and fortunately still alive. A young woman named Jena McCain. And that wasn't all we found."

"Carla Rosi's body?" Manuel asked.

Hodge silently nodded. "We received a positive match from her dental records later this morning."

"So, how in the hell did her body end up in the Salem Cemetery?"

"Well, the thing is, I believe Carla's body has been in that grave all these years," Hodge explained. "I think whoever murdered your sister did the same thing to Carla and buried her body there. The question is *who* dug up that grave?"

Manuel's mind raced back in time, to the day he watched his sister climb in the backseat of that green Camaro. It led to the dreadful arrival of the police and the shocked expression on his mother's face, to the morgue where they identified his sister's body, and back to the mysterious discovery of Carla's body.

"How did Ms. McCain end up in that grave?" Manuel asked, the cop in him coming out.

"She stated that she accidentally fell into it."

"So," Manuel blew out a deep breath. "What made you think those remains were Carla's anyway?"

"This is where it gets even more bizarre." Pausing, Hodge sighed, and then rubbed his forehead. "Ms. McCain claims she's a spiritual medium. She and her friends went to the cemetery to try to communicate with Carla's spirit. They wanted to find out what happened to her years ago."

"Well, did she? I mean, did she actually say she spoke with Carla's *ghost*?"

"Yes, but you have to understand Ms. McCain wasn't exactly coherent when we pulled her out of that grave. She was hysterical, babbling on about a curse and that she'd been bitten by some kind of creature."

Manuel's eyes rounded. "What kind of creature?"

Another uneasy silence fell between them. Hodge lowered his head and stared at the floor for several moments, rubbing his forehead again. Then he looked at Manuel and said, "A werewolf."

"A *werewolf*?"

"Yeah," Hodge replied. "I know that sounds crazy, but Detective Ratcliff was standing beside me when she said it."

"Jesus," Manuel muttered. "What do you make of this, Captain? Do you really believe Ms. McCain saw a werewolf?"

Hodge snorted. "I think Ms. McCain is suffering from severe trauma. Whatever she *thought* she saw was definitely not human. It had to be some kind of wild animal. Maybe a pack of coyotes. Hell, I don't know." He shook his head. "The victims looked as though a damn Kodiak bear attacked them. Whatever it was, it ripped out their throats. Mr. Blackmon's injuries were the worst. It appeared that some of his organs were missing."

"My God," Manuel gasped. "Was there any sign of animal tracks?"

Hodge shook his head. "Not a damn thing, which makes it even more baffling. The murders seem to be similar to all the homeless victims we had not too long ago. There is a possibility both are related. We'll know more after forensics examine the victim's bodies."

Manuel knew it wasn't related to the homeless murders, although he couldn't tell his captain. He'd sworn to the Breedline Covenant to keep it a secret. The Fury—a trio of supernatural beings that were responsible for all the murders—had surrendered to five battle angels. Manuel and his partner, Frank Perkins, had witnessed the angels take them captive. The *thing* in that cemetery had to be some other kind of monster.

"What about Ms. McCain's injuries? You mentioned she said she was bitten."

"The physician on duty at the Bates Memorial Hospital..." Hodge paused for a moment as though he was thinking, and then finally said, "I believe her name is Dr. Helen Carrington. Anyway, she is supposed to contact me after Ms. McCain's examination. Hopefully, she'll be able to pinpoint *what* kind of animal we're dealing with, if that's what *this* is."

Thank God, Manuel thought. *Dr. Helen Carrington was exactly the right physician for this type of situation. She was a Breedline, and if indeed something supernatural caused the attack, it was imperative that he notify the Breedline Covenant as soon as possible. This was way over his department.*

"I've met Dr. Carrington," Manuel finally said. "She's the same physician that was at my nephew's bar when Perkins and I came across that freaky homicide. You remember, don't you? The one where the victim's head was nearly severed."

"Yeah, I remember," Hodge said, cocking a brow. "There's no way I'd forget that incident. I still cannot figure out how in the hell someone could throw a punch that hard. The whole damn thing never made any sense. Not to mention how several witnesses reported seeing the suspect vanish into thin air, and that he looked like *Aquaman*."

"You mean the actor Jason Momoa?" said Manuel.

Hodge nodded. "Yeah, that's his name. My niece has the biggest crush on that guy," he said, rolling his eyes. "The walls of her bedroom are plastered with his posters. Of course, our suspect is obviously not the actor. I think everyone in the bar was tripping on acid that night."

Manuel smirked. "You could be right, Captain. So, you thinking the case with Ms. McCain could be cult related?"

"It's a possibility," Hodge replied. "At this rate, nothing would surprise me. That's why I want you and Perkins on this one. You two are already familiar with all the homeless murders, including the other gruesome homicides that still remain a mystery, so I want you guys in charge of this investigation."

"I'd hope so," Manuel simply said. "I've been working my sister's case since I joined the force. Now that Carla's body has been discovered, and with Ms. McCain's cooperation, I might actually get a break in the case."

"Let's keep our fingers crossed," Hodge grumbled as he got to his feet. "All these unsolved murders are starting to test my sanity."

As Manuel stood, he extended his hand. "Thanks, Captain. I'll do my best."

Hodge took Manuel's hand in a firm shake. "I'm counting on it. I want to put a closure to all this chaos. I'll expect you first thing in the morning... and *sober*."

"Will do, Captain." Manuel chuckled a little and said, "Have you contacted Perkins yet?"

"I just came from his place," Hodge replied. "And actually, it was perfect timing. His wife Missy had just made a homemade peach cobbler." He rubbed his stomach. "You should think about settling down yourself, unless you're planning on living the rest of your life as a bachelor."

"Oh, I'm pretty content, Captain." Manuel chortled. "Besides, Ira keeps me company."

The sounds of nails clipping across the hardwood floor caught their attention. As they turned around, Ira came bailing down the hallway, only to melt into a puddle of wagging tail and excited whines as Manuel called out to her.

Hodge bent down as the dog rushed to him. "Keep 'em in line, old girl," he said as he looked up at Manuel and smiled. After a few moments of petting Ira, he stood straight and patted Manuel on the shoulder. "Enjoy the rest of your evening, Detective. I'll see you and Frank bright and early."

"Sure thing, Captain."

"By the way," Hodge said. "We need to keep a lid on the *werewolf* thing. If we tell people what Ms. McCain said, after all this is over with, she could end up wearing a straitjacket in a padded cell, if you know what I mean."

Manuel nodded. "Yeah, I get what you're saying. I wasn't planning on relaying that information to anyone."

As soon as Hodge left, Manuel grabbed his phone and initiated a call. While he waited for Perkins to answer, he poured some bourbon into a glass and slugged it down.

"Hey, partner," Frank said as he answered Manuel's call. "I take it Captain filled you in on the recent homicides at the Salem Cemetery."

"Yeah," Manuel grunted. "As a matter of fact, he just left."

"So what's your intake on all this?" Frank asked. "I can't believe Carla Rosi's body has been in that cemetery this whole time."

Manuel sighed into the phone. "I'm still trying to process all the other crap we've been through. I mean, who would ever guess vampires and werewolves actually existed? Not to mention the thing with my sister—" He caught himself, the image of her fiery black wings permanently embedded in his head. "Never in my wildest dreams would I ever imagine

Lailah coming back from the dead and transformed into a battle angel. Now, we've got a double homicide to deal with," he continued to rant. "You would agree that we can safely rule out any possibility that a human is responsible." He let out another long sigh. "For the love of God, we deal with human criminals, not supernatural ones. I'm surprised I haven't lost my damn mind over all this."

"I hear ya, partner. I'm still trying to process all this myself," Frank said, exhaling a deep breath. "You think we should notify Tim Ross?"

"As much as I hate to admit it, this is way out of our league," Manuel told Frank, reaching for the bottle of bourbon, but then drew back his hand, remembering the warning his captain had given him about his sobriety. "We're going to need the Breedline Covenant's help. We have no other choice but to contact them."

"I agree, and as soon as possible," Frank said. "Captain mentioned Dr. Carrington is Ms. McCain's physician. It might be a good idea to visit the Bates Hospital before we head to the station in the morning. So, you want to meet me at the hospital in..." he paused to check his watch, "...say in an hour?"

"I'll see you in an hour." When he ended the call with Frank, he searched through his contacts and located Helen Carrington's cell number.

After checking with Helen to make sure they could visit Ms. McCain, Manuel grabbed a quick shower and a cup of coffee.

An hour later, Manuel entered the main entrance to the Bates Hospital with his partner. After they checked in at the front desk, they waited for Helen.

Chapter Six

When Jena woke, she could not remember where she was. Then dark events of the cemetery began to re-form in her mind. What had been out there this morning? From the moment she entered the eerie graveyard, everything had seemed dreamlike. She remembered bits and pieces of muddled memories: Todd attacked and dragged off by some kind of creature; Sophie's screams; then some kind of animal chasing her, yet the face of the *thing* blurred in her memory. Was it a man, or an animal? The two impossibilities mingled with reality, leaving her swirling in confusion.

Oh God… Todd and Sophie… were dead…

She couldn't think straight. She couldn't get those horrible images out of her head.

Maybe it didn't really happen. Maybe it all was a nightmare.

Jena wanted to believe that. Wanted to believe that with every fiber of her being, because what she remembered didn't seem real. Nothing seemed real anymore, not the creature, not the death of her fiancé, not the decision to abandon her dear friend, not the grave, not the body of Carla Rosi, and not the *Rougarou curse.*

Yet, it all *had* been real, and now she was cursed to become the same monster that had savagely murdered the two people she'd loved in this world more than anything.

Carla's warning echoed back to her, chilling her to the bone.

"If you give in to human blood—and I promise, you will crave it with a burning desire—you will shift into the beast."

"No," Jena whispered to herself. "Please, God, help me."

She took a deep breath and closed her eyes, but she couldn't shut out the dead girl's words.

"You have one hundred and one days to control your hunger. If you resist the urge within that time frame, the curse will be lifted."

With difficulty, she pushed through the pain and opened her eyes. As she focused on her surroundings, she saw a tube attached to her right arm. It hung from a metal pole that connected to a clear bag. That's when she realized she was in a hospital but couldn't remember how she'd gotten here.

Suddenly, out of nowhere, a tall shadowed figure appeared above her—the face a blurred, dark silhouette, and without features.

Jena's eyes were huge in her face and found she could not move. All she could do was watch in terror at a sight too immense to comprehend or explain, like something out of a dream where what you witnessed was possible only because it wasn't real.

Oh God. This is really happening.

He was leaning over her now, the contours of his face forming into a man's. The paleness of his skin appeared smooth and flawless, as if sculpted from stone. His long hair was thick and dark, falling in loose waves over his broad shoulders.

Jena could see a pair of golden eyes gazing down at her with deep intensity. High cheekbones accentuated the angles of his mysteriously attractive face... a face far too dangerous and seductive for reality. Yet his face seemed oddly familiar. It was as if she had met him before, but she couldn't place where.

Her heart was racing and her thoughts spinning in all directions. *Who is he? Is he the creature who killed Todd and Sophie? And is he here to kill me?* A strangled cry caught in her throat. She wanted to scream but found she couldn't move her lips.

"I've been waiting centuries for you." His voice was like some faraway echo, which made it all the more frightening.

Jena managed to choke out a few words, barely above a whisper, "Who... are you?"

"I'm the one who made you the way you are," he said, his voice ending in a soft purr. His eyes narrowed slightly, yet the alluring stare never wavered, even when Jena began to tremble.

Jena's voice rose. "What do you want?"

"I am your *death*, and your *life*, Jena. And I'm here for... *you*," he murmured, staring at her with such emotion—such profound emotion in his hypnotic eyes—but Jena couldn't tell if he intended to do her harm, or toy with her sanity.

His statement caught her by surprise, and she stared at him openmouthed.

When Jena attempted to reach for the nurse call button beside her bed, he caught her with a gentle but firm grip on her arm. The feel of her skin against his fingertips was like satin. He was a creature of instinct and she called to that primal part of him in a way he could not resist.

He inhaled sharply, then whispered, "Jena—"

The sound of the latch on the door turning caught his attention. With no time to spare, he pulled his hand away and transformed himself back into a shadow. Jena watched in horror as he slowly vanished before her eyes.

In sheer panic, Jena grabbed her head with both hands and screamed. Her voice echoed into the hallway, alerting the two detectives that were standing outside the doorway next to Helen.

"Jena?" Helen called out from the other side of the door.

As she and the detectives pushed their way in, they could see the hysteria in Jena's eyes.

"You're all right, Jena," Helen said in a soothing voice. "You're safe now. I'm Doctor Helen Carrington, and you're in the Bates Hospital." Helen turned to the detectives who stood close by and said, "This is Detective Manuel Sanchez and his partner, Detective Frank Perkins."

Finally, Jena's face seemed to ease as she looked up at Detective Sanchez. His features reminded her of the handsome actor Antonio Banderas.

Manuel moved closer and peered down at her with kindness in his eyes. "Ms. McCain, I promise, we're not going to let anything happen to you."

"I know this is going to sound crazy," she said, trying to clear the tears out of her eyes with her hand. "I swear I saw something in this room just now." She paused, building the courage to continue. "I think it's the *thing* that murdered my fiancé and my friend. He was here one minute and then... he was gone."

Manuel stared at her for a moment and asked, "Can you give us a description?"

"It's hard to describe. It was a shadow, yet I'm sure it was a man. He had golden eyes, and long, dark hair. For some strange reason, I feel like I've met him before."

Jena turned to face Detective Perkins. She was not surprised to find the bewildered expression on his face.

"Do you think I'm mad?" Jena asked him.

"Of course not," Perkins said reassuringly. "I'm sure there is a perfect explanation for this."

"Ms. McCain, can you tell us what you saw this morning?" Manuel chimed back in. "Do you remember *what* attacked you and your friends at the cemetery?"

"It was a man, only he was inhuman," she said wearily. "I saw it stand on two legs. It was covered from head to toe with thick, black hair." She exhaled a sigh. "Maybe it was more like a dog's fur. And it's face..." Jena was beginning to tremble all over. "It looked like the creature in that remake horror film, *The Wolfman*. You know." She shrugged. "The one with Anthony Hopkins and Benicio Del Toro."

Frank cringed at the image that displayed in his head, remembering the movie Jena had just mentioned. "Well, all the physical evidence points to something inhuman," he said. "Something with the strength of a grizzly bear. We have no doubt that no man could have possibly done this."

"What about Carla Rosi?" Detective Sanchez queried. "You told my captain you went to the cemetery to try and communicate with..." he paused as though he was trying to find the right word, and then said, "...her *ghost.*"

Jena silently nodded. "I've been able to speak with the dead since I was a child. My parents knew Carla Rosi's family. After her folks passed away, I wanted to use my gift and find her body so she could finally be laid to rest."

"My captain had the dental records checked this morning," Manuel told her. "It turns out the body found in that grave was a positive match for Ms. Rosi."

Instantly, Jena clamped a hand over her mouth, shocked by the detective's words. Without a doubt, everything she had hoped was a nightmare had truly been real.

Manuel waited and then asked, "Did you communicate with Carla?"

Jena could not look directly into Manuel's eyes. She could not tell him the truth. Revealing it meant exposing her curse. Through all the atrocities of the day, there was no one she could turn to, and she had to keep everything that Carla had told her to herself. *Except for maybe my friend in Arkansas,* she thought. *But getting her involved might put her life in danger.*

"I'm sorry," she finally said, shaking her head. "My memory is somehow strange and incomplete. I can't remember everything."

Manuel's eyes darted about her suspiciously as though he knew she wasn't telling the truth.

"Are you sure?" Manuel asked. "When Captain Hodge and Detective Ratcliff pulled you from that grave, they mentioned you saying you spoke with Carla's spirit. Is that not true?"

"All I can remember is her warning me."

Manuel cocked a brow. "Warning you about *what*?"

"The creature," Jena said, her lips quivering.

"What about your injury?" Manuel continued to question Jena. "You stated to my superior that you were bitten by the *thing* that murdered your friends."

"Detectives, Ms. McCain should get some rest," Helen cautioned. "When she's up for more questions, you'll be the first to know."

"Of course," Frank said, then turned away from Helen and focused on Jena. "We appreciate all your help, Ms. McCain."

"Yes, thank you, Ms. McCain," Manuel said, placing his card on the table next to Jena's hospital bed. "If you remember anything, please don't hesitate to contact me. Even the smallest thing can be helpful."

Jena found she couldn't stop herself from saying, "Why did it kill Todd and Sophie, and not me?"

"Maybe something distracted it," Frank replied. "We don't know, but you're one lucky young lady, Ms. McCain."

Jena slowly nodded.

Frank stepped out of the room, but Manuel paused with the door open and turned toward Jena. She seemed troubled and tense.

"I'm sorry about your friends, Ms. McCain," Manuel regretfully said. "I don't think you're aware of this, but my sister was best friends with Carla Rosi. The same day Carla went missing, the police found my sister's body. I believe the person that killed your friends is the same person that murdered my sister and Carla. You have my word..." He swallowed the lump that had formed in his throat. "...we'll do our best to bring them all justice."

Jena's eyes softened. "Thank you, Detective. And I'm sorry about your sister."

Manuel nodded and held the door open for Helen.

"I'll be right back, Jena," Helen said. "I need to speak with the detectives for a few minutes. Please, try to get some rest. Oh, I almost forgot. I put your satchel in the closet. Captain Hodge brought it by this morning. His men found it in the cemetery."

"Okay, thanks." Jena sighed in relief, praying her cell phone was still in there. If so, maybe all her contacts were still intact. The only person left in this world she could trust was her longtime friend, Angie Hawkridge. Even though they lived miles apart, they had always kept in contact, and occasionally visited one another. Jena had known Angie for years, and now, she needed her help more than ever. There was no way she could do this... *curse thing*... all alone.

As Helen followed Manuel into the hallway, she said in a hushed voice, "I've already contacted Tim Ross. He is gathering the council for a meeting."

"Have you heard from the coroner on the two bodies they found in the cemetery yet?" Frank asked Helen.

Helen nodded. "Before I could make sure one of *ours* was in charge of the examination, some of the DNA was taken by a human lab tech. After reviewing the injuries reported, I'm positive a human is not responsible. We can only pray it doesn't leak out to the press. Somehow, Jena's statement about the man-wolf got out. We could have a widespread epidemic on our hands."

"Shit," Manuel said. "So what are we dealing with?"

"I'm not exactly sure," she remarked. "The claw and teeth marks left on the victims did not come from a wild animal, and we're positive it's not a Breedline. I plan to do more extensive testing on the hair samples that I found on the victims' bodies. With luck, we'll be able to determine the species."

Manuel let out a long sigh. "Do you think Ms. McCain really saw something in her room?"

"Maybe," Helen stated. "She has been through a lot. Just as a precaution, I'll make sure we have Breedline guards posted outside her room at all hours."

"There's something she's not telling us," Manuel said. "She looks scared to death."

Helen nodded. "I agree. I made a suggestion to Tim that after Jena is released from the hospital she's taken to the Covenant for a precaution."

"I think that's a good idea," Manuel replied. "Just make sure you let me know before she leaves here."

"What about Ms. Rosi's body?" Frank cut in, changing the subject. "Do you know her cause of death?"

Helen slowly shook her head. "Since there was no tissue left on the body, it could be hard to determine, but we're still working on it."

Manuel extended his hand to Helen. "Thank you, Dr. Carrington, for all your help. Please, keep us informed."

She shook his hand and said, "Of course, Detective. I'll be in contact."

Chapter Seven

As Sebastian lay in a dreamlike slumber, he had no idea what lurked in the shadows of his deep state of unconsciousness. Yet he sensed something unsettling and sinister. He could feel it clawing with icy fingers, tearing at his mind, a twisted feeling all too familiar. A *hell* he would never escape.

Something clamped tight around his throat, and haunting words whispered in his ear, "*You belong to me.*"

Sebastian gasped silently. Not just from the alarming strength of the stranger's grip, but the images that exploded through his brain—memories of the merciless, recurring nightmares of his childhood past. The pain stabbed through his head and pierced his heart.

As hard as he tried to prevent them, more unwanted memories flooded in. He had kept this particular memory locked away, to be forgotten forever. The images came in a torrent, flooding his consciousness with scattered fragments of Eliza's death—by the hands of his biological mother—and the painful expression on Anna's face as she watched her mother's life slip away. While the dreadful nightmare of his past flashed before his eyes, an unbearable sorrow weighed down his shoulders. The sight of Anna, who he loved like a sister, led away, perhaps to her death, tore his heart into a million pieces.

His mind raced feverishly, and the song "Cry Little Sister" strangely blasted in his head at the same time the grip on his throat squeezed tighter and tighter. Struggling for air, Sebastian's lungs burned, and an unrelenting agony struck every inch of his body.

"*Give me your son,*" the stranger demanded.

Now, as the true horror of the voice sank in, he realized it was... *Lucifer.*

Meanwhile, in the same room, unaware of the dark and evil presence, Frigg was about to wear a path in the floor. Impatient for Lailah's return, he paced back and forth, before a flash of light, as if someone had turned a lamp on and off, stopped him in his tracks. From out of nowhere, three people appeared in the room. Apollyon and his fraternal twin sisters, Callisto and Electra, materialized out of thin air.

By the expression on their faces, it was hard to decide whether their arrivals were with good intentions or bad. Considering their past transgressions, it was most likely the latter. All three of them narrowed their eyes on him.

"What the..." Frigg paused, startled by the savage trio, and puffed out his chest and crossed his arms. "How in the *hell* did you get in here?"

When Apollyon moved closer to the hospital bed, Frigg gave him a nasty look—then he stood over Sebastian. Leaning this way and that, Apollyon surveyed the tubes going in and out of Sebastian's nose and the wires attached to his chest.

Just as he was about to reach for them, Frigg quickly put a hand out and said, "Stop right there, asshole."

"There's no time," Apollyon gritted out. "We've got to wake him before—"

Then the strangest thing happened. It seemed as though everything went into slow motion.

In a series of events that Frigg no doubt was going to remember for the rest of his immortal life, the center of his chest suddenly yanked forward from his spine. His torso bowed back so hard it felt as though his rib cage was about to explode. As he fought to keep his balance, his arms flailed like a pinwheel. Before he ass-planted the floor, he was levitated off his feet by an unknown force.

Abruptly, Frigg's head slumped forward as if the impact had taken all of his strength.

Without making contact, Callisto used her powers and created a protective shield, praying it would protect the enormous, black-winged angel. At first, she didn't think anything was happening, acknowledging the fact that she and her sibling's gifts had been restricted in the heavens, but then there was a subtle sound that rose up. Taking advantage of the situation, Electra quickly extended her hand and wrapped the invisible force field that held Frigg prisoner with an electrical current. Like magic, the force that held Frigg in midair began to crack as if being subjected to some kind of pressure, even though there was nothing visibly solid surrounding him. As

Electra and Callisto kept up whatever it was they were doing, the sounds of glass breaking grew more intense.

"It's working," Electra said as she looked away from Frigg and focused on Apollyon. "Hurry, brother! Wake him *now*!"

While Apollyon hurriedly tugged at the tubes and the wires that kept Sebastian in a deep slumber, the tight hold around his neck mysteriously vanished. Finally, to Sebastian's relief, his lungs filled with air, creating a needy sensation in the back of his throat, his mouth opening with a string of raspy breaths. Then he opened his eyes and looked up at Apollyon. Just as he was about to say something, Lailah opened the door, stunned in disbelief at the sight before her.

"Frigg—" Lailah called out as gravity took hold of his limp body.

Before Frigg hit the floor, Electra was the one who caught him and carefully eased him down.

"What happened?" Lailah asked as Electra moved away.

Lailah knew the answer to her question as she rushed over to Frigg and dropped to her knees. It couldn't have been the Fury's doing. After she'd spoken to the Creator, she knew without a doubt it was Lucifer who had created all the chaos. Somehow, he'd found his way into Sebastian's subconscious, spinning an evil web of threats to get to his son Arius.

"Frigg?" Lailah put her hand on his shoulder and shook him. "Frigg... can you hear me?"

When there was no response, she looked up at Callisto and Electra. "Help me," she pleaded.

"Let me take a look," Callisto said as she knelt down and thumbed Frigg's eyelids up, one by one.

Electra crouched down. "He can't be dead. He's immortal."

Lailah briefly shut her eyes and thought, *Please, God. Don't let him die. I beg you. Help him.*

Suddenly, groans rose, and there was a rustling as if Frigg was coming to. His eyes flipped wide open and he took a deep breath. "Lailah," he gasped.

"I'm right here, Frigg."

When he turned toward her, he sagged with relief and asked hoarsely, "Bloody hell, will somebody please tell me what just happened? My body feels like it's been ripped in half."

Sebastian grabbed the side of the mattress and pulled his torso upright. Then he rubbed his face, took a deep breath and blurted, "It was Lucifer."

Everyone, including Apollyon, turned toward Sebastian, who appeared angry.

"He's using me to get to my son, Arius," Sebastian continued, his voice raspy. "I'll die before I hand him over to that bastard."

"No one is going to die," Lailah said as she rose to her feet. "And no one is going to sacrifice an innocent child." She cleared her throat. "I promise, as God as my witness, Lucifer will never get his hands on your son."

Frigg directed his attention toward Apollyon. "I have a question. Why in the *hell* did you help us? It's no secret that the three of you are nothing but bloodthirsty killers."

"Frigg," Lailah cut in, her voice scolding.

Apollyon held up his hand. "It's fine." He let out a heavy sigh. "He's right. Our father created us for a sole purpose: to be used as a weapon. Our lust for human blood was uncontrollable. When he could no longer contain us, he locked us away. We were to be forgotten forever, but our mother, who was kept from us since birth, set us free."

"What happened to your father?" Lailah queried.

"He was killed by one of his experiments, a young woman he'd tortured since she was a child for his own scientific greed," Apollyon continued. "As she grew up, the she-wolf within her became far greater than he bargained for."

"How did you regain your powers?" Frigg pressed further. "It's impossible for you to be able to use them here."

"Your Creator gave them back to us," Electra chimed in.

Frigg narrowed his eyes. "Why the hell would he do that?"

"To save Sebastian from Lucifer," Electra replied.

"We are forever indebted to your Creator," Apollyon said. "He took away our suffering. We no longer lust for the blood of humans."

"Our Creator is forgiving," Lailah said softly. "All of you have been granted a second chance. He only asks for one favor in return."

Then Lailah proceeded to tell them of the Creator's plan that involved the Fury and Sebastian. After she explained the dangerous task they were about to face on earth, she volunteered her winged, comrade in arms to go with them.

Frigg was the first one to open his big mouth. "Oh hell no," he barked. He groaned as he slowly maneuvered himself upright. "I'm not going back to that dreadful place."

Lailah wanted to slap him. "I think it's a good time to have that talk," she told him. "Your attitude needs an adjustment, Frigg." Her tone took on a serious note. "Our purpose is to sacrifice for the sake of others, especially the weak and innocent. You think more about yourself instead of others. Are you truly that selfish?"

He stared up at Lailah, and the look in his eyes seemed to be miles away. This time, Frigg wasn't thinking of himself. No, in fact, he was thinking of what Lailah had said to him. Maybe she was right. Deep down, Frigg knew he'd always been a selfish bastard, even in his human life. He was well aware of what kind of hell had transpired and was transpiring down below—a century-old creature had come back to wreak havoc on the innocent, and nothing could stop it, not even his kind. He figured that's why the Creator wanted the Fury. Their allegiance hopefully wasn't a front. After all, the Creator did allow them to live, and they saved his life.

Beneath Frigg's calm mask, he was on the verge of breaking down, and the energy to keep his emotions at bay created a pain at both his temples. *Damn, the truth really does hurt,* he admitted. Now, though, he felt connected to his feelings on an entirely new level.

"You're right," he finally said and struggled to his feet. "I am selfish, but I am not heartless." He lowered his head and exhaled a curse. "I will go with you, Lailah."

Lailah smiled. Frigg's words were like a cool glass of water on a hot day in the driest desert.

She walked over and embraced him. "Thank you, Frigg."

When she pulled back, his eyes, those intense blue eyes, roamed around her face as if checking to see if there was a show of fear. But no, he did not pick up on fear. No, Frigg sensed something else... *someone* else. She was in love with a man back on earth. The *Adalwolf*. Her infatuated sentiments caused a repulsive reaction deep in his gut. He rolled his eyes but kept his smug comments to himself.

Meanwhile, Apollyon stared out of the open door, wishing that the visit to earth would eventually lead him back to his beloved, Yelena.

"Are you all ready to risk your lives for others?" Lailah asked, shifting Apollyon's thoughts back to their task ahead.

He was suddenly compelled to say, "I am ready."

Lailah looked at Apollyon and then to Electra and Callisto. "I know that you would never let personal enmity stand in the way of what the Creator has asked of you. If you promise to help us destroy the creature, which will involve the Breedline, and dedicate your life back on earth to protect and serve others, he will grant all of you a full pardon."

Apollyon's jaw ground hard, but he didn't disagree. "You have our word."

Chapter Eight

As Lawrence and Roman stood outside Melanie's front door, patiently waiting for her to open it, Roman turned to Lawrence and said, "You don't think I'm crazy for chasing after an angel, do you?"

"Roman, for the hundredth time I don't think you're crazy. I would be a hypocrite to think that, considering my own sister claims she was an angel in another life. So it certainly doesn't sound like an insane thing to have bonded with one. We cannot control who we fall in love with. It's as simple as that." He reached out and clapped a hand over Roman's shoulder. "Except it for what it is, buddy."

When the door opened, Roman immediately squared his shoulders and forced a smile.

"Roman, you looked scared to death," Melanie said, looking at him with caring, brown eyes. Roman had known Lawrence's sister since they were teenagers, and she reminded him of the beautiful movie star Halle Berry. Her athletic, petite frame and pixie haircut gave her a youthful appearance. Dressed in a pair of torn jeans and a T-shirt with the *Metallica* album cover on the front made her look even younger.

"Don't worry, honey," she told Roman. "You can trust me. I promise I'm going to do everything I can to help you."

He sighed at her soothing words. "Thank you, Mel."

"Yeah, thanks, sis," Lawrence said, peeping his head inside. "Is that pie I smell?"

She moved aside and gestured them in. "Come on in." She chuckled. "I've got a pumpkin pie with your name on it, brother."

As Lawrence walked in behind Roman, he tugged Melanie into a tight embrace and whispered close to her ear, "Thanks for doing this, sis."

She pulled back and lightly patted Lawrence's cheek. "You're welcome."

When Melanie sat down in the chair that faced the couch Roman and Lawrence were sitting on, she lifted her gaze to

Roman's to see he was staring intently at her. He looked tense and ill at ease.

"Are you sure you want to do this, Roman?" Melanie asked in a quiet tone.

Roman went stiff in response to her question. Not even a breath escaped him.

"Yes... no..." He trailed off and then expelled a long breath. "Okay, yes, damn it."

Melanie sat forward, her expression earnest. "I need you to have faith in me, Roman." She reached out and placed her hand over his. Instantly, warmth traveled up his arm, filling him with undeniable heat. Roman snatched his hand back, shocked by what he'd felt.

"I'm not going to hurt you, Roman," Melanie said, moving her hand back to her lap. "But you may feel a bit uncomfortable."

Roman glanced helplessly at Lawrence, almost as if he was pleading for some kind of guidance.

Lawrence nodded reassuringly. "Remember, you've known my sister for a long time. You can trust her, but you have to let her inside your head. Mel needs to see what you've experienced in order to find the angel you're looking for."

Without further hesitation, Roman moved from the couch and knelt down in front of Melanie so they were eye level. Regardless of the fact that he felt uneasy, nothing about Mel's odd gifts contradicted his assessment of her character. Besides, if she was truly a guardian angel in another life, how could he *not* trust her?

Then he simply placed his hand over hers and whispered, "I trust you, Mel."

She locked gazes with him and then laced her fingers through his. She could feel how terrified Roman was that something would go wrong and that she would not be able to connect with the angel he was desperate to find.

"Clear your mind, Roman, and think of her," Melanie told him, squeezing his hand in an effort to give him some encouragement.

It was like an electric shock to Melanie's system as she meshed with Roman's mind. She was assailed by desire, lust, love, and all things he'd felt when he first saw the beautiful, redheaded angel. She was one of God's battle angels, and her name was Lailah. It was almost too overwhelming for Melanie as images of the angel flooded her mind. One thing she knew for sure, the bond Roman experienced was real, and definitely not one-sided. Lailah had indeed bonded with him too. Then more images, more like messages, came rushing into Melanie's subconscious as clear as if written down for her to read.

Her mouth rounded in shock. "Lailah... is coming back."

Roman's brows shot up. "Wh-what—" he stammered. "When?"

"Very soon," Melanie replied. "And there's more."

Lawrence got to his feet and moved next to Roman. "What do you mean there's more?"

"She has been tasked by God to help destroy a creature."

Roman shrugged. "What creature, Mel?"

"An age-old creature similar to the legend of the Lycanthropy curse," she explained. "It's not just a savage killer like the lycanthrope. It stalks its victims with tactics and cunning skills. The creature stays dormant for years, buried underground in a comatose state until it's time for it to feed again on humans."

"Are you saying this creature is here, in California, roaming the streets, and killing innocent people?" Roman asked. His expression appeared worried and grim.

Melanie nodded. "And it's bitten someone."

"It's not capable of infecting others is it?" Lawrence queried.

"I'm sorry, brother, but yes. The creature's venom is very contagious. Once it has spread the virus, the victim becomes cursed. They have one hundred and one days to resist the urge to feed. If they are successful, then the curse will no longer exist. But if not..."

Tension radiated from Roman in waves. His mind was a jumbled mass of chaotic thoughts and fears. He rose to his feet and said, "Can Lailah destroy this creature?"

Melanie shook her head. "She can only use her powers to trap the creature with her gift of holy fire. She's bringing three supernatural beings with her called the Fury, a half-breed, and another male angel. With their combined powers, they might be able to destroy this creature."

"What the hell?" Roman's voice raised, echoing through Melanie's small apartment. "Why would God trust the Fury after what they did? They're savage killers!"

Lawrence lifted a restraining hand. "Calm down, Roman. Let her explain."

Roman exhaled a heavy sigh, and an apology reflected in his eyes. "Sorry, Mel."

"It's okay, Roman. I know what the Fury has done. But you have to understand. God gives everyone a second chance when asked for forgiveness. The bloodlust they were born with is gone. The Fury will no longer kill the innocent. It's like…" she paused as if she was thinking of the best way to explain, "…they've been reborn."

"We need to contact the Covenant," Lawrence said. "They need to be notified ASAP."

Roman shifted his gaze from Melanie and narrowed his eyes at Lawrence. "Shit never ends does it?"

"Unfortunately, no," he said to Roman and then looked to his sister. "Thanks for all your help, sis." He wrapped his arm around her. "Is it possible to get a piece of that pie to go?"

She leaned into his embrace and murmured, "Anything for you, big brother."

Roman's expression softened, his eyes losing some of the harsh glint. "Don't forget about me, Mel."

She laughed a little. "Don't worry, Roman. I'm sending the whole pie home with both of you."

As Melanie turned to go into the kitchen, Roman cleared his throat and called out, "Hey, Mel."

When she whirled around, he said, "You helping me is not going to get you in trouble with the big guy upstairs, is it? I mean, didn't God tell you to keep the angel thing a secret?"

"Technically, I'm only supposed to keep it from humans," she told him, cocking a brow. "Considering you're an Adalwolf and my brother is a Breedline, you would agree that I'm not breaking the rules."

"Yeah, I guess you're right," he said, grinning like a Cheshire cat. "So, Mel..." Roman hesitated, wondering if he should ask. "I've always wondered. What does God look like?"

"I don't know," Melanie replied, shrugging. "I've never seen him. Very few angels get the opportunity to witness his glory. But I've heard his voice."

"What does it sound like?"

"It's hard to put it into words," she said. Then Melanie closed her eyes and smiled. When she opened them, a few tears slowly trickled down her cheeks. "Imagine you're listening to a beautiful symphony, but the instruments are vocal cords."

Roman was speechless. After a few moments of silence, he said, "Thank you, Mel."

* * *

Now that the unexpected had happened, deciding to curse Jena instead of killing her outright, *he* would stand and claim what was rightfully his. And she was to blame for it all, her carelessness and desperation to connect with the spirits of the dead that lay forever rotting in their graves.

He closed his eyes and his mind shifted immediately to the attack in the cemetery. He reveled in his savage brutality. If only Jena had the gift to see how much worse, how much darker and sinister, the tragedies that lay just ahead of her.

Guilt and regret are your weaknesses, Jena.

He sighed and opened his eyes again, his glance going at once to the Breedline guards outside Jena's room. As he hovered above in silent menace, like a thin fog barely visible to the eye, he felt more restless by the minute. It was time to feed again. Before he floated through the vents to hunt for his next meal, he paused, consumed with an ache so deep it clawed at the pit of his stomach. Something had changed since he laid eyes upon her. Despite her weaknesses, Jena made him feel a human emotion he hadn't felt in ages.

He couldn't help wondering why she caused him such a profound emotion in so short a time. *No matter*, he thought.

This newfound feeling will only serve to be more challeng-ing... more interesting... more worth waiting for.

Now his venom flowed through her veins, spreading the virus, and fueling the gift he'd given her. Jena's lust for blood would be slow at first, and she would scarcely recognize the growing desire that would eventually take hold. It was *already* happening, in fact.

Soon she would welcome his embrace and crumble in submission.

Meanwhile, on the other side of the guarded door, lying in a hospital bed, Jena nearly let despair overwhelm her to the point of surrender. A sick taste of guilt welled up inside her, and she swallowed, forcing it down. Todd's and Sophie's deaths would forever haunt her memory.

She pulled herself into an upright position and propped her elbows on her knees. Instantly, she cradled her face into her palms and fell apart.

Why did I bring them to that cemetery? Jena asked herself. *It's my fault they're dead.*

Without warning, a voice whispered in her subconscious. It was so realistic, so compelling, that Jena covered her ears, desperate to silence the words.

"I am your death, and your life, Jena. And I'm here for... you."

I don't want any of this, she was thinking. *This curse... I can't deal with it by myself. My life is slipping away from me. I can't...*

A chill settled over Jena. No one would possibly understand or believe what she'd experienced. Nobody could. Except maybe the creature that had attacked her in the cemetery. She briefly closed her eyes as a memory came back to her of the same creature moving through the dark cemetery, brutally killing Sophie and Todd with its fangs and claws, and then that deep horrific pain of something biting into her flesh. *Why did the man-beast let me go?* she painfully thought. Now, she was to become that *thing*. It was only reversible if she could last one hundred and one days without killing for human blood. Then a horrifying thought came. *Did the creature plan for this to happen?*

All this was maddening. It took Jena a second to pull herself together and gather her thoughts before she completely lost her sanity. *Why did he let me live? What does he want from me?*

Why couldn't she understand his meaning? And why—despite what he'd done to Todd and Sophie—did she feel compelled by his presence? It was as though she was spellbound.

"Jena..."

Jena lowered her hands and looked up. For an instant, she heard his voice again, piercingly vivid, almost as though he'd whispered her name into her ear—the alluring stranger with mesmerizing eyes, with that look of desire in them.

He *couldn't* be the creature that murdered Todd and Sophie, Jena tried to convince herself. *Surely, I would have sensed or felt something evil, or got a sign if he'd been the person responsible for their deaths.*

"Yes, Jena," the stranger's voice whispered in her mind again. "*You need me... the only one who can satisfy your desires...*"

It seemed as though her inner subconscious was playing tricks on her, driving her to the brink of madness.

Jena decided immediately that her sanity—and her life—were over.

In realization, she didn't know who the man was that mysteriously appeared in her room. He could be anybody. He could be a madman that escaped from the mental ward. He could be a hospital employee with a criminal past, or a serial killer preying on innocent patients. It could have just been her imagination. It was also a possibility she was losing her mind. Maybe he didn't exist at all.

Frowning, she thought, *what do my gut instincts tell me?*

With a burst of courage, Jena came back to reality and said, "They're telling me to give Angie a call." Then she reached toward the nightstand, unhooked the charger to her phone, and searched through her contacts for her friend's number.

Right after high school, both of them had moved apart from one another to live out their separate dreams. Although

Jena had moved to California for art school and Angie joined the Navy, they never lost contact. Sure, they were busy with life—juggling careers and relationships—but they always found the time to maintain their friendship.

Holding her breath, Jena held the phone to her ear for several seconds, praying Angie would answer.

"Hey, girlfriend," Angie said at last. "I haven't heard from you in a while. Is everything okay?"

"I'm fine," Jena lied, holding back tears. "How are you doing?"

"What's going on, Jena? I can tell something's off by the tone of your voice. Talk to me, girl. You and Todd didn't break up, did you?"

Jena bit hard on her bottom lip, fighting the urge to fall apart. She could feel a lump in the back of her throat building, but she was determined not to cry.

"Angie," she managed to whisper. "I'm in trouble."

"You're not pregnant, are you?"

Even though the situation was grim, Jena couldn't help but crack a little smile.

Angie had always been so straightforward and *blunt*. That was one of the characteristics Jena loved about her. No beating around the bush. Angie told it like it was. She was honest and upfront, with a heart of gold. Angie wasn't fake or the type to put on a front. She was the kind of friend that always had your back no matter the circumstance. When you think of Angie, the word *fun* comes to mind, among others: spontaneous, witty, and flirty, with the most contagious laugh and a stubborn determination. Jena had always admired Angie's disregard for rules and routines. It *was* her way or the highway. Jena never experienced what it was to have a sister, but Angie was the closest thing, not to mention her very best friend. Without her, Jena felt completely alone in the world. In the last few days, Todd's and Sophie's deaths had taken a toll on Jena, and right now Angie was the only person she could trust. She definitely couldn't go to her parents. They hadn't spoken in years. Besides, they'd never believe her. They'd always blamed her ability to speak with the dead-on mental illness. Sometimes she wondered if they even cared whether she lived or died.

"No, it's not that," Jena finally said. Her mind was spinning. "It's about Todd and Sophie. Something bad has happened."

Angie grumbled something under her breath. "Jena, please don't tell me they're screwing behind your back. I swear—"

"They're dead," Jena cut her off.

"What—"

"Angie, th-they were murdered," Jena stammered. "It was h-horrible."

"Oh my God, Jena. I'm so sorry. What the hell happened?"

There was a moment of silence after Jena explained to Angie what had happened at the cemetery. She left out the part about the curse and the man-wolf. Jena thought it best to tell her in person.

"Hang tight, girlfriend," Angie simply said. "I'm booking the next flight out there."

Jena blew out a sigh of relief. "I knew I could count on you. Thank you, Ang."

Before she ended the call, Angie said, "Don't worry, Jena. I got your back."

Chapter Nine

Tara looked over at the speedometer and then cast Brandon a sidelong glance.

"Brandon..." she grumbled.

"What?"

"Slow down. The roads are wet. You're going to get us killed."

"Take it easy, Tara." He chuckled. "It's just misting. I'm not going to wreck."

"No, I mean it, Brandon. Please."

He slid his hand across the seat to reach for her. "Come here, honey."

She sighed and scooted away from him. "Damn it, Brandon."

"What?" he echoed.

"Will you please keep both hands on the wheel?"

She saw a half-smile form at the corner of his mouth.

Tara stuffed her hands into the pockets of her fleece jacket and fixed him with a worried frown. "I'm serious," she said. "It's not funny."

"Okay, okay," Brandon said, easing his foot off the accelerator.

She looked up at him and let out a deep breath. "Thank you," she said quietly.

He quickly looked away from the dashboard, winked an eye at her and said, "Sure thing, princess."

Tara groaned. "I hate that."

"Hate what?"

"When you call me *princess*," she said, her voice laced with irritation. "It's like you're categorizing me as a drama queen."

He cocked a brow. "Well, you've got your moments."

"Whatever..."

Brandon smirked. "Why don't you lay your head back and get some rest. You've got to be exhausted after pulling a double shift at the hospital."

"Nah, I'll be fine," she said around a yawn. "Besides, we'll be home in fifteen minutes."

He shrugged. "Suit yourself. So, anything exciting happen at work?"

"Nope," she shot back. "Unless you consider giving sponge baths and changing bedpans exciting."

He grimaced. "Sorry, honey."

"Hey, it's just part of the job."

He briefly took his eyes off the road and looked in her direction. "You have a big heart, Tara. I've never met anyone that cares for people the way you do."

She smiled. "Thanks, babe."

Her smile touched a private spot in his heart. With a nod, he turned away and focused his eyes back on the road. Silently, he wondered if he'd made a big mistake; the kind that could change a course in their relationship. After all, they had been living together for almost two years. Sure, they had their share of problems, but maybe this year he would find the courage to ask Tara to marry him. Maybe...

As they sailed along the highway, Tara leaned against her door and stared out the window of the pickup. The moon among the tops of the trees seemed to be watching her through the clouds, and the red color was both eerie and hypnotizing at the same time. Tara shivered and burrowed deeper into her jacket. Why did full moons make her think of creepy things like... ghosts, vampires, and werewolves?

"Hey, are you falling asleep?"

Tara turned to Brandon and muttered, "No, I'm not falling asleep." She rolled her eyes and turned back to her window.

A few minutes later, she closed her eyes. The hum of the motor mixed with the sound of the windshield wipers and the rocking motion of the truck made her drift off. Tara was in a pleasant state between sleep and awareness, where everything seemed warm and safe. She forced her eyes open and gazed out into the darkness, out at the bloody moon. Then something fast-moving caught her eye. She focused on the side of the road. Something *big* was traveling swiftly through the tall, thick weeds, keeping pace with Brandon's truck, but it was so foggy she could barely see a thing.

Tara looked over at the speedometer. They were going... *sixty*.

Her hands were gripping the edge of the seat, and there was a growing tightness in her chest.

Oh God...

"What the—" she gasped.

"What's wrong?" Brandon mumbled.

Tara opened her mouth and tried to warn him, but never got the chance.

As a dark shape, the size of an enormous animal came out of the fog, Brandon hit the brakes and Tara screamed. The tires screeched and the truck skidded across the wet, black asphalt and began to spin. Whirling around in circles, Tara could see the monstrous, dark silhouette standing on all fours, statue-like in the middle of the road watching them with yellow, glowing eyes. *Waiting...*

Everything seemed to move in slow motion. As Brandon desperately tried to reach for Tara, his head slammed into the window, and the truck careened off the road, landing in a deep, muddy ditch. The impact nearly jarred Tara's teeth loose. She screamed in protest when her body whipped against the seatbelt. All Tara could think in those last few seconds before she went unconscious was... *we're going to die.*

He crouched on the road and waited. The image of the two humans, who appeared wounded, fueled its rage and gave the creature direction. The rage blended with hunger and consumed his mind in flames. Quickly, his crouching form slipped into the grassy, open field and moved in behind some bushes to watch his prey more closely. *This is better*, he thought, *better for surprises, better for an attack.*

Brandon and Tara did not see or hear the creature as it crept out of its hiding place on all fours like a tiger on the hunt, stalking its prey. After his visit at Jena's room, he'd spotted the young couple leaving the hospital and followed their vehicle.

He circled around and around the pickup with the moon shining above him, deciding which one he was going to take first. He finally stopped outside the driver's side and peered into the window. Inside, the couple lay unconscious and unaware of his presence. Preparing to strike, he paused, taking notice of his own reflection in the window staring back at him. Dark hair covered his face, and his amber eyes steamed with hatred. The humans were oblivious to his long, black claws that reached for the door handle.

As Brandon opened his eyes, they rounded in sheer terror. The creature's mouth opened into a white grin of sharp teeth, and a low grumble that sounded almost like cackling issued from its hideous mouth. It looked like a wolf with distinctive human features, but it was as big as a horse. Its lupine ears came to a point atop its huge head and its pupils appeared split like a cat's.

The predator and the prey stayed there staring at one another as though time had suspended. Savoring the moment, the man-wolf could already feel its fangs gorging on the warm flesh of the man's jugular. As it tore the door completely from its hinges, Tara suddenly roused by the distinctive sounds of creaking metal and Brandon's voice.

"Oh, God, Tara—run!"

He screamed in a voice she couldn't believe was his. It grew into a long spiraling cry of agony as if being ripped apart. In the end, there was only a garbled wail streaming from his throat, joined by a terrifying howl of rage, followed by dead silence.

With a ragged cry, Tara tried to lift her head, praying Brandon was still alive. In desperation, she searched the driver's side for him but found it abandoned. Blood took his place, coating everything. The seat... the steering wheel... the dashboard...

"Brandon," she said hoarsely. "Brandon!"

As though she was in a dream, her sight blurry and mind disoriented, she saw something dark and sinister dragging Brandon across the grassy pasture as if he was nothing but a lifeless, flimsy doll. Then the sickening sounds of flesh and muscle tearing from bone echoed across the open grassland to Tara.

She moaned, swallowing back the pain. "H-help," she breathlessly pleaded. "Someone please, help us."

Lying there on her back, all alone in the dark cab of the truck, her head throbbed, and she struggled to comprehend what she had seen. Her brain felt short-circuited. All Tara could sense was the cold, wet mask of her face, and she wasn't sure if it was tears or blood.

Finally, after several attempts, she managed to unfasten her seatbelt and reach for the steering wheel. She winced at the searing pain coming from her torso as she pulled herself up. It hurt just to draw even the shallowest of breaths. Just as Tara looked to where the door had once been, she saw Brandon's murderer in the distance rise on its hind legs. It glared in her direction as if she was its next victim.

Oh, please... God...

When it set off after her, she grabbed the passenger's door handle and pushed it open with the strength and ability brought forth by pure adrenaline. It drove her willpower to keep moving. A sense of calm descended, washing away the paralyzing fear. Before, she had Brandon to protect her. Now it was up to her to save herself.

No one can save you now but you, she tried to convince herself.

Tara fell to her hands and knees on the wet, mucky ground. On all fours, she forced her injured body onward and crawled until her bare hands felt the rough exterior of the road. Despite the pain and the loss of blood from a cut on her forehead, she managed to get to her feet. She was shaking so she could barely trust her legs to support her weight. All the while, feeling dizzy and lightheaded, she kept waiting for the feel of the beast's sharp claws, knowing it was getting close.

Without warning, a horn blared behind her. Tara flinched and whirled around as a black Hummer screeched to a stop only three feet away. She put her hand above her eyes to block its bright headlights, noticing another SUV as it pulled up alongside it. Then one of the windows slid down.

"Ma'am, are you all right?" said a man. His voice was a deep baritone.

Tara shook her head. Even though it was a complete stranger, she felt an immense sense of relief. When she turned to look for the creature, it was gone. It simply vanished, leaving nothing but empty shadows.

"P-please, I need help," was all Tara could think of to say as she toppled forward and dropped to her hands and knees.

Seconds later, the sound of doors opening, voices exchanging, and heavy footsteps came next. Then she felt a pair of strong hands gently cradle her body as if she was a small child. The stranger lifted her off the ground effortlessly.

"Don't worry, ma'am," the man told her, carefully placing her inside the large SUV. "I'm a trained medic."

As he placed a cloth on her forehead and applied pressure to the deep cut, she caught a glimpse of his face. He had the oddest color of eyes. They were so green the color glimmered in the darkness. He was dark-skinned and ruggedly handsome, reminding her of the character Raze in the movie *Underworld*.

His emerald-green gaze looked upon her with kindness as he began to examine her with professional efficiency. "Are you injured anywhere else?"

Tara moved her hand on her left side and gasped in pain.

"Easy there," he soothed Tara, softly caressing her shoulder. "You may have some broken ribs." Then she heard him speak to someone else. "We need to get her to the Bates Hospital."

Tara listened to the other man say, "Shouldn't we check to make sure no one else was in the accident?" He spoke with some kind of European accent.

An overwhelming feeling suddenly took hold of Tara. Her body felt as though she was floating and her lids started to close.

The *Raze* doppelganger lightly shook her shoulder and said, "Miss, I need you to keep your eyes open for me. Can you tell me your name?"

Forcing her eyes to stay focused, she muttered, "T-Tara." She cleared her throat. "Tara Hood."

"Tara, my name is Lawrence Colbert. And my friend here is Roman Kincaid," he said in a reassuring voice. "I promise we're going to get you help. But before we take you to the hospital, we need to know if there was anyone else with you."

For a brief second, the world went hazy. Suddenly, the sounds of Brandon's nightmarish screams and the image of the creature dragging his lifeless body flashed inside her head. As her lips began to tremble, tears spilled down her cheeks. "Oh God," she cried out. "Brandon..."

Lawrence looked away from Tara and shifted his eyes toward Roman. "Stay here with her," he said. "I'll go check."

Tara grabbed ahold of Lawrence's shirt with a tight grip. "It's too late," she said, sobbing. "It killed him."

Lawrence narrowed his eyes. "*What* killed him, Tara?"

Her eyes rounded in fear. "I tried to warn him, but it ran out in front of us. I... it just came out of nowhere," she stammered. "Brandon tried to stop. H-he swerved. He tried not to hit *it*."

"*Hit* what?" Lawrence queried.

Fiercely, she shook her head as more images pounded in her subconscious. "It was dark... foggy." Her voice was trembling, her whole body shaking. "It was something... big!"

She buried her face in her hands and struggled to breathe. It was too much shock for her to process. God, she wanted this to be only a dream.

"Please, Ms. Tara," Lawrence pressed further. "Try to calm down. This is very important. What was it you saw?"

As Tara lowered her hands, she stared at Lawrence in mute horror. Then she exhaled a deep breath and said, "It was some kind of wild animal. It looked like a wolf, yet it stood like a man."

Lawrence shot Roman a look that told him without words what he was thinking.

Shit! Roman silently mouthed.

"I need you to think, Tara," said Lawrence. He had a seriousness to his tone. "Did this animal *bite* you?"

When she shook her head, Roman exhaled, realizing he'd been holding his breath.

"Okay, good," Lawrence said, breathing a sigh of relief. "Let's get you to the hospital."

"What about..." she briefly paused, her lips quivering, "Brandon's body?"

"Don't worry, Tara," Roman said, trying his best to console her. "While Lawrence drives you to the hospital, I'll stay here and see to it he's properly taken care of."

She frantically shook her head. "Please, it's not safe." She raised her voice. "That *thing* could still be out here. You need to call the—"

"Trust me, Ms. Tara," Lawrence interjected. "Roman will be just fine. He'll call for help."

There was a rock-hard assurance to his voice and a comforting look in his eyes. Despite her fears, the unwavering confidence in his words soothed her.

Tara sighed. "Thank you, both," she said, her voice laced with gratitude. "If you hadn't gotten here when you did." She swallowed back tears. "You saved my life."

Chapter Ten

He had to act quickly. He'd been forced to seek cover, hiding in the dark shadows as two men intervened with his next kill. Yet, they were not human, he realized.

He could smell their scent, too—as surely as he smelled the blood from the remnants of the raw meat of his victim's flesh.

Should he attack and take what rightly belonged to him? As the desperate need to kill surged through every vein, filling him with agony, he did not.

No matter, he thought. He would follow them. They would lead him to the girl.

As his mind drifted to Jena, he closed his eyes and remembered the last time he had gazed upon her face. It wouldn't be long now. Her life as she knew it was drawing near the end, and finally, she would be his. The anticipation was almost more than he could bear. Just thinking of it made him ache. She would learn submission and oh, how she would love him. He would take her to his own private world of eternal darkness.

"Jena," he whispered and then turned at the sound of approaching footsteps.

In a kind of fascination, he watched as three men engaged in conversation only a few feet away. They were different from the ones before. But they too were not human.

He narrowed his eyes and listened.

The one with a dark Mohawk sounded frustrated, his words tinged with discontent as he stood addressing two men with long, blond hair who were obviously identical twins.

"I just got off the phone with Tim," Drakon said. "Instead of taking Ms. Tara Hood to the hospital, he's having Lawrence deliver her to the Covenant. Helen is meeting them there."

Both Jace's and Jem's eyes rounded.

Jace huffed in exasperation. "What the... but she's human," he protested. Then he cast a glance at his twin, who stood next to him, his expression grim. "I think it's a bad idea."

Jem shifted uncomfortably and heaved a sigh. "I don't see any way around it. We can't have her talking to the police. They'll think she's lost her damn mind. We already have enough to deal with. If human reporters find out the girl's identity that was attacked in the cemetery, they'll hound her relentlessly. Besides, she'll need our protection. It's possible *whatever* this creature is, both girls could be in danger. It may see them as a threat and try to finish what it set out to do in the first place."

"I agree," Drakon confirmed, smoothing a hand over the spiked strip of hair down the middle of his head. "They'll be safe in the Covenant. Tim is going to have Helen relocate Ms. McCain in our care after she's released from the hospital. She'll need to be monitored for the next hundred or so days."

Jace shrugged. "What for?"

"Because..." Drakon paused, clearing his throat, "Ms. McCain was bitten by the creature."

"You're not talking about the curse of the Rougarou are you?" Jem queried.

Jace's eyes narrowed and he turned to stare at his brother. "I thought that was just a myth."

Drakon shook his head. "No, it's real. The creature can stay dormant underground for years until it's time to feed again. This savage killer has preyed on humans since the 1800s. He's been responsible for several unsolved crimes throughout history," he continued to explain. "Among the Breedline, he is known as *The Werewolf of New Orleans, The Louisiana Vampire, The Blood Moon Killer,* and *The Beast Man.* It's said that he was thought to be the notorious serial killer, *Jack the Ripper.*"

"Holy shit," Jace muttered. "Are you serious?"

"He's right," Jem pointed out. "And what's worse, *we* cannot destroy it."

Jace made a dry sound of amusement. "That's messed up. So, what the hell are we going to do?"

"*We* are not going to do anything," Roman said as he walked up behind them.

Everyone turned to Roman in surprise.

Jace narrowed his eyes in confusion. "What do you mean *we* are not going to do anything? Why the hell not?"

Roman moved closer. "Hold on," he fired back, holding a hand up. "Let me explain."

Jace cocked a brow. "Well, I'm waiting." His voice sounded impatient. "Let's hear it."

"Earlier today, Lawrence and I went to see his sister, Melanie," Roman hesitantly said. "She has a special ability that is supposed to be kept a secret from humans, but considering the dire situation, and the fact that we don't exactly fall into that category, I think it's safe to say I won't be breaking any rules by telling you."

"What are you getting at, Roman?" Drakon chimed in.

Roman let out a deep breath and simply said, "Melanie can speak to angels."

Jace leaned in and held up his hands in question. "And?"

"Remember the redheaded battle angel that took Sebastian?"

When Drakon, Jace, and Jem nodded at Roman, he continued to explain. "Well, her name is Lailah, and Mel contacted her. She and another battle angel, you know the one that looked a lot like Billy Idol?"

When they nodded, he continued, "Anyway, they are coming back to help us destroy this creature."

"Thank God," Jace said with a sigh of relief.

"There's more, isn't there, Roman?" Drakon asked in a deep baritone.

Roman looked agonized. His jaw clenched and he glanced at all of them as if weighing whether or not to tell them the rest.

Jem placed his hand on Roman's shoulder. "Roman, we need to know everything Lawrence's sister told you. Whatever it is, we're not going to judge or otherwise say anything negative about Melanie." He eyed Jace, making sure he understood the implied suggestion.

Without voicing his opinion, which was rare, Jace nodded an understanding.

"None of the battle angels have the power to destroy this creature," Roman said. "Lailah can only trap it with her holy fire. I'm not sure what the other angel can do, but apparently God has tasked them to bring four others along who possess the ability to help take down this creature."

"Do you know who they are?" Jem asked.

"Sebastian and the Fury," said Roman.

Jace shot forward, and he was about to explode, but Jem flung his hand out to silence his brother, his expression fierce. Jace's lips tightened but he stepped back and didn't further interrupt.

The look on Drakon's face ranged from incredulity, to doubt, to *what in the hell is Roman smoking?* He shook his head. This whole thing sounded crazy. He couldn't even wrap his head around it. But the important thing was that Lawrence believed his sister, and Roman believed her too.

"What did Lawrence's sister say about the Fury?" Drakon asked Roman. "Won't they be just as dangerous as this creature we're dealing with?"

"Melanie said God has lifted their lust for human blood. She explained it as if they'd been reborn."

"So, I guess this means Sebastian is alive," Jace finally said. "How is that bastard tied into all this?"

Roman looked at Jace, despair gleaming in the shadowed depths. "I'm sorry, Jace. Mel didn't say."

"Did she... did she give you any idea when this is all supposed to take place?" Drakon hedged.

"Mel just said soon," Roman replied.

Shit! Drakon thought. "Okay, this is what we're going to do," he said, taking charge. "I'll call Tim while you guys finish cleaning up the body so we can tow the truck to the Covenant. Between Tim and Tessa, maybe they can figure out what the hell we need to do next."

"Someone needs to tell Eve and Anna about Sebastian," Jem spoke out, changing the subject. "They deserve to know he's still alive. Especially since it's a good possibility he'll show up at the Covenant."

"I don't know." Jace shook his head. "I think it's a bad idea. Besides, if I catch him near my family—"

"Come on, Jace," Jem cut him off. "Put yourself in their shoes. What if it were you? Don't you think Tessa and Cassie would want to know the truth if they thought you were dead?"

"He's right, Jace," Drakon pointed out. "I agree with your brother. They need to know."

Jace threw his hands up in defeat. "Alright, alright," he grumbled. "I get it already."

"I'll tell Mia as soon as we get back to the Covenant," Jem said. "I think it would be best for Eve to hear it from her sister. Since Eve has become close to Sebastian's sister, I'm sure she would want to be the one to tell her."

Drakon nodded. "I agree. Thanks, Jem."

As *he* watched the four men walk away, a sinister smile curled his wolfish lips. *They were all mistaken,* he thought. *Only my own kind has the power to destroy me.*

* * *

Panic splintered through Yelena, and she came awake with a gasp. For a moment, she thought she was having another dream, reliving the mournful memory of the battle angels taking Apollyon and his siblings away. Now, she realized it was not a dream, but a vision. This time, the black-winged angels were bringing them *back*.

"Oh, Apollyon," she cried out.

As she scrambled to sit up in bed, her entire body shook. Then she swallowed back the knot that suddenly formed in her throat. She felt... sick.

Seconds later, she was in the bathroom on her knees leaning over the toilet bowl, one hand holding back her hair, the other braced on the seat. It seemed forever that she strained and suffered through a series of violent heaves.

Every time she thought the nausea was over, she'd go back to bed—and two minutes later, she was on her knees again, heaving up absolutely nothing.

Finally, her stomach settled. Lying in bed, she put her hands on her belly and said in a faint whisper, "Could I be pregnant?"

A persistent knock at the door made her flinch. Then a soft voice called out, "Yelena, darling... are you okay?"

Recognizing Sonya's voice, Yelena got to her feet and opened the bedroom door.

Distress radiated from Sonya like a beacon. Her face was as white as a ghost and she looked as though she'd been crying.

Yelena frowned. "Sonya, is something wrong?"

Sonya sighed and then her lips turned up into a blissful smile. "Oh, Yelena," she choked out and flung her arms around Yelena, holding her so tight that for a moment she couldn't breathe. "I knew it was true!"

"What are you talking about?" Yelena asked.

Sonya pulled from their embrace to face Yelena, her eyes drenched with tears. "You're going to have my grandchild."

Yelena's eyes rounded. "H-huh?" she stuttered. "B-but, how do you know?"

"I had a vision," Sonya said. "It was so beautiful. I saw Apollyon holding his son. My grandson." She placed her hand on Yelena's belly and whispered, "Your unborn child."

Yelena felt her mouth drop open. "Well, I..."

As Sonya caressed Yelena's stomach, she had a moment of total, stunned disbelief. *Is it possible I'm really carrying Apollyon's child?*

"He's coming back," Yelena finally said. "I had a vision too. The same angels that took Apollyon, Callisto, and Electra are bringing them back."

Sonya's eyes filled with more tears. Her hand trembled as she removed it from the place that held her grandchild and covered her mouth. "Thank God," she sobbed.

"I'd be more than happy to help you find an excellent physician, one that deals with our species of course. I know a great ob-gyn in Berkeley—a woman. Between you and Apollyon sharing the genetics of a succubus, I'll feel more comfortable knowing you're getting the best care."

Yelena nodded. "Thank you, Sonya."

"Your welcome, darling," Sonya murmured. "I'll make the appointment first thing this morning. In the meantime, I want you to promise you'll get some rest. Remember, that's my grandbaby you're carrying."

"Don't worry, Sonya," Yelena said, placing her palm over her belly. "This child is a part of Apollyon. They both mean the world to me."

Chapter Eleven

It was seven o'clock in the morning when Jena turned on the television in her hospital room. A familiar face on CNN news came into view, although Jena could not recall her name. She appeared to be interviewing a criminal psychologist going by the man's name and credentials displayed at the bottom of the screen.

The female newscaster asked, "Dr. Gunneman, do you believe the Salem Cemetery murders were some kind of an animal attack?"

"No, I don't," he simply replied. "I truly believe we're dealing with a cult."

"Are you talking about a *satanic* cult?"

The expert nodded. "The DNA is unequivocal, but I have no doubt the ones responsible are human. Somehow, the evidence has been contaminated to make us believe there's a supernatural creature on the loose."

"But what accounts for the person's strength?" the newswoman asked. "I mean what kind of human being has the power to do that to a body. The evidence states that two bodies were left mangled and some of the body parts were missing."

"Again, we are rushing to conclusions." The physician's voice sounded irritated. "Clearly, we're dealing with disturbed individuals. It is unimaginable of what a psychopath can be capable of doing. They possess much more strength than the average person, and probably the most dangerous."

"What about the witness at the crime scene?" The newswoman shrugged. "According to the police records, a young woman, whose identity has not yet been released, was the only survivor. What do you make of the astounding statement she made on that dreadful day when officers pulled her out of that open grave?"

"It's all a bunch of nonsense," Dr. Gunneman protested. "She's clearly distraught by the dreadful incident. It's a possibility the perpetrator could have suffered some type of hideous affliction at some point or they could have been born with extreme deformities. Whatever the case," he continued to explain, "after what the poor girl witnessed, I don't doubt she's suffering from major psychological trauma."

"So you don't think there's a possibility that a large animal, maybe a mountain lion, a wolf, or some other type of *thing* could have done this?"

Dr. Gunneman smirked. "If you're asking if I believe a werewolf or some mythological creature is responsible for the murders, your answer is no. It's absolutely rubbish," he grumbled. "And if anyone buys that line of bull, I'd say they're on the borderline of insanity."

As Jena listened to the psychologist's rants coming from the television, her thoughts drifted. She remembered the creature's howls, that savage sound when it had attacked Todd and Sophie. Although calls came in from people claiming to have heard howling that night, there were no witnesses to the killings except for her. The fact of the matter was, no one could possibly fathom whatever did this, but speculation about the mysterious animal would continue.

She changed the channel and muttered under her breath, "If only you knew, doctor smarty pants. You have no idea what it is to see someone you love to be ripped apart."

No matter what bad situation a person suffered in their lifetime, she thought, *enduring or witnessing the vicious ugliness of that kind of death would never compare.*

At once, a woman's face filled the screen. It was Sophie's mother. Her expression was of grief and despair. "I don't care what the police say," she said, her eyes flooded with tears. "I know my daughter was breaking the law when she broke into that cemetery, but still, she didn't deserve to be torn apart by some crazed lunatics." She started to sob. "My Sophie deserves justice."

The camera closed in on Sophie's father. "Please, if anyone knows anything..." He briefly paused and wiped his tear-stricken eyes. "...I beg you. Help us bring justice for our daughter. She was a beautiful person with a bright future ahead of her." His lips quivered. "We've put up a fifty-thousand-dollar reward for anyone who has information that will help the authorities identify the person responsible for Sophie's murder."

Jena switched to another channel, unable to bear the pain Sophie's parents were going through. When she came to an image of another female reporter addressing a camera, talking about the Salem Cemetery murders, Jena hit the OFF button.

"I can't take this anymore," she said, overcome with grief.

All Jena could think about was the curse. When would it begin? Would she hurt the people she cared for? When it started, how bad would her lust for human blood get? Deep down, she knew she was already feeling it.

If only I knew, she thought. *Could I really be capable of this? Was there a way to predict or control it?*

Jena wanted to reach out to Sophie's and Todd's parents, but Dr. Helen Carrington and the detectives assigned to her case suggested she wait a few days. For now, it was imperative that her identity remained anonymous. Her safety was a priority. Whatever attacked her, and brutally killed Sophie and Todd, might still be out there. It was possible the person or *thing* responsible could be gunning for her. Somehow, it had already leaked out to the press that the survivor of the Salem Cemetery murders was at the Bates Hospital. More than likely, someone at the hospital traded the information for money in return. Fortunately, Helen listed Jena as Jane Doe on all the hospital's medical records in order to keep her identity private. Helen also sternly cautioned Jena against agreeing to give DNA samples unless she ordered the tests. With every new revelation concerning the murders, the reporters grew bolder in their search for a story and a comment from the only survivor.

Last night, Dr. Carrington had offered Jena a safe place to stay until all this blew over. *The fact of the matter was,* she thought, *sooner or later, no one would be safe around me.*

A knock at the door startled her, followed by a familiar voice. "Hey girl, you dressed?"

Jena fought back tears when she caught sight of Angie's face peeking through the cracked doorway. "Oh, thank God you're here."

As Angie came into the room and moved next to Jena's hospital bed, she looked just the same as Jena always remembered her. Although it had been over a year since they saw one another, it seemed as though Angie hadn't aged since their senior year in high school. She had her shoulder-length hair arranged into a thick braid, and her tanned skin was flawless as always. Built like an athlete, Angie's frame was long, lean, and strong. Her eyes were the color of the bluest ocean. Not only was Angie beautiful, but she was also smart and confident. Jena could definitely see her friend as a sports model.

Angie tried not to show any negative emotions, no matter how bad her best friend might look. Seeing Jena now was like viewing a chaotic display of cuts and bruises, stitches and bandages, and Angie could feel her good intentions crumbling away. She attempted to keep from frowning and instead, faked a smile.

"Do I look that bad?"

"Sorry, girlfriend." Angie sighed. "But you look like hell."

Jena let out a half-suppressed laugh. "Thanks." She patted the covers, though her voice and movements were still weak. "Sit. I need to tell you something. *Something* just between us two. What I say here is sealed."

Angie placed her hand over her heart. "Amen, that's without question." Then she slipped out of her jacket, tossed it on a nearby chair, and perched on the edge of the bed. Placing her hand over Jena's, she said, "Haven't I always had your back? For crying out loud, woman, I practically had to jump through hoops to get in to see you. Your doctor is one tough cookie."

Jena's heart was aching, and all she could do was nod her head. As she opened her mouth to speak, her heart crept into her throat. She tried to swallow it back down as Angie lightly squeezed her hand.

Angie frowned. "Jeez, girl. Whatever this is, you know you can tell me. I'll keep it locked in the vault."

"It wasn't a man who attacked me and killed Sophie and Todd," Jena finally said.

Angie shook her head. "What are you talking about, Jena?"

"You're going to think I've done lost my mind."

"Jena—"

"I saw it, Angie. I looked into its evil eyes. At first, I thought I was dreaming when I saw it attack Todd. It was like someone else's nightmare. But it wasn't. It was real. I had to leave Sophie behind," she continued to ramble, her words mixed with tears. "I thought I was going to die. And it... bit me."

"What *bit* you, Jena?"

Jena wanted to answer but couldn't. The air seemed to be getting thicker. The room seemed to be growing smaller. Her throat was tightening, and her pulse began to quicken.

When Jena felt the steady grip of her friend's hand, she could feel her own hand trembling.

"I know what I saw, Angie," Jena continued, her eyes wide with terror. "I'm not crazy."

"Please Jena," Angie said, her voice soothing. "I promise. Everything is going to be all right. I'm not going to think you're crazy."

Jena nodded. "It chased after me, and the pain... I have never felt pain like that. Like my entire body was on fire. And then I fell into an open grave."

Angie's eyes stared straight into hers, filled with that unconditional love and trust Jena always found so comforting. "You've told me things before—private things—because you knew I'd believe you, right?"

"Yes," Jena replied.

"Well, why wouldn't I believe you now?"

"Because," Jena's voice cracked, "it sounds so *damn* crazy."

"Try me, Jena."

"Okay." She swallowed back tears. "It was a werewolf."

For a long moment, neither of them said a word, just sat there in silence, staring at one another.

"I believe you, Jena."

Jena's expression immediately eased. "Y-you do?"

"Yes, I do."

"Thank God." Jena released Angie's hand and settled back against the pillows. "But," she released a heavy sigh, "there's more."

As Jena explained to Angie about speaking to Carla Rosi's ghost and the curse, the hairs lifted on Angie's arms. She leaned toward Jena, her voice urgent, "What the hell are *you* going to do?"

Jena was silent. Just thinking of what Sophie's and Todd's families was going through—and what worse things were about to happen—she turned and looked off toward the window.

"Hey, girl." Angie's voice drew her firmly back again. "Don't worry. I'm not leaving you. There is no way you are going through all this alone. I may know some people who can help you."

"But I could be a danger to others." Her voice trembled. "That *thing* cursed me. I'm going to turn into some sort of..." Jena's voice broke. "I might hurt you. I couldn't live with myself if I—"

"Don't start flipping out on me, Jena. We can deal with this. We'll figure it out."

"For Chrissake, Angie. This is serious. I've been lying in this bed all morning, listening to the news about Sophie and Todd's death. I can't even reach out to their family. It's my fault they're dead. I took them to that cemetery. I brought all this—"

"Stop it, Jena," Angie cut her off. "Stop blaming yourself. It's not your fault."

"Angie, I can already feel the virus spreading inside of me. I don't know how much longer I will be able to control it. What if I kill *you*?"

Angie heaved a deep breath. "You won't."

"What are you saying? How could you know that for sure?"

"Because..." Angie paused, thinking of the right words to say, "...I'm not exactly human."

The two girls stared at each other in utter silence.

Angie, watching her friend's expression, already knew what Jena was going to say.

"What the *hell* are you talking about?"

For the first time, Angie felt relieved to be able to tell her friend the secret she had been keeping from her all these years. Yes, she knew it went against their laws, but in this case, she had no choice. Jena was in danger and she needed the Covenant's help.

"I'm a Breedline."

Jena furrowed her brows in question. "What?"

After Angie told her all about the Breedline species, they just sat and held on to each other's hand, as though, between the two of them, they were each other's anchor.

"So, do you actually turn into a wolf?"

"No. Not yet anyway," Angie said with a chuckle. "It's different for us chicks. Sure, the guys get their first change at age eighteen. We get our wolf when we make love to our bonded mate. So, considering I lost my virtue *years* ago and I haven't yet produced a tail or sharp teeth, I guess you can honestly say Mr. Right hasn't crossed my path."

Jena felt blindsided. She stared back at Angie, unable to muster up a single word. Finally, she found her voice and said, "Whoa. I thought my problem was going to sound crazy. Damn, girl."

"You ain't kidding," Angie said. "The good news is you're not alone. I know a place that will keep you safe. They will help you, Jena. Trust me."

"Where did the Breedline originate from?" Jena queried. "I mean, your people are kept a secret from humans, right?"

"We come from the same place as everyone else," Angie explained. "God created all mankind. He created us for a special purpose. To help protect humans. It's written in our book of True Laws. And yes," she went on, "our kind is supposed to be kept on the down-low, but sometimes, like in your case, our secret is revealed."

"This is all so surreal," Jena said, looking past Angie as though she was lost in thought. "I can't believe all this is really happening." Then her eyes went wide. "Wait a minute. I thought you said only Breedlines born with an identical twin could shift. You don't have a twin, do you?"

"I did." Angie sighed. "My mother had a miscarriage during her second trimester. Her name would have been Alyssa."

"I'm so sorry, Ang. How come you never told me?"

Angie shrugged. "My mother had a hard time accepting Alyssa's death, so we just never talked about it. It was one of those things my family tried to forget."

"Losing a child must have been hard for both your parents. I can't imagine."

"Yeah, things were tough growing up in my house. Well *hell,* I don't need to tell you. I'm sure you remember what it was like."

"My family wasn't exactly *normal* either," Jena said regretfully. "You know how my parents treated me growing up. They were ashamed of my ability to speak to the dead. For years, they thought I was schizophrenic. And that's not even the worst of it. After I graduated, they pretty much didn't have anything to do with me. I haven't heard a peep from them in years."

"What doesn't kill us makes us stronger, right?"

"Ain't that the truth," Jena replied. "So, this place you were talking about," she said, changing the subject. "Are they like you? I mean, are they Breedline?"

"Yep," Angie said shortly.

"Man, it's going to take me some time to wrap my brain around all this. I feel like I've crossed over to another realm."

"Kinda like an alternate universe, huh?"

Jena chortled. "Yeah, something like that."

"What am I supposed to tell my physician? She offered me a safe place to go after I'm released here."

"Jena, she's talking about the same place I am."

She looked at Angie perplexed. "But how does Dr. Carrington know about this *place*?"

"Girl, Dr. Helen Carrington is a Breedline too. Do you really think she would let me see you otherwise? Hell, the hospital has two guards posted outside your door twenty-four seven. This shit is serious."

Jena just shook her head. "It gets more bizarre by the minute."

Angie laughed a little. "Yeah, it's a lot to take in at first. But trust me, you'll get there."

Jena had welcomed her dearest friend to her secret with wide-open arms, trusting her completely, and that was exactly what she got. *Trust*.

"Thank you, Ang." Jena was obviously relieved. "I knew I could count on you."

Angie lightly squeezed Jena's hand again. "That's what friends are for."

Chapter Twelve

When Detective Manuel Sanchez got out from behind the wheel of his unmarked car, the morning sun was unmercifully bright. As he covered his eyes with a pair of Ray-Bans, he felt the vibration of his phone. He retrieved it from his back pocket and recognized the caller ID. *Shit!* It was the head of the Breedline Covenant, Tim Ross.

He checked his watch, noticing it was a little after eight o'clock, which meant the fun was just getting started. In about fifteen minutes, he and his partner, Detective Frank Perkins, were supposed to meet with their captain, who would skin their asses if they showed up a minute late, to go over Jena McCain's case. Captain James Hodge was not a man who took kindly to tardiness.

Manuel looked up at Frank and said, "Go on ahead. I'll meet you there in a few. I've got to take this call."

"What do you want me to tell the captain?"

"Hell, I don't know." Manuel shrugged. "Tell 'em I'm in the shitter."

Frank nodded and headed toward the station while Manuel stayed back to take the call.

"Detective Sanchez," he answered.

"Detective, this is Tim Ross. Can we talk, off the record?"

"Yeah," Manuel replied, leaning back against the car. "I've got a few minutes."

"We had another incident last night, similar to Ms. McCain's."

"Shit!" Manuel stood alert and then asked, "Any survivors?"

"Her name is Tara Hood," Tim said. "Roman and Lawrence happened to come upon the accident in the nick of time, but her boyfriend wasn't so lucky. He was ripped to pieces just like the couple in the cemetery."

Manuel heaved a heavy sigh. "So, did they actually get a look at this *thing*?"

"No," Tim replied. "I guess it got spooked when Lawrence and Roman showed up."

"I take it they didn't call this one in," Manuel prompted.

After a few seconds of silence, Tim finally said, "Detective, this is way over your department's head. We took Ms. Hood to the Covenant, where she is safe. She suffered a few broken ribs and a nasty cut to the forehead. She's lucky to be alive. Helen is taking care of her injuries. On that note, I thought I would let you know I'm having Ms. McCain transported here when she's released from the hospital. It's crucial that we watch over her as well. I believe Ms. McCain is not only in danger, but she could possibly be dangerous to others."

"And why's that?"

"Trust me, Detective," Tim reluctantly said. "It's a bit of an odd story. I'll explain later in person."

"What about the body?" Manuel asked, the cop in him coming out.

"We've got the body stashed in the Covenant's mortuary."

"You have your own funeral home?"

"Let's just say..." Tim briefly paused, "we're prepared for just about anything."

"You got an ID on the victim?"

"His name is Brandon Coghill. He and Ms. Hood lived out on Highway 59, about two miles from the scene."

"I'll want to ask Ms. Hood a few questions as soon as possible," Manuel said, checking his watch. "And I want to hear this *odd* story regarding Ms. McCain. Right now, I have a meeting with my captain. I'll call you—" He paused when he caught sight of a news reporter moving in his direction. Beneath his unshaven jaw, a muscle worked in aggravation. "Damn it!"

"Is something wrong, Detective?"

"Damn reporters," Manuel grumbled into the phone. "They're probably after Ms. McCain's story. I gotta go. I'll be in touch."

He started to walk away, but a TV news reporter with a camera crew blocked his path.

"Detective Sanchez," said a nerdy reporter sporting coke bottle eyeglasses, a navy blue suit, and a matching pinstriped tie. "I'm from the Mercury News. Do you have a few minutes to answer some questions about the Salem Cemetery murders?"

When he didn't answer, the reporter pushed it, taking one step closer toward Manuel. "Can you give us an update on how the girl is doing that survived the attack?"

"No," Manuel gritted out, his eyes narrowing to slits.

Sensing the aggravated tone of Manuel's voice and the stone-cold look on his face, the reporter took a few steps back.

"What do you think about the girl's statement?" the reporter asked, further irritating Manuel. "Do you really think she saw a *werewolf*?"

Manuel removed his sunglasses and glared at the reporter with such intensity that for the smallest second he wondered if the detective was going to throw a punch.

"Our sources tell us the victims at the crime scene were torn apart, and one of them was half-eaten. What do *you* think, Detective? The public deserves to know the truth." He held the microphone closer to Manuel's face. "Are the police searching for a man or is there some kind of wild animal on the loose?"

Manuel took a step forward, towering over the reporter, imposing and seething. "This case is not up for questions." His temper sparked and he couldn't help but add, "Take your camera crew and get the hell out of here."

The reporter drew a breath and lowered the mic. He wanted to ask one more question, but instead, backed up a step, his lips forming into a thin line.

Manuel pointed a finger right at the reporter's chest and said, "Let's just make something clear right now. I don't want to see you or your cameras here again."

The reporter shrank back as Manuel pushed past the camera crew and headed for the entrance to the station.

With his mind focused on Captain Hodge's office, Manuel started down the hall when he heard shouts as two officers led a guy in handcuffs toward the conference room. As Manuel stopped and cast a glance in their direction, the prisoner glared at him and shouted, "What the hell are you lookin' at, pig?"

One of the detectives that were guiding the convict said something back, but Manuel didn't hear it. Whatever he'd muttered was effective, as the shaved head scumbag immediately shut up. He was a witness in the Benedetti crime family, who had been trafficking guns, drugs, and prostitution for generations. His name was Jimmy Fratianno III, grandson of the late Aladino "Jimmy the Weasel" Fratianno. Three years ago, they brought him in on cocaine and heroin transportation charges. Captain Hodge had offered him a deal in exchange for a bigger fish. If Jimmy gave up the names of his connections, it could take five years off his sentence.

When Manuel turned around, his partner was motioning him over.

"Get your ass in gear, Detective," Frank told him. "You've got exactly thirty seconds before Captain rips you a new one."

"Keep your pants on. I'm coming." Manuel was about to start for the door when he heard a shotgun go off.

He instantly ducked. "What the f—"

In the corner of his eye, Manuel caught sight of his partner's torso twist like a rope. Frank went with the force of the blast, spinning to the ground with his hand covering his shoulder.

Moving fast and low, Manuel got Frank the hell out of the way, managing to take cover behind a desk in case the shooter was ready for round two.

"Stay down," Manuel told Frank as he quickly took stock of his injury. It was nothing too serious. Fortunately, it was just a graze.

Frank winced. "It burns like a son of a bitch."

Manuel slipped out of his jacket and pressed it against Frank's wound. "Oh hell, Perkins," Manuel grumbled quietly. "Suck it up. The slug barely grazed you. It's bleeding like a sieve, but it'll slow if you keep pressure on it."

As Frank held the jacket over his wound, Captain Hodge shot around the corner on his hands and knees like a bat out of hell.

"What the hell is going on?" Hodge demanded. Then his eyes homed in on Frank's bloody shoulder. "Shit! You all right, Detective?"

Frank nodded. "It's just a flesh wound, Captain."

Hodge let out a heavy sigh. "Did either of you get a look at the shooter?"

With his eyes locked on the captain's, Manuel shook his head. "No, but I think I have a pretty good idea who the asshole is," he said to Hodge. "It's Jimmy Fratianno."

Hodge checked his watch, realizing it was time for Mr. Fratianno's deposition. "Shit," he cursed through gritted teeth. "I almost forgot about the damn Beneditti case."

"Yeah," Manuel said. "Jimmy was supposed to give up those names, but it looks like he suddenly had a change of heart."

"For Chrissakes," Frank chimed in. "How in the *hell* did he manage to get his hands on a damn shotgun?"

Manuel reached for his Colt .45 and kept his voice low, "I don't know, but I'm gonna find out. Captain, stay here with Frank. I'm going in."

Captain Hodge nodded in agreement. "Head around the back," he said as he put a hand on his holster that held a Glock .40 caliber. "I'll cover you from the rear."

With his weapon in hand, Manuel slipped out from behind the desk and made a run for it while Hodge covered his back.

Craaack! The blast from a shotgun split the silence and hit Hodge's office door, sending wood splintering into pieces.

Blam! Blam! Blam! Captain Hodge immediately fired back.

Shit! Manuel cursed as he swung around a corner and flattened himself against the wall. Then, more shots fired. Thinking quickly, he jogged down a narrow hallway, past several armed officers who were crouched behind their desks and came to the backside of the conference room. When he peered around the corner, he saw the two detectives from earlier, lying on the floor, appearing unconscious. Beside them was Jimmy's attorney. Blood pooled on the floor beneath him.

As Manuel looked away, he saw Jimmy Fratianno, setting up, taking aim at the desk where his captain and partner took cover.

"Jimmy!" Manuel yelled before he could fire off another shot.

Jimmy heard his name and turned just in time to see Manuel, a semiautomatic in his grasp and the barrel aimed in his direction.

"Drop your weapon, *now!*" Manuel ordered.

Jimmy turned to fire his weapon, realizing it was over. In that nanosecond before he pulled the trigger, Manuel unloaded his.

It seemed as though everything moved in slow motion. He watched as Jimmy's body took the impact and the shotgun flung from his hand. Blood spurted from his head and torso like a crimson geyser as he toppled to the floor.

Manuel moved next to Jimmy's body with his weapon drawn and kicked the shotgun away. As he crouched down to check for a pulse, something *strange* happened.

Straining muscles rippled beneath Jimmy's face, while the tendons in his neck stood out like thick cable. Then, one by one, the gunshot wound in his left temple and chest contracted, disgorging the embedded fragments. The bloody bullets clattered onto the floor and rolled across the tile toward Manuel's boots.

"What the—"

In the blink of an eye, Jimmy's body began to expand like something within him was overtaking his natural form. As his orange prison jumpsuit came apart at the seams, coarse black fur sprouted from his pale skin, covering the two bullet holes and various prison tats throughout his body. All the flesh-twisting carnage took Manuel by surprise.

The detective's eyes widened in alarm as he finally became fully aware of what was happening. In that moment, the 1981 British-American horror film, *An American Werewolf in London* suddenly came to mind. Whatever Jimmy had shifted into, it looked similar to the grisly werewolf in that movie. Acting on instinct, Manuel raised his gun, but the snarling creature swatted it away with a sweep of its massive paw. Knocked off balance by the force of Jimmy's newfound transformation, Manuel staggered backward.

As the wolfish beast stalked toward Manuel on all fours, police officers swarmed forward with their guns raised. When the creature heard the distinctive sounds of rifles cocking, it stopped in its tracks and growled. The rogue wolf in Jimmy wanted nothing more than to lunge for Manuel's throat. Regardless of the odds against him, the wolfish fiend realized that, even with his supernatural strength, he could very well be at a severe disadvantage if their weapons were loaded with silver. Although, silver wasn't lethal to his kind, but it burned like hell. Searching for an escape route, its glowing eyes seized on one of the windows. The hideous beast growled at Manuel one last time, then sprang through the window. Glass shattered and rained down onto the floor with the force of the monstrous impact. Police officers shouted, and opened fire, missing the mysterious creature by mere inches.

Damn it! Manuel watched in disbelief as some sort of *werewolf* managed to escape a precinct full of armed men and women.

Did it really matter? he thought. Whatever Jimmy Fratianno was, the son of a bitch somehow survived a bullet to the head, not to mention the one that hit him square in the heart. The question weighed heavily on his mind. Did Jimmy's transformation have anything to do with the creature they were after? It couldn't be the same creature, Manuel figured. Jimmy Fratianno had been behind bars during all the recent attacks. It was bad enough having to deal with one freak of nature. Now there were two? *Shit!*

Chapter Thirteen

As Lawrence pushed his way into the Covenant's exam room, his heart fluttered, and for a split second, he stopped in his tracks, wondering if he was overstepping his boundaries. Maybe he should have asked Dr. Helen Carrington's permission before barging into her patient's room. Shrugging it off, he moved forward and perched on a rolling stool next to a bed that resembled one from a hospital. Stretched out under several blankets, resting peacefully, was probably the most beautiful woman he'd ever laid eyes on. Pulled back into a ponytail, her jet-black hair hung in thick waves next to her head. The golden undertone to her skin appeared to be of Italian descent, and in spite of all the bandages on her face, she was breathtaking.

"Lawrence?"

Helen's voice was right behind him as she came through the door, but Lawrence felt as if she were miles away. In fact, the whole world seemed nonexistent except for the young woman he and Roman had rescued earlier. Was it just a coincidence, he wondered, that they arrived at the right time to save her life, or was it God's way of performing a miracle? According to Lawrence, God's miracles were not coincidences.

All his life, he'd set aside his personal life and dedicated it to saving others, never taking the time to fall in love. Now, he knew why. He'd been waiting for this moment, for this woman, for this time.

Ms. Tara Hood, he thought. *My heart belongs to you.*

And even though that might sound ridiculous to others, the connection he felt for her was so strong he couldn't deny it if he tried.

Tara opened her eyes. "Are you the one who saved my life?" she said in a weak voice that just about stopped his heart.

"Yes, I am." Lawrence quickly rose to his feet and placed a shaky hand over hers. The instant he made contact, his whole body turned to mush. Damn, she was getting more alluring by the minute. If this kept up, he was going to end up losing his mind. Period.

On that note, he leaned in close and caught a whiff of her perfume. Nothing fruity or flowery, but nothing he could place commercially either. Was it her shampoo, or just the natural scent of her skin? *Dear God, where's my head at? Apparently, not between my shoulders.*

"Is there anything I can get you, Ms. Tara," he finally asked as he looked into her amazing, chestnut eyes. "Are you in pain?"

His voice was quite deep and familiar to her, but her brain struggled to process everything that had happened. After the accident, she remembered hearing the same soothing voice. And then a blurry recollection of a pair of strong hands cradling her body as though she was a delicate piece of glass in fear of shattering. As bits and pieces of her memory came to her, images of someone putting her inside an SUV and then being driven to what appeared to be a castle—similar to the one in her favorite childhood bedtime story—flashed before her eyes. Inside the spectacular, massive structure, someone carried her down a long corridor to some type of attached medical facility that was as clean as any hospital and everything smelled like Lysol. That's when Tara's instincts kicked in. It was obvious whoever lived here wanted it kept secret. *But why?* One thing she knew for sure. The owner definitely had big money. How they managed to live here without someone from the outside finding out was certainly a mystery. Whatever the case was, the man who had brought her here made her feel safe and protected.

"Where am I?"

"Don't worry," he told her. His voice sounded reassuring. "You're in a safe place."

While he spoke to her, he leaned down into her field of vision, and she recalled the odd color of his eyes. They were shimmering green, like two polished emerald gemstones. The mesmerizing shade complimented his dark complexion.

"Ms. Tara, do you understand what I'm saying?"

Tara nodded and glanced over as far as she could toward the doorway. The physician that had treated her injuries stood back with a slight grin on her face. Then something suddenly registered in her mind. Her name was Dr. Helen Carrington. She was a physician at the Bates Hospital. With a sense of relief, Tara refocused her eyes back on the handsome man that had saved her life while Helen quietly stepped out of the room.

She cleared her throat. "I'm sorry, what did you say your name was?"

"Lawrence," he replied. "Lawrence Colbert."

"Thank you, Lawrence... for helping me."

"You're welcome, Ms. Tara."

As more memories came to her, Tara looked at Lawrence in question. "There was someone else with you that night you found me," she said. "He spoke with a European accent."

"Yes," Lawrence replied. "He's a good friend of mine. His name is Roman Kincaid."

Tara nodded, and then suddenly remembered what *this* Roman had promised her.

"Did he..." She paused as her chin began to tremble. "...take care of Brandon?"

Lawrence nodded and looked at her gravely. He knew more than a little something about how losing one felt, so yeah, he understood the kind of pain she was in.

"Don't worry," he said, trying his best to console her. "Everything has been properly taken care of. And I'm sorry for your loss, Ms. Tara."

She swallowed hard as one tear slipped out of the corner of her eye. On instinct, Lawrence reached forward and wiped it away.

She took a halting breath and nearly broke down. "Thank you," she finally said.

A moment passed in silence, though Tara's heartbeat echoed in her ears. Then, with his gaze intently studying hers, he asked on impulse, "Were you married?"

Tara went very still, her expression frozen. It hit her then. Brandon's death came to her, and the memory of how distant their relationship had become. She closed her eyes to gather strength, and said, "Uh, no—"

"I'm sorry, Ms. Tara." Lawrence nearly bit his own tongue. "I didn't mean—"

"No, no," she interjected. "You're fine, Lawrence." For some strange reason, he made her want to open up, if only a little, about her and Brandon's relationship. Perhaps this would give her closure. "Brandon and I lived together for a few years, but we were not married," she continued, her tone dismal. "Sadly, our relationship was not what it used to be. But I guess it doesn't matter anymore, does it?"

A lump grew in his throat, and his eyes gleamed with a worried look. *Uh-oh. Had he pressed too far?* He felt like an idiot. A yellow light suddenly flashed inside his head. *Proceed with caution.*

"Do you have any next of kin living close," Lawrence reluctantly asked, changing the subject. "I mean, do you want me to contact anyone?"

Tara sighed and regretfully shook her head. "Both Brandon and I have no one. He left his family years ago due to an unfortunate situation, and I ran away from my foster family when I was fourteen."

He lightly squeezed her hand. His touch was soothing, careful, and everything about him softened. "I'm so sorry. What about friends or coworkers?"

"Most of my friends are coworkers. If you don't mind, can I use your phone to contact the Bates Hospital? I'm a nurse there, and I still have several vacation days that I haven't used. I need to ask for personal time off."

Lawrence nodded. "I'm sure that can be arranged, but right now, you should rest, Ms. Tara. I could come back later if you like." The huskiness of his voice drew a blush to her cheeks.

"Yes, I would like that, Lawrence."

Still holding her hand, he smiled and said, "I'll be back in an hour."

Before he released her hand, he gave it a final squeeze. As he turned to leave, Tara said, "You know what killed Brandon, don't you?"

When he looked at her, the expression on his face clearly answered her question.

"What was *it*, Lawrence?"

"Please, Ms. Tara." His eyes were pleading. "Get some rest. I'll explain everything when I return. All you need to know now is that you're safe here."

Her brows furrowed with confusion. "Where's *here*?"

"You're in a..." he briefly paused, thinking of the right word to say. The last thing he wanted was to confuse her more. "This is a safe house," he continued. "I promise. Nothing can harm you here."

Tara was confused and yet comforted by his words. In fact, something in his eyes made her feel warm on the inside.

After she accepted his word that he would explain everything later, Lawrence took a last look at her and then stepped out into the hallway where Helen was waiting.

As Lawrence's bonding scent wafted over, Helen knew without a doubt, he had feelings for Tara.

"You feel something for her, don't you?" she asked Lawrence.

If it weren't for his dark complexion, Lawrence's cheeks would have flushed beet red.

"How can you tell?"

"The look on your face," Helen said. "It's the same way Alexander looks at me."

"Oh, I—"

She held up a halting hand. "It's okay, Lawrence. I think it's sweet."

He tilted his head a little. "You do?"

"Yes, I do."

Lawrence exhaled a deep breath and then settled back against the cinder block wall, his eyes still focused on Helen. "So, would it be okay with you if I come back and check on her in an hour?"

"You can visit her as much as you like. Aside from a few bruised ribs, she should make a full recovery in two to four weeks," Helen explained. "But that doesn't mean she's free to leave the Covenant. Tim strictly said under no circumstances was Ms. Hood to be released. It's for her protection that she stays put until *whatever* is out there killing humans is destroyed."

"I agree."

There was a moment of silence, as if Lawrence wanted to ask Helen something. She could practically feel the awkward tension in the air between them.

"Lawrence, is there something else you want to ask me?" Helen finally spoke out, breaking the ice.

Stiffening his resolve, Lawrence forced himself to ask Helen what had been on his mind since he'd first laid eyes on Tara.

As he inhaled a deep breath, he spoke on an exhale, "Do you think it's possible that Tara might have inherited the Breedline genetics but doesn't know anything about it?"

"It's possible," she replied. "A lot of our species are out there without the slightest clue. They carry the gene but never have the knowledge of it, especially if they're born without an identical twin. It could be because it's kept secret or their family doesn't know. Look at Detective Sanchez for instance. He only found out a short time ago. His father carried the gene but never told his mother. It's possible that even his father never knew of his lineage."

Lawrence sighed. "Yeah, I guess you're right."

When he said not another thing, the quiet was now making Helen feel uneasy. Then she said, "Would you like me to run a DNA test?"

His eyes rounded. "You would do that?"

She nodded. "Of course, this would have to be just between us."

"Yes, yes, of course," he said with a hint of excitement in his voice.

Before Helen walked away, she placed her hand on his shoulder. "I'll let you know when I find out. Oh, and tell her not to worry about her job. I've taken care of everything at the hospital. When this is all over, she'll be able to return to work."

"Thank you, Helen."

As Lawrence stood outside Tara's room, grinning like a Cheshire cat, he felt his phone vibrate in his back pocket. When he retrieved it, he saw it was Tim calling.

"This is Lawrence," he answered.

"We've got a situation," Tim said. "I just got a call from Detective Sanchez. His precinct was attacked."

"Attacked?" Lawrence questioned. "By what?"

"Going by Detective Sanchez's description, it sounds like we're dealing with a rogue wolf," Tim explained. "I need you and Roman to check this out ASAP. The guy's name is Jimmy Fratianno. He's a convicted felon brought in to turn over state's evidence on a big mob case. In exchange, he would receive time off his sentence. After checking our records, I found out he's a rogue wolf from the Chiang-Shih demon's army that we apprehended two years ago. Jimmy had agreed to do his time in a human prison facility without shifting. It's my fault," Tim regretfully admitted. "I let this one slip through the cracks. I should have known better than to trust his word. He's always been nothing but a damn criminal. Hell, his entire family raised him in that environment. I guess I just felt sorry for the bastard. When he refused to join the demon's army, he'd been relentlessly tortured." Tim let out a heavy sigh. "Now we have a whole damn police department to deal with. It's just a matter of time before all this leaks out. The damn press is already having a field day over the Salem Cemetery murders. They will *eat* this shit up."

"You can count me in," Lawrence said.

"Thanks, Lawrence. Detective Sanchez will fill you in on all the details," Tim said. "The good news is, we've got Jimmy's location. Before he went off to prison, the council planted a tracking device on him. It's inside his chest cavity. If he tries to remove the microchip, it will detonate."

"Damn," Lawrence shot back. "Does Jimmy know the device is an actual explosive?"

"Yeah, he knows."

"I've got a feeling you're about to tell me the bad news, am I right?" Lawrence sounded reluctant.

"Jimmy is hiding out at his Uncle Vincent Scarpelli's estate."

"Aw, shit," Lawrence gritted out. "That place will be loaded down with security. It won't be easy getting in there."

"I'm sending Drakon, Jem, and Jace to meet you and Roman at the police station," Tim explained. "Detective Sanchez knows you're coming."

"I'm on it," Lawrence said.

After Lawrence ended the call with Tim, he headed toward Tara's room. Before he left the Covenant to meet up with Roman and the others, he wanted to let her know Helen had taken care of her time off at the hospital. Mostly, he wanted to make sure she knew he was a man of his word. He promised to explain everything to her when he returned.

Chapter Fourteen

Hours later, after Angie had left the hospital, Jena suddenly came awake, her eyes searching through the dark room. She could have sworn she heard a faint movement on the other side of the door.

She hesitated for a moment, unsure of what to do. Finally, she rose from the bed, covered herself with a robe, and quietly crept toward the door. Then she heard that muffled sound again. It wasn't exactly footsteps, but something softer... lighter... gently stirring the air.

As Jena pressed close to listen, she felt a cold draft on her bare feet coming from under the door. She crouched down and felt along the floor. *Yes,* she thought. *I can feel it, but where is it coming from?*

Contemplating whether she should investigate, Jena slipped out of her room before she could change her mind. Standing outside of the door, she took a nervous glance around. It was dark, except for a few flickering fluorescent lights that hung from the ceiling and a lamp on the receptionist's desk.

That's strange, she thought. There wasn't a sign of life anywhere. No guards, no nurses, no one at the front desk. Not a soul in sight. *Where did everyone go?*

Instantly, the hairs on Jena's arms lifted and goosebumps rose at the cool breeze that crept over her skin, as though someone had breathed down the back of her neck.

She whirled around, her eyes searching every corner. "Hello," she called out. "Is anyone there?"

"Shhh... come this way."

"Angie?"

Jena turned toward the soft echo of her friend's voice and saw a distant shadow of a person standing in a narrow hallway, holding the door open that led to a stairwell.

"In here, Jena," the familiar voice said, motioning Jena to follow.

Bewildered, Jena began to walk slowly, curiosity building inside her. Before she managed to get close, the dark figure of what *looked* like her friend disappeared through the door.

Jena rushed onward. "Angie, wait!"

Surely, Angie saw that I was coming. Why didn't she wait for me?

Jena opened the door and nervously peered up the poorly lit stairwell. She couldn't hear or see anyone. Deep inside, she knew she should turn back around and run to her room. Instead, she kept her feet moving up the stairs, one step at a time. She was compelled to find her friend. What was Angie doing? Why did she come back so late?

When she finally reached the top, she came to a door with a sign that read PRIVATE.

After a timid glance around, Jena slowly reached for the doorknob. It was cold to the touch. Pushing her fears aside, she went in.

She stood in a large room filled with shadows and damp, cool air. Jena shivered and shoved her hands inside the pockets of her robe.

"Angie?" she whispered, exhaling steam from her parted lips. Her gaze swept from one end of the room to the other. There were file cabinets, lab tables with computers, piles of books stacked on top of one another, and medical instruments she could not easily identify going by the odd shapes of them.

As Jena waited, her ears tensed for the slightest noise. She couldn't hear anything but the rhythm of her heart beating and the hum of illuminated glass doors that were across the room. It reminded her of refrigerated shelved storage units in grocery stores until she moved closer.

That's when she realized what was inside. It was *blood*.

Rows upon rows of bags of it stored and locked away. Shelf after shelf of dark red liquid kept chilled like the finest of wines.

Sweet wines that someone would sip with great pleasure, she thought as she ran her tongue over her lips.

Jena froze as a lone, tall figure suddenly appeared from out of the shadows and moved into the light. She could see his elegant profile and was certain she'd seen it before.

In my dreams, Jena reminisced. "In my nightmares," she whispered.

His handsome features were too beautiful and seductive to be real. The soft illumination from the glass clung to him like a shining aura.

It was at that moment she realized *who* he was: the stranger from her dreams... the *monster* in her nightmares.

Like a distant observer, she watched as he reached to open the glass door. Her mouth watered as he took out a precious bag of blood. He then slightly tilted his back and poised it delicately above his mouth. With his brows clenched, he curled his lip off his front teeth. His fangs positively gleamed in the light as he silently punctured the plastic. As the crimson gold ran down his throat, he let out a satisfied sigh.

After downing all the contents, he ran a hand over his mouth, and said, "Would you like a taste, Jena?"

The room faded around her. She struggled to breathe, to think, or to move, yet she could hear his velvety voice and recognized it at once.

He dropped the empty bag at his feet and held out his hand. "Come closer," he told her. His tone was rich, deep, dominating.

"Where's Angie?"

He made no reply.

"W-what do you want from me?" Jena cautiously asked, trying to hide the trembling in her voice.

"I want all of you," he murmured. "We were destined to be together since the beginning."

"What the *hell* are you?" she said, glaring at him. Her tone suggested *monster* could easily be the descriptor.

Leveling his stare on her, he said in a sultry voice, "You know what I am. I'm your destiny." His words rolled off the tip of his tongue like silk.

A chill slithered down her spine. She wanted to escape, but she yearned for the truth. "You're the one who took Todd and Sophie's life, aren't you?"

A sinister grin formed his lips. "But I spared yours." He sounded pleased. "I gave you a gift."

Jena gritted her teeth. "You damned my soul."

"You're very courageous, Jena, in spite of your fear. I find it quite arousing."

"Tell me your name then," she demanded.

With a powerful yearning flashing in his gleaming eyes, he whispered into her mind, *"Jena, I am your beloved."*

"I don't believe you," she cried out. "You're lying!"

Just then, Jena felt a warm sensation closing all around her, searing all the way through her. Her entire body was shaking. She could hardly stand.

"You feel it, don't you?" His voice was hypnotic. "It's a part of me flowing through your veins."

"No..."

"Don't you see, Jena? I've given you eternal life."

In the blink of an eye, he was upon her. Jena's breath caught in her chest. She looked up at him and froze. His glowing eyes were on her throat, and they were burning with a passion that wasn't just sexual. A dark, spicy scent came out of his skin in a rush. As she drew it in, she could feel his whole body shaking with restraint.

When he took her by the arm and pulled her against his body, the element of surprise shocked her into surrender. Although she was trembling, she freely tilted her head to the side while his lips moved slowly down the length of her neck. Her skin tingled at his touch, and a faint moan escaped her lips.

"You know you crave the taste of blood," he said as her body felt the merciless, ravaging lust. "And your body aches for me."

Jena found that she could not fight it anymore. His lips created wave after wave of desire everywhere they touched her. Taking his time, he kissed the throbbing pulse at her throat so tender, so teasing... so demanding. He made a noise in the back of his throat, a purr that rolled through his chest. Her strength was rapidly fading away, drifting in a swirl of heated and painful longing.

Overwhelmed by his boldness, she gasped as he swept her off her feet and scooped her into his arms. As he carried her across the room, it was as though he floated in midair, his feet never touching the floor.

Carefully, he leaned her against a table and stripped the robe off her, handling her as gently as he could while her body willfully submitted. As he positioned himself between her thighs, she could feel the hardness of him pressing against her.

Her breathing began to quicken.

"Look at me, Jena," he said in a sensual, disembodied drawl.

As if he controlled her eyes, they obeyed and rose to meet his.

"You hunger for me." His voice dropped deeper. "Don't you, Jena?"

She briefly closed her eyes. For a split second, her defense went down. Dear God, she wanted him—No, she didn't.

Yes, she did.

He reached out with his mind and forced his way into hers. The vision was of him. And she was aching. She was aching for *him.*

"Yes," she finally answered.

"Close your eyes." His voice flowed like black satin.

As Jena closed them, he caught her off guard when he flipped her around. Her gasp was first one of shock, then one of ecstasy as he bent her over and splayed her legs apart. She felt his arousal against her core, the rigid length pressing in through the thin material of her panties. His hand found her breasts, then moved down to her stomach, and down lower to her hips. Then down farther...

She cried out, arching her back as two sharp points suddenly ran up the column of her neck to the curve of her jaw. Anticipation and a needy sensation flooded her veins. He was the master of her body, the driver, the one controlling her emotions. He knew exactly what he was doing to her.

"I'm going to take what belongs to me," he growled as he buried his hand into her long blonde hair and pulled back. As she gasped in pleasure, wetness bloomed within her.

She wanted this. She wanted him. "Please," she pleaded, her eyes squeezed tight.

He roughly positioned her neck to the side and exposed her throat. "Beg for me, Jena." His tongue was warm and wet as it rode up her neck.

Jena opened her mouth but could only pant.

He licked her throat again, and then gently nipped at her earlobe. She flinched at the delightful twinge. "Beg me *now*," he demanded, tugging at her hair.

She nearly sobbed, so aroused she could barely speak. "Please, take me."

Then Jena felt his palm grip her shoulder. As he pulled her upright, his hand moved up her throat, locked onto her chin, and tilted her head back.

"Soon," he whispered softly into her ear. "You'll be *begging* to be at my side."

When Jena opened her eyes, she was shocked to find herself back in her hospital room, lying in her bed alone.

The hazy, but realistic images lingered and frustrated her like she'd lost her mind. As she sat up slowly, she was completely overwhelmed by the bizarre and unbelievable experience she'd just encountered. Looking around the dark room, she realized with dread that the whole thing had to have been a dream. Maybe her mind was just playing tricks on her. But the arousal she felt though? That was real. *Was the mysterious man real or just a figment of my imagination?* As she thought about it, she wasn't sure what was real and what wasn't anymore.

Jena inhaled a deep breath and smelled something *delicious*. Her stomach immediately roared. She followed the sweet aroma and noticed that there was a tray set up next to the bed. As she lifted the silver lid off the platter, she saw a plastic container of blood.

Maybe this was all a horrible nightmare. She waited, praying she would wake up.

Instead, the crimson liquid that was in her dreams was now taunting with her sanity and her weaknesses. Jena closed her eyes and breathed in deep. *Calm down. It's just a dream,* she tried to convince herself. Although the hunger still rose deep in her gut.

Disgusted with herself, she scrambled out of bed and hurried to the door. After Jena flipped on the light, she tried the knob but found it wouldn't turn. *What?* Someone had locked her inside.

Damn it, she cursed to herself. *This is not a dream.*

She panicked and banged on the door. "Please, is anyone there?" she cried out. "Open this door!"

When the doorknob turned, she immediately stepped back as a stalky man, dressed in a uniform, peered inside and said, "Ma'am, is everything all right?"

"Th-the door." Jena's voice trembled in fear. "I-it was locked. I couldn't get—"

The guard held up his hand in a reassuring gesture. "Ma'am, please, calm down. The door wasn't locked." He pointed to the knob. "See, there's no lock on the outside."

Jena looked at it confused, and then her eyes rose to meet the guard's. "But I swore it was locked."

"It could have been jammed," he told her. "Don't worry. Everything is just fine. You're safe. There are two of us posted outside your door twenty-four seven."

Her brows furrowed. "No." She shook her head. "That's not true. I came out of my room not long ago, and there was no one here. No guards, no nurses, no one. I swear to you, the hospital looked vacant."

"I'm sorry," he reluctantly said. "We've been stationed outside your door since this morning, and all the hospital staff has been here as well. We were here when your visitor came to see you today."

"Angie?" Jena cocked her head a little. "Did she come back later?"

"No, ma'am. She hasn't been back."

Jena looked down and stared hard at the floor. What good would it do to ask anything else or continue this conversation? The guard didn't know what she knew, hadn't seen the unexplainable things she'd seen. The reality of it all was simply too much for anyone to believe or comprehend.

"I am your destiny..."

His words—the stranger in her dreams—still haunted her.

The room started to spin. Jena put her palm over her forehead and stumbled back. The guard quickly reached out to steady her. "Ma'am, I think you should lie down. You don't look well."

With his hand tucked under her arm, Jena went along as he walked her to the bed. "Should I call for a nurse?"

"No, no," she quickly replied, climbing into the bed. "I'll be fine. Thank you."

Then it suddenly dawned on her. *The bag of blood!* As she looked to the tray next to the bed, she saw nothing.

Oh God, what happened to it?

Jena's eyes frantically searched around the small room. *That blood had to be somewhere. It couldn't have just disappeared. Someone must have taken it. But how?* Her brain scrambled to come up with a practical explanation. *It was here just a minute ago.*

"Did you or anyone else take a silver platter from my room?" she asked the guard.

He shook his head.

She nodded and slowly eased back against the pillows.

"Would you like me to leave a lamp on?" the guard asked her.

"Yes, please."

When the guard stepped out of the room, Jena glanced desperately at her phone. She wanted to call Angie. But what good would that do? There was nothing her friend could do right now. Besides, she was coming to pick her up in the morning.

Frustrated, Jena let out a deep breath and closed her eyes, thinking she was beginning to lose the only bit of sanity she had left. "Please, God," she prayed, "give me strength."

Chapter Fifteen

Detective Manuel Sanchez started toward the parking lot after he watched the ambulance leave with his partner, taking him to the hospital. Although Manuel had parked his unmarked car at the front of the police station, he headed in the opposite direction. In the event of what just went down in his own precinct, he needed some air.

Man, just a few months back, he never guessed that werewolves and vampire-like creatures existed, much less protected humans, or lived in a mansion the size of a castle. They had one in all fifty states with their own laws, but they also had enemies.

As he went along, the heels of his black leather boots ground against the concrete of the sidewalk that surrounded the precinct. When he got to the far side of the building, he paused at the sound of a revving engine coming from the street alongside him.

Acting on instinct, Manuel spun around and unbuttoned his suit jacket so he could get a hand on his heat. Considering the incident at the station earlier, he wasn't taking any chances. He might be pushing fifty-four, but the cop in him wasn't dead yet.

This is quickly going to get ugly, he thought.

A black SUV with tinted windows headed in his direction, moving at a high speed. The moment Manuel palmed his semiautomatic, the passenger window started to come down. When the muzzle of a gun emerged from the inside, he dove for the ground before it discharged. The first bullet ricocheted off the pavement, barely missing him. Just as he scrambled to take shelter behind a parked car, a second shot ripped through his shoulder.

Manuel ducked lower and gritted his teeth. *Son of a bitch!* His arm felt like a hot, fire poker had drilled through it. At the sound of doors opening and footsteps pounding, he swallowed back the pain and leveled his gun.

As a man's head popped around, Manuel put a slug into his chest, spinning the bastard away, landing him face-first on the ground. Seconds later, he heard a door slam and tires screeching as the other man made his getaway.

Manuel cursed through the pain while he managed to get to his feet. When he approached the shooter, who was lying facedown on the pavement, he heard moans.

"Good," Manuel said, his upper lip curled into a snarl. "You're still alive."

After Detective Sanchez kicked the shooter's pistol away, he knelt beside the bastard, grabbed a fistful of his hair, and tilted his head off the sidewalk. He roughly twisted his head to the side, and got up in his face, pegging him with a hard stare.

"Tell me who the *hell* you're working for, or I'll send your *sorry* ass home in a pine box!"

When there was no answer, Manuel put the muzzle of his semiautomatic against the base of the man's skull. "Start talking." He raised his voice. "*Now!*"

The man slammed his lids shut and gasped in pain. "Okay, okay," he choked out. "Just don't kill me."

As police sirens alerted his attention, Manuel turned to look, aware that his left sleeve was soaking wet from his own blood.

Cursing again, he pressed the gun further into the gunman's head. "Spill it! I haven't got all *damn* day!"

The shooter tilted his face toward Manuel with his eyes rounded. "It was Vincent Scarpelli," he sputtered, swallowing compulsively, and then fell completely limp.

The perpetrator's face fell forward as Manuel lowered his gun and released his hair.

When Manuel felt a hand clamp over his uninjured shoulder, he looked around to see his captain.

"I can't leave you or Detective Perkins alone for one minute, can I?" Captain Hodge said to him.

Manuel smirked and shook his head. "It's been one *helluva* day."

After his captain called for an ambulance, he said, "So, what the *hell* happened?"

"Vincent Scarpelli ordered a hit on me," Manuel grumbled. "That's what happened."

"Shit." Captain Hodge let out a deep breath. "I'm guessing this has something to do with our furry friend, Mr. Fratianno?"

Manuel furrowed his brows and nodded.

As the paramedics arrived, they placed the unconscious hit man on a gurney while another EMT checked Manuel's gunshot wound.

"Looks like the bullet went clean through," the paramedic said. "You've lost a lot of blood, Detective. We need to get you to the hospital."

Damn, Manuel thought as his captain and the paramedic helped him to his feet, *this has been a long, long, very bad day.*

Moments later, the ambulance arrived at the Bates Hospital. Helen's physician instincts came online as the paramedics wheeled the hired gunman inside. When she met them at the emergency entrance, she saw the soles of a pair of men's Italian leather shoes hanging off the gurney. By the expensive style, they was obviously Prada.

She pushed ahead so she could get to the man who appeared to be unconscious and said, "What do we have?"

"Male in his twenties," the paramedic said to Helen. "Gunshot wound to the chest. He crashed on us once on transport. I shocked him at two hundred joules. BP is sixty over forty and falling."

A nurse sitting at the front desk began to record everything. Two others were on standby to take Helen's directions, and a pair of residents hovered to help as needed.

"Do we have an ID on the patient?" Helen asked.

"I got a wallet," the other paramedic said, handing it over to the closest nurse. "His name is Sammy Caruso."

"Do whatever you have to do to keep that SOB alive," Manuel interjected as he walked in behind everyone with his arm in a sling, "he's a witness to a hired hit."

Helen looked over her shoulder and rolled her eyes when she got a look at the detective. "And what happened to you?"

Manuel pointed to the man lying on the gurney. "That sucker shot me."

Helen cursed under her breath and directed her attention to the EMTs. "Take him to bay two." Then she turned to a nurse standing nearby. "I want a blood type on the patient and a chest X-ray right away."

Dr. Helen Carrington's commands snapped the staff into action.

As Helen followed behind the patient that was being wheeled to the operating room, she focused on another nurse and said, "Nurse Kathryn, please see to Detective Sanchez's injuries."

She quickly nodded. "Yes, Dr. Carrington."

Helen paused and looked back at Manuel. "By the way, your partner is getting stitched up. It looks like you two have had one hell of a day."

He cocked a brow. "You ain't a-kiddin'."

"We've got some things to discuss, Detective. I'll be back to check on you after I take care of Mr. Caruso," Helen said before she turned to leave.

* * *

Jena sank deep into the padded mattress of her hospital bed. The layers of blankets enveloped her like a warm embrace. Somewhere in slumber, she dreamed a familiar smile. *Was it Todd's?* As his smile finally faded away, something dreadful and disturbing took its place.

The agonizing sounds were muffled and faraway... powerless and defenseless, harsh and deep. The way a man might cry out in torment.

"Todd!" With a frightened cry of her own, Jena sat upright, her eyes rounded with fear. Her breath came out in a panicked rush. It was pitch-dark. The only light in the room came from the pale glow of her phone's screen saver. She could barely make out the image. It was a photo of her and Todd, taken a month ago.

Did I only imagine Todd's screams, or was it another nightmare taunting my sanity?

Despite her confusion, she instinctively looked to the lamp on the nightstand. It was at that moment she remembered the guard turning it on before he left the room. Could the bulb have burned out? Maybe the nurse came into her room while she was sleeping and turned it off.

Jena slipped out of bed and padded cautiously over to the nightstand. Her hand trembled as she reached out to turn the switch.

Click, click...

Without warning, she caught a glimpse of a shadow in the corner of her eye. The next instant she felt the impression of warm hands from behind, wrapping around her waist. Startled, she stepped back and looked down, but there was nothing. Jena could feel her heart starting to pound.

The uneasiness building inside of her was becoming unbearable. Danger clawed at the outer edge of her consciousness, warning her to get out of this hospital.

I can't stay here any longer.

Completely distraught, she reached for her phone and unhooked the charger, then sat on the bed and searched through her contacts for Angie's number.

Come on, Angie! Pick up!

It wasn't like her friend not to answer her calls. Even at this hour.

Maybe she was out of range, Jena tried to tell herself. *Maybe Angie was away from her phone. Considering the situation, surely she wouldn't turn it off.*

In spite of her rationalizations, Jena became more and more paranoid.

Please, Angie. Please answer my call.

Before it went to Angie's voice mail, Jena ended the call and curled up on the bed, her heart beating so fast she could feel it in the back of her throat. Her eyes filled with so many tears that the room went out of focus.

A sudden chill worked at the base of her spine, lifting the hairs along the back of her neck. That's when Jena realized the truth. If she stayed here alone in this room tonight, *he* would surely come back.

In sheer panic, Jena reached for the phone. She screamed as it began to ring just when she grabbed it.

Relieved that it might finally be Angie, she quickly answered, "Thank God, I tried to call—"

"Jena... Jena... I'm coming for you," the stranger's voice cut her off.

She dropped the phone on the bed. "No!" she cried out, recognizing that voice. It was *him*. She was sure of it. She'd heard that voice many times before, whispering and taunting her. And he knew exactly where she was.

"Jena?" Angie's voice sounded fuzzy as her words crackled through the static over the phone. "I can barely hear you."

Jena's hands were shaking so much she could hardly hold onto the phone.

She managed to hold it steady. "Angie?" Her voice trembled. "Is that really you?"

"Yes," Angie replied. "Is something wrong?"

"Please, Angie." Jena's heart fluttered. "I need you to come get me. The monster that killed Todd and Sophie is coming for me."

"Hang on, girlfriend. I'm heading your way now."

Jena found relief to hear the urgency in her friend's voice. "Thank you, Angie. And please *hurry*."

Chapter Sixteen

Tara glanced at the clock on the wall, surprised at how late it was. A little past midnight and everything seemed quiet around her. She hadn't seen or heard from Lawrence since he last visited her. He promised when he returned he would tell her all about this mysterious place, and *what* had brutally attacked Brandon.

She tried to close her eyes and rest, but she didn't feel like sleeping. She wasn't even tired. She was mostly frustrated. She couldn't get her mind off the *thing* that killed Brandon. *What was it, and will it come back for me?*

Feeling more restless by the minute, Tara winced in pain as she eased off the bed and stood up. She held herself on the IV pole until it shook from the effort of keeping her body upright. She carefully put one foot in front of the other until she got to the door. As she placed her ear against it, all she could hear were the sounds of buzzing coming from the fluorescent lights on the other side.

Tara wondered how big this place really was and what the rest of it looked like. Her curiosity got the better of her. *Maybe I'll just take a quick peek around.*

The door made a creaking noise as she slowly cracked it open and stuck her head out. The coast was clear. She let out a deep breath, realizing she had been holding it, and made her way into the hall.

When she finally made it down to the end of a long corridor, she cautiously pushed open a set of double doors. Beyond them was a gym big enough to fit an entire football team. The room housed a variety of cardiovascular machines and tons of weight equipment, some of which she had no clue what they were. Black mats were stacked against the far end of the wall, and there were at least a half a dozen red punching bags hanging from the ceiling.

At a snail's pace, she moved to the far side of the gym and stopped in front of a door marked WEAPONS ROOM. As she reached to open it, she paused before her hand made contact with the elongated handle. Although her gut instincts warned her otherwise, she pushed her way inside.

Her eyes rounded in amazement at the number of shelved weapons. An arsenal of military weaponry was stored on racks and locked in glass cabinets. As all kinds of terrifying scenarios went through her head—wondering why in the hell they needed weapons of this magnitude—she heard a man's voice echo from behind, calling out her name.

"Tara..."

She twisted her head to the side and said, "Lawrence, is that you?"

"Lawrence is not here, Tara." The voice pronounced each word with a deep drawl. "He cannot protect you *now*."

She could hear the smugness in his tone. He had an American accent with a slight hint of the south.

Her pulse leaped and her fight-or-flight reflexes screamed inside of her. It took every ounce of courage she possessed to keep herself calm.

In a cold voice, he said, "No one can protect you."

Tara's hand trembled as she braced herself against the portable medical device and shifted around. A tall, dark figure stood in the dark shadows.

Her voice trembled. "Who are you?"

"You know *who* I am, Tara." Another hint of smug superiority bathed his tongue.

"Y-you're the one who killed Brandon, aren't you?"

For an endless moment, there was silence. Then, out of nowhere, *he* was on her in an instant.

Tara gasped in shock, her ability to move suddenly drifting into a weary fog.

As her knees began to buckle, a pair of strong hands held her up. She could feel sharp nails digging into her skin and warm lips tracing the curve of her neck. Her mouth opened to call for help, but strangely, she could not muster a single word. Tara hadn't realized she'd been holding her breath until the grip around her arms loosened and his fingers glided down the back of her thin gown.

Trapped in a web of terror, her only awareness was a sinister voice that whispered in her ear, "You'll be with your beloved Brandon soon."

Tara clenched her lids shut, preparing for him to strike, but instead, he hesitated and inhaled a deep breath.

On a quick exhale, he let out a disgusted groan. "You're not *human*." His words ended in a guttural growl.

Before Tara could open her eyes, *he* simply vanished, leaving her limbs weak and helpless. Moaning at the effort to stay on her feet, she felt she could no longer find the strength. She heard the dull echo of a clatter as she fell to the floor, taking down the portable iron pole along with her.

The sound of a door opening brought her head upright. Footsteps began to move in her direction. Tara felt sick with dread, sick with the killer's promising words of death. His voice echoed mockingly in her head. She could still feel his lips on her throat.

Oh, God, was he coming back?

Tara panicked when she saw the shadowed silhouette of someone getting closer and closer. With her mind focused on an escape, she maneuvered herself on all fours and slowly crawled as if she were trudging through thick mud, getting absolutely nowhere.

"Ms. Hood?" a woman's voice called out. "Are you okay?"

Tara froze in confusion and looked around. Then she breathed a sigh of relief. Standing before her was a woman with long brown hair and bright emerald-green eyes that expressed concern. Perched over her left hip was a blond-haired little boy that didn't look much older than a year. He was pointing his finger and mumbling gibberish.

She felt utterly exhausted, yet still terrified. Brandon's killer could be out there right now, watching and waiting.

Tara stared nervously at the woman and finally managed to speak. "I swear, something was just here, and it disappeared into thin air." Her voice trembled. "It was the *thing* that killed my boyfriend. And I think it wants to kill me."

For a brief second, the woman stood in silence. With concern brimming in her eyes, she knelt down with the little boy in her arms. "Are you saying someone was here in this room with you?"

Tara reluctantly nodded.

"What did this *thing* look like?"

"It was a man," Tara told her. "But I'm positive it was the same creature that killed Brandon."

"How can you be sure?"

"Because..." Tara's voice wavered. "...he said I would be with Brandon soon."

The woman placed her free hand over Tara's trembling shoulder. "Did he hurt you?"

Tara shook her head. "No, but he said something strange to me. It didn't make any sense."

She looked at Tara confused. "What did he say?"

"He said I wasn't *human*."

"You're safe now, Ms. Hood." The woman's voice was firm, trying her best to keep her reaction calm and collected. "I give you my word. No one is going to harm you here." Her voice seemed genuine. "I'm Tessa, by the way. And this is my son Jax."

"Do you live here?"

"Yes," Tessa replied. "I guess you could say I oversee everything. Each and every one of us here is like a big family." She lightly squeezed Tara's shoulder and then rose to her feet. "Tara, you really shouldn't be out of bed. Please, come with me. I'll help you back to your room."

She became at ease with Tessa's soothing words. Tara suddenly realized she was no longer in danger. Before she got to her feet, she heard a light meow. A black cat slunk out from the shadows to rub affectionately against Tara's arm.

"Don't worry," Tessa said. "He's very friendly. His name is Buddy."

"Kitty," Jax murmured, directing his finger at the cat.

Tara smiled and reached out to the furry feline. It arched its back as she smoothed her hand over his sleek, soft fur.

"Looks like you've got a new friend." Tessa laughed a little. "Although my husband brought him home, Buddy kind of adopted us."

"He's beautiful," Tara said. "He reminds me of a stray cat that used to hang around my foster parents' old barn when I was a little girl. I brought him milk every morning before I left for school. I named him Midnight. I think that cat was the only real friend I ever had as a child." Her eyes stared in the distance as though her mind was miles away.

"What happened to him?" Tessa hesitantly asked, bringing Tara back to focus.

"I don't know." Tara shrugged. "When I went to feed him one morning, he never came. It took me a whole month before I finally realized he wasn't coming back."

Tessa looked at her sorrowfully. "I'm so sorry, Tara. That must have been painful as a child."

"Oh, that was a long time ago," Tara said as she struggled to stand.

Tessa quickly put Jax down, reached for Tara's IV pole, and stood it upright. "Here, let me help you," she said, offering her hand to Tara.

As Tara took ahold of Tessa's hand, she slowly got to her feet and said, "Thank you, Tessa." She reached for the intravenous pole to help steady herself. "And please, call me Tara."

"You're welcome, Tara. Now, let's get you back to bed," Tessa said as she picked up Jax. "I'll make sure you have guards posted outside your room."

"Do you know when Lawrence will return?" Tara bluntly asked.

"Uh, well..." Tessa stumbled with her words, caught off guard by Tara's question. She didn't want to share too much information with Tara since the Covenant hadn't decided what all they were going to tell her just yet. "I'm not exactly sure. I know he went with my husband and some of the other men to help Detective Sanchez with a case earlier."

Tara's brows furrowed. "Does it have anything to with the *thing* that killed my boyfriend?"

"No, Tara. It has nothing to do with the creature that is responsible for your boyfriend's death. But I promise we are doing everything we can to give Brandon and the others it has killed some justice," Tessa simply said. "And I know you're confused and you have a lot of questions. As soon as Lawrence and the others return, we will do our best to explain everything we can. Right now, my main concern is keeping you and my family safe."

Tara nodded and let out a deep breath. "Thank you, Tessa."

Hidden in the dark shadows, *he* watched in silent fury as Tara and the other woman with the child in her arms exited the room. His body craved the taste of human blood, and his patience was running thin. The two women and the child were anything but human. Left with no choice, he would have to search for another.

Before his ghostly apparition completely vanished, he hesitated when a pair of glowing green eyes peered in his direction.

It cannot be, he thought as the mysterious, green-eyed stalker moved closer. Then, from out of the shadows, a black cat appeared, but *he* knew it was no ordinary house cat.

The cat then arched his back and hissed at the unwelcome visitor. Out of nowhere, magic flared in a surge of power, forcing the feline to shift into its human form. A blinding light suddenly burst from the small animal, and when it faded, a man took its place. His glowing eyes were slit-pupiled, and a pair of black wings unsheathed from his back.

The ghostly creature's chest lifted and fell on a deep breath. "Raphael—"

The black-winged angel flashed a wicked smile, revealing two sharp teeth. He stepped forward with a warning. "Leave this place, evil creature. You are not welcome here."

"You hold no power over me," he went on, ignoring the angel's warning.

Raphael's nostrils flared in anger. "Not only do I possess the power of healing," he said, extending his hand. "I have the power to bring forth pain."

Instantly, the Angel of healing released an invisible barrier of magnetic energy from the palm of his hand. The weight of the blow sent the bloodthirsty phantom flying several feet away. Winded and in terrible pain, he recoiled, lurching back as white-hot agony pierced his chest like a burning blade.

Impossible, he thought as pain sliced through him. The place on his chest where the angel had struck him burned as if he'd been hit by lightning. Soon after, a rush of weakness coursed through him that he had never felt before.

As the evil creature's body began to dematerialize, he tossed his head back and howled in silent agony.

Chapter Seventeen

After Jimmy Fratianno caused a ruckus at the police station, Tim Ross had Drakon form a team to go hunt him down. The tracking device implanted inside Jimmy gave them his exact location. By the looks of things and the family's criminal history, it wasn't going to be easy getting into his Uncle Vincent Scarpelli's place without a confrontation.

As Drakon, Lawrence, and Roman worked their way to their destination, Jem and Jace hung back, waiting for their signal to move forward with the plan. Once they reached the rendezvous point—an unguarded passage that led to the back of Scarpelli's estate—they would give them a thumb's up, using a two-way radio. It wouldn't take but a few seconds to meet the others, considering Jem had the ability to use a portal to get them where they needed to be.

A half-hour later, the others finally reached a large tract of land covered with trees and underbrush. Drakon stopped to check his map. He pointed out to the others an area that ran alongside a creek. "Once we get around to the north side of that creek, we'll be within range of Scarpelli's estate."

Roman looked to where Drakon had directed them and said, "You want me to radio Jem and Jace?"

Drakon nodded. "Tell them to get to the place we agreed to meet in fifteen minutes. From here, it shouldn't take us much longer."

"Don't you think it would have been quicker if we just had Jem take us all there using a portal?" Roman queried.

"Yeah, it would have been quicker," Drakon replied. "But considering Scarpelli's manpower, it's better if we split up. We could run into trouble. Plus, I'm not particularly fond of portals. Have you ever traveled through one?"

"No, I can't say I have. Oh, wait a minute. I did when Jem took us through a portal after we battled it out with the Fury." Roman shrugged. "Why do you ask?"

"Because, the last time, it threw my equilibrium completely off," Drakon told him. "I felt like I was on a bender from hell for two days."

Roman smirked and then radioed Jem and Jace.

As they waited on Roman, Lawrence stared out over the woodland and said, "Keep your eyes peeled, guys. At this close range, we could run into some of Scarpelli's men. He's well known for taking extreme measures when it comes to his security."

A mile out, Drakon slowed, getting his water bottle out of his pack and swigging half of the contents down in one big gulp. As he paused to put the bottle back, he heard a rustling noise coming from behind. Without hesitation, he turned with his pistol raised, but it was too late.

At least a half a dozen men dressed in camouflage had their guns on Drakon, Lawrence, and Roman as if daring them to make a move. Their expressions came across as harsh as they seemed to weigh the opposition. And they looked way too damn trigger-happy.

One of the men barked an order. "Drop your weapons *now*!"

As Drakon lowered his gun, he hoped to hell that Jem and Jace weren't stuck in the same predicament. This could all go to shit at a moment's notice, and he damn sure didn't want to have to shift into his rogue wolf in front of all these humans.

A stalky man stepped forward that Roman instantly recognized. He had a cigar tucked between his lips. "This is how it's going to play out." He blew out an agitated puff of smoke and then threw the still glowing stogie to the ground. "You're going to do exactly what I say. Anyone tries anything stupid..." He paused and pointed his gun at Drakon. "...I'll put a silver bullet through his head." Then he shifted his weapon in Lawrence's direction, aiming it at his forehead. "Yes, I know what you all are. Isn't that right, Mr. Roman Kincaid?"

Roman straightened, his face going tight, his nostrils flaring. Anger boiled up in his throat until the bitter taste of acid saturated his tongue. For a moment, he stood glaring at a man he believed to be dead and buried years ago. At first glance, it was as though a ghost from the past had come back to haunt him. But it wasn't a ghost he was looking at. It was Ethan Renshaw. The shady bastard had his fingers into damn near everything: dirty politics, illegal drugs, gun running, and sex trafficking. There isn't much he hasn't done, and most of the shit would turn the stomach of a serial killer. He did all of Vincent Scarpelli's and his cousin's, Gino Beneditti, dirty work.

Ten years ago, the military contracted Roman to hunt down the POS. He'd never forget the blistering Sahara Desert. Along with four of his team members, they spent several agonizing days tracking Renshaw through Northern Africa, until finally they caught up with him and his pack of bodyguards. Their mission was to bring him in alive, but under grave circumstances, they were forced to do otherwise. During a sandstorm, Roman and his men took Renshaw's guards by surprise. Inside a tent that looked like King Tut's, they found the dirty bastard raping a young civilian girl that he kidnapped two days prior. His dead corpse was the last of Ethan Renshaw that Roman set eyes on. Now, he was staring into the bastard's cold, evil eyes once again. He could have sworn Renshaw was dead because he had been the one that pulled the trigger that supposedly ended his life. Considering the current situation, it appeared that the asshole had nine lives.

Renshaw pushed forward until he was just inches from Roman's face and raised a speculative eyebrow. "I bet you never expected to see me alive, seeing that you killed me and all," he said mockingly. "How does it feel to be at my mercy, Kincaid?"

Drakon's eyes widened in surprise and then he looked at Roman as if gauging his reaction to Renshaw's statement.

Lawrence stiffened beside him, but he didn't react.

"Fuck off," Roman gritted out.

Renshaw laughed. "The feeling is entirely mutual." Then he nodded at his men and said, "Cuff 'em. And if they give you any trouble..." He pointed at Drakon. "...shoot that one in the head."

Roman glared in hatred and turned to meet his comrades in arms. Lawrence stood there looking like you could break a rock on his face. Drakon looked... pissed, for lack of a better word, his hands wound into tight fists and his lips drawn in a straight line.

Renshaw's cell went off just as his men were about to secure Roman, Lawrence, and Drakon in handcuffs. As he pulled it from the inside of his jacket and answered, his entire body tensed and his expression became dark and hostile. Renshaw's hand curled so tightly around the phone that his knuckles whitened. To Roman's surprise, he moved closer and extended the phone in his direction.

"It's Vincent Scarpelli," he grumbled between gritted teeth. "He wants to speak to you."

Roman took the phone from Renshaw's hand and barked, "Kincaid speaking."

Vincent Scarpelli was short and to the point. "I have something you want, and you have something I want. If you want your men to stay alive, give me the location of Mr. Tim Ross. He's the sorry bastard that put away my nephew. And he's the only one that can safely remove the explosive tracking device that's planted in him."

Roman's lips curled into a snarl. "You can go fuck yourself."

Scarpelli smirked into the phone. "Have it your way, Kincaid."

In the brief silence that followed, a gun going off in the background was all Roman heard, and then Jace screaming his twin brother's name.

Roman's face fell, and he sucked in a wavering breath. "You son of a bitch!" he roared into the receiver.

"Do I have your attention now?" Scarpelli asked in a smug tone.

Despite the fact that a silver bullet wasn't lethal to Jem or Jace, it galled Roman to the deepest pit of his core that Scarpelli thought to have murdered one of his friends. He lifted his gaze and sought out Drakon, who stood as still as a statue, wondering what in the hell was going on. Lawrence had the same look of bewilderment stamped all over his face.

Then, as if gathering himself, Roman straightened. His eyes went flat and no hint of emotion reflected in the dark color. "I want to talk to you face to face... man to man," he told Scarpelli, stalling the bastard. Roman knew it was just a matter of time before Jace's beast reared its ugly head. "Give me that," he continued, "and I'll tell you what you want."

"I will agree, but if you screw with me, Mr. Kincaid," Scarpelli threatened, "I'll order the rest of your men to be put down like the dogs they are. Do I make myself clear?"

Roman nodded against the phone. "Yeah, we're clear alright." His voice was tight with anger. He lifted his gaze and focused them on Renshaw.

Before Roman could hand the phone back to him, Renshaw jerked it away and put it to his ear. "What the hell was that all about?" he all but roared at Scarpelli.

Not long after, all the color leeched out of Renshaw's face. You could hear Vincent Scarpelli's voice thundering over the phone.

"Yes, sir," Renshaw painfully choked out. As he ended the call, he looked at Roman with pure distaste and said, "When Scarpelli is done with you, I've got a score to settle."

Roman's lips curled into a sneer, but he didn't say anything. He just stared at Renshaw, his eyes seething with rage. He'd like nothing more than to shift into his Adalwolf and rip the bastard's throat out.

After Renshaw's men forced Roman, Lawrence, and Drakon in the back of a dark SUV at gunpoint, they finally rolled up to the gates that led to Vincent Scarpelli's massive estate.

When Renshaw spoke into the security camera, he became curious as to why there was no immediate reply. As minutes passed, his curiosity turned to hostility.

"What the hell is going on?" Renshaw shouted. "Will someone open this damn gate?"

Out of nowhere, something crashed into the windshield with a loud bang.

Renshaw flinched. "What the f—"

Lying on top of the vehicle's hood was a *human* head. Its glassy stare met Renshaw's wide eyes. It was Vincent Scarpelli. At least what was left of the guy.

"H-holy shit," Renshaw's guard that was sitting in the passenger seat of the SUV said. He made the sign of the cross with his hand. His entire body trembled as he pointed toward the windshield. "Is that Mr. Scarpelli?"

Just as Renshaw opened his mouth to make a reply, a bone-chilling roar cut him off. When he looked away from the severed head, he caught sight of an enormous creature climbing over the gate. Covered in white shaggy fur, it towered at least seven feet tall or so, with teeth the size of daggers and a slashing pair of front claws.

"Shit!" Renshaw cursed under his breath. Without further delay, he quickly reached to the door panel. After he rolled up his window, he hit the button to lock the doors.

"Will someone tell me what the hell that is?" the guard sitting next to Renshaw said as he fumbled with the door, checking the lock.

"It's Jace," Drakon muttered from the back. "When he's pissed off."

The guard felt his heart pounding in his chest. "Can that *thing* get in here?"

"If he's hungry enough," Drakon replied with a clear smirk in his voice.

When the Beast cleared the gate and charged at the SUV, running on two legs, the guard checked the door one more time. The rest of Renshaw's men were gone. The sounds of tires squealing pissed him off. *Damn traitors!* Renshaw thought, watching his own men desert him.

The Beast came up to Renshaw's window and pressed his massive face so close his hot breath fogged the glass as he exhaled. Renshaw stiffened in his seat, taken aback by the unholy creature before him. Yellow glowing eyes glared out from the creature's wolfish face, and dark blood dripped from its monstrous jaws, staining its milky fur.

With his eyes locked onto the white beast, Renshaw reached for his weapon.

"I wouldn't do that if I were you," Drakon warned him. "Silver bullets are useless."

Shit! "Are you saying that *thing* is indestructible?" Renshaw asked, trying to keep his voice low.

Drakon cocked a brow. "Yep. I'd say all of you are pretty much fucked."

Renshaw ignored Drakon's warning and gripped his pistol. When he turned to the door, the Beast slammed his clawed hand through the window. The immense force caused the entire SUV to bounce up off its wheels. The gun slipped from Renshaw's grasp as he flew across the cab, knocking the guard into the passenger's side window. Glass shattered against his skull, rendering him unconscious.

Before Renshaw could react, the Beast tore the door off its hinges and sunk his claws deep into his back. Renshaw howled in agony. The white beast jerked him from the SUV and tossed him like a rag doll. He crashed into the side of an abandoned vehicle close by, denting the metal panel. When he hit the ground headfirst, pain exploded inside his skull, causing his vision to blur.

Renshaw looked up and found the Beast looming over him with a hungry expression in his eyes. He covered his head with his arms, afraid to watch… afraid of becoming the Beast's next meal.

Someone yelled, "Jace! Stop!"

The Beast's head whipped around as his twin brother's voice traveled from the other side of the gates. Then his attention shifted to Drakon and Lawrence as they stepped out of the SUV. Roman stood back, anxiously waiting to be the one to witness Ethan Renshaw as he finally met his maker, and this time for good.

"I'll distract Jace," Drakon said to Lawrence. "You get Renshaw out of the way."

The Beast turned toward Drakon and positioned itself in an attack stance. The muscles in its legs quivered, waiting for Drakon to make a move.

Drakon took a step forward as Lawrence readied himself to grab Renshaw.

The Beast crouched lower and snapped its jaws.

Jem shot around the corner. "Drakon, stand back!"

When Drakon stopped moving, the Beast looked toward Jem.

"Brother," Jem murmured with his hand outstretched, "it's me. Jem."

The Beast's eyes narrowed and its lips curled up into a snarl.

"Everything is okay, brother." Jem used his telepathic voice as he approached the Beast slowly, hoping he could get to his brother and talk him down. He knew Jace was in there *somewhere.*

The Beast heaved in a big breath and then eyed Renshaw once again.

"Look at me, brother," Jem said in a low voice. "He's not going to be a threat to you, to me, or anyone else ever again."

In that moment of distraction, Renshaw made a move for another weapon he had tucked behind his back. Before he could fire a shot, the Beast lunged at him.

Jem and the others immediately ducked.

The sound of the Beast's thunderous roar went silent as he took Renshaw's head between his jaws.

Jem turned away from the horrible killing, cringing at the sounds of flesh torn and bones crunching.

Moments later, Jem felt something nudge at his arm. The Beast was pushing at him with its wolfish paw.

Jem looked up into the Beast's glowing eyes and sagged in relief. "It's okay, brother," he said. "Now, bring Jace back."

The Beast heaved a deep breath and dropped to its knees. There was a flash of light and then Jace appeared in his human form. Before Jem could reach him, Jace pitched forward and collapsed on the ground.

Jem shrugged out of his jacket and covered Jace's naked body as Drakon, Lawrence, and Roman rushed over.

"Jem..." Jace called out in a weak voice.

"Don't worry, brother. I'm right here. Everyone is going to be fine."

Jem looked up from Jace's body and focused on the others. "I'll take him back to the Covenant while you guys wrap things up here."

"I'm guessing there's no one left alive inside Scarpelli's estate, am I right?" Drakon asked Jem.

"Yep," Jem replied. "After Vincent Scarpelli shot me, Jace went ballistic. Be warned before you go inside. It's not a pretty sight."

"It's nothing we haven't seen before," Lawrence chimed in.

Before Jem summoned a portal, Roman knelt down beside Jace and said, "Thanks for saving our ass." He patted Jace's shoulder. "But I've got to say this." He chuckled a little. "That *thing* you turn into. That's one ugly son of a bitch."

Jace smirked in triumph. "You only wish you could be as great."

"Yeah, you said that right." Roman stood up. "I owe you one, buddy."

"Don't mention it," Jace said, heaving a deep breath. "It's what I do."

Chapter Eighteen

As Helen pushed her way into Detective Manuel Sanchez's hospital room, a nurse standing next to his bedside looked up. "Hello, Dr. Carrington."

Helen smiled at her. "Nurse Kathryn, how's our patient?"

"Stubborn as hell," the nurse replied. Her mouth curved and her blue eyes sparkled as she winked at Manuel. "Other than that, he's patched up and ready to go."

Manuel's cheeks and neck suddenly appeared flushed.

"That's good to hear," Helen said. She moved to the opposite side of Manuel and put her hand on his shoulder. "I just examined your partner in crime. It looks like Detective Perkins is going to make a full recovery."

Manuel eased back against the pillow, seemingly relieved to hear the news of his partner's condition.

"What about the bastard that put this hole in my arm," Manuel grumbled, getting straight to the point. "Please tell me he didn't kick the bucket. He's my only witness to whoever put out a hit on me."

Helen cocked a brow. "I'm sorry to say, Mr. Caruso took a turn for the worse. I know I'm not supposed to give out this information, but considering the situation and everything we're dealing with, I'm going to bend the rules here. I trust you'll keep this confidential." When Manuel nodded, Helen's tone was grim as she continued, "We've got him in ICU on a ventilator. I don't expect him to make it through the night."

"Shit," Manuel cursed low. "Have you heard back from Tim?"

Helen looked up at Nurse Kathryn and said, "Kathryn, will you please excuse us. I need to speak with Detective Sanchez in private."

Kathryn nodded. "Of course, Dr. Carrington." She reached out and lightly patted Manuel's hand. "I'll get your release forms ready, Detective."

Manuel's face bloomed again. "Th-thank you, Kathryn."

Helen noticed that Manuel's eyes never left the nurse as she exited the room, her long braided hair swaying gently. Not to mention his reaction to her touch.

"Detective Sanchez," Helen said with the biggest grin on her face. "I think Nurse Kathryn is a little sweet on you."

Manuel took his eyes off the door and refocused them on Helen. "I'm sorry, what did you say?"

Helen chuckled. "She's single. I can get her number if you like. I'm sure she'd be thrilled if you asked her out on a date."

His brows furrowed in confusion. "Who?" he mumbled. "What?"

"I was talking about Nurse Kathryn," Helen raised her voice a little. "I think you should definitely ask her out."

Manuel's face turned three shades of red. "If you don't mind, I'd like to keep this conversation professional and get back to my question."

"Whatever you say, Detective." Helen snickered under her breath. "But if you change your mind, just let me know."

"About Tim Ross," Manuel said firmly, changing the subject. "Have you heard from him?"

Helen's expression dropped. "Unfortunately, no," she sighed. "But I did hear from Tessa."

"So, what did she say? Did they find Jimmy Fratianno?"

"Tim sent Drakon and four others to Mr. Fratianno's hideout. Apparently they were apprehended by a group of bad guys," Helen told him. "To make a long story short, they pissed off Jace. He turned into his Beast, and everything went to hell."

Manuel shook his head. "Did they manage to catch Jimmy?"

"Yeah, they got him alright. The parts of him that were left."

"Shit," Manuel gritted out. "I take it Jimmy's rogue wolf was no match for Jace's beast."

"Don't worry about it, Detective." Helen crossed her arms. "They've got everything covered."

"What about the bodies?"

"As I said, Detective..." Helen briefly paused, her lips forming into a slight smile. "...they've got it covered."

In frustration, Manuel rubbed his eyes and groaned. "So what you're saying is it's out of my hands, right?"

"No, Detective. That's not what I'm saying. Right now, you and Detective Perkins need to take a day or two and rest. You need to heal. Let them take care of things in the meantime." Then she tacked on, "Doctor's orders."

"I think I'll take you up on that," Manuel said.

"You mean you're actually going to take my advice and rest?"

"No," he simply said. "I was referring to the nurse's phone number."

Helen shot Manuel a look. "You got it, Detective. Oh," she went on, "before I leave, I wanted to tell you that I had Ms. McCain transported to the Covenant. She's not safe here."

Manuel looked at Helen in question. "Why in the hell wasn't I informed?"

Helen held up her hand in a reassuring gesture. "Calm down, Detective. There was no time. The creature somehow got into her room last night. We thought it best to get her out of the hospital as soon as possible."

"Is she all right?"

"Jena is fine, Detective. She's just a little shaken up."

"How in the hell did it get past the guards?"

"That's a good question. So far, we think the creature has the ability to transform into a fog-like substance. If so, it's possible it could have gotten through the vents."

"Shit," Manuel grumbled. "You mean to tell me we are chasing after a creature that not only can shift into a werewolf, the damn thing can make itself change into *fog*?"

"Sorry, Detective. But that's the only explanation I can come up with."

"How is Tim going to keep this *thing* from getting into the Covenant?"

Helen shook her head. "I don't know, Detective. At least we'll be able to contain Ms. McCain in the Covenant. It won't be long, and she'll be a threat to humans."

He heaved a deep breath. "Yeah, I guess you're right, Helen. Thanks for letting me know. Sorry I barked at you."

"You're welcome, Detective, and don't worry about it. I know you're just concerned about Ms. McCain's safety. As soon as Nurse Kathryn gets your release forms ready, you're free to check out."

"What about Perkins?" Manuel asked. "How long before he gets out?"

"If his vital signs continue to improve," Helen said as she headed to the door, "he should be good to go tomorrow afternoon."

"Has anyone called his wife, Missy?"

"As a matter of fact, she came to see him as I was leaving his room."

"Thanks, Helen. You're a damn good doctor."

"Why thank you, Detective." She opened the door. "I'll have Tim give you a call."

Before she stepped out of the room, Manuel said, "Uh, Helen," he briefly paused, "about that nurse. Is she a—"

"Breedline?" Helen finished his question before he could get the words out.

"Yeah," he said. "I was just curious. I mean, in case I had to keep all this stuff a secret."

"She's just like you." Helen smiled. "Kathryn was born with the Breedline genetics, but she does not have an identical twin."

He nodded. "Thanks, Helen."

"You're welcome, Detective."

* * *

As Tessa escorted Tara back to her room, so many questions plagued her mind. How did the creature find its way into the Covenant? And why didn't it kill Tara like it did her boyfriend? Was it true what *it* had told her? That she wasn't human.

After Tara carefully got back into bed, she eased her head against the pillow and asked Tessa, "How old is your son?"

"Jax and his twin brother Jem turned a year old on Groundhog Day."

Tara's eyes widened. "You have twins?"

137

Tessa brushed Jax's hair back, tucking it behind his ear. "Yes, and they're identical."

"He's adorable." Tara's eyes softened. "You and your husband must feel very lucky to have such beautiful children, and so well behaved."

"Oh, we are truly blessed." Tessa smiled a little. "But this one here," she dropped a kiss on the side of Jax's cheek, "he can be a little ornery at times."

Jax crinkled his nose, stuck his tongue out, and blew a raspberry.

Both Tessa and Tara laughed. Then their attention went to the sound of a light knock coming from the door. Seconds later, a familiar voice called out, "Ms. Hood, it's Tim Ross. May I come in?"

"Yes," Tara replied. "It's open."

When the door opened, Tessa turned to meet Tim as he stepped inside the room. Jax smiled ear to ear and extended his hands.

"Hey, little guy." Tim smiled back and tentatively reached for Jax, taking him from Tessa. He hugged Jax close, giving him a light squeeze. "What are you doing up so late?"

Jax placed his thumb in his mouth, a habit he'd recently adopted.

"He's been up for hours," Tessa said, releasing a long sigh.

"Where's his brother?" Tim asked.

Tessa cocked a brow at Jax. "He's *sleeping* like a baby."

Tim shifted Jax in his arms. "Are you keeping your mama up late?"

Jax grinned around his thumb, and Tim chuckled. "Well, I hope I'm not intruding," he said, his eyes meeting Tessa, and then Tara. "I came by to check on our guest and heard voices." He moved next to Tara's bedside and smiled down at her. "I was just making sure you were all right, Miss Hood."

"Please, call me Tara," she told him.

"Tara, this is Tim Ross," Tessa introduced them. "He's a close friend of mine and he helps me take care of this place."

Tim repositioned Jax and offered his hand to Tara. "It's a pleasure to meet you, Tara. I hope you're comfortable here."

Tara took his hand, and said, "It's nice to meet you, too. And yes, everyone has been so nice to me."

"Good to hear," Tim said, and then turned to Tessa. "So, what are you doing here at this hour? Is there something I should be aware of?"

"The reason I'm here is that..." Tessa hesitated for a moment, trying to figure out the easiest way to tell Tim about Tara's recent incident. She knew this was going to put the Covenant on high alert. "The creature tried to attack Tara here in the Covenant."

Tim's eyes rounded. "What?" He shifted his eyes away from Tessa and focused them on Tara. "When did this happen?"

"Just moments ago," Tara told him.

Tim heaved a deep breath. "Are you all right?"

"I-I'm fine," Tara nervously said as the images of the terrifying ordeal came crashing back. "Just startled, that's all."

"Do you think the creature could have followed Jena back here?" Tessa asked Tim.

"Who's Jena?" Tara interrupted.

"She's the survivor from the cemetery attack," Tessa told her. "I'm sure you've heard about it on the news. She's coming here to stay with us for her protection."

Tim's hold tightened around Jax. "It's a possibility the creature has some kind of link to Jena. We are going to have to beef up security, and I want everyone to report to a meeting first thing in the morning, before breakfast. I'll send everyone a text." Then he asked, "Have you heard from Helen?"

"I spoke with her earlier," Tessa replied. "She'd just got out of surgery. Both Detective Sanchez and Detective Perkins are doing fine. And I gave her permission to inform them about the situation with the Scarpelli thing." She cocked a brow, not wanting to say anything further in front of Tara.

Tim nodded an understanding. "Thank you, Tessa."

Tara cleared her throat, catching their attention, and then said, "Tim, why are you doing all this for me? I mean, you don't really owe me anything, and you hardly know me. No one here knows anything about me."

Tim frowned. *Because you are human, and you wouldn't make it a day without our help*, he thought.

Keeping that to himself, he leaned over and placed a hand on her shoulder. "Because, Tara, we care about your safety and the safety of our family."

"But—"

"Just let us help you, Tara. And don't worry about a thing." He pulled back his hand and straightened. "I know you have a lot of unanswered questions. Considering the circumstances, it's perfectly understandable."

Tessa reached for Jax and whispered, "Come to Mommy, sweetheart."

He disentangled himself from Tim's grasp and reached for Tessa.

"There you go, buddy," Tim said as he placed Jax in her arms.

"Look, Tara, I have to go meet with my security," Tim said. "But I assure you, we will do our best to answer all your questions tomorrow after our meeting. Until then, you get some rest. I will post two guards outside your door twenty-four seven."

"Thank you," Tara whispered, her eyes heavy with exhaustion.

Tessa patted her hand. "Get some rest, Tara. I'll check on you first thing in the morning."

As they shut the door behind them, leaving Tara to get some rest, Tessa said, "We need to have Helen run a DNA test on Tara."

Tim's brows furrowed. "Why's that?"

"Tara had mentioned something rather strange. She said the creature told her she wasn't human."

"You think that's why he didn't kill her?"

Tessa shrugged. "I don't know, maybe."

"And she didn't say anything about what we are?"

"No, nothing." Tessa shook her head. "As far as Tara thinks, we're human."

"Have Helen do a DNA test as soon as she returns. It's a possibility Tara was born with the Breedline genetics without her knowledge," he said.

"Mama," Jax mumbled around a noisy yawn.

Tim looked down to see Jax rubbing his eyes.

"I think it's way past someone's bedtime," Tim said, chuckling lightly.

Tessa stroked Jax's blond curls and pressed a kiss to his head. "Let's get you back to bed, sweetheart."

Jax pulled away from Tessa and glanced over at Tim. "Night-night," he murmured, waving his hand.

"Good night, little guy."

"I'll see you in the morning, Tim," Tessa said, cuddling Jax in her arms.

"Good night, Tessa."

When they left, Tim buried his face in his hands, briefly giving in to the crushing despair that hovered over him like the darkest cloud. What in the hell were they going to do? How was he going to keep everyone in the Covenant safe? They depended on him, and not knowing how to destroy the creature was eating a hole in his stomach. Whatever he had to do to keep his family safe, he was willing to do, even if it killed him.

Chapter Nineteen

As the creature materialized a mile from the Breedline Covenant, hidden among acres of trees and undergrowth, he noticed a solitary light in a corner window upstairs at the front of an old Victorian, two-story house. Pine trees hid the lower half of the place, but the second floor glowed from the glorious rays of the moonlight, drawing him onward.

His clawed feet clicked as he quickly ducked underneath the house's wooden, rickety porch and stood sniffing the air. The smell of a human nearby was almost too overwhelming to bear. That scent released the hunger within him and drove him on. Every muscle in his body wanted to rip the human limb from limb. He had to grit his teeth to keep from tearing down the door to get at what he craved. He briefly lowered his lids, calming the fury inside as a low growl rumbled deep in his chest.

Slowly, he reached for the door and found that it was unlocked. With his clawed hand, he turned the knob and edged the door open. He lowered his head to keep from brushing along the top of the entrance and crept inside like a wild animal stalking its prey.

Meanwhile, upstairs, and unaware of what was transpiring below, Cobi settled back into his pillow with a sigh. The night seemed especially weird, he thought, the way the moon looked at him through the bedroom window and the wind blew the pines outside, making the two-story house creak.

Before he called it a night, he decided to relax in bed and enjoy a good mystery novel or, even better, a scary ghost story.

As Cobi opened the book, he heard an eerie scratching sound. He quickly sat up in bed and listened. The noise was coming from the window. He let out a sigh of relief when he realized it was only a twig tapping on the pane. Easing back into his pillow, he focused on the novel in his hand and turned to the first page.

It was late, nearly two o'clock in the morning, but he managed to get to the third chapter. Despite the large quantities of caffeine, he could feel himself getting drowsy.

His eyelids felt heavy and the room had gotten darker, as though the lights had magically turned themselves down. With a halfhearted effort, Cobi forced his eyelids to stay open while he stared sleepily out the window.

The moon illuminated the dark sky, glimmering softly into the window. Closing his eyes, he let the book rest on his chest as he drifted off to sleep.

In the dark shadows of the open doorway stood the creature, his cunning eyes shifting rapidly around the room. The moonlight coming through the bedroom window struck the glowing orbs of his yellow eyes. He was beyond furious. After the painful confrontation with the Angel Raphael, he couldn't wait to unleash his fury on the foolish human—who was oblivious to his presence—lying just a few feet away.

The floor creaked as the creature moved forward, waking Cobi from his slumber. His head bolted up. He peeked over the foot of the bed and saw nothing but the moon shining through the window. *How strange*, he thought as he rubbed his eyes. Then his attention went to the sound of heavy breathing. As Cobi turned to look, he instantly wished he hadn't.

"Oh God…"

His mouth rounded in sheer terror as he stared into a pair of glowing eyes that peered out through wiry, thick black hair. Cobi watched in disbelief as a huge hulking monster, the embodiment of evil, stalked closer and stood over his bed. It was *hideous*. It had some features of a man but more elongated like an animal, resembling the creature in the original 1941 American horror film *The Wolf Man*. With high-pointed ears atop its huge head, its black leathery lips formed a ghoulish grimace, revealing sharp-pointed canines, and a deep gargling growl broke from its throat.

Before he could move, the creature's claws reached out and caught him by the arm, lifting him up into the full glare of the moonlight.

"P-please," Cobi stammered, his feet dangling off the floor.

At the same time, Cobi squeezed his lids tight, praying with his eyes shut.

The monster opened its jaws, preparing to sink his fangs into the human's flesh. As he moved in for the kill, a dark and sinister voice came from behind that froze him in his tracks.

"Put the human *down*."

The wolf-man dropped Cobi and spun around on the balls of his feet, heels high, knees positioned in an attack stance.

On his hands and knees, Cobi scrambled to a small corner of the room. With his heart in his throat, he merely watched as something immense and deadly stepped out of the shadows, reeking of pure evil, one utterly devoid of humanity. It slightly looked like the devil in the American dark fantasy film, *Legend,* except this devilish creature was scarier, and it didn't have horns atop its hideous head. Although, the size of the thing was enormous. It towered at least seven feet tall, bigger than the wolf-man that was about to devour him, with sharp protruding teeth and glowing eyes. Dark fur partly covered his skin, and it had leathery, bat-like wings that made the hair on his neck stand. While Cobi took this in, he swallowed nervously, wondering if this monster was friend or foe.

A pink tongue flashed behind the wolf-man's white teeth as he flexed his powerful thighs. "Who dares to interfere with my meal?" His voice was grotesque, the cultured, southern drawl coming from such a bestial face.

The bat-like creature took a step forward, and to his surprise, the wolf-man reflexively stepped back. "My name is Apollyon." His voice went on with a maddening restraint. "We are here to send you back to *hell*."

"We?" the wolf-man asked.

Again, Apollyon advanced, but this time, the wolf-man stood firm, narrowing his eyes in an aggressive warning.

A female with long red hair and feathery black wings ducked under the doorway. When she stepped inside, she towered above Apollyon, barely able to fit into the room. With resentment in her eyes, she glared at the wolfish creature.

The wolf-man's eyes rounded in astonishment. Then, a giant black-winged male with blond spiked hair moved next to the female. He crossed his arms over his chest and curled his top lip as though he was daring the wolf-man to make a move.

Before he could process the trio, two more females came up behind Apollyon and stood on the opposite side of him. They did not have wings, but one of them had a muscular physique, and her eyes sparkled like diamonds. The other one was feminine; her beauty was almost hypnotizing. Both women appeared connected to the creature that called himself Apollyon. Closing in behind them was a pale-faced, tall male with a lean muscularity and long black hair. His golden eyes narrowed with pure hatred. The wolf-man heard the red-headed angel whisper out to him, using the name Sebastian.

What a dreadful spectacle this must make for the human huddled in the corner, the redheaded angel thought as she glanced his way. A room full of supernatural beings sparring with ghastly words surely was terrifying for him to witness.

When she pressed closer, the wolf-man kept his feet firmly planted in place. His thighs flexed, and his hands lifted as though he was ready to attack.

"Remember me?" the winged female asked. Her tone was bitter. "I'm the innocent, young girl you murdered over forty years ago."

"Lailah," the wolfish creature said through gritted teeth.

"I'm surprised you remember my name," she replied.

"Oh, believe me. I could never forget you." He gave her a look filled with self-satisfaction. "Your beauty made the kill all the more challenging."

Apollyon said nothing. It was now, he thought, now that they should strike.

The wolf-man spoke again. "Don't think that makes you special though," he said, baring his teeth as if in an ugly smile. "Had I chosen you for my mate, you would have been magnificent, the most breathtaking of my kind, but I did not choose you." His voice was angry but steady. "You were not worthy to be at my side."

"That's enough," Lailah said impatiently. "It's time for you to pay for your sins. And now you will die for them." She leaned in and cocked a brow. "But first, do tell me. Were all those innocent lives you took worth it?"

This infuriated the wolf-man. "You think you have the power to destroy me?" he said with a spiteful cackle. "I've been around for centuries. None of you have any idea what powers I possess. But you will find out soon."

A low rolling growl escaped Apollyon. "We're done talking!" he roared.

The wolf-man lowered his head and shook his hands in fury. "What are you waiting for, devil man?" A gnashing mocking sound came out of him, fully as forceful as his words. "Bring your worst!"

Cowered in the corner, Cobi tucked his knees into his chest and covered his ears.

Apollyon looked to the female with overwhelming beauty and muttered, "Cover me, Callisto."

She nodded in silent understanding.

In a snarling outrage, he rushed at the wolf-man, claws out, and lunged for its throat.

Before he made contact, the wolf-man kicked at Apollyon with such a powerful force, it drove him back and slammed him into the wall.

The wind went out of Apollyon, realizing his sister's protective shield was useless up against the wolfish creature. Instantly, he recovered and sprang at the wolf-man, his powerful thighs catapulting him forward. Using his fierce claws, Apollyon slashed wildly at the evil creature, gashing open his thick hide.

The wolf-man bellowed, then lunged at Apollyon and drove his fangs deep into his shoulder. Apollyon felt the wetness of the blood as it gushed from his flesh.

I refuse to let it overpower me, Apollyon thought fever-ishly as the wolfish beast tore at him with fits of rage.

In a savage frenzy, Apollyon broke loose of him, and this time he kicked at the wolf-man as it had kicked him, landing a blow at his lower gut with tremendous force.

As the furious creature doubled over, Apollyon yanked by the hair of his mane and hurled him backward. He cursed in anger as his head struck the wall.

Faster than their eyes could perceive, the wolf-man rose up and charged forward. In a heated fury, he pummeled Apollyon with his monstrous paw. The thundering blow sent him sailing across the room. Apollyon crashed against the paneling, and crumpled to the floor, his gaping mouth full of blood.

Using a portal, Sebastian vanished in thin air. When he reappeared, he stood behind the wolf-man with a silver wire in his grasp. In one swift motion, he wrapped it around the creature's throat and pulled with all his strength. Unexpectedly, the monstrous creature disappeared, leaving nothing but a puff of smoke in his place.

"What the—" Sebastian muttered, spinning in circles, his eyes searching for the creature.

Apollyon rose to his feet and gritted his bloodstained teeth. He had never seen anything move that fast. One second the wolf-man simply vanished; the next, he reappeared behind Sebastian. With unbelievable speed, the wolf-man put Sebastian in a blistering choke hold and hauled him into the shadows.

It seemed as though the darkness had swallowed them. As Sebastian struggled to breathe, the wolf-man spoke in a deep, accented growl, "You should have stayed out of my way, half-breed." He narrowed his eyes at the others and raised his voice, "You *all* should have stayed out of my way!"

Sebastian clawed at the iron hold and choked, desperate for air. The massive arm locked around his throat was squeezing the life right out of him.

A minute later Sebastian stopped resisting altogether, his arms dropping and hanging loose. He wanted to fight, but no longer had the strength. If this was his death, he was okay with it. It was better and quicker than ending up back in Lucifer's possession, reliving his tortured past. He was willing to die to save his soul.

With his last bit of strength, Sebastian tried to speak.

The wolf-man loosened his grip and leaned in to listen.

"Go to hell," Sebastian gasped.

Then, an authoritative voice called out, "Let him go!"

As the wolf-man lifted his chin and looked ahead, Electra's diamond eyes brightened with such intensity, it blinded him for a moment. He instantly removed his arm from Sebastian's throat to shield his eyes. Sebastian fell to his knees, and what little breath he'd been able to steal got kicked out of his lungs in a rush.

In the short time he took to look away, Electra knew that she had not a second to spare and reached for her silver whip. She used her cunning skills and whirled it at the evil creature with lightning speed. When it struck his chest, a bolt of electricity burned his skin like a red-hot coal, paring his flesh to the bone. He clenched his teeth to keep from howling out. He'd be damned if he'd give them the satisfaction of seeing him cry out like a whipped dog. Before he could recover, Electra stuck him again. He dropped to his knees as steam rose from his scalded hide. Then his glowing gaze lifted up and searched his enemies around him. Before he could react, Lailah extended her fiery wings and trapped the wolf-man with a circle of flames.

In his weakened, but not defeated state, he used the strength within him and took on the form of a vapor-like fog. As the mysterious phantom suspended into the air, it slipped through the vents and escaped his adversaries below.

Once he fed and regained his strength, he would prove more powerful than any opposing force that challenged him. And this time, nothing would stop him.

Chapter Twenty

The wolfish beast stood shaking as he materialized back into the thicket, surrounded by darkness. Thoughts of killing and feasting on human blood occupied his mind as he staggered through the woods. He wanted something else. He *wanted* Jena. He wanted her now more than ever. Soon, he would have her. It wouldn't be long before her lust for human blood took over. Only one drop and the transformation would be complete.

About fifty yards away, and with his acute hearing, he picked up voices. As he stopped to listen, he heard two people passing through the dense growth of trees, getting closer to where he stood. He moved in behind some bushes and watched. They were barely visible, like dark silhouettes in the thick fog. Their bodies were steaming in the cool morning air as they trudged onward, speaking in low tones. One of them carried a weapon.

They were hunting, he realized, and by their scent, they were young males. Not virginal blood, but a tasty meal all the same.

Soon the tables would turn. If only they knew what lurked in the shadows, stalking them. The predator would soon become the prey.

As he continued to watch them, he licked his lips. His tongue played around his sharp canines for a second, then slipped back into his mouth. Without a sound, he began to track them, keeping himself at a fair distance.

Would they dare have the courage to be out at this hour if they knew there was something preparing to spring out from the bushes and turn them to corpses? It was crazy really. They were roaming in the dark as though their young lives and souls were not in mortal jeopardy. Yet here they were.

He curled his lip into a snarl. *Humans seemed stupid and their lives worthless,* he thought. *What fools they are.* He could sense all their weaknesses clearly and viewed them only as food.

The man-wolf filled his chest with air and looked up at the sky.

Suddenly, over the tops of the trees, an arc of the moon emerged, and with it, a long eerie howl broke the silence. It seemed to last forever. The noise halted the two humans in their tracks.

One of them, wearing a pair of thick glasses, whispered to the other, "Did you hear that?"

The other one with the weapon nodded in silence and then motioned for his brother to hunch low. For a long time, they just waited, not speaking, and listened. Filled with anticipation and a twinge of dread, they wondered what was out there.

Then the staccato of snapping branches came from behind.

Both of them instantly looked over their shoulders. "Listen," one of them said, barely above a whisper.

They could hear something creeping slowly upon them. It was like the sound of twigs being broken underfoot, one after the other. As they listened, it started to move toward them at a steady pace.

"What do you think it is?" the one wearing glasses asked, his wide eyes probing his brother with alarm.

"I can't tell," he whispered. "But it sounds like it's moving on all fours."

As they waited, a sense of uneasiness made the hairs on the back of their necks stand on end. Then the sound stopped dead, as though whatever was out there was waiting too.

"Damn it," the kid gripping the rifle said. "This is ridiculous. It's probably a coyote tracking a deer." He couldn't stand waiting any longer and inched up to look.

Forty yards away, hidden in the tall grass, and peering out of the fog, he saw a pair of glowing eyes. With precision, he aimed his weapon forward and looked through the scope to get a better look at what was out there. As he kept it steady, scanning the area, the muscles in his jaw felt ready to cramp. When he pulled the cocking piece back, the slide action of the bullet chambering made a distinctive sound.

"What the hell is it?" the other kid impatiently said.

He didn't answer right away, but finally lowered the rifle, and looked at his brother. "It's hard to see through all this fog. I think it's just a coyote, or maybe a bobcat."

"Logan, are you sure?" Greg reached for his brother's weapon. "Let me take a look."

Logan rolled his eyes. "Why the hell did you leave your rifle in the truck?"

"I wasn't planning on using it. Besides, you're the one that wanted to go hunting, not me. I came along for the nature hike." Greg let out an aggravated groan. "Come on, already. Just let me see it for a minute."

"Be careful, it's cocked."

Greg gave his brother a look. "I know how to handle a gun."

As he handed Greg the rifle, whatever it was started moving again. They could hear it in the grass.

Greg pushed himself to his feet. His muscles were sore from crouching, the way they felt after a bad cramp. When he put the scope against the left side of his glass lens, he saw the hairy back of an animal tearing through the tall grass about twenty yards away. And it was *big*.

"Well?" Logan shrugged. "What do you see?"

"Shit," he cursed low. "It's definitely not a coyote."

"Damn it, Greg." Logan raised his voice, "Just shoot the damn thing!"

Greg froze with his finger on the trigger. His mind and reflexes didn't seem to be working together. He kept looking through the scope, but he couldn't see the animal anymore. It simply vanished into the thick fog.

"I-it's gone," Greg finally said. "It must have got spooked off."

When he lowered the rifle, a thickly muscled, hairy arm ending in five sharp claws, quickly emerged from the brush. It caught Greg by the arm and tore it completely off.

In a state of shock, Greg's mouth opened in utter horror.

Then the animal's hairy form stepped into full view, the moon shining down on the beastly thing. It towered above them.

Logan went into sensory overload and helplessly watched as it viciously attacked his little brother. It stood on two legs and had the features of a man and a wolf. Covered in thick, black hair, its nose ended in leathery nostrils.

Greg's screams of agony only seemed to fuel the creature's rage. In a matter of seconds, it tore at his throat, turning the boy's screams into a wet gurgling hiss of air.

"Greg!" Logan desperately cried out, reaching for his brother.

The brutality of it all seemed to move in slow motion as the savage creature ripped his brother's lifeless body into pieces. Distraught and powerless, Logan shrunk back in disbelief.

The grisly sight of his brother's head dropping down onto the dismembered parts of his body sickened Logan and nearly drove him to the brink of madness.

"No, no, no..." Logan mumbled, the words coming out like someone had slowed time.

He tripped and stumbled back. Staring into his brother's glassy dead eyes, Logan felt himself falling... falling... yet never reaching the ground. It was as though he fell for an eternity, suspended in a web of terror while images of his childhood past flashed before his eyes—memories of his little brother trying to carry the puppy he'd got for his third birthday, which was almost as big as he was, and the excitement he'd expressed. Then another memory came to him, only this time, it had happened only a year ago. It was Greg's sixteenth birthday. He would never forget the look on his face when their dad brought home a beat-up, canary yellow, Ford Maverick. His little brother had been ecstatic. Greg cherished that damn car just as he did his big brother— the same brother that was supposed to look after him, and kept him out of harm's way.

Everything sped up to normal when Logan hit the ground. His eyes zoned in on the rifle. It was lying in the weeds only a few feet away. Using all his strength, he dove for it with his arms outstretched.

Without hesitation, he quickly grabbed for it. As he spun around with the barrel aimed at the creature, he pulled the trigger. The blast thundered and filled the forest chamber. Soon after, an ear-shattering roar broke loose.

As the man-wolf angrily slashed it claws at the night, Logan felt the wetness and warmth of its blood splattering down on his face. With the gun in his grasp, he got to his feet and forced himself to run. As he trudged onward his only thought was, *Oh God, my brother is dead.*

Logan seemed lost in thought for a few moments, and then he looked over his shoulder. He found that only the darkness followed him and wondered if he had killed that *thing.*

For a moment, his grief stopped him. Logan lowered the rifle to the ground and leaned against a tree. He buried his face into his hands and sobbed. He wept not only for the loss of his brother but the savagery of his death.

"Damn it, Greg," he whispered to himself. "I'm so sorry, little brother."

Out of nowhere, something touched his hair. Logan flinched and whirled around.

"It's okay," a soft, delicate voice said. "I'm not going to hurt you."

With his mouth gaped open, he couldn't believe his eyes. Standing over him, towering at least ten feet tall was a woman. She had long red hair that flowed past her hips and giant, black wings with smoke rising above them as though they had recently been on fire. Her broad shoulders and toned arms were marked with odd symbols that he did not recognize. It was unreal. She looked like some kind of warrior out of a sci-fi movie.

As he took all of her in, he found that he couldn't speak, much less move.

"You're safe now," the beautiful, angel-like female said. "The creature is gone."

Logan sagged in relief, and then asked, "W-who are you?"

"My name is Lailah."

"Are you..." He briefly paused and swallowed the knot in his throat. "...supposed to be an angel?"

"Yes," she replied. "I'm one of the Creator's battle angels."

"What the hell was that *thing* back there?" He raised his voice, "Is it dead?"

"No," she reluctantly said. "But I promise it's gone. It can't harm you now."

"Please tell me." He let out a ragged breath. "What was *it*?"

Lailah hesitated to tell the poor human what had brutally murdered his brother, but at this moment, he deserved the truth. She'd been granted permission from the Creator to bring life back to his brother. Afterward, she would erase all the horrible events from their memory of this night, including the one of her.

"The thing that took your brother's life," she began to explain, "is a creature that has lived for centuries. I was sent here to try and destroy it."

He narrowed his eyes. "How do you know about my brother?"

She smiled and brought her hand toward his face.

In response, he took a couple of steps back.

"Don't be afraid." She halted her hand before it made contact with the surface of his skin. "I'm here to help you."

He nodded in silence and slowly moved closer.

"There's blood on your face." She gently placed her hand against his cheek. "Are you injured?"

With tears in his eyes, he shook his head. "It's not my blood. I shot that thing that killed my brother."

Lailah's face softened. "I'm sorry."

Suddenly, he fell apart. "Please, can you help me?" His lips trembled. "You're an angel. Surely you can bring him back."

She placed two fingers under his chin and tilted it up. Her eyes held many kinds of love. "Have faith, Logan."

"H-how did you know my name?"

"The Creator knows all of his children," she said as she lowered her hand and stood straight.

"Are you saying, *God* told you?"

She nodded and simply replied, "It's not Greg's time."

He looked at her bewildered. "What are you talking about?"

Then Logan heard footsteps in the near distance. His eyes searched through the thick fog until suddenly, a lone, dark figure stepped forward as though it had magically appeared out of nowhere. As the person moved closer, Logan finally recognized who it was.

"Greg?"

"Yes, brother," a familiar voice called out. "It's me!"

As the brothers embraced, Lailah did her thing and erased all the traumatic memories that had happened to them as well as Cobi's nightmarish encounter with the creature earlier. She replaced Cobi's memories with a peaceful night of rest, and Logan and Greg's with a glorious morning of two brothers enjoying nature. Not long after, she went to meet up with her comrades in arms. They had a task to complete, but unfortunately, destroying the creature was going to be more challenging than they had foreseen. Even her powers of holy fire couldn't contain the creature. That's when she decided she needed Cronus's help.

Chapter Twenty-One

The sun was shining through the cracked blinds, rousing Jena from a deep and peaceful slumber. She hadn't remembered the last time she'd slept so soundly and undisturbed. She had been so exhausted when Angie checked her out of the hospital and brought her to the Covenant she didn't even bother turning on the bedroom lights. Jena barely managed to change into her nightgown; she practically passed out as soon as her head hit the pillow.

Jena slowly sat up, pulled the covers back, and slid off the bed. The hardwood floor was cold against her bare feet. When she felt steady enough to stand, the muscles in her long, lean legs shook as they worked to balance her weight. Before she took a step, she glanced around the spacious room.

Her eyes rounded. *Holy... Queen of England.*

Long silk draperies hung from the Victorian windows in swaths of burgundy and gold. There were matching Oriental rugs on the floor, which looked expensive, and oil paintings on the walls.

Good lord, she thought. *Was that one of Pablo Picasso's original paintings?*

In the corner of her eye, something sparked her attention. When she turned to look, her mouth gaped open. Spread across the length of the entire wall was a bookshelf that housed numerous old leather bounds. Jena wandered over and scanned the titles in awe.

She covered her mouth and mumbled into her hand, "Oh my—"

Pride and Prejudice by Jane Austen, *To Kill a Mockingbird* by Harper Lee, *War and Peace* by Leo Tolstoy, *Moby Dick* by Herman Melville, *The Adventures of Huckleberry Finn* by Mark Twain, *Invisible Man* by Ralph Ellison, *The Chase* by A.P. Von K'Ory, *The Creator's Plan* by Rebecca Williams, and her favorite Christian poetry by Roy Owens.

Her eyes roamed over the lower shelf, and the list of outstanding authors was endless. Then her eyes spotted a book she had been dying to read. Her eyes rounded in sheer joy. It was *Mirrors of Life* by Neal Owens.

I'm definitely reading this later, she thought, admiring the hardback. *Someone in this house definitely has fabulous taste and big money.*

In the corner of the spacious room, she noticed an artist easel and a studio chair. Positioned on the easel's stand, as though it was waiting just for her, was a blank canvas. As Jena moved closer, she was surprised at the variety of paintbrushes, and an assortment of acrylics, not to mention a paint palette. At that moment, she knew this must have come from Angie. It was like her to do something like this. The thought made her smile. Jena could not ask for a better friend.

As she went into the bathroom and flipped on the lights, her eyes rounded in pure astonishment. A Jacuzzi tub the size of a boat was smack dab in the middle of the monstrous room, which also had a humongous shower, a double vanity, and an enclosed space with a private bidet.

She heard a soft knock at the door and then Angie's voice, "Hey girl, you up?"

"Come on in," Jena called out.

When the door opened, Angie walked back to the bathroom and stood next to Jena. "How are you feeling?"

"I feel rested. Last night was the first I've slept in days."

"That's great, Jena."

"Hey, thanks for all the art supplies. Have I told you lately what a great friend you are?"

"You're welcome." Angie smiled. "I just wanted to make sure you feel at home here. So, whatcha doin'?"

"Oh, I was just checking out this tub. It's freakin' huge." Jena shook her head. "The people that live here have to be loaded. Have you seen the book collection? It's priceless." She turned toward the bedroom and pointed at the oil painting. "And please tell me that's not an original Picasso."

Angie shrugged. "Hell if I know."

"A girl could get real comfortable here if you know what I mean. I could spend days just reading all those books."

Angie laughed a little. "I knew you'd like this room."

"Are you kidding me? I love it. You're the best, Ang."

"Don't mention it, girl. Whenever you get dressed, I'll take you down for breakfast and introduce you to some of the others. Oh, and don't worry. You will love everyone here. They've always treated me like family."

"So, is everyone in the Covenant a Breedline?" Jena asked, looking at Angie curiously.

Angie's lips curved up. "Mostly, but not everyone."

"I thought you said the Breedline are kept secret from humans."

"They are, except in cases like you," said Angie. "We have other species residing here. You remember the woman with long brown hair and piercing green eyes?"

"Her name is Tessa, right?"

Angie nodded. "She's our queen."

Jena's eyes rounded. "You have a queen?"

"Yeah," Angie replied. "She's one badass queen, too. Her wolf is twice the size of an ordinary Breedline. The good-looking blond you met is her husband Jace. He was born a Breedline, but he is also the Beast."

"What the hell is that?"

"It's something you don't want to piss off," Angie told her. "I've never seen it, but I've heard several stories. I guess you could say he's a mixture of the abominable snowman and a seven-foot werewolf on steroids."

Jena let out a long sigh. "Remind me not to piss that guy off."

Angie chuckled. "His twin brother Jem is not exactly an ordinary Breedline either. He has the power to conjure a portal and can create a firebomb out of the palm of his hand. He's called the Chosen Son."

"Why do they call him that?"

"Jem and Jace's father, Alexander Crest, was possessed by an ancient demon before he was even born," Angie explained. "To make a long story short, he kidnapped their mother—who was engaged to Alexander's twin brother—killed him, and raped her. They inherited the Breedline genes from both biological parents and inherited some of the demon's powers. Later on, Zadkiel, the archangel of mercy, released him from the demon's possession. The Covenant did not blame Alexander for the demon's crimes."

"Oh my gosh." Jena shook her head. "That must have been hard for Jace and Jem to forgive him."

"It's taken some time, especially for Jace. He hated Alexander for what he did to his mother, but he eventually, like everyone else, has come to love Alexander for the good man he truly is."

"Tell me more," Jena said. "I'm dying to know what other species live here."

"Well," Angie said, shrugging, "Tessa's brother Steven is an Adalwolf, and so is Roman Kincaid. They are wolf-like creatures except they walk on two feet and have the strength of ten men, not to mention super speed. Casey Barton has the genetics of a Breedline and a Therimorph. Instead of shifting into a Breedline wolf, he turns into a giant black panther. Abbey, Steven's mate, is a Lupa. When provoked into anger, kinda like Jace, she shifts into a dangerous she-wolf. Celina Baldolf is a Breedline with the power of a white Wicca. Tim's wife, Angel, is a half-breed, along with Mia and her twin sister, Eve. All three were born half-Breedline and half-succubus. A full-blooded succubus feeds off the blood of a Breedline. Although, in most cases," Angie went on to explain, "a Breedline doesn't naturally get along well with a succubus, but sometimes you can't help who you fall in love with."

"Wow," said Jena, staring at Angie, leaving her nearly speechless. "That's incredible. If someone other than you told me all this, I wouldn't believe a word of it. So tell me, do you visit the Covenant often?"

"Not really, but I need to. I miss everyone. The last time I was here was almost a year ago. I've heard new people have moved in. And I hear some of them are not bad on the eyes." Angie nudged Jena's arm and batted her brows. "If you know what I mean."

Jena smiled. "You haven't changed a bit, girlfriend."

"Hey, a girl's got needs, right? Besides, you never know. There might be someone here that catches your eye."

"Right now, I've got other things on my mind." Jena sighed. "Getting laid is the last thing I'm worried about. My first priority is to resist *other* urges."

Angie made a face. "You mean... human blood?"

"Uh-huh," Jena grudgingly replied.

"Don't worry, girl." Angie wrapped her arm around Jena's shoulder and pulled her close. "That's what I'm here for. I'll keep you straight."

Jena rested her head on Angie's shoulder. "I don't know what I'd do without you. I owe you big time."

Angie pulled back and said, "Come on now. Don't be getting all emotional on me. Get your ass in gear and get dressed. I'll be back in twenty. Please don't dawdle. My ass is starving."

"Okay," Jena said with a slight chuckle. "See you in twenty."

* * *

Downstairs, everyone else gathered in the formal dining room. When Tim walked in, he looked tense. His dark eyebrows pinched together as though something weighed heavily on his mind.

"Everyone is accounted for," Tessa told him.

Tim nodded in her direction. "Let's meet in the library. We've got a lot to discuss."

As they filed into the library, Tessa went to the head of the table that was large enough to seat thirty. Before she sat down, Jace pulled out a chair for her. Tim stood beside her, his arms crossed as he waited for everyone to take a seat.

Jace sat next to Tessa, and Jem sat down beside him. Drakon took the seat across from them, and Roman settled in the chair beside him while Lawrence, Justice, Lena, and Bull sat close to one another. Kyle, Casey, and Steven sat in the chairs closest to Jem. Alexander, Helen, and Detective Manuel Sanchez came in last and sat down in the three empty chairs next to Casey.

When everyone that Tim invited was accounted for, he said, "I know all of you are wondering why Tessa and I called this meeting. First, I would like to thank Detective Sanchez for all your patience. We're glad to have you here. I'm sorry for your and your partner's unfortunate incident with Jimmy Fratianno. It's a relief to hear you two managed to come out with only minor injuries, but I can't say the same for Mr. Fratianno and the rest of his criminal companions." His voice took on a grim tone, glancing in Jace's direction. "I'm sure Helen has filled you in on most of the details. Thanks to Drakon, Roman, Lawrence, Jem, and of course Jace, or should I say the *Beast,* they will no longer be a problem."

"Wish I could have been there to see that," Kyle muttered in a low voice, looking in Jace's direction. "The Beast is a savage."

"No kidding," Casey chimed in.

Jace cocked a brow and smirked at them.

"Thank you, Tim," Manuel said, and then he turned to the others. "You all did society a big favor. As I see it, justice was served, and you saved the taxpayers money."

Everyone nodded in agreement.

"We'd also like to thank Helen for doing a super job keeping everyone here in one piece," Tessa spoke out, focusing her eyes on Helen. "I know we've kept you busy lately. You've been a godsend to this Covenant."

Alexander reached under the table for Helen's hand and lightly squeezed. She smiled at the comforting gesture of support.

"Yes, thank you, Helen," Manuel added. "And I also speak for my partner, Detective Perkins. I have to say, Helen is one helluva physician. We own you one."

Helen nodded. "You're all welcome. That's what I'm here for."

"I want to make sure everyone here is aware of our current house guests," Tim continued. "Ms. Jena McCain and Ms. Tara Hood will be staying with us for a while. You already know Ms. Angie Hawkridge. Those of you that don't, we will get you acquainted. She'll be staying with us as well, considering she's close friends with Jena. Angie will be a big help in keeping her focused. I'm sure I don't have to tell you to make them all feel at home." Tim let out a long sigh. "Both Jena and Tara have been through hell."

"What about Ms. McCain's curse?" Jace interjected. "Shouldn't we be concerned? How are we going to keep her contained when she starts craving blood?"

"We keep you contained, don't we?" Jem said mockingly.

Drakon let out a short laugh. "Yeah, *barely*."

"Whatever," Jace muttered, rolling his eyes.

Tim frowned. "She's only a threat to humans. I've alerted our security. Ms. McCain will not be allowed to leave the Covenant until the curse is lifted."

"What about Tara?" Lawrence asked. His voice was low, insistent. "She's human. Won't she be in danger around Ms. McCain?"

"That's another reason why we called this meeting," Tessa chimed in. "Last night, Tara was attacked by the creature."

"What?" Lawrence rose from his chair, feeling a growl working its way up his throat. "Is she all right?"

"How the hell did that *thing* get into the Covenant?" Jace said abruptly.

Tessa held up her hand in a reassuring gesture. "Don't worry, Lawrence. Tara is just fine. Please, sit down and let me finish." Then she turned to Jace and gave him a look.

He shrugged and silently mouthed, "Sorry."

Lawrence worked his molars, grinding them together. He lowered his head and simply said, "I apologize for interrupting." Then he sat back down.

Tessa nodded at Lawrence. "As I was saying, the creature did not hurt Tara. Of course, she was frightened, but no harm came to her. I don't know how the creature found the Covenant's location. The only explanation I have is somehow it's linked to Jena. And according to the Rougarou Curse, this is what we know. Any human bitten by the creature will soon crave human blood. If they can resist it for one hundred and one days, they are no longer cursed. If not, they will be damned for eternity with the urge to feed on humans. It's possible for the creature to go dormant for years, living underground until it wants to feed again, and it can kill for many years before it's ready to..." She paused as though she was searching for the right word. "I guess you'd call it hibernate?" She shrugged. "Not only does the curse bring forth the creature, it gives them the power to transform into various nocturnal animals, such as taking on the forms of bats, and even rats. It can also assume a cloud of smoke or fog. I think this is how it managed to get into the Covenant undetected."

"And I thought *Dracula* was just a made-up story," Manuel pointed out.

Tessa looked at Manuel with a raised brow. "There are definitely similarities, but you can rest at ease, Detective. *Dracula* doesn't exist."

Helen raised her hand. "May I speak?"

"Yes, of course, Helen," Tessa said.

"The creature has also been visiting Jena in the hospital," Helen told them. "And there's no way it could have gotten past security or the hospital staff. I think it shifted into some type of fog or transparent mist and traveled through the vents."

Alarmed by Helen's theory, everyone looked at one another in silence.

"Are you sure *Dracula* isn't real?" Manuel asked. "It sounds like the prince of darkness to me."

Tessa chuckled a little. "Yes, Detective."

"Sorry to interrupt," Steven spoke out for the first time. "So, if Tara is indeed human, why didn't the creature kill her?"

Tessa looked at her brother and exhaled. "That's a good question, Steven. Tara told me the creature said something strange to her. It told her she wasn't human."

Jace cursed while several others inhaled sharply.

Lawrence glanced at Helen, his eyes rounding in surprise.

"If Helen will agree, I would like a DNA test done on Tara," Tessa said. "I think it's a possibility she may carry our bloodline but was never told." She glanced at Manuel. "As you and I both know, Detective, that happens a lot."

"Actually, I've already tested Tara," Helen admitted.

Lawrence's heart raced, praying the test was positive while everyone at the table waited in anticipation.

"I suspected Tara might share our genetics, so I took some of her blood during her exam," Helen continued. "I hope I wasn't overstepping the boundaries."

"Of course not, Helen," Tessa quickly replied. "We trust your judgment."

"Well?" Jace said impatiently. "Is she a Breedline?"

"The test was positive," Helen replied.

Lawrence blew out a deep breath and sagged in relief.

"Someone needs to tell her," said Helen. "Tara also needs an explanation of why she's here, and about the creature. It killed someone she cared for. She deserves to know the truth."

Tessa nodded. "Thank you, Helen. And yes, you're right. I promised her I would visit this morning. I have no other choice but to tell her about us, especially since she carries our DNA."

Lawrence felt the tension building inside him. The temptation to blurt everything out, to reveal his feelings for Tara was suddenly unbearable. He cleared his throat. "Ms. Tessa, can I tell her?"

Tessa looked at Lawrence bewildered, as so did the others at the table. Before she could utter a single word, he forced the words out, "I have... bonded with her."

The room fell silent and then Helen finally said, "I think it's a good idea." She smiled at Lawrence. "He should be the one to tell her."

"I trust your instincts, Lawrence," Tessa said. "I like Tara." A hint of a smile crossed her face. "She seems to be a very nice person. I think she'd make a great addition to our family. Congratulations."

"Thank you, Ms. Tessa," Lawrence replied. "Hopefully she feels the same about me."

Roman shook his head. "Well hell, buddy," he said with a light chuckle. "It's about damn time. I'm sure she feels the same. What's not to like? You're like a freakin' big ol' teddy bear."

"I know she does," Helen said. "I saw the way she looked at you, Lawrence. The feeling is certainly mutual."

Lawrence simply smiled at Helen's reassuring words.

Drakon reached behind Roman and tapped Lawrence on the shoulder. "Way to go, buddy. It feels great doesn't it?"

"There's no comparison," Lawrence replied. "I never expected this to happen to me."

"I know firsthand how that feels. We're very fortunate." Drakon smiled a little, remembering the first time he met Cassie. "It's not easy for our kind to find that special one… our beloved."

Jace turned to Tessa and said, "I remember the first time I saw you. When you walked into the room, it seemed like the whole atmosphere changed."

Tessa's eyes softened. "That day changed my life."

Manuel shrugged. "I don't understand. Is this a Breedline thing?"

"It's hard to explain," Jem said to Manuel. "It's like this individual energy that completely consumes your entire body. The word *beloved* will immediately enter your subconscious. It's the same thing as a soulmate. When I met Mia, it was like a physical shift in the air. I knew instantly she was the one."

Lawrence gave a curt nod, fascinated by everyone's stories. He wanted to hear more.

"Do you know anything about Tara?" Tim asked Lawrence. "Did she mention having a twin sister?"

"Tara didn't say anything about having siblings. But I do remember her mentioning her foster parents." Lawrence's tone was sympathetic. "I don't think she had a happy childhood. She told me she ran away at a young age."

Tim heaved a deep breath. "It's a possibility Tara is a full-blooded Breedline."

"I hate to change the subject, but has anyone had a chance to check the security cameras?" Manuel asked, the cop in him coming out as always.

"Yes," Drakon said. "Before the meeting, I rolled back the video footage of last night. It did capture Tara leaving her room a few minutes after midnight and entering the gym. Although when she went into the weapons room, the footage was scrambled. I couldn't see anything that happened in that room."

"Are you saying our camera's malfunctioned?" Tim queried.

Drakon shook his head. "I checked them again this morning. They're working just fine. Someone or *something* kept the camera's in the weapons room from capturing what happened to Tara."

Tim's brows furrowed. "Do you think the creature had something to do with it?"

"There's no other explanation, "Drakon replied. "The cameras outside the weapons room were working. It did get a video of Tessa and Jax entering the room, and fifteen minutes later when they came out with Tara."

"Did the cameras catch anyone else leaving or entering that room after we left?" Tessa asked Drakon.

"Nope," Drakon said, and then added, "except for the cat."

"How'd Buddy get in there?" Jace bluntly asked.

"Oh, yeah," Tessa said. "I forgot about Buddy. When Jax and I found Tara, Buddy came into the room behind us. He took to Tara right away. His presence seemed to calm her. The poor girl was terrified."

"What about the video surveillance at the hospital?" Tim pointedly asked Helen. "Has anyone thought to check those?"

"I had our security check them last night," Helen replied. "There was nothing but scrambled footage."

"Shit," Tim said. "It looks like our mysterious phantom has outsmarted us." His eyes shifted toward Lawrence. "I hope your sister was right about the battle angels. At this rate, I believe they're our only hope at destroying this damn creature."

"Did Melanie happen to mention when the angels would come back to earth?" Tessa asked Lawrence.

"I'm sorry, Tessa. Mel didn't know the exact day. All she said was that they were coming soon, bringing along with them Sebastian and the Fury."

"Hopefully *soon* will get here fast before this *thing* kills more innocent people," Tim said. "I need everyone to keep a close eye on Jena. Now that she's here, I'm sure it will be back. It appears the creature has chosen her for a reason, and it's obvious it doesn't want to kill her."

"Do you think it's looking for a mate?" Alexander suggested.

"It's a possibility," Tim replied. "Or maybe it needs someone to take its place. Whatever the case, I want everyone in the Covenant to stay accounted for at all times. Those that are not here will be updated on the situation we're facing. As of now, I'm starving. Since we don't have much of a plan, let's take this to the kitchen." He focused on Manuel. "Detective, please join us for breakfast."

"Thanks, Tim. Sounds like a plan to me."

Bull hung back and held the door open as everyone left the meeting. He followed behind his sister Lena and her boyfriend Justice as they were the last ones to leave. When Bull rounded the corner, he stopped in his tracks as Angie and Jena came downstairs. The second Angie caught sight of Bull, she immediately came to a halt and placed her hands on her hips.

She grinned like a kid on Christmas morning. *Damn*, Angie thought. "Well, hello there," she said, batting her brows in Bull's direction.

Chapter Twenty-Two

While everyone gathered in the kitchen for breakfast, Tessa greeted Lawrence with a smile and said, "Helen went to check on Tara, and before she left, she asked if you would like to have breakfast with her. I'm sure Tara would love your company, and I can have a tray of food brought to her room."

His eyes lit up with excitement. "I'd love to. Thank you, Ms. Tessa."

Tessa smiled again. "I'll take you back to see her." She motioned for him to follow. "I'm heading that way myself. After what happened last night, I promised Tara I would stop by this morning to check on her."

Without so much as a backward glance at the others, Lawrence walked alongside Tessa with a little giddyup in his steps, eager to see Tara. Not only was he excited to see her, but he also had to make good on his promise and answer all her questions about the Covenant, the creature that had attacked her, and not to mention the part about her DNA results. He prayed she would take the news well.

Tessa lightly knocked a couple of times and then peeked through the cracked door. "Is it all right if Lawrence and I come in?"

"Of course," Helen said, motioning her inside. "Please, come in."

When they stepped inside, Lawrence's mouth formed a smile that was a mile long as he caught sight of Tara, who Helen was monitoring by her bedside. He whispered a thank-you to God for protecting her when he couldn't.

Tara turned in Lawrence's direction, her eyes instantly going warm as she registered his presence.

Helen smiled and then gestured him over to the other side of Tara's bed.

"How are you feeling, Ms. Tara?" Lawrence asked in a soft voice.

"I'm better," she said hoarsely. "Now that you're here."

He felt a rush of heat as though the temperature in the room had suddenly shifted.

"Your blood pressure is normal," Helen said to Tara, tucking a stethoscope in her lab coat pocket. "I'm going to leave the IV out as long as you promise you'll take it easy. It's important that you get plenty of rest."

Tara nodded. "I promise. Thank you, Dr. Carrington."

"You're very welcome, Tara." Helen patted her on the shoulder. "I'll be back to check on you this evening."

As Helen discreetly stepped out of the room, Tessa moved next to Tara's bedside.

"Now that I hear you're doing better, I won't take up much of your time," Tessa said as she looked over at Lawrence and smiled a little. "I have a feeling someone wants you all to himself."

Tara's eyes sparkled at Tessa's observation despite the grogginess from lack of sleep.

"I just wanted to make sure you're comfortable," Tessa continued, refocusing her eyes on Tara. "If there's anything you need all you have to do is press the call button by your bed."

"Thank you, Tessa. I appreciate everything you've all done for me."

"Don't mention it." Tessa briefly placed her hand on Tara's. "We all just want you safe and sound."

Before Tessa left the room to give them privacy, she said, "By the way, your breakfast should be here shortly."

Lawrence waved at Tessa and said, "Thank you."

As the door clicked shut, Lawrence gathered Tara's hand in his and lightly squeezed. "I'm sorry," he choked out, "that I wasn't here for you when you needed me."

Tara lifted her hand to his cheek and gently caressed his face. "It's not your fault, Lawrence. You couldn't have known something like that was going to happen. Besides, I owe you my life." Her eyes filled with tears. "If you and Roman hadn't come when you did that night—"

He reached up for her hand and pressed his lips to her delicate skin. She shuddered at the warmth and softness of his touch.

"You might think I'm crazy, Tara, but I believe somehow we were destined to meet."

She smiled up at him, so much emotion in her eyes it took his breath away. "I don't think you're crazy at all." She swallowed back tears. "When I first saw you, I felt something... something I've never felt before in my life. It's hard to put into words. Somehow I feel safe with you, almost like I've known you my whole life."

Lawrence had to take a moment to compose himself, to try to rid himself of the emotion knotting his throat so tightly.

The funny thing was he was already envisioning a life with her.

"Tara, in all my years, I never dreamed of meeting someone like you," he said, sincerity ringing clear in his voice. "You're like a gift from God. And I'm so damn grateful for it."

Tara's smile broadened and her heart swelled. "So, what do we do now?"

"Well, first, we need to talk about a few things," he said. "I promised I would answer all your questions. And I think now is a perfect time."

"And I'm ready to listen," she replied.

Lawrence nodded and started talking, telling Tara about the creature that had killed Brandon, and attacked her. Then he went on to tell her all about the Breedline, and that she was too born with the same genetics along with other things that seemed entirely impossible. When he finally fell silent, Tara could only stare at him. Her instincts were telling her that he wasn't lying, but it was all too hard to accept.

Tara pondered Lawrence's words and then asked, "If I am indeed a full-blooded Breedline, will I shift into a *wolf*?"

He lifted one eyebrow. "Yes, if we make love."

Her eyes widened, and her cheeks flushed. "Oh, I see."

He leaned over her just as she was rising off the bed to meet him, but a knock at the door halted their kiss. Then a familiar voice called out, "Tara... Lawrence... you guys in there? I've got breakfast for two."

Great timing, Mr. Roman Kincaid, Lawrence thought. "It's open, Roman," he said with a slight groan. "Come on in, buddy."

Roman pushed open the door with a tray on wheels and muttered, "I wasn't interrupting anything, was I? I mean, I can come back if—"

"No, no," Tara quickly replied. "You're fine, Roman. Thank you." She inhaled deeply. "It smells wonderful."

As Roman wheeled the cart into the room, he glanced over at Lawrence, who sat close to Tara's bedside with a look of contentment on his face. A surge of pride washed over Roman as he thought of his close friend. After all the years of putting everyone before himself, this time, he was finally getting what he deserved—a bonded mate. That particular notion brought Lailah to mind. He wondered if he would ever see the beautiful, redheaded angel again.

"Thanks for bringing us breakfast, buddy," Lawrence said, bringing Roman back to focus.

"It's no problem," he replied. "It's my pleasure. Besides, it gave me an excuse to stop by and see how our guest is getting along." He placed his hand on Tara's shoulder and said, "You feeling better, Tara?"

Tara had to force herself not to grab for the cup of coffee on the tray full of covered dishes. Instead, she smiled and said, "I'm feeling much better. Thanks for asking, Roman."

Roman noticed her eyeing the cup of coffee. "Would you like some coffee, Tara?" He picked up the mug and held it out to her.

"I'd love some." She reached for the hot beverage and took a slow sip, then moaned. "Oh, my. This is the best cup of coffee I've ever tasted."

After a couple more sips, she briefly paused, her shoulders sagging a bit as if all the air escaped her at once. "I'm glad you stopped by, Roman. I want to tell you how thankful I am to you and Lawrence for saving my life. If it weren't for you two, I wouldn't be alive today."

Roman's expression softened. "I'm glad I was there to help. And you're very welcome, Tara." He included Lawrence in his gaze as he looked between them. "And in my opinion, it was fate that brought us there that night. Just looking at the both of you is enough proof to believe in destiny."

"I think we should give the good Lord all the credit," Lawrence said as he looked away from Roman and focused his eyes on Tara. "I believe he's the one that led us to you, Tara. I have no doubt about it."

Tara teared up, her eyes going glossy and bright, but there was also a joyous smile on her face. "I believe it too," she said.

Lawrence leaned over and gently pressed a kiss to her lips.

"I think that's my cue to hit the road," Roman said. "Enjoy breakfast."

"Thanks, buddy." Lawrence chuckled. "I'll catch you later."

As Roman left the two lovebirds alone, he headed back to the kitchen where everyone gathered for breakfast.

He could hear chatter, laughter, and bustling around, all the way down the end of the hall. When he got to the opening of the kitchen, the thirty-foot-long table in the center of the room was full of nearly everyone in the Covenant, except for Lawrence and Tara.

On the far side, he noticed an empty chair next to Jena and her friend, Angie, who was staring at Bull with a flirtatious smile. *Hmm,* he thought. He would definitely have to ask Bull about that later.

As he sat down next to Angie, he stared across the table at Bull and batted his brows.

Bull looked at Roman with a shit-eating grin.

When a plate full of food was set in front of Roman, he looked up and saw that it was Tim Ross's beloved standing over him. Angel was beautiful. She closely resembled the country singer, Crystal Gayle, except for her eyes. Angel's eyes were the color of fire with gold specks around the irises. And her black, almost-floor-length hair, reminded him of the fairy-tale story of "Rapunzel."

"I hope you're hungry," she said. "We made enough to feed an army."

"Thanks, Angel," he said, patting his stomach. "I'm famished. The food smells delicious."

As Roman chewed his food, he listened to everyone while they engaged in conversation and watched as the mothers at the table fussed over their children. So far, there were two sets of twin boys, one belonging to Jace and Tessa and the other twins were Eve and Sebastian's sons. Since Sebastian was... well... supposedly with the battle angels, everyone in the Covenant, especially Sebastian's sister, Anna, helped Eve with the boys. Over the last few weeks, he'd noticed Zeke Rizzo—the owner of the Cat Club, and a.k.a. the sin eater—stopping by to visit Anna. It was obvious the two had some kind of love connection. Ever since Yelena quit her job at Zeke's bar and moved in with Apollyon's mother, it was like Zeke had accepted the fact that she had moved on. He didn't blame her for falling in love with Apollyon. In fact, they'd recently found out Yelena was carrying his child. Sometimes love took you on a journey that couldn't be explained. It was fate's way of deciding for you. Besides, Zeke had Anna on his mind, and things seemed to be moving in the right direction.

Tim and Angel's little girl, Natalie, was the oldest child in the Covenant, nearly two years now. Soon, she would have playmates. Jem and Mia were expecting a little girl soon. Since Mia was half-succubus, the fetus grew at a phenomenal rate, even after it was born. Her species carried a child for no more than four months. Once the child reached the size of a two-year-old, they would then develop at the rate of a normal child.

Steven and Abbey were expecting too, but they didn't know what the sex of the baby was. They wanted it to be a surprise, although it was apparent they were hoping for a boy. Abbey was born a Lupa, and if the baby happened to be a girl, she would inherit her mother's genetics. Even so, it wouldn't make any difference. Everyone in the Covenant would love her just the same. But there would have to be precautions when she reached adulthood. A Lupa, also known as a she-wolf, can be a threat if provoked into shifting. Anger was the creature's worst adversary, and the Covenant made sure they kept tranquillizer darts well stocked.

As Roman roamed through all the faces at the table, his eyes stopped at the couple sitting at the far end. They looked the complete opposite. Drakon was a mountain of a man, who had to be at least six-foot-seven with a black, three-inch Mohawk on top of his shaved head and a look that said without words he wasn't a person you wanted to piss off. His wife,

Cassie, was a tiny thing, and full of life. She worked in prenatal care at the Bates Hospital. She was the type of person that would give a stranger the shirt off her back. And she adored everyone at this table, especially her husband. Eager to be married, Drakon and Cassie decided to skip the traditional ceremony, and instead said their vows on the Courthouse Steps. They had been married for a year, and now they were ready to start a family of their own. Roman envied their relationship. He had always admired his and Drakon's friendship for years and hoped he would have the same kind of luck his friend had.

For no particular reason, Roman took note of how attentive the men were with their mates. Sitting next to Drakon was a young couple that were obviously smitten with one another. He had met them when he came to help the Covenant track down the ruthless and notorious drug and weapons dealer, Valkin Steele. Casey Barton was a pro-fessional male model and was the keyboardist in the band Chaos. His girlfriend, Lila Demont, worked as a lab technician and was well known for her family's wealth and prestigious bloodline. Her father, Victor Demont, was a retired council member of the Pennsylvania Covenant who wasn't too happy about his daughter dating Casey since he was not a full-blooded Breedline. Casey was a Theriomorph. That was definitely not something the Demont family accepted. Due to certain circumstances which Roman was not aware of, Victor had suddenly reasoned with his daughter's decision to be with Casey.

Then Roman's attention went to another young couple sitting across from Casey and Lila. Clearly, by the way they looked at one another, it was evident they were in a serious relationship. Kyle Jones was Casey's best friend and worked as a mechanic and the bass player in the band Chaos. Kyle's girlfriend, Celina Baldolf, was not only a Breedline, she was a white Wicca. She worked as an editor at a local publishing company. The couple seemed head-over-heals for one another.

Roman noticed Detective Sanchez—who was sitting next to Celina—reach for his cell phone. When he answered, it wasn't long before his expression turned grim. Whatever was being said on the other end didn't appear to be good news.

As the chatter surged among Roman's newfound family, he felt himself receding, stepping behind an invisible screen that dimmed the sounds and the senses. His mind was on Lailah, wondering when she would come back to earth, and *if* he would get to see her.

"Hey, Roman," Tim said as he stood next to Roman. "You okay?"

When he didn't answer, Tim gave Roman's enormous shoulder a squeeze.

Roman flinched and looked over his shoulder. "Oh, sorry, Tim. Did you say something?"

Tim chuckled and said, "You look like you're miles away. Is there something you want to talk about?"

"Ah, nah," Roman muttered, waving it off like it was nothing. "I was just admiring all the couples here. It must feel good to have someone special, you know, to be in love."

"Yes, it is," Tim replied. "And you're next, Roman."

A female voice called out from across the room, distracting them. "Honey, your daughter wants you."

As Tim turned to the sound of Angel's voice, Natalie slipped out of her highchair and took off at a dead run, smiling at her daddy as she ran in his direction.

Tim scooped her up in his arms and pressed kisses to her forehead. "Hey there, sweet pea."

Natalie giggled and kicked her feet.

"Just think, Roman." Tim looked down at him, arching a brow. "This could be you someday. It'll happen before you know it. When you least expect it."

Roman nodded and smirked. *Yeah*, he thought. He had no idea how to make that happen. It was impossible to be with Lailah. She was a battle angel for crying out loud. How could he be with someone he could never really have?

When Detective Manuel Sanchez rose from his chair and began to address the table, Roman shifted back to focus.

"I hate to interrupt everyone's meal," Manuel said. "But I just received some news from my captain. The surveillance footage of the incident at the precinct is missing."

"Please don't tell me you're talking about the footage of Jimmy Fratianno shifting into his rogue wolf," Tim reluctantly said.

Manuel nodded. "The evidence storage facility was compromised."

"I don't understand," Tessa spoke out. "I thought you were going to get rid of that video."

"I'm sorry, Tessa," Manuel regretfully said. "I was going to take care of it first thing right after our meeting. I was sure the video would be secure until then. Apparently I was wrong."

"Do you have any idea who could have taken it?" Tim queried.

"There are only two other people, including myself, my partner, and my captain that have access to the precinct's property and evidence room," Manuel replied. "And I know Perkins and my captain are the two most trustworthy people I know."

"Who are the two others?" Tessa asked Manuel.

"Detectives Nicolas Ratcliff and Meagan Lacher."

"Do you think one of them could be capable of taking it?" Tessa asked.

"I've known Detective Ratcliff for fifteen years," Manuel said to Tessa. "He's not the type of man that would betray anyone. I'm not so sure about Detective Lacher. She's only been with the precinct for a year," he went on to explain. "It's possible someone made her an offer she couldn't refuse. After all, the love of money is the root of all evil. In my line of work, I've seen people do just about anything for it."

"Whatever the case, we've got to get that video back," Tim demanded. "If this gets out to the press—" he released a deep breath. "I'm going to have faith you'll get this taken care of, Detective."

"I'll do whatever I can to make that happen," Manuel said. "But before then, prepare yourselves for the worst. If this gets out, they'll link it to the cemetery attack. It's a possibility we'll have a mass panic on our hands."

"What's done is done," Tessa simply said. "Besides, we still have all those witnesses at the police department, of which some were human. If we're lucky, most people will think it's fake."

"Yeah," Manuel sighed. "If we're lucky." Then he added, "There's something I want to bring up about this mysterious creature that's been bugging the hell out of me."

Tessa shrugged. "What do you mean, Detective?"

"If this is the same creature that killed my sister and Carla Rosi, I don't think it acted alone."

"Are you saying there's another creature?" Tim asked.

"I'm not positive, but I do know the last time I saw my sister she got in a car with two males."

"Did the police ever get a lead on who they were?"

"The two suspects were never found," Manuel told Tim. "There was no evidence at the crime scene, no fingerprints, nothing. It was eventually listed as a cold case."

Tim shook his head. "Let's hope to hell we're only dealing with one creature. For now, let's focus on getting that surveillance video."

Chapter Twenty-Three

It was almost one the following morning when Sebastian used his powers to conjure a portal to get inside the Breedline Covenant. The place was quiet, not a single person stirring. Lailah had agreed to let him visit his sons while the others took refuge at the estate where Apollyon, Callisto, and Electra's mother lived. Their next plan of action was crucial. It would include the Breedline Covenant. Sebastian was not only here to see his family, he came here to inform everyone in the Covenant of their plan to destroy the creature. Although, killing it involved the human female. She was the only key to the destruction of the creature, and they weren't going to like what had to be done.

As Sebastian stood outside the door to Arius and Tidus's nursery, tears formed in the corners of his eyes. It had been so long since he last cried he barely recognized what tears were. He quickly reached up to wipe them before they spilled down his cheeks.

God, he felt like shit for not being there when his family needed him, just because of his greed for power. He was ashamed of himself now... ashamed of missing precious time with them. His past had affected the decisions he made, replacing the light in his heart with anger and darkness. Now, he wanted more than anything to be the father they never had. His sons deserved nothing less.

Sebastian took a hard breath and reached for the door. As he slowly opened it and walked in, an overwhelming sea of emotions swept over him. His face transformed into an absolute glow of happiness. Arius was standing up in his crib with one hand locked on the rail and the other outstretched as though he was reaching for him.

"Arius," he said in a low, trembling voice.

He closed the door quietly and went over to the crib. When he scooped Arius into his arms, he settled instantly in Sebastian's hold, wrapping his arms around his neck and cuddling into his chest. Having his son in his arms was so natural, and he realized how much he needed him.

Sebastian put his mouth to Arius's ear and whispered, "I'm so sorry I wasn't here for you."

With Arius snuggled against him, Sebastian looked over the lip of the crib. The instant he peered down at the toddler dressed in a blue-footed pajama sleeper, his chest filled with renewed purpose.

When Sebastian reached inside the crib and lightly stroked his hand over Tidus's arm, he opened his eyes. As he looked into a stare the exact golden color of his own, Sebastian's heart skipped a beat. "Hello, son," he whispered as he bent down with Arius in his arms.

From out of nowhere, Tidus mumbled, "Dada."

"They've missed you," a soft, but all-too-familiar voice said.

As Sebastian looked to the door, the rhythm of his heart skipped again, but for a different reason.

"Eve," he gasped.

Tears were streaming down Eve's face and her trembling lips pursed tight as if she were trying her best not to fall apart.

Sebastian reached out to her with his free hand. "Come here, beloved."

Without further hesitation, she went to him freely. "Oh, Sebastian," she quietly sobbed as he tucked her in against him. "I thought I'd never see you again."

As Sebastian held on to Arius and Eve, his world seemed complete. His family completed him by filling a gap in his heart he lost so many years ago.

He leaned in and inhaled the scent of her hair. "I love you, Eve."

While embraced, Sebastian felt the brush of a tiny hand. When he looked down, Tidus was standing in the crib with the most adorable look on his face.

Sebastian reached down and caressed Tidus's cheek with his thumb. "You make everything wrong in this world right."

At that very moment, everything seemed to fall into place. Sebastian felt as though his life had a new meaning and a fresh beginning. One was his heart and the other two a piece of himself, and they all gave him a purpose to be the man he needed to be.

Now all he had to do was convince the Breedline of his changed ways, even after all the low-down, rotten things he had done to them, and pray they would give him a second chance. He wouldn't blame them if they killed him outright. Especially his half-brother Jace. Betraying others you hardly knew was one thing, but betraying your own family... that was another.

* * *

It was almost dawn, and Yelena found she couldn't sleep, so she decided to get up. Her mind seemed consumed with worry and her chest ached with sadness. She wondered when or *if* she would ever see Apollyon again. Would their unborn child grow up without a father? The succubus side in her said he was coming back, but the rational side said otherwise. She had less than a month—to think, to plan, to process everything—before the baby was born.

As she swung her feet to the floor and stood, a flash of dizziness came out of nowhere, blurring her vision. Before she lost her balance, she plopped back down on the bed. Lowering her head and exhaling a deep breath seemed to help a little. After a moment, her head cleared and she got back to her feet. Moving toward the bathroom, she slipped out of her nightgown and opened the shower door. Switching the faucet on, she waited until the water built up a warm steam.

When she stepped in, the baby moved as though he was trying to find a better position inside such a small space. She looked at her belly and smiled. Smoothing her hand over the precious life nestled in her womb, she vowed with everything she had that her child would grow up with love no matter the circumstances. Already she loved her son so much.

The shower she took was heaven. Her body relaxed under the warm and penetrating spray. Hanging her head, she let the rush of soothing water run down the back of her neck.

By the time she got out, she felt more at ease with her thoughts. That quickly changed when she looked across the room at the reflection staring back at her in the full-length mirror.

180

Yelena put her hands on her belly and sighed. Under her palms, her stomach was rounded, the protrusion such that it was obvious she was in her third trimester. Since she was born a full-blooded succubus, the fetus developed faster than any other species. Instead of carrying the baby for nine months, Yelena had less than two months until the baby was full-term.

As she reached out to grab a towel that was hanging on the rack next to the shower, the ring Apollyon had given her slipped off her finger.

Yelena looked down and watched as it bounced on the tile floor. After she wrapped the towel around herself, she carefully stepped out of the shower and bent down to pick the silver band up. *Please come back to me, Apollyon,* she thought, admiring the symbol on the signet ring. *I need you, and your son needs you.*

"Yelena," a familiar, dominating voice said.

The second she heard that voice, her head shot up. Yelena looked stunned. On some level, she thought it had to be a dream, or maybe her imagination was playing tricks on her. Yet, as she rose on shaky legs, her brain could not deny what her eyes were telling her. She was shaking so badly she reached for the shower door to keep from dropping to her knees.

Yelena looked at him, her eyes pleading. "Apollyon?" she said with wonder.

He stood in the open doorway and held out his arms to her. "I'm right here my beloved."

With her eyes locked onto his golden gaze, she muttered, "Is it really you?"

Apollyon snapped into action and went forward. Gathering her gently in his arms, he lifted her from the floor and murmured into her ear, "Yes, my Yelena."

Her heart leaped inside her chest. "Oh, Apollyon," she sniffled, resting her head against his chest. "Thank God you're back."

Yelena's towel opened down the middle when he laid her on top of the bed. He could tell by the shape of her belly that she was with child. His eyes rounded in disbelief. *How was this possible?*

His eyebrow went up and he studied her for a moment. "Are you?" He fell silent, swallowing the lump in his throat.

There was a long pause, and then Yelena reluctantly said, "You're going to be a father soon."

Apollyon looked a little gobsmacked. His mouth opened as though he was about to say something, but instead he reached out and smoothed his hand over the swell of her belly. Then his gaze met hers, and she seemed surprised by the tenderness in his eyes. He took her hand and squeezed it.

"A father?" he finally said.

Her thumb stroked back and forth over his palm. "It's a boy," she said in a small voice.

Apollyon put his hand over his heart as if struck by something. *A son? They were having a son.*

He shook himself back to awareness and blurted, "A son…"

Yelena nodded with a peaceful smile, picturing their son, big and tall, strong as his father.

"Your son will need his father."

Her statement seemed more like a question, wondering what fate had in store for their future.

That's when Apollyon teared up, the droplets falling off his hard jaw onto the place that held the tiny life inside of his beloved. He was prepared to fight with the battle angels to destroy the creature, but nothing had prepared him for the reality of the woman he loved carrying *his* child.

In response, he lifted her off the bed and cradled her protectively against his chest. "I promise," he whispered close to her ear, "I will be here for you, and our child."

Yelena closed her eyes and inhaled his comforting scent. Tears leaked down her cheeks, absorbed by his shirt.

Apollyon stroked her hair with one hand and held her tightly with the other.

"But how is that possible?" She whispered into his embrace. "What about the battle angels? Don't you have to face some kind of punishment?"

As he slowly lowered her back down, he leaned in to kiss her on the forehead. "The Creator…" he paused as though he was fighting back more tears, "has given me and my sisters a second chance. If we help the battle angels destroy an age-old creature, and dedicate our lives to serving and protecting others, we will be allowed to stay on earth."

Her brows furrowed, and Apollyon could see the conflict so readily apparent on her face. "I don't understand." She shook her head. "What about your lust for human blood?"

"It's gone, my beloved." His eyes softened as he spoke, and Yelena relaxed a little. "The Creator released us from our hunger. I'm finally *free*."

Hope and excitement welled in her chest, and ridiculously, Yelena felt like crying all over again. It was like a weight had been lifted off her shoulders.

Yelena reached up to his face. "We're a family," she whispered, wiping his tears away.

Apollyon started to smile, and then he found her mouth, kissing her. He held her even closer, next to his beating heart, which now belonged to her. Yelena made him feel alive in a way he had never been in his entire existence. Somehow, he would find a way to keep his promise. Not only was he never letting go of his son, he wasn't letting go of Yelena either.

"Forever," he murmured against her lips.

Chapter Twenty-Four

Jena hadn't been the least bit afraid since Angie brought her to the Breedline Covenant. She felt relaxed and self-confident in a way she hadn't felt since the creature had taunted her sanity in the hospital... *until now*. After the Covenant told her about Tara's attack, things took a turn for the worse. It was obvious the monster who had bitten and cursed Jena had knowledge of her whereabouts.

He wanted her, and she realized there was nothing she, or anyone else for that matter, could do to stop him. Other than feeding on human blood, the creature had a one-track mind. And it was *her*.

Lying awake in her bed, for the first time in her life, Jena felt utterly helpless and alone—more alone than she had ever been, and more unsure about the future. A sense of sadness consumed her until tears formed in her eyes.

Then a wave of sickness came over her. Jena thought of the slaughtered bodies of Todd and Sophie. Her thoughts then went to Carla Rosi's corpse. The poor girl had been missing for over forty years. Carla's spirit had been the one who warned her about the Rougarou curse. Jena didn't want to become that *thing*... a savage creature that preyed on innocent people. Maybe she could resist her newly found urges and beat this dreadful curse, although she still had more days than she could bear. The thirst for human blood was already burning in her veins.

Suddenly, she felt warm all over, and restless. She heard the low hum of the refrigerator coming from downstairs and the pitter-patter of the raindrops falling down on the rooftop. She could hear the hushed voices in the other rooms as though they were speaking directly to her. *How is this possible? Is all this just my imagination?*

Something startled her. It wasn't a sound exactly but something she couldn't quite make out. It was coming from the balcony outside of her room.

Her curiosity got the best of her. She got up and quietly crept over to the sliding glass door. When she opened it, the night air was gusty and moist. The light rain that struck her face and clung to her thin nightgown was soothing to her skin. As Jena moved forward, her acute sense of hearing astounded her. It was so sensitive, and powerful... and enlightening.

All the sounds of the night were sharpened: the chorus of noises rising around her mingled with the whistling sounds of trees blowing in the wind, the harmonic vibrations of flying insects, and footsteps of nocturnal animals foraging through the grounds far in the distance. In fact, she was picking up all kinds of scents too. Jena could smell the rain and all the scents of the outdoors the way she had never smelled them before.

So, she thought, *I'm going to be like this from now on. I'm going to pick up scents like a dog, and sounds, too, no doubt.*

That's when she heard a voice whispering to her. *"Come, Jena... come to me."* This was an alluring, hypnotizing voice.

Jena peered over the balcony and searched for the voice calling out to her.

He stood back in the darkness invisible to the human eye, watching her... desiring her... ready to take her. Jena was tall for a female, her legs long as a gazelle's. Her blonde hair hung in thick waves, falling to the small of her back. Her flawless skin was pale cream, and she had a mouth just made for his lips. The silk nightgown she wore was delicate and clung to her small waist, firm hips, and perfectly proportioned breasts. The fabric had dampened in the fine mist, meshing to her skin, leaving nothing to the imagination.

His heart was pounding. The desire for Jena was as strong and uncontrollable as the desire to kill or the craving to feast on human blood. He wanted her, wanted to rip the silk material off her and get her underneath him.

"You belong to me," he murmured into her thoughts.

Jena panicked at the voice in her head but found she could not move.

From behind, something smoothed her hair back, revealing the pale skin of her neck.

In reaction, goosebumps trailed down her skin. Suddenly, there was the strangest scent in the air—something rich and heady.

Then she felt something warm tease her bare skin as if someone was breathing down her shoulder.

She gasped at the wonderful sensation and whirled around.

Unexpectedly, *he* appeared before her like a ghostly apparition suddenly becoming corporeal. The element of surprise froze Jena in her tracks.

His eyes roamed over her long, delicate neckline, and beyond to the swell of her breasts. He dragged air into his lungs and briefly closed his eyes, feeling a sexual stirring in his gut. Her scent was seductive and addictive, reminding him of the sweetest fragrance of night-blooming roses. It reminded him of *someone* else, a scent from the past.

As he boldly reached out to her, a rush of desire hit her hard. It was the curse, she thought numbly. Whatever he had done to her, it was unstoppable.

Curious to touch him, Jena shockingly went to him freely. As his chest expanded, she knew he caught the scent of her arousal.

He trailed his finger from Jena's jaw to her throat, to the point at her collarbone where her pulse beat. "I ache for you, Jena," he said, the words sliding off his tongue like silk.

Jena swayed, hypnotized by the luring sound of his voice and his soft touch. How easy he made it to fall under his spell.

She was past all self-control. As he laid kisses on her neck and on her breasts, her body began to writhe with a burning desire. It was rather like stoking a fire until it became a blaze.

"Why do you continue to taunt me?" she moaned, her head tossing back. "Please... free me of this curse."

When he placed his open mouth to the skin of Jena's throat, covering the throbbing blue artery, he appeared to kiss her. As he drew back, however, his lips were bloody.

Her eyes widened for a moment. She felt paralyzed, staring into his golden gaze for what seemed to last for an extended time. Jena studied the mysterious stranger, not fearfully, but in fascination.

He was handsomely beautiful in a decadent old blue-blooded, aristocrat fashion. His jaw was masculine and his lips full. His hair was jet-black, falling to his broad shoulders from a widow's peak. The piercing color of his eyes beamed like scarlet coals.

Although she knew he was a savage killer, something told her he wasn't here to do her harm. Jena felt powerfully drawn to the stranger, bound to him by some unnatural force, that she wanted him with an intensity she could not explain. Denying him now was unthinkable.

He reached out with his pale hand and took hers. "Come with me." He spoke with a sliver of the South.

Jena begged her body not to obey, but regretfully it betrayed her. She went with him freely as he guided her through the opening of the sliding door and into her bedroom.

As they stood next to the bed, she was shaking all over. He tentatively brushed her hair back from her face, and then ever so gently, lifted the damp nightgown over her head.

His eyes raked over her body approvingly. Jena was so beautiful, he thought, with the dim light of the lamp falling on the soft lines of her face. Her nipples stood rigid in tiny rosebud points. Her nakedness and vulnerability maddened him. Then his eyes locked onto her mouth. Her lips looked as soft as rose petals.

Shivers went through her when he reached out and cupped her cheek. His touch was frigid and cold.

He slid his tongue over his upper lip. "I'm going to kiss you, Jena." There was a razor-sharp edge beneath his soft-spoken words.

Overwhelmed by his determination, she took a step back. He followed. She retreated until the back of her calves came against the edge of the bed, and then he bumped into her.

Jena raised her hands in defense, fully intent on shoving him back. When they came up against his chest, she stood still, anticipating his next move.

He leaned down and wooed her with his mouth before his tongue gained entrance. He felt her flinch, although she did not turn away. His tongue savored hers as if she was something decadent and delicious.

This was ridiculous, Jena thought. She should be furious with him. He'd murdered her loved ones and left her with a curse. Now, they were kissing. When she tasted her own blood, it ignited a flame inside her. Her breathing started to quicken.

Jena clutched her chest. The pain was so intense she nearly fell to her knees. It was as though her heart was suddenly pierced and divided in half with a burning blade. Then, just as quickly as it had struck, the agony was gone, leaving her breathless and dizzy.

Working her like a puppet attached to his own set of strings, he gently eased her down on the bed.

After a moment, he curled his lip off his front teeth. His white fangs were sharp and fine at the points, like needles. As Jena breathed in deep, she recognized the mix of heady scents from earlier.

"Please," she said on a shaky breath, shame constricting her voice.

Lost in her sensual gaze, he could not fight his needs any longer. His desire rose, surprising him in its burning ferocity. It was a feeling he remembered from a long, long time ago.

An all-powerful need to mark her lit him up. Lifting his shirt over his head, he wrenched the thing off and shrugged out of his pants.

He lowered himself on top of her, but lightly, not letting his weight hurt her. When her breasts hit the wall of his chest, her body surged under his. As he shifted in between her legs, Jena absorbed his weight with a light moan.

He looked down at her, wondering if she would give in to his curse, and join him for eternity.

Suddenly, he felt her hands on his shoulders, pulling at them as though she was begging to feel his lips against hers.

He leaned closer and kissed her again, feeling his fangs pressing against her. He ravished Jena with kisses all over, on her lips and her breasts and her belly, and on the insides of her silky, warm thighs.

She nearly sobbed, so aroused her legs started to shake.

While lavishing her body with attention, Jena let out a breathless gasp that brought his head up just so he could look at her beautiful face.

With her eyes closed, and her lips slightly parted, her body clenched. In the midst of her climax, she shuddered in silence, fighting the urge to cry out. Before her pulses faded, he rose above her, and entered in a single thrust, sliding in deep. With no pause whatsoever, he started to move in a rhythm that nearly made her lose it all over again. It was like nothing she had ever experienced.

His mouth broke open as he found his own release. As he climaxed, he stared at her neck, resisting the temptation to bite her... to taste her blood once again.

When he finally pulled from the warmth of her body, he shifted on his side. He wanted desperately to take her again, but he did not want to press. He'd managed to lure Jena in this far, and soon she would be at his side forever. Instead, he asked, "Will you welcome me again?"

"Yes," she whispered, staring up at the ceiling, seemingly lost in thought. It was as though her body was present but her mind was miles away.

Jena finally turned to him, her eyes full of questions. "Please, tell me. What is your name?"

He lifted her hand and kissed it. "My name no longer matters," he answered. "It's only a faded memory of the man I used to be."

Jena placed her hands to his face, staring at him with tears in her eyes. "Then I will call you..." She briefly paused, exhaling her breath. "...my beloved."

He smiled to himself. At that moment, he knew without a doubt she was *his*.

Chapter Twenty-Five

Wound tighter than a rusted spring, there was no give in Angie's determination to relieve some of that tension. Earlier, when she got a look at the newcomer in the Covenant that everyone referred to as Bull—she wondered how he managed that nickname—she had only one thing on her mind. It was to get Mr. Tall, Dark, and Handsome naked and in her bed.

The big lovey-dovey fest that had gone on at the table during breakfast this morning, complete with enough kissy-face and handholding and baby talk to make her green with envy, hadn't helped. It seemed that everyone in the Covenant—minus her and Jena—had found their soulmate.

Not that she was a big believer in true love. Of course, she loved romance and had dreamed since she was a little girl of finding that special one, *her beloved*, but she wasn't getting her hopes up. There was no reason to sugarcoat the shit. It wasn't easy falling in love. In the end, feelings got hurt and hearts got broken. That pretty much summed up her past relationships.

The truth of it was she felt out of place here. All the couples in the Covenant only made her think of what she wanted but did not have. She always wondered if anyone here ever argued or got pissed off. If so, she'd never seen or heard it. The Breedline clan was all nothing but unconditional love and support. *Damn it!* She so desperately wanted that too.

She was reaching for the door to her room when she heard a deep voice from behind.

"It's Angie, right?"

When she turned to look, her stomach plummeted like a rock and her cheeks flushed red. She briefly considered making a break for it and hightailing it into her room.

Why in hell was she contemplating hiding for? Hadn't she been eager for this opportunity? Wasn't she dying to get this man naked earlier, and in her bed? All of a sudden, she felt like a blushing teenager. What the hell? That wasn't her style. She was always straightforward and Ms. "Get-down-to-business." She had never been bashful in her life. *Damn it, woman, get your shit together.*

Angie forced her nerves to calm before she made a complete fool of herself.

She cleared her throat and said, "Yeah, but you can call me Ang." Her lips curled up like a bow, and she had that awestruck look on her face. "And your name is... Bull?"

He nodded. "Everyone calls me that, but my real name is Ben," he nervously said. "Benjamin Calvero. If you want, you can call me Bull."

Angie cocked a brow. For some strange reason, she repeated his name over and over in her head. *Benjamin Calvero, Benjamin Calvero, Benjamin Calvero...*

When he moved forward with his hand outstretched, she came back to focus, her heart pounding in her chest.

"It's nice to officially meet you, Ang."

She quickly reached out with a shaky hand. "It's my pleas—"

Before Angie could finish her sentence, she felt a balmy rush blooming out all over her skin. It even spread all the way down to her toes, and she found herself swaying.

Bull did his best to steady her, as he too was experiencing the same effect. When their hands made contact, the word *beloved* rang loud and clear as though an elaborate musical composition was playing inside his head, soothing him... comforting him. It was the most wonderful feeling he had ever felt. For some reason, he suddenly had the urge to kiss her.

Instead, Angie got her bearings and took over the reins. She tugged at his hand, pulling him closer. Bull immediately responded and sank his lower half into hers, trapping her with his massive body against the bedroom door. She released a gasp as their bodies meshed together in a heated fury.

When their lips collided, her breath came out in a rush. Bull's kiss was electric, his lips moving sensuously over hers until her knees shook and her heart pounded. Never, never in her life had someone kissed her like this.

He curved his hand around her nape and dug his fingers into her silky hair as he held her in place. Inhaling a deep breath, he caught the scent of her arousal, a lovely sweetening in the air, and his body instantly reacted.

"I want you," he moaned against her lips, rubbing his arousal on her belly, increasing his ache and her desperate need.

To show her approval and complete submission, Angie pressed into him. When her hand moved underneath his shirt and rubbed over his back, he growled low in his throat.

She shivered at the masculine sound and wondered what he would feel like inside her.

His head came down and his breath tickled the side of her neck. Then she felt a soft, moist stroke that created goosebumps all over her body. *God, I want him*, she thought. "I want you *now*," she said with urgency, and tacked on, "naked, and in my bed."

Bull nudged her chin up and stared into her deep blue eyes with a burning intensity. "Are you sure?" he said in a hushed voice.

"Yes," she quickly replied.

He followed as she took hold of his hand and guided him into the bedroom.

"Make yourself comfortable," Angie said, gesturing grandly toward the big king-sized bed in the middle of the room.

He merely winked and looked at her with an unholy gleam in his eyes. "Ladies first," he murmured. "Unless, of course..." He cocked a brow. "...you need my help undressing."

A smile hovered at the corners of her mouth. "Oh, I definitely need help undressing."

As she moved past him, she sat down on the mattress and zipped out of her favorite pair of Christian Louboutin ankle boots. Then she gave him a look of pure desire, wiggling her finger in silence, beckoning him over.

He wasted no time stripping off his shirt and shrugging out of his size fifteen leather boots and strode over in her direction, moving with powerful shifts of his muscular arms and legs.

She eased back on the bed anticipating the feel of his hands all over her body.

As the bed dipped, Angie found herself staring up at Bull while he loomed over her. He had both hands planted on either side of her shoulders and his knees were straddling her.

His piercing green eyes mesmerized her. *God, he is magnificent,* she thought. Built like a brick house. All muscled, lean at the waist, broad at the shoulders, and his hips... *damn*, he made her mouth water. It was all she could do not to roll him over and take a bite out of his ass.

He slowly closed the distance between them and brushed his lips against hers. His tongue came out and stroked over her mouth.

Mindless, out of control, she grabbed on to his broad shoulders, and he changed the kiss, going in deep, moving in a rhythm that got her even more ready for him.

With his lips hovering over hers, he whispered, "And just so you know, I want the last thing you feel before you go to sleep is me inside you, and the first thing you know when you wake up."

She sucked in her breath and licked her lips nervously. "Mmmm, that sounds wonderful."

When his hand slipped under her skirt and found the right spot, a moan broke out of her.

He pressed his lips to the soft skin of her throat. "I want to make you feel good," he murmured close to her ear.

As her eyes closed, she gasped for air, realizing she was on the verge of losing it.

His mouth found her lips again, and it was a while before his long fingers went to the bottom of her blouse. As he pushed it up and tugged the thin fabric over her head, her bare breasts rose and fell as his eyes took her in.

"You're beautiful," he whispered and ran his tongue around one nipple.

Angie was aching as Bull worked his way to the other breast and took it into his mouth.

In a matter of moments, Bull had Angie and himself completely naked, his jeans and boxers gone, her skirt gone, and her panties tossed aside.

Then he rubbed his thumb over her cheek and gave her a doubtful look. "Are you sure this is what you want? Angie, you know what will happen if we do this, right?"

She smiled up at him. Angie could not believe she was looking into the face of her bonded mate, who at this moment was about to change everything, and yet at the same time, she had never been so sure of something in her life.

"I know," she said, swallowing the lump in her throat, "and I'm ready. I want this. I want this with you."

Bull started to speak, but she pressed her mouth to his to hush him.

His breath escaped in a long hiss and every muscle in his body tightened as he slowly glided inside of her.

She gasped and tensed at the instant fullness.

His hips went completely still. "Are you okay?" he whispered, waiting for her response.

"Please don't stop," she groaned.

He leaned down to kiss her at the same time he pushed forward again.

She panted frantically as his hips moved rhythmically, pushing her harder and getting her closer to the edge. With her eyes squeezed tight, she gripped the sheets and arched up as high as she could while his weight pressed down on her.

Then the pressure that had built up within her finally gave way. It was like nothing she'd ever known—wave after wave of ecstasy splintering through her. It was good. Oh, so very good.

The sounds she made brought him to his own release. As he shuddered inside of her, he gently grazed her shoulder with his teeth like he was a wild animal marking his mate. She was his, and he was *forever* hers.

When he finally pushed himself up, he watched the series of emotions that flickered across Angie's face. The purposeful look in her eyes told him she was close to shifting.

He reached out to her. "It's okay, honey. I'll be right here with you every step of the way."

Every particle in her body was changing... changing in a way she had never experienced in her life. Angie's entire body began to expand and stretch by the second. Her fingernails and toenails tingled, and her skin itched as soft, dark fur began to burst out of every pore, covering every inch of her bare skin. She could even feel her teeth descending and her mouth lengthening.

As Angie's transformation continued, Bull watched in amazement. There were no words to express her Breedline wolf. She was simply *beautiful.* God, it made such sense that he'd bonded with her.

In her new form, Angie felt her throat open with a howl, but she did not give in to it. Instead, she moved toward Bull on teeter-tottering limbs and let out a light whimper.

"You're beautiful, sweetheart," he said, smoothing his fingers through her soft-coated fur.

Moments later, when Angie shifted back into her human form, she stared up at him and sighed in utter contentment at the look in his eyes. No words could simply replace the way he looked at her. It was as though there was no one else in the world for him.

Words bubbled up inside her. She was grateful and amazed that a man like him actually existed. She leaned forward and kissed him warmly, pressing her mouth softly to his. "I don't know what to say," she said. Her voice grew shaky with emotion. "This is all so new to me."

Bull reached for her hand and laced his fingers through hers. "I know we've just met, but I'll do whatever it takes to have you in my life."

Angie glanced down at their entwined fingers, watched as his thumb caressed the top of her hand. Then she raised her head back up and took a deep breath as she drowned in those intense green eyes of his. "I would like that... for us to be together."

A smile quivered on his lips. "You know what this means, don't you?"

She shook her head. "No, but please, do tell."

"You're stuck with me," he said with a light chuckle.

Angie pretended disappointment. "Oh, I suppose I can learn to live with that."

After another round of intense lovemaking, Bull pulled Angie closer and murmured in her ear. "I've got a great idea."

She raised an eyebrow. "Is that so?"

"How does you, and me, and a tub full of hot water sound?"

Angie was quiet for a minute, but he could tell by the way her hips surged against his that she was tempted.

"I'll wash your back," Bull murmured, nipping at her earlobe. "And your front. Not to mention all the other parts in between."

She shivered at his touch and made a soft, breathy sound. "I'll go run the water," she said.

Angie put out towels and arranged long-stemmed candles around the bathroom while the tub that would easily fit more than two people filled with water.

Shortly after, she turned the water off and called out, "The bath is ready."

As he entered the bathroom, his eyes widened when he took in the huge tub on an elevated platform. "This is nice," he said as he looked around, noticing all the candles.

"Are the candles too much?"

Bull turned to look at her. "Nope, it's perfect."

She smiled and nodded toward the bath. "You first."

When he climbed over the edge and lowered himself in the water, she got a prime view of his backside. *Damn.* Even as large as the bathtub was, he seemed to fill every inch.

He stretched out with an appreciative groan. "Damn baby, this feels good."

Her head cocked to the side in question. "It's not too hot?"

"Not yet," he said in a husky voice, looking at her through half-lidded eyes. "I'm waiting for you to make it hotter." He reached out to her. "Come here."

When Angie approached the bath, he held up his hand to help her over the edge. As soon as she eased into the steaming water, she moaned with sheer pleasure.

Bull tugged her forward, closer to him... facing him, and between his thighs. There was a predatory gleam in his stare. And she loved that look. Like he wanted to devour her entire body and savor the taste.

"I'm making you a solemn promise," he said. "You will never doubt for one moment that you belong to me. I'm going to spend every day making sure you know that."

Angie leaned forward and kissed him, letting her lips melt over his. She breathed a sigh into his mouth and whispered, "I can't wait."

Chapter Twenty-Six

A golden hue peeked through the blinds of Yelena's bedroom window as the sun gradually crept over the horizon. Apollyon lay on his side, his head propped by a pillow as he stared to where Yelena slept. Curled on her side, she faced him with her arms wrapped around her belly as though she was cradling the tiny life inside.

While he watched her sleep, there was a sense of peace to her expression. Her features were relaxed and her lips slightly parted. Yelena had barely moved the entire night. He knew because he'd woken every hour to check on her, worried he'd wake up to find that all this had been nothing but a dream, or maybe just a figment of his imagination. Miracles like this didn't happen to him, he thought. For all the horrible things he had done, he didn't deserve a second chance in life, much less a family of his own.

She released a breathy sigh when he reached over and smoothed a loose strand of her hair away from her face. He swallowed painfully, overcome by the newfound emotions he'd never felt in his life. Falling in love simply wasn't him, until now. It was like Yelena hung the damn moon. He found himself hugely possessive and protective of her and their unborn child. There was no doubt there.

When it came to Yelena, it was as if his soul had transformed overnight—from a savage killer, that lusted for human blood, to this mushy, softhearted fool. No matter what challenges they faced, it was all worth it when he looked into her eyes.

As he leaned in to press his lips against her forehead, Yelena's eyes opened and her amber gaze found his. When she smiled, warmth instantly spread through his veins.

Apollyon was quiet for a moment before he cupped her jaw and feathered his thumb across her cheek and then her lips. "So beautiful," he whispered. "You're beautiful, Yelena. I'm so lucky you're *mine*."

His words sent a blast of heat up her spine to her neck and over her cheeks. Yes, she thought. She was his, and he was hers.

Yelena turned her face so that her lips brushed over his hand. Then she reached out and trailed her fingers across his cheek, glancing up at him to see his reaction. It was a mixture of desire and a state of fulfillment.

Apollyon flinched when she put her hand close to the scar above his left eyebrow. When he tried to turn away, she said, "Don't hide from me, Apollyon. Tell me. What happened?"

His brow furrowed.

Her eyes pleaded. "Please."

For a moment, he'd forgotten that Yelena could use her skills as a succubus to get inside his head. The thought of her seeing the ugliness of his past made him sick to his stomach. He wondered, how much did she already see? Shame immediately crowded in that she'd seen all his demons, his pain, and his moments of weakness.

He hesitated, but then took her hand and slid it down to his chest, holding it firmly over his heart. "My father," he simply said. "It was a form of punishment." His eyes looked tortured, and to her shock, they glittered with tears and grief.

Yelena sat up, holding the sheet over her bare breasts. "My God, Apollyon, what you went through." Her expression was so fierce, almost angry. "I'm so sorry."

"It was a long time ago," he murmured. "Now that I have you, and our child..." He paused, placing his palm over the swell of her belly. "...things have changed. You're both the most precious part of *my* world. For the first time in my life, I have hope."

Apollyon stared in wonder as Yelena edged toward him, letting the sheet fall from her chest. The sight of her nipples, puckered into hard rosebud points, brought him to sudden arousal. Heat flushed from his body as she swiped her tongue over her swollen lips. Even though they'd made love not long ago, he still ached for her. It took all his restraint not to pull her into his arms and lavish her entire body. He wanted her more than he wanted to breathe.

He sucked in a breath as she lowered her head and pressed her lips to the scar over his brow. Her kiss was so tender and loving.

"I need you, Apollyon," she whispered, craving his touch and remembering the first time they'd made love. He made her feel as though she'd been dominated and taken. "Make love to me again." She moaned, her tone almost begging him.

Unable to resist, he pulled her against him and kissed her hungrily. Shivers ran down his spine as her plump breasts pushed into his bare chest. She inhaled deeply and arched into him when his mouth claimed one of her taut nipples.

Apollyon couldn't get enough of simply touching her, yet he didn't feel worthy, although he wanted it more than anything. No part of her was left untouched as he caressed, kissed, and licked up and down her soft, flawless skin. Apollyon could no more deny Yelena than he could deny the burning desire deep within himself.

They made love, gasping and panting as their intertwined bodies came together again, and again. Using her succubus-side, Yelena whispered in his mind that she belonged to him, the words nearly sending him over the edge.

He held his weight above her as he slid in and out of her body, fearing he was too heavy for her. The last thing he wanted was to hurt the tiny life they had created. He thought, at this moment, he'd never experience something so beautiful. There were no words to describe how he felt.

Yelena rose up, curled her arms around his neck and pulled until their lips almost touched. "I've dreamt of this moment every night," she said, barely above a whisper. "Of us, together again."

He lowered his face to the crevice of her neck and inhaled her sweet scent, wanting it embedded into his senses forever. "We're going to be together forever," he vowed.

As Yelena ran her hands over Apollyon's wide, bare shoulders, he made a sound deep in his throat. Smoothing her hands from his shoulders to his neck, she sank her hands into his hair. The long waves were so soft like the most lustrous satin.

After their blissful lovemaking, he went quiet for several long moments. Wrapped in his arms, Yelena could feel the beat of his heart as his mind worked through a tangle of thoughts. She could feel the tension radiating from him in waves. Apollyon was thinking of his promise to God. In order to stay on earth with his family, he had to help destroy the creature. It was going to be a difficult task, which also involved one of his biggest rivals, the Breedline Covenant.

Forcing his mind back to focus, he kissed and nuzzled Yelena's neck, enjoying the warmth of her skin. He murmured close to her ear, "I love you, Yelena. You're everything to me."

Apollyon's words made her heart squeeze. As she snuggled into his warm embrace, his hold tightened around her.

"I love you too," she whispered back, barely able to keep her eyes open. She felt safe in his arms... protected... cherished.

He leaned in and kissed the top of her head. "Go back to sleep," he murmured. "You need your rest. Soon this will all be over and we can focus on our future."

Yelena let out a small sigh and shut her eyes. She clung to Apollyon as though he was her lifeline, but in fact, she was his.

Two hours later, pain splintered through Yelena's spine, and she came awake with a gasp. For a moment, she thought she was just stiff from sleeping too long on her back. Then she felt it again, a stabbing ache that radiated from her lower back down to her legs.

With all her strength, Yelena pulled herself upright in the bed, and breathed through the discomfort, bumping into Apollyon's sleeping form.

Apollyon's eyes flew open and he quickly sat up. "What's wrong, Yelena?"

Her breath exploded from her lips in harsh puffs. "I'm not sure," she said, barely managing to get the words out. "My back... it hurts."

A surge of panic burst through Apollyon like a beacon. Unsure what to do, he eased his arms around her and stroked her back, trying to comfort her.

"Please, Yelena." His hands shook as he pulled her close and slid one hand down to cup her belly. "Tell me what to do."

Her entire body started to shake and Apollyon realized with alarm that Yelena was in a great deal of pain. Then his mind took a turn for the worse. Was there something wrong with the baby?

When Apollyon got no response from Yelena, he took control of the situation. He gently cupped her jaw and tilted her head to meet his stare. Her eyes were drenched with tears and distress. "Listen to me, Yelena," he said as he rubbed her cheeks with his thumbs, wiping the tears away. "I want you to stay here." He leaned forward and kissed her forehead. "I'll be right back. I'm going to get help."

Yelena suddenly reached for his hand and gripped it with enough force to cut off his circulation. "Hurry, Apollyon," she said as she took in several light breaths through her nose. "I think I'm in labor."

Panic hit Apollyon in the gut like he'd been punched with an iron fist. He could handle a battle single-handed with the least amount of fear, but the thought of losing his child, or worse, Yelena dying in childbirth, was like ripping his heart straight out of his chest. He felt sick just thinking about it.

"It's going to be all right, Yelena." He prayed he was right. "I'm going to get Lailah. She will know what to do."

When Yelena's contraction passed, she took a deep breath and exhaled. Then she released his hand and nodded.

Apollyon gathered her hand back and brought it to his lips. "I love you," he said against her soft skin. He released her hand and got to his feet. After he scrambled to get dressed, he left Yelena alone in the room to go for help.

A few minutes later, Lailah entered the room with Apollyon.

"Please help her," Apollyon said, sitting on the bed next to Yelena and gathering her hand.

Lailah nodded at Apollyon, although her eyes focused on Yelena. As she moved forward and stood on the other side of her, she could see the anxiety etched in Yelena's expression.

"May I?" Lailah asked with her hand hovering close to Yelena's rounded belly. "I need to see if your child is in danger."

Apollyon put his arm around Yelena and lightly squeezed her shoulder reassuringly. "It's okay, Yelena. You can trust her. I give you my word."

Yelena grimaced and nodded at the beautiful yet intimidating angel who towered at least ten-feet-tall, with enormous black wings.

As Lailah placed her palm over Yelena's stomach and kept it there for several minutes, Apollyon silently waited, his patience getting the best of him. "Is the baby okay?" He asked.

"He's just fine," Lailah said in a calm voice. "He has the heart of a lion and he's ready to come into this world."

Apollyon looked over to Yelena at the same time she turned toward him. Her entire face lit up and Apollyon could see the tension ease in her expression.

"We don't have a name for him yet," Yelena said, looking to Apollyon as though she was searching for an answer.

He studied her for a moment and then laced his fingers with hers. "I would like to call him Tobias." He smoothed his hand over her swollen belly. "It was my grandfather's name. My mother told me it means goodness of the Lord."

Yelena nodded her approval and leaned in to kiss him. "It's perfect," she said softly.

A commotion coming from the doorway caught their attention. Apollyon breathed a huge sigh just as his mother Sonya, and sisters, Electra and Callisto, stepped inside.

"Yelena?" Sonya said as she moved next to Apollyon and peered down at Yelena. "Are you all right, darling?"

"I'm just fine, Sonya," Yelena told her. "The baby is ready to be born."

Sonya immediately covered her mouth. "Oh, my," she muttered into her palm. Tears spilled from her eyes as she lowered her hand. "But the baby..." She wearily shook her head. "He's not due for three more weeks. Is he okay?"

Lailah patted Sonya on the arm. "No need to worry. Your grandson is going to be fine."

"Thank goodness," Sonya said, exhaling a deep breath.

"Congratulations, brother," Electra said as she came forward, her diamond eyes illuminating the room.

"What are you going to name him?" Callisto asked, standing in the doorway with a big grin on her face.

Yelena turned to look at Apollyon and said, "We're going to name him Tobias."

"That's wonderful," Sonya said, and then looked at Apollyon. "You're naming him after your grandfather."

Apollyon nodded and smiled at her.

"I hate to interrupt," Lailah said, "but we need to prepare Yelena for delivery. I'll need everyone to wait outside the room."

Apollyon swallowed. "I want to stay with Yelena… to see my son born." He tried to keep the nervousness from his voice but knew he failed miserably.

"Of course you can stay, Apollyon," Lailah said. "I was referring to everyone else." She raised her voice, peering over her shoulder at Frigg, who was peeking into the room. "And I'll need your help, Frigg."

Frigg rolled his eyes and cursed under his breath, wondering how in the hell he'd gotten himself in the middle of childbirth.

As Frigg ducked under the doorway to assist Lailah, Apollyon took Yelena's hand and said, "I'll be right here with you, my beloved. I'm not leaving your side."

"Thank you, Apollyon," Yelena whispered, resting her head rested on his shoulder.

"What for?"

"For loving me," she simply said as she drifted into a peaceful sleep.

An hour later, Lailah placed a small bundle into Apollyon's arms. As he looked down into his son's eyes, the same color as his own, his heart skipped a beat.

"I have a son," he heard himself say. "Welcome to the world, Tobias. I'm your father."

As Yelena came around, feeling lightheaded from the dreamlike sleep Lailah had magically placed her in during the process of giving birth, she looked beside her when she heard Apollyon's voice. He was sitting in the bed next to her, holding their son. Tobias was beautiful, the spitting image of his father. In that instant, nothing in the world seemed to matter but this moment... this very precious interval of time.

"He looks just like his father," Yelena said in a weak voice.

Apollyon looked over at Yelena and smiled. "He's perfect."

As Yelena reached for Tobias, Apollyon carefully placed the tiny bundle in her arms. Tears trickled down her cheeks when she saw his eyes. The pupils were the same beaming, honey-yellow as his fathers. "You are so beautiful," she whispered to her son.

"Congratulations," Lailah said, her eyes looking between the new proud parents. Her gaze settled on Yelena. "You'll need to rest today. Tomorrow you should be fine as long as you take it easy for a few days."

"Thank you, Lailah," Yelena said, and tacked on, "you too, Frigg."

Lailah smiled and Frigg said, "It was no big deal, but if you want, you can name the little bugger after—"

"We were honored to help," Lailah cut him off. "We'll give you some privacy."

When Lailah stepped out of the room with Frigg following behind her, Yelena said, "Apollyon, you should tell your family. I'm sure they're dying to see the baby."

Apollyon nodded, and then he found her mouth, kissing her. "I love you, Yelena."

"I love you too." She stroked his face. "I love you both."

Seconds later, Apollyon got out of the bed and rushed into the hallway where his family was waiting. A smile hovered over his mouth, the corners lifting as his eyes sparkled with excitement.

"Yelena's had the baby!" he announced.

Sonya looked over at Apollyon and then reached out. "Oh, son," she said with a wide grin. "I'm so proud of you."

Apollyon embraced his mother. "Would you like to meet him?"

"I'd love to," she said in a trembling voice. "Are they okay?"

"Yelena and our son are doing fine." He motioned everyone inside the room. "Come, and I'll introduce you to Tobias."

When everyone came into the room and crowded around the bed, Yelena was cradling the baby against her chest. As Yelena looked up, Sonya was smiling so wide and proud. Her hands covered her heart as though she was dying to hold her grandson.

"Would you like to hold him?" Yelena asked her.

Sonya put her hands up to her face. "Oh, yes." She sniffled. "I would love to."

That's when Apollyon teared up. Witnessing his mother holding her first grandchild was pretty much the best thing in the world next to witnessing the birth of his son.

Chapter Twenty-Seven

He watched with cunning eyes as the moon was just beginning to peek over the edge of the trees. Lying on the cushioned forest floor, his thoughts of Jena and the tantalizing pleasure they shared only moments ago consumed him down to his core. She was so naive, so foolish, so careless. There was no turning back now. He sealed her fate with a simple kiss. The blood kiss of eternal life. Finally, the curse was set into motion, and Jena was *forever* his.

As he inhaled a deep breath, the scent of pine needles and distinctive green things invaded his senses. He closed his eyes, and for a second, he thought he heard voices. His lids flipped open and a sinister smile came over his face. He felt his skin crawling with a tingling sensation. Then the hunger in him instantaneously came to life, releasing the monster within. The transformation rapidly took over. His clothes ripped apart as his chest expanded, and his limbs began to stretch and lengthen. Thick, black fur sprouted from his pores, spreading like wildfire. When he rose to his feet, he stripped the remains of his shirt away and brushed off the torn fragments of his pants. The transition had taken full possession of him, bringing with it the inevitable doom. Nothing in his path would survive.

He flexed his powerful thighs and perked his lupine ears to listen more carefully. The voices grew louder now, the chorus rising and falling as they moved closer to him.

Using his razor-sharp claws, he climbed a large oak with a long leap and moved as fast as he could to the top. As he peered down from above, he caught a strong scent, something flowery that mingled with the smell of a man's cologne.

The pungent odor of humans quickly ignited his hunger. Every muscle in his body wanted to leap, to spring out and devour them instantly. Instead of killing them outright, he watched and listened to the couple below, who spoke in low voices. They were seemingly oblivious of his presence as he waited for the right moment to attack and end their worthless lives.

"This looks like a good spot," Chad said, spreading a blanket over the ground. "There's not a single person for several miles." He turned to look at the wide stretch of nothing but a vastness of trees, plants, and a grassy meadow sprinkled with bright, colorful wildflowers. Although the darkness surrounded them, the star-filled sky lit up the woodland like a canopy of sparkling lights. The peaceful quiet in the urban forest of the Presidio National Park compared to the sounds of the city made him feel as though they had magically discovered their own private world.

"I hope you brought something to cover up with," Debi said as she began to undo the buttons on her blouse. "It's a little chilly."

"Don't worry, babe." He dropped his jeans to his ankles and batted his brows. "I've got something that'll keep you warm."

Debi arched an eyebrow as she caught sight of his enormous erection hidden behind his tight-fitted briefs.

"I'm serious, Chad," she smirked. "If you want me naked..." She paused with her fingers on the last button. "...you better promise to keep me warm."

Chad wasted no time stripping off his shirt and slipping out of his shoes. When he stepped out of his jeans and came forward, he looked at her seductively. "Oh, I promise." Sincerity rang clear in his voice as he wrapped his arms around her and lightly squeezed. "Cross my heart and hope to die."

"Oh, you," Debi said reproachfully, as she reached around and smacked him on the butt.

They both laughed, but then Debi's face suddenly went rigid and the hair lifted at the back of her neck. As she quickly turned away, Chad asked, "What is it, baby?"

She held up a hand to silence him. "Listen."

After a few moments of stillness, Chad shook his head. "I don't hear anything."

"I could have sworn I heard something rustling," she said, her fearful eyes probing through the darkness.

"It's nothing, honey," he said. "It's probably just a rabbit, or maybe a squirrel. Remember, we are miles from the hiking trails, and it's the middle of the night. I'm pretty positive we're the only ones here."

Debi didn't respond right away. Her eyes continued to glance around wildly. Finally, she looked up at him. "I don't know." She released a deep breath. "I have this weird feeling that something is out there, somewhere... watching us."

Chad shook his head again, amazed at how beautiful his fiancée looked, although she was stoned and paranoid. "Honey, it's just your imagination. I told you not to smoke that joint before we left."

She rolled her eyes. "Whatever," she groaned. "It's not the pot. I'm being serious, Chad. I think we should go."

He blew out an aggravated sigh. "Jeez, you've got to be kidding me, Debi. You're the one that dragged me all the way out here. Didn't you say we should put some adventure in our lovemaking?"

She drew back from him. "I know, I know. It seemed like a good idea at first, but now, I don't know." She shrugged. "I guess I was wrong." She noticed the disappointed expression on his face. "I'm sorry. It's just... I'm spooked, that's all."

He took her hand. "Come on, baby. Let's get out of here."

"You're not mad, are you?" she hesitantly asked.

Chad put his arm around her and gave her a squeeze. "No, I'm not mad, honey. I just want you to be happy. Hell, the last thing I want is for you to get bored of me before we tie the knot."

She smiled a little. "I could never get bored of you, babe. You always make me feel wonderful."

As they gathered their things, Chad caught sight of something that looked like pieces of clothing lying in the grass. He pointed toward a tree a few feet away. "What the hell is that?"

Debi looked in the direction he was pointing and spotted the bits of clothing scattered around a tree. "Are those some-one's clothes?" she asked.

Chad moved forward to get a closer look. "They look like they've been through a shredder. I wonder where they came from."

"Okay, this is really creeping me out," Debi said. "I think that's our cue to get the hell out of here."

He turned to face her and replied, "Yeah, I think you're right."

Suddenly, the full moon emerged from behind the clouds, drawing Debi's attention. Her mouth opened as the light shined down on them. "Oh my, it's so big."

Chad chuckled. "You're not the first one to tell me that."

Debi put her hand on her hip and eyed him sternly. "I better be the last one too. And for your information, I was referring to the moon, smart-ass."

He frowned. "Ouch," he said in amusement, placing his hand over his heart. "That hurt."

She lightly snickered and pointed toward the sky. "Look at that. I've never seen anything like it."

When Chad turned to look, he heard something—or he thought he did. It was a rustling sound, like something moving in the tree where they'd found the clothes. As he lifted his chin and looked up, his eyes rounded in sheer terror. What he saw threatened his sanity.

Positioned at the top, Chad saw two glowing orbs staring back at him. The head of the thing was hideous—like Lon Chaney's *Wolf Man.*

The creature smiled down at him, its white canines flashing against its thick, black fur.

Chad opened his mouth to warn Debi as the *thing* dropped from the tree and knocked him to the ground. In a savage frenzy, the creature slashed its claws mercilessly, ripping through flesh and bone.

Debi screamed, but they were lost in the sounds of the creature's own thundering roars and Chad's shrieks of pain.

Her body seemed frozen in place, watching helplessly as the unholy beast tore at Chad's body and sank its teeth into his throat. At the sound of bones cracking came a dying gasp as Chad's lips opened and closed.

For one brief moment, she wavered between hysteria and total collapse. Debi stared at Chad's body through a numb haze of detachment. Then she stumbled back, her mind struggling with what her eyes were telling her. The images of her fiancé ripped apart and eaten were too unbearable, the sounds driving her mad. She covered her ears and cried out, "Chad!"

Her pitiful cries alerted the creature, fueling its rage. With fury in its eyes, it twisted away from Chad's body and faced her. The hideous beast had the features of a man and a wolf. Its matted fur was soaked in blood. Chad's blood.

He watched her eyes go wide as she swiftly clamped a hand over her mouth to muffle her screams.

Torn between fight or flight, she looked around, trying to decide what to do. If she was going to try to make a run for it, time was ticking. *Tick-tock, tick-tock.*

With a rush of adrenaline and a determination to escape, she quickly pulled herself together. As Debi spun around and took off at a dead run, the creature did not go after her. He stood in his tracks *watching*. He had the patience for a chase tonight. For his amusement, he gave her a head start. The thrill of the hunt surged through him—that for one minute of her worthless life, he'd let her think she might actually get away.

As Debi ran through the dense growth of trees and underbrush, using the full moon and the starlit sky to guide her, fear began to rise in her and take hold. *Was that thing following behind me?* she feverishly thought. If so, she prayed she could outrun it. Maybe she would be able to make it to the car.

At first, her pace was steady. After a half-hour's run, her thighs and calves began to cramp as the ground became increasingly hilly. When she could run no further, she stopped to catch her breath and whirled around, preparing to meet her death. Surprisingly, nothing was pursuing her.

"Thank God," she said, heaving a sigh of relief.

While she trudged along, jumping at every sound, the savage memory of Chad's death came to mind. She saw his dead eyes, as though they were staring at something far beyond, and his disfigured face that was once handsome. She shuddered at the images in her head. They would forever haunt her. He was the love of her life, and now he was gone, taken by something unnatural... something derived of pure evil. No matter how much she tried, she could never forget the horror of his screams. The thought quickened her pace and kept her moving.

With heavy gasps, she struggled forward along the trail as fast as she could, not bothering to look back. It took another half hour of climbing before the hill began to level off. Every muscle was taut with fear and alertness. All around her, thick fog rose from the ground, clouding her visibility. Then finally, she caught sight of Chad's Toyota Camry.

She looked longingly in its direction, to the safety of the car and whispered a prayer, "Oh God, please let me make it."

Debi guessed it was only twenty feet away, but as she kept going, it looked no closer than when she first saw it. The silver Camry seemed to hang in the distance like a shiny mirage. *Surely, it isn't too far*, she thought.

Suddenly, the sound of an unearthly howl froze her heart in her chest. It seemed to last forever, coming from behind. Debi tore through the darkness, shoving wildly to fend off the branches in her path. For a brief moment, her escape came to an unexpected halt when her blouse tangled around a thorny bush. In a desperate attempt to get free, she tugged at the trapped material and pulled it over her head. As Debi moved on without a shirt, a trail of goosebumps covered her exposed skin.

Abruptly came a second howl. It rose to the treetops and ended in a guttural snarl. When she turned to look, cold chills raced down her spine. Of all the terrors she felt, the most terrifying one, as she stared up into that hellish face, was how she would die. Would the creature end her life quickly, or make her suffer?

Then the *thing* leaped into the air. As it landed on the ground with a loud thud, Debi stopped dead in her tracks. The monstrous, black-haired beast stared at her with glowing eyes.

Oh God, I'm not going to make it, she painfully thought as she eyeballed the distance between her and the car.

Frantically, she turned to run away. Behind her, she could hear the creature's savage pursuit, its heavy footsteps bounding after her, getting closer and closer.

She ran erratically, cutting sharp turns and weaving around trees, hoping to gain some distance. In her efforts to escape, she lost her footing on a broken branch and fell to the ground. Trembling with fear, she pushed herself up on her hands and knees. Forcing her eyes to look up, she came face to face with the wolfish fiend as it crouched before her. Its breath was warm against her skin and it smelled like rotting flesh.

Debi screamed and tried to fight as the creature slowly brought its claw-like hand to her throat, but she was defenseless against his strength. At first, she struggled, choking violently, but the creature's grip was mighty, and she could not move her head. Her chest was tightening, her heart and lungs about to explode. The world around her spun away as though she was a lonely passenger on an endless carousel. She was spinning... spinning until the night descended with dizzying speed.

As she slipped into a state of unconsciousness, the creature released his firm hold and eased her limp body to the ground. "You will live yet another day," his lips whispered next to her ear. "Your blood is a gift. A precious gift for my *beloved*." Then he smiled. A cold, smug smile of satisfaction.

Chapter Twenty-Eight

Hours after the stranger vanished from Jena's room—who Jena now referred him as her beloved—he left her feeling as though he had branded her as his. Then the images of him taking her, dominating her, marking her... brought her to awareness. She *belonged* to him now.

Guilt crashed down on her. *Dear God, what have I done? What will become of me? Have I lost the strength to resist the curse?*

Suddenly, feelings of betrayal consumed her. She'd betrayed her fiancé Todd, and her dear friend Sophie. The memory of their lives darkened, and their brutal deaths brought to light. How could she? *What* was she? At this moment, Jena knew it was already too late. She could feel her thirst for blood growing by the minute. She felt the powerful aching in the back of her throat and the gnawing pain in the pit of her stomach.

Jena rolled over in bed and let out a moan. Her body felt like she'd been on a bender from hell. When she reached for her phone on the nightstand, she noticed it was nine o'clock in the morning. *What?* She had slept in, which was unusual for her. Normally, Jena was up before six, ready for her daily run. It took her almost half an hour just to motivate herself enough to get out of bed.

On shaky legs, Jena moved toward the bathroom feeling completely drained of energy. She reached for a robe draped over the door and slipped her arms into the sleeves. Her hands shook as she secured it around her waist. Jena eyed the shower but decided against having one. Although the thought of warm water massaging her skin seemed like heaven, she was just too exhausted to make the effort.

Instead, Jena decided on a hot bath in the Jacuzzi tub that was big enough for at least four others. As she turned toward the king-size bath, she caught her reflection in the mirror. Her eyes rounded in shock, and her legs nearly gave out from beneath her.

She put her hands up to her face. *No,* she feverishly thought. *This cannot be.*

The reflection staring back at her was not her own. It was someone... *something* she did not recognize. She slowly inched forward and brought her face closer to the glass. It was Jena, of course, but she didn't look like the person she used to be. This was a wolfish creature—a monster staring back at her.

Jena's heart caught in her throat as she studied herself in the mirror. *My God,* she painfully thought. *I look like the creature.* Thick, matted fur covered every inch of her skin. Only seconds ago, she'd seemed normal, but now...

Although she recognized the blue eyes, *her blue eyes,* they were glowing like the irises of an animal in the night. Jena smoothed her tongue over the black-rimmed edge of the mouth of this *thing* she'd become and felt two, sharp-pointed teeth. *Oh God!*

Jena immediately covered her mouth. She gasped at the misshapen form of her hand. Dark hair covered it, and long, deadly claws were at the tips of her fingers.

When she looked up, pointed lupine ears were atop her head, half-hidden by thick, rooted hair.

"What am I?" she whispered, her voice sounding rough.

"Oh, you knew this would happen, didn't you?" her inner voice said. *"You invited him. You wanted this!"*

A strong feeling in the pit of her gut told her she knew, and she had welcomed it. She had known it deep down in her very soul.

Jena began to laugh with utter madness, the sounds wicked and sinister, until she broke down into an overwhelming emotion of despair. As tears gathered in the corners of her eyes, she felt herself drifting into a state of confusion and uncertainty.

How can this be? she thought as she gripped her long, wolfish fingers around the porcelain sink, and watched the endless river of tears roll down her fur-covered cheeks. *Surely, this is nothing but a bad dream.*

Jena closed her eyes for a moment. Then realization escaped her suddenly. It was the blood... *her* blood.

Why hadn't it crossed my mind before? He bit me, and then he... kissed me.

"Oh, dear God—" she gasped. *He* tricked me.

Am I to be this *thing* for the rest of my life? Jena prayed it wasn't so. She felt sick to her stomach. She wanted to kill him, but something inside her made her feel drawn to him as though they had bonded somehow. Then it came to her. *I'm going to be a bloodthirsty killer.* For a second, Jena thought she was going to lose her mind, but then she realized there was nothing she could possibly do to stop this curse. There was no way out of this. The fact was, the life she once knew was over now.

At that moment, coming from the bedroom, she heard her phone ringing. *Shit!* Jena knew it was Angie calling going by the ringtone. Suddenly, panic shot through her. What in the hell was she going to do? She couldn't possibly talk. Not in this state. The change in her voice would send Angie on alert. She wasn't ready to explain to her best friend that she'd weakened.

As it went to her voice mail, Jena expelled her breath as if she'd been punched. She slowly shook her head. "I've got to change back," Jena found herself saying. Although she had no idea how to make that happen.

* * *

Angie left a message on Jena's voice mail and rolled over in bed, her hunger pangs gnawing at her like she hadn't eaten for days. It made sense after all the extra physical exertion between her and Bull. Her body felt as though she had run a marathon, and it hurt in a good way. The two of them had stayed up most of the night making love, talking, and laughing as if they had known each other for years. They shared memories of their past, traded each other's life stories, and made plans for the future together.

God, she wished she'd woken up lying next to him.

Bull had thought it best to leave before everyone in the Covenant woke this morning. He didn't want to make the wrong impression, especially for Angie, which she completely understood and respected the hell out of his decision. Going by the way he kissed her goodbye this morning, he was head over heels for her. She had a feeling that when word got out, no one would be surprised, especially by the way they looked at each other yesterday morning during breakfast. They practically undressed each other with their eyes.

Angie stretched in bed. Feeling the satin sheets against her naked skin made her ache for him. After last night, she could not pretend she wasn't already emotionally invested in Bull. She was half in love with him.

Now that it was already after nine o'clock in the morning, Angie decided to get out of bed and head for the kitchen. She was famished. First, she would make a pit stop by Jena's room to check on her. Knowing her, Angie wouldn't be surprised if she'd already been up for hours. Unlike her, Jena was a creature of habit. Ever since Angie had known her, she'd been early to bed and early to rise. Angie was the complete opposite. Funny, she'd never considered how different they were in some ways but nevertheless shared a lot in common in more ways than one. Perhaps it was the reason why they'd always managed to remain the best of friends. No matter what, words unspoken, she had Jena's back, and Jena had hers. That was just the way it was between the two of them.

She cursed aloud, feeling the soreness radiating through her body as she maneuvered herself from the bed and to her feet. Hell, even her toes ached. Pushing it aside, she managed to get dressed. As she headed to Jena's room, she was eager to relay the exciting news about her and Bull.

* * *

Jena flinched at the rapping noise that came from the balcony, as though someone was knocking on the sliding glass doors. *Shit!*

Then her attention suddenly shifted to the sounds of someone knocking at the bedroom door. *Christ almighty!* In a state of panic, she didn't know what to do. Should she answer the door, or see who was at the balcony? *Decisions, decisions.*

Cautiously, she stuck her head outside the bathroom and looked to the door when she heard Angie's voice, "Jena, are you in there?"

Her head swung back toward the balcony when the noise persisted, getting louder.

Shortly after, the door handle jiggled as if someone was trying to open it. "Jena, it's me... Angie."

Thankfully, she'd thought to lock the door last night. She didn't want Angie to see her this way, and to know that she'd weakened to the curse.

On a split-second decision, Jena went to the balcony. Her first thought was the stranger, her *beloved,* had come back to visit her. If so, maybe he could help her. She prayed he would.

When she drew back a peephole section of the drapes, there was someone at the glass doors. Someone big, towering at least ten feet tall.

"What the—" she gasped, stepping away from the covered glass. She rubbed her eyes. *It can't be,* she thought.

Jena wished she had answered the door instead, but to her disappointment, the knocking ceased. Angie had obviously given up.

The man standing on the balcony wasn't the stranger. It was a man with giant black wings. His features were handsomely regal, and he had an intense look in his eyes.

"Jena?" His voice was deep but friendly. "I give you my word. I'm *not* going to harm you."

This time, Jena didn't flinch. At that moment, she decided to take a chance on the man-angel standing outside of the balcony. Besides, what did she have to lose? She was desperate. At this point, she was willing to accept help from a total stranger.

"Here goes nothing," she muttered. Letting out a deep breath, she went forward and pulled back the drapes. So far, she had witnessed many bizarre things. But an angel? This was way off the charts.

"I'm here to help you," the black-winged angel said.

As he smiled, Jena was overcome with comfort and something else she couldn't quite pinpoint. *Was it trust?* Then she freely opened the sliding glass door.

"My name is Cronus." The angel stuck his hand out. "I'm first commander-in-chief of God's battle angels."

Not sure what to say, Jena nervously extended her hairy hand and shook his.

"Uh... P-please come in," she said in a guttural voice.

He bowed. "Thank you."

The giant angel... battle angel—*shit, whatever he was*—ducked his head and stepped inside.

"I-I'm not a monster," she stammered with her words, trying to come up with a good explanation to her appearance. "I mean, there's a reason why I look this way."

Cronus grinned at her as if he knew what she was trying to say.

Before Jena could utter another word, he held up his large hand to silence her. "You don't have to explain. I already know everything."

She shrugged. "You do?"

He nodded. "Yes, Jena. I know about the creature stalking you." His nostrils flared and he frowned, staring at her hard. Then his expression eased a little. "And I'm aware of the curse he's placed upon you."

Her shoulders sagged in relief. "Are you here to take it away?"

When he didn't immediately reply, and by the look on his face, it told her without words the answer to her question. A sick feeling of disappointment hit her hard.

Finally, he said, "I'm sorry, Jena. I cannot reverse what is already done, but there is some light at the end of the tunnel."

Jena furrowed her brow. "What's that supposed to mean?"

"With my help, and with your compliance..." He briefly paused, scanning the open sliding door with his sharp eyes, as if he were looking for someone. "...you will not kill innocent humans."

Her eyes rounded. "Are you saying I won't become a killer?" *God, she hated that word.*

Cronus shook his head. "No, Jena. That part I cannot take away. You're still going to kill humans for their blood."

She threw her wolfish hands up in defeat and let out an aggravated groan. "I don't understand." Jena's voice had hardened then. "So what part of this is supposed to be helping me?"

"You will only kill evildoers," a strange deep voice from the balcony said.

When Jena looked away from Cronus and focused her eyes on the man—who resembled the other giant angel—peering into the opening of the sliding glass door, she found herself speechless. It was like she couldn't move. *There are two of them?*

Words could not describe the angel staring back at her with strange silver eyes that shimmered like crystals, which accentuated his handsome face. And he had the most fantastic head of hair, the kind most women would die for. The long, colorful shades of his golden-toned hair were outrageously gorgeous.

Jeez, are all angels this attractive? Jena thought.

As the angel ducked his head to enter the room, Jena took a few steps back. Then, to her amazement, another angel appeared in the opening of the balcony. As he ducked under the doorway and stepped inside, Jena looked up at him in awe. When he stood straight, he towered above the other angels by at least two feet. He had shimmering eyes and braids that trailed past his bare chest as thick as rope. The way he stood firm and mighty reminded Jena of an African King.

"Who are you?" she asked, looking between the two angels.

"My name is Icarus," the blond-headed angel said. He bowed his head and then turned to the other angel. "And this is Helios."

Helios bowed to Jena in silence.

"Cronus is our commander." Icarus's eyes shifted to Cronus and then back to Jena. "We're here to help him, help *you.*"

Jena swallowed the knot that had formed in her throat. "What did you mean by what you said just a second ago?"

"In our world, 'evildoers' refers to the worst of sinners," Icarus said, and he added, "child molesters, serial killers, rapists, and anything that walks on two feet with the intent of performing the most perverse acts on the innocent. I'm sure you get my meaning."

When Jena nodded, he went on, "We need you to help us rid the earth of these evil beings before they are sent to hell."

Jena smirked. "Why not just let them go to hell? Won't that be a worse punishment?"

Icarus laughed a little. "I'm sure burning for eternity would be far worse than being killed outright by you. But the curse you bestow will destroy their souls before Satan gets his hooks in them."

Jena narrowed her eyes. "But isn't that how it works?" Her voice sounded frustrated. "You're confusing me here. Why would you care if the devil gets the bad people? Don't they deserve it?"

"Yes, they deserve to burn in hell for eternity," Cronus told Jena. "But what you don't understand, some of those *bad people* will be converted into demons. Not all of them will burn in eternal fire. Satan unleashes his chosen to do his bidding. He wants to destroy us and take over. He sends powerful demons to a place called the In-Between. It's the outer surrounding of heaven. That's where all the battle angels like us reside, where we guard heaven's gate. You will be doing us a big favor by eliminating Satan's soldiers. As of now, his numbers are rising. If you agree to this, you will not kill innocent people, and you'll be helping us."

"So what you're saying is..." Jena momentarily paused to let out a deep breath. "...I'd be sort of like God's grim reaper?"

Cronus cocked a brow and Icarus made a noise in the back of his throat as though he was holding back a chuckle.

"Yeah," Cronus chortled. "Something like that."

Jena shrugged. "But how I am supposed to know if a person is good or bad?"

"Trust me," Icarus said to her. "You'll know. The evil will call out to you."

Jena looked to the angel named Helios. "Are you always this quiet?"

"He doesn't speak," Icarus stated. "He was born without vocal cords, although now he's telepathic."

"You mean he can communicate with his mind?"

Helios focused on Jena and spoke to her using his special gift. *"Yes, Jena."* His voice was a deep baritone, softly whispering in Jena's head. *"I can communicate with everyone in this room at the same time, using my inner voice."*

Jena's eyes rounded. "Wow. That's incredible."

Helios smiled at her.

"Seeing all of you here is amazing, but I can't help but feel like this is my fault," Jena regretfully said. "I feel guilty every single day because Todd and Sophie died and I didn't. I'm the one that led them to that cemetery. They died because of me. I'd give anything if I could go back in time. I would have never gone there. I—" she began, then broke off with a gasp. "I don't deserve to live."

Cronus drew closer to Jena and kept his voice low. "I regret what's happened to you, but what is done is done. There is no turning back. You have to know this is not your doing. The wicked creature had you spellbound. You had no other choice but to submit to his bidding."

"You were born with a purpose, Jena," Icarus chimed back in. "Your ability to speak to those who have passed on is not coincidental. God gave you this gift for a reason."

Jena narrowed her eyes in question. "But why?"

"To help them move on," Icarus explained. "Those who cannot pass on to the other side turn to people like you that are gifted with sight."

"You mean like that girl, Carla Rosi?" she asked.

Icarus nodded. "Yes, Jena. And you're not to blame for anyone's death. You went to that cemetery for the sole purpose of helping Carla's family. You had no idea something evil was lurking in the shadows." He loomed over her with tenderness in his mesmerizing gaze. "Jena, you gave Carla and her family what they desperately needed."

"And what's that?"

"Peace," Icarus simply said. "Carla can finally rest in peace, and her family can heal from her death."

Jena held steady. She drew in her breath and reached for the last of her strength she had left. "All this time, I thought I was a freak," she muttered, her words ragged and choked. "My family thought I was crazy."

"You're anything but that," Cronus said, his words soothing. "You have a special gift."

Jena's eyes softened. "So, I guess all this leaves me with no choice. I have to do what I have to do. Even though the thought of becoming this *monster* makes me sick to my stomach, it's the right thing." She sighed again. "At least I won't be killing innocent people."

"There's one more thing," Cronus went on to explain. Before he continued, he reached out and placed his hand on her shoulder. The instant he made contact, Jena shifted back to her human form.

She looked down at her body, and her eyes went wide. It was as if she'd just witnessed a miracle. *Thank goodness she'd put on a robe this morning*, Jena thought. Otherwise, she'd be standing buck naked in front of three angels. Then her eyes lifted to meet Cronus's stare.

Jena let out a long breath as if all the air in her lungs expelled. Tears immediately gathered in her eyes. "I don't know what to say," she said in a low voice. "Thank you."

Cronus smiled and removed his hand from her shoulder. "You're welcome, Jena. But in order for all this to work," he began to explain, "the creature that cursed you can no longer exist. You *must* destroy it. You're the only key to its destruction."

Her face grew pale at the horror of what he told her. It was so inconceivable. *No,* Jena painfully thought as she slumped and looked down. Her unease was growing with each passing moment. Then tears fell from her eyes. Swallowing back the sobs that welled in her chest, she lifted her chin. As her eyes roamed the faces before her, she finally managed to say, "I'm sorry." The words came out as shaky as her hands were. "I cannot kill *him*."

"*You have no choice, Jena,*" Helios said, his inner voice a deep, resonant baritone. "*Innocent lives depend solely on you. We depend on you.*"

Chapter Twenty-Nine

When Sebastian woke the next morning, he automatically reached for Eve. As time passed while he was away, separated from her was like having a part of his soul ripped out. Now, she was here, and he'd be damned if he'd let her go again. Sebastian had ached for so long to hold Eve, to touch her, and to make love to her. Things were different now. Although they had experienced more suffering than any person should, they no longer lived in the past. Eve had changed. *He* had changed. Letting go of the pain had led them to a better place.

Despite his burning desire to make love to Eve, they stayed up most of the night talking. Just being in her presence again was more than he had ever hoped. After Sebastian explained to Eve the reason he'd been given a second chance to do the right thing—which involved the human who had been bitten by the creature—she told him all the things about the boys that he'd missed out on. Then there was the matter of showing his face to the Breedline Covenant. The battle angels had given him a huge task. It was Sebastian's responsibility to relay to them the details about Jena. And they weren't going to like what he had to say. He'd be lucky if Jace didn't kill him before he got a word out. After the vile things he'd done to him and his bonded mate Tessa, who could blame him.

Eve had only been asleep for a few hours, and he hated to wake her, but time was ticking, which meant she needed to be awake and prepared for the worst case scenario. It was crucial that he speak with the Covenant about Jena. She was their only hope of destroying the creature.

Sebastian pulled Eve into his arms and molded her tight against his chest. At last, he was holding her, and he had never felt something so right in his life. She stirred with a small sigh and melted into his embrace, her body so soft and warm against his.

Eve looked up and their gazes locked. Her crimson eyes filled with love.

"I can't believe you're really here," she whispered to him. "I was afraid to open my eyes this morning."

As he reached for her hand, he intertwined his fingers with hers and said, "Why would you be afraid?"

Eve sucked in a breath. "I was afraid to wake up and find all this to be nothing but a dream."

The sadness in her voice made Sebastian's gut tighten. "Everything is going to be okay, Eve," he murmured, smoothing his thumb over her cheekbone. "I'm here now, and I don't plan on going anywhere." He prayed he was right as he lowered his mouth to hers, kissing her softly.

When he pulled away, he said, "As much as I would love to spend the rest of the morning here in this bed with you making love, it's important that I speak with the Covenant. I have to tell them about Jena."

"But what about Jace?" she asked, a protest forming on her lips. "I'm scared. What if he—"

"Shhh." He briefly put his fingers against her lips. "I know, I know," he whispered, nodding an understanding.

Sebastian knew all too well what he was getting himself into. Facing his half-brother was like poking at a hornet's nest. Pissing Jace off would most likely bring forth his Beast, and the outcome would not be pleasant.

"I don't want you to worry, Eve." He released her hand and then smoothed it up her arm and squeezed her shoulder. "We'll work this out, okay?"

She went quiet for several long moments. It seemed as though Sebastian wasn't looking at the seriousness of the situation. Almost as though he had blinders on. He was walking straight into the line of fire without a plan.

Eve hesitated a moment and then said, "We need to talk about our options."

"Okay, what do you propose we do?"

She sat up and let out a deep breath. "Let me talk to my sister first. Mia will explain everything to Jem. Surely, he will understand. Maybe Jem can talk some sense into his brother. So far, Jace has come a long way. He has accepted me and the boys living here. Maybe he'll have a change of heart after he sees that you've changed."

Sebastian shook his head, his lips twisted into a grimace. "I don't think my brother will ever forgive me. He still thinks that I..." He briefly paused, barely able to stomach what he was about to say. "... raped Tessa."

Eve eyed him steadily. "But I know you didn't. You have to tell him the truth."

"I still hurt her, Eve." He let out a ragged sigh. "I used my succubus-side and put those images in her head, leading her to believe I did, just to hurt Jace." He swallowed back the tears that were building in the back of his throat. "I wanted to punish him, and I wanted to punish Jem. What I've done is unforgivable." His lips trembled and he brought his hand to his face to wipe at his eyes. "I was jealous of my father's love for them," he went on, shame evident in his voice. "All I wanted was for my father to love me. I was willing to do anything for him. He used me to do his dirty work, and then discarded me as if I was nothing. After what my mother had done to me, I just couldn't bear the thought of feeling abandoned again."

Eve's blood ran cold hearing the pain in Sebastian's voice. "All that is in the past," she said as she took hold of his hand and lightly squeezed. "Sebastian, your father is not the same man he was before. The demon that possessed him is gone. Alexander is a good man with a loving heart. He is a wonderful grandfather to our boys, and they love him. When my sister and Jem announced their engagement, Alexander knew she did not have anyone to walk her down the aisle. He offered to take the place of the father we never had," she went on to explain. "Even Jace has accepted him. Everyone in the Covenant respects and adores him. He has put his life on the line more than I can count to protect everyone here."

Sebastian looked at Eve with total bewilderment. His mouth opened, but then shut it as though he had no idea how to respond to what she'd just told him. Then he finally said, "Does my father remember anything? I mean, when he was possessed by the demon?"

"No, he doesn't, which is best."

"Does he ask about me?"

"Of course he does," she murmured. "He told me he feels responsible for everything that has happened to you, even though all the terrible things were not his doing. He loves you,

Sebastian. And he wants nothing more than to be the father you always deserved."

"I want to believe that, Eve. I want to believe it more than anything."

"I know you do. Maybe soon this will all be over and you can get to know the family you never had."

Sebastian gave her a half-smile. "I would like that." He stiffened as though he had remembered something horrible… something completely despicable that he had done in his past. A painful, faraway look instantly took hold of him. Images were crowding his mind, filling him with remorse and despair. Sebastian thought of what he had done to Tessa and the people whose lives he had taken, which included his birth mother, his spoiled half-siblings Camille and Edward, and his stepfather, although he did not regret killing him. William Montgomery was a monster. He'd raped Anna as a child. She was like a sister to Sebastian. William deserved his fate. He deserved to burn in hell for eternity. Sebastian started to speak about it to Eve but decided against it.

"Has Tessa forgiven you?" he asked, coming back to focus as a mixture of grief and uncertainty rang clear in his eyes.

"Yes, honey," she honestly replied. "And so has everyone else."

Sebastian stared at Eve in a way that made her want to wrap her arms around him and tell him everything was going to be all right.

"What about my sister?" he asked in a nervous voice. "Does Anna know what I've done?"

Eve nodded. "Anna knows all about our past, and she doesn't judge either of us. She knows I am not the same person I used to be. She knows deep down who you truly are. She loves you with all her heart. Anna has always considered you her brother even though you are not blood. And she has done some healing herself. Anna has found true love."

"With who?" Sebastian asked, cocking his brow.

"His name is Zeke Rizzo. You'd like him, Sebastian. He's a good man. And he is good to your sister."

Sebastian sighed. "I've missed out on so many things. How can I ever make up for all that I've done?"

"Honey, both of us have suffered more than anyone deserves," Eve continued. "Yes, we have hurt others and done terrible things, but God has forgiven us. He healed our broken hearts and brought us together again. He gave us two beautiful sons as proof. This is our second chance at life. You have to start forgiving yourself."

Sebastian's fingers tightened around hers as tears streaked down his cheeks. He loved that she didn't seem turned off by his moment of distress, and all the sins of his past. She gave him strength. She made him feel *whole* again.

"You're right, Eve." His lips curved up into a smile. "I didn't think it was possible to love you any more than I already do and yet here you are, proving me wrong." Then he leaned until his forehead touched hers. "I love you to infinity and beyond."

"You are my love," she whispered. "My only love."

A few minutes later, they made the decision to reach out to Mia and Jem. Eve went through her contacts and found Mia's number, irritated with how nervous it made her feel to make that call. As Eve explained the situation over the phone to her sister, the irrational part of her didn't want to involve Mia, but she was left with no choice. Mia had already given her more help than she ever deserved, especially after what she'd done to her not so long ago. Then again, who else could she have turned to? At this point, Eve was desperate, and she knew her sister would do whatever it took to keep peace within the Covenant. And having Sebastian under the same roof as Jace could end up in disaster. She couldn't dispute that. Eve knew she was treading on thin ice bringing the two together.

When Mia had agreed to talk to Jem, Eve sagged in relief. Mia was everything that she had come to know when she needed the support of a loving family. She was the kind of person that Eve came to trust, no matter the circumstances.

A year ago, Eve wouldn't have ever imagined she had a twin sister. They'd been separated at birth, living apart all these years, but now she was the only family—other than Sebastian and their twin boys—that Eve had. Although her mother discarded her at birth, and her foster parents tortured her, Eve wanted the same things other children wanted growing up—to be loved. Now, she had a real family, something to look forward to every day, instead of praying for death to end her suffering.

As the call ended, they waited for whatever came next. If they were lucky, Jem would agree to help Sebastian without confrontation. In truth, Sebastian wasn't looking forward to a reunion with his half-brothers. He figured Jem would be more lenient, in spite of the fact that he was born with an extraordinary gift. Jem had the power to burn him to the ground with a single flick of his wrist. On the other hand, Jace was the one he was most worried about. Nevertheless, both of them were going to be understandably angry knowing he was in the Covenant. If he could do his part and help the battle angels destroy the creature, he'd take whatever ass-kicking they wanted to dole out.

It wasn't long before the sound of a knock came from the bedroom door, followed by Mia's voice. "Eve, it's Mia... and Jem."

While Eve went to open the door, Sebastian waited in an area that adjoined the bedroom and served as a small dining room with a table and several chairs. He stood back, feeling nervous as hell, and listened to Eve as she spoke to Mia. There was a thread of worry coming from her loud and clear. Then he heard Jem say, "Where's Sebastian?"

As Eve invited them in, Sebastian thought of all the things he'd planned to say, but when Jem approached him, the only thing that came to his lips was the simple truth. "Please, Jem, I need your help."

Jem's brow wrinkled. "Because of the situation, I'm agreeing to listen to what you have to say," he bit out. "But this doesn't mean I give a shit about you. When it comes to my brother, I cannot promise anything. Jace has more than enough reasons to rip you into pieces."

There was a long silence as guilt weighed heavily on Sebastian. "Look, I know this has to be difficult," he told Jem. "And I'm ready to accept whatever punishment you or Jace seem fitting for what I've done to the people you love."

When Sebastian turned to face Mia, shame crowded into his eyes, remembering the awful things he'd done to her.

Before Sebastian's dark heart changed, he kidnapped her, threatening to use her as his own personal concubine against her will. "I know there's nothing I can do to make up for what I've done to everyone that I've hurt, and that includes you, Mia." Empathy laced his voice. "I'm sorry."

Jem frowned and looked as though he was going to argue, but Mia grasped a hold of his hand and squeezed it as though she was pleading with him to hear Sebastian's side. In a silent understanding, he lightly squeezed back.

Mia acknowledged Sebastian with a nod. "I believe in what my sister has told me about what's happened to you, but that doesn't mean I trust you. I'll need some time."

Sebastian nodded an agreement. "I don't expect anything more. But I can promise you this," he said earnestly. "I swear it on my life I love Eve, and I love my sons. I'll do whatever it takes to protect them. And if it means giving my life for them, then I'm willing to give it."

Eve smiled then. Hearing Sebastian's devoting declaration of words melted her heart. God, she loved this man.

"Not to cut short on your apologies," Jem cut in, glaring at Sebastian. "But maybe you better get to the point of why you're here. The shorter version if you don't mind. We need to relay this information to Tim and Tessa as soon as possible. We can go over all the details when we meet up with them."

Sebastian exhaled a deep breath and explained why he'd been sent. There was a lot of doubt reflected in Jem's face, but not Mia. Her expression seemed one of shock.

When he got to the part where Jena was their only hope at destroying the creature, Jem's expression blackened, and Mia's mouth fell open.

It didn't surprise Sebastian that they had such an upsetting reaction to his explanation. Jem wasn't the type of man to put an innocent person in harm's way, so when Sebastian was candid about what Jena had to do, it was almost too much for him to comprehend. Mia just shook her head in denial.

Jem turned his sharp stare to Mia. "There's no time to spare," he said gravely. "This shit is urgent. I need to inform

Tim. He's going to want to gather everyone in the Covenant for a meeting."

"You've got to do that now," Mia said to Jem.

Jem nodded and turned toward Sebastian. "Until we say otherwise, I want you to stay put. We can't take the chance of Jace's reaction if he sees you. Things could get out of hand, and right now we've got more pressing issues to deal with."

"Trust me, you won't have any arguments from me," Sebastian replied.

"Keep your phone handy," Jem told Eve. "I'll contact you as soon as I know more."

Eve quickly nodded.

Mia reached out to Eve and placed her hand on her shoulder. "Don't worry, Eve," she said softly. "We'll figure this out. We always do."

Eve's lips formed a slight smile. "Thank you, Mia."

With her nerves on pins and needles, Mia followed Jem to the door. When he opened it, her eyes rounded in alarm, so shocked she wasn't sure how to respond. Jem just froze where he stood.

"There you are," Jace said as he stood outside the open doorway, facing Jem. "I've been trying to call—" He halted in mid-sentence while his gaze drifted inside the bedroom, his thoughts interrupted by the person standing next to Eve. Then his entire expression instantly hardened. His gaze narrowed and a frown marred the line of his mouth. "You *son of a bitch*," he said through gritted teeth.

The fury in Jace's voice, the *anger* evident in his tone, worried Sebastian.

Chapter Thirty

By the look on his half-brother's face, Sebastian knew he was in deep shit. Oh yeah, Jace was definitely pissed-off. His nostrils flared, and he bared his teeth into a snarl. He was like a seething ball of fury ready to explode.

As Jace lunged forward, Jem grasped his shoulders and held him back.

"Listen, brother," Jem pleaded with Jace, "before you lose your temper, let's step out into the hall and talk."

Jace's jaw ticked and he turned to stare at his twin brother.

"I know you're pissed, and you have reason to be," Jem continued in a low voice. "I get it, okay? But there's a reason why Sebastian is here, and it has to do with Jena. Please, just give me a few minutes to explain."

Jace sent him a disgruntled look. "Get the *hell* out of my way."

Blunt as ever, Jace—who gave new meaning to the term "bull in a china closet"—as always, wasn't one to hold back on what he was thinking. He didn't see the value in pussyfooting around what was looking him square in the face. He tended to act out his emotions first rather than thinking them through.

Jem kept a firm hold on Jace's shoulders and leaned in closer. "I don't give a shit what you do. I'm not letting you inside this room."

Jace flipped Jem off and shoved past him, nearly knocking Mia down in the process. With fast reflexes, Jem quickly grabbed Mia by the arm and tugged her out of the way.

When Jace put the person who was soon to be the mother of his child in harm's way just to get at Sebastian, there was no way in hell Jem could let that shit go. Without hesitating, he spun away from Mia and tackled Jace from behind. The two brothers went down, grunting and cursing as each wrestled for the advantage over the other.

Mia gathered closer, overwhelmed by what was transpiring before her and cried out, "Please, stop this!"

Ignoring her frustrated demand, Jace and Jem rolled on the floor, knocking over everything that got in their path.

Eve moved next to Mia, her eyes rounded in fear and said, "I'm going to go for help before they kill one another."

Frantic with worry, Mia looked at her and said, "Hurry, Eve."

Taken aback, Sebastian kept his distance and merely watched as his half-brothers grappled on the floor like two five-year-olds, fighting over who was right and who was wrong.

Jem flipped Jace over his head and then rolled to his knees about the time Jace caught him in a scissor lock. After a period of struggling, Jem finally broke the hold and snaked an arm around Jace's neck, holding him in a headlock while he gasped for breath. As he finally went completely still, Jem was ready to call it quits and released his grip. Then, to his surprise, Jace suddenly came to. With one swift motion, he curled his fingers into Jem's shirt and practically lifted him off the floor and tossed him across the room.

Sebastian's eyes widened at the sheer strength it took for Jace to toss his brother aside as though he was nothing but a rag doll.

"You need to back the hell off," Jem barked when he saw Jace coming after him. Then he gave Jace a look that told him without words that things were fixing to get *real* serious. He gave him a final warning, "Don't make me repeat myself, brother."

Jace got the hint, knowing his brother's powers were something no one in their right mind wanted to screw around with and stopped in his tracks before he took another step. "All right," he gritted out, shifting his eyes to Sebastian with a hateful glare and then looked back at Jem. "Then explain to me why *he's* here. And it better be a matter of life and death."

"It is, damn it!" Jem let out an aggravated sigh as he moved to his feet. "He's here to tell us how to destroy the creature."

"Well—" Jace threw his hands up in defeat. "Why the hell didn't you say so in the first place?"

Jem rolled his eyes and groaned. "You idiot. For once in your life, try listening before you overreact." There was a protective note in his voice. "You 'bout knocked Mia down."

"Shit," Jace grunted as he swiveled on his feet, and turned to Mia. Pain flashed in his eyes. He hadn't meant to hurt her. "I'm so sorry, Mia." He looked at her like a whipped dog. "Please, forgive me."

Mia silently nodded. "Please, Jace. Listen to what your brother is saying. Sebastian wouldn't have come here if the situation wasn't grave."

Jace shifted his eyes back to Jem and sighed. "Okay, I'm listening."

Just as Jem was about to explain, Eve came back into the room and brought Tessa and Tim with her.

"Will someone please tell me what in the *hell* is going on in here?" Tim demanded as he stepped into the room, his eyes roaming over all the disarray. There were pictures lying on the floor, broken glass, and chairs toppled over. "It looks like a damn tornado went through this room," he tacked on.

When Tim noticed Sebastian, he scowled at him, letting the full force of his aggravation bleed into his expression. "How the *hell* did he get in here?"

Sebastian looked down at the floor, afraid to pick his head back up.

"Like I said," Jem spoke out. "I was just about to explain the situation to this asshole..." He narrowed his eyes at Jace. "...before he lost his temper and all hell broke loose."

Jace rolled his eyes and heaved a deep breath.

Disappointment surged over Tessa as she looked at Jace, and then her eyes shifted toward Sebastian. "Why don't we let *him* explain," she said in a bitter tone. "Tell us, Sebastian." She crossed her arms over her chest and lifted an eyebrow. "*Why* are you here?"

Sebastian lifted his chin and started talking, explaining to Tessa and the others why the battle angels were summoned by the Creator to return to earth, bringing him and the Fury with them. Then he went on to tell them about Jena, and that she was their only hope at destroying the creature.

When he fell silent, Tessa turned away from Sebastian and looked to Eve. Her instincts were telling her that Sebastian was lying, but it was all too much to take in.

"I know you don't trust Sebastian," Eve said to Tessa. "He has done terrible things." She paused and looked at everyone in the room. Then she focused her eyes back to Tessa and went on, "After all the horrible things I've done to the Covenant, and my sister, everyone believed that I could change. You gave me hope. You even took in my children. You all gave me a second chance." She glanced at Sebastian. "I know in my heart Sebastian is not the man he was before. Please, for the safety of the Covenant... for all humanity... believe him."

"If you're asking us to forgive him," Jace chimed in, "you can forget it. What he's done to Tessa is unforgivable, not to mention all the other rotten shit he's done."

"I'm not asking for anyone's forgiveness," Sebastian said. "But you're right. What I have done to everyone is unforgivable. And if I have to give up my freedom or my life to ease the suffering I have caused, I will give it freely."

As Tessa listened to Sebastian, she felt an unnerving shiver pass through her. Her head felt light and her skin flushed warm. And from some very distant place came a suppressed memory, buried deep in her subconscious.

Tessa's breath caught in her throat as though she'd just awakened from a dream. "You didn't do it, did you?"

Jace moved next to Tessa and wrapped his arm around her. "Honey, he's not worth upsetting yourself over. Don't give him the time of day."

"You didn't *rape* me," Tessa continued on, keeping her eyes focused on Sebastian as she pulled away from Jace. "That's why I couldn't remember that day you kidnapped me until days later." She stepped forward and stood face to face with Sebastian. "You used your succubus skills to play tricks with my mind."

Jace quickly moved in behind Tessa and stared hard at Sebastian with his hand balled up into a tight fist just daring him to make a move so he could punch him in the face.

Sebastian lowered his head, pausing there for a moment. Then he peered up at her in silence. His eyes flickered dimly, and Tessa recognized the depth of his sorrow, an emotion she knew all too well.

"No," he finally said, "I did not rape you, but the other thing is true."

"But why?" She looked at him painfully. "Why would you want me to believe such a thing?"

"I'm sorry, Tessa," Sebastian solemnly said. "No excuse could ever make up for what I've done." His eyes shifted toward Jace. "I put those horrible images in Tessa's subconscious to hurt you, Jace. It was wrong. I was jealous of my father's love for you and Jem. I would do anything to take it all back, but I cannot change what's been done."

In heated silence, Jace glared at Sebastian. Before he opened his mouth to speak, Tessa cut in, "This is not the time nor the place to discuss this. The past is where it should stay. Right now, we have important things to sort out." Then she changed the subject and said, "How can Jena destroy the creature?"

"She must give in to the curse," Sebastian regretfully said. "It's the only way."

"That doesn't make any damn sense," Jace said abruptly. "What the hell is that supposed to mean?"

"The only thing that can destroy this creature is one of its own," Sebastian explained. "In order for that to happen, Jena must turn."

"But if Jena becomes this *thing*," Tim said, looking at Sebastian in question. "How are we supposed to control her? Won't she be taking its place?"

Sebastian looked at Tim gravely. "Yes. Jena will become a killer, but she will only kill the wicked."

"This is a lot to ask of her," Tessa pointed out. "Doesn't she get a choice in the matter?"

Sebastian shook his head again. "Jena has already given in to the curse."

"What?" Jem shot back in startled response. "But how? There's no way she could have got out of this Covenant undetected."

"Jena did not leave the Covenant," Sebastian quickly replied.

"Then how did she manage to get human blood?" Tim queried. "That's how the curse takes over, right?"

"And everyone here is anything but human," Mia pointed out.

"The creature..." Sebastian briefly paused, swallowing the knot in his throat. "...came here."

"Son of a bitch," Jace blasted. "Don't tell me that thing brought in a human for her to feed on."

"No, but it somehow tricked Jena by using her own blood," Sebastian told them. "She's spellbound by the creature. After she was bitten, the virus soon created an unbreakable bond between them."

"So if this thing has her hypnotized, and if they are truly bound to one another," Jace said, "how are we going to convince her to kill this *damn* thing?"

"That's where the battle angels come in," Sebastian said. "They are here to convince her."

"They're here?" Jace's eyes rounded. "Like right at this very moment?"

Sebastian nodded.

Jace furrowed his brows. "How in the hell did they get inside the Covenant?"

"Well," Sebastian said, shrugging one of his shoulders, "they *are* angels."

"Yeah, ten-foot angels." Jace smirked. "They couldn't have just walked through the freakin' front door. They'd be kind of hard to miss, don't ya think?"

"Where are they?" Tim bluntly demanded.

"They're with Jena," Sebastian hesitantly replied. "She let them in through the balcony of her room."

Tim blew out a deep breath. "I think it's time we get some answers. We need to know what all we're dealing with."

"That's why they came here," Sebastian said. "They're going to need the Covenant's help."

"Where's the Fury?" Tim asked.

"They're staying at the Hothburn estate with the two angels, Lailah and Frigg," Sebastian replied.

"So which angels are here?" Tessa inquired.

Sebastian gazed back at her. "I'm not exactly certain," he murmured. "But I know Lailah asked Cronus, Icarus, and Helios for help."

Jem cast Sebastian an inquisitive look. "Are they one of the same that helped render the Fury powerless?"

"Yes." Sebastian nodded. "Cronus carries the sword of truth. He's like the right hand of God."

"All right then," Tim said to Sebastian, motioning in the direction of the open doorway. "Since you seem to know so much, by all means, lead the way."

Jem was the last one to exit the room while the others headed to speak with the battle angels. As he came out, he glanced up to see Jace waiting in the hallway with his hands shoved in his pockets. He had a concerning look on his face.

Jem stared dully at Jace as he walked up to him and said, "Look, man, I'm sorry." He let out a long breath. "You know I'd never intentionally hurt Mia, right? I mean, when I saw Sebastian, I just lost it. I didn't mean to…"

"I know," said Jem as he gripped Jace's shoulder. "It's forgotten."

Jace grabbed his twin brother in a bear hug and lightly pounded him on the back. "Thanks, bro."

"Okay, ladies, enough," Kyle said as he came down the hallway, catching a glimpse of his best friends embracing. "By my guess, this looks like an apology." He chuckled. "So, who started the fight this time?"

The brothers looked at one another and rolled their eyes.

Jem waved Kyle over and said, "Follow us. We'll explain later."

"Where are we going?" Kyle asked as he stood next to them.

"To Jena's room," Jace told him.

Kyle shrugged. "What for?"

"We're meeting the battle angels."

"W-what?"

Chapter Thirty-One

Debi opened her eyes with a gasp. For a brief second, she hovered between a state of unconsciousness and waking, her mind a complete whirlwind.

Dazed and confused, she did not recognize her surroundings. *Where am I? How long have I been here?*

She heard the questions, but she wasn't sure if she'd thought it or said it aloud. Then she remembered the dark events of what had happened to the man she was engaged to marry.

"Oh, God... Chad..."

The horror of his death was overwhelming. The brutal attack swept through her brain: his face, all the blood, his agonizing screams, and his glassy dead eyes.

Crumbled on her side with her knees drawn up to her chest, Debi tried to force the images out of her head. From the moment she and Chad had decided to leave Presidio Park, everything had seemed dreamlike. She remembered hearing him calling out to her, warning her, and then the sharp, piercing screams. She struggled to cut out the noise inside her head, but no matter how hard she tried, it wouldn't go away. She couldn't stop sobbing, couldn't stop the shaking that wracked her body with grief and shock.

Her pulse pounded loud in her temples. In an effort to drown it out, she clamped her hands over her ears. "Please, God," she pleaded. "Make it stop."

Then, the memories of something horrible chasing her came to mind. Was it an animal or a man that had pursued her? The two impossibilities left her swirling in confusion. Was that *thing* still out there?

When a distant rustling noise caught her attention, she lowered her hands and looked to the sound. In a burst of panic, she jerked upright and screamed as rats scurried on the floor around her.

Suddenly, the stench of rotting flesh flooded through her. As Debi searched her surroundings, the only thing she could see was a horde of rats crowded around something beyond the shadows.

She struggled to move. Her arms and legs felt stiff and sore as though she'd been to hell and back. And her throat still ached from being choked by the monster that murdered her fiancé.

When Debi managed to get to her feet, she felt the tension draining from her muscles. As she took a step, she nearly slipped and fell. The floor seemed to be wet, coated with something thick and sticky. Peering down, she could see what looked to be a bloody trail leading out in front of her. Chills crept up her spine. Was something bleeding or injured dragged along the floor?

She hugged herself tightly and prayed the blood was from a dead animal. The thought of that hellish beast dragging Chad's body sickened her.

Cautiously, she planted one foot in front of the other and moved on. Focusing on the things all around her, Debi soon recognized where she was. The hair on the back of her neck rose. She was inside a mausoleum.

How did I get here? She feverishly thought. *Did that thing bring me here?*

Not far away, the glow of candles flickered on the floor, lighting a path through the dark and damp burial chamber.

As she slowly trudged onward, the putrid smell grew thicker. Bile rose into the back of her throat, making her gag.

Debi stopped and quickly covered her mouth. "Dear God," she choked.

She flinched at the sound of approaching footsteps. They were getting closer and closer. Then suddenly, they stopped.

Swallowing back the knot that had formed in the back of her throat, she knew at once that she wasn't alone. That there was someone—*something*—waiting and watching her. She sensed someone hidden among the flickering candlelight and all the crypts that housed the dead.

Out of nowhere, a smooth voice called out to her, "Come closer." His voice echoed as though it was coming from all around her. "I have something you'll want to see."

"Who are you?" she cried out. "What do you want?"

His voice spoke again, louder this time. "Come here, Debi." He seemed to be taunting her. "Your beloved is waiting."

A moment of silence hung between them. His words muddled her thoughts. Beloved? What did he mean?

Her heart began to pound, leaving her breathless. "Please," she sobbed. "I beg you... please, let me go."

"You can never leave," he said with a slight, humorless laugh. "But if you promise to behave yourself, I'll let you see your beloved again."

His words mocked her, filling her with doubt. Maybe Chad was still alive. Was he here... suffering... dying?

"Chad?" she murmured, swallowing hard.

"Yes. Chad is waiting for you."

"I don't believe you!" Debi cried. "You're lying! He's dead!"

Holding back her sobs, she surveyed her surroundings again, searching for a door, a window, anywhere that would lead her out of this dreadful place.

There has to be a door, she prayed. *Please, God. Help me find a way out of here.*

"There is no way out." His voice was gentle but firm. "Come. Before it's too late."

When she took a step forward, she felt something scamper over her feet. She gasped when she looked down. The floor seemed to be moving. It was then she realized that what was moving were the rats.

She screamed and kicked at them. Squeaking in protest, the horde of rodents backed away and scuttled toward whatever was reeking of death. Desperate to block out the repulsive stench, she brought her hand up and covered her nose.

With her nerves on pins and needles, Debi took shallow breaths and forced herself to keep moving. Though her rational side told her Chad was dead, the false hopes she had—wanting to believe he was still alive—gave her the courage to go on.

She followed the flickering pinpoints of glittering lights that seemed to circle around something that led up a stairway.

As she started to climb, the foul odor became more evident with each step. It was almost too much to bear.

Debi barely made it to the top before her legs gave out. "No!"

On her knees, she let out a strangled cry and covered her eyes. The concrete walls of the burial chamber echoed the sounds of her sorrow.

Enclosed by candlelight and gnawing vermin, a scene of horror was set out before her. What was left of Chad's body, his head practically severed, had been torn to pieces. Both arms were completely gone, chewed off at the shoulders, and one leg was missing. It seemed the only thing holding his remains together at all was threads of muscle and tendons.

Stricken with grief, she wrapped her arms around herself and slowly rocked back and forth. "Please, God," she begged. "Please..."

"God?" a guttural voice said behind her. "Do you really believe *he* will help you?"

On sudden impulse, Debi whirled around on her hands and knees. What she saw was so frightening she could barely catch her breath. She felt paralyzed there, her heart pounding wildly, and her breath finally coming in short, sharp gasps.

It was a man—his face twisting and converging into something terrifying. She watched in horror as his features formed into some kind of beast—half-man, half-wolf—with glowing eyes and thick, black, matted fur.

As it moved toward her, she was vaguely aware of someone grabbing her from behind. The next thing she felt was a sharp sting in her left arm, and then everything started to fade and blur.

* * *

After Detective Manuel Sanchez showered and shaved, he was on the road before six in the morning. The rain kept a steady drizzle as he drove to the Presidio National Park to meet up with his partner, Detective Frank Perkins.

An hour ago, he had received a call from his captain about a possible homicide and one missing person located in the vicinity. A 911 call had come in early this morning. About six miles off the park's trails, in a thick, wooded area, a group of hikers came upon a gruesome discovery. They had reported a blanket covered in blood, one bloody tennis shoe, and a human leg. It looked to be a man's shoe going by the size. They found it lying next to the dismembered body part. There were also clothes found nearby that were torn to pieces.

When police got to the scene, they found a silver Toyota Camry parked alongside the road three miles from the crime scene. The registration listed Chad Morgan as the owner of the vehicle. Inside the car, police discovered a purse belonging to a female in her early twenties. Debi Flynn was the name on the license they recovered. Not far from the vehicle, police retrieved a woman's blouse, the material tangled in a thorny bush.

A sick feeling suddenly came over him. Manuel thought of the bodies of Sophie Turner and Todd Blackmon discovered in the Salem Cemetery and the body of Brandon Coghill of which all were ripped to shreds and half-eaten. Their deaths had been brutal, similar to the findings located in the park. Then his thoughts went to the corpse of Carla Rosi his captain and Detective Ratcliff had found. The remains were in the same open grave that Jena McCain had fallen in.

Questions plagued his mind, giving him an unsettling sense of reality. Were all the murders connected? Could this be the same creature from years ago that murdered Carla and his sister? They were all possibilities, yet he could not shake the feeling that there was more than one supernatural creature working together and killing innocent people.

As he drove along, his mind went to the stolen surveillance video of Jimmy Fratianno. Manuel swallowed back the uneasiness that had settled in his stomach. He suspicions were set on Detective Meagan Lacher. Someone must have paid her a hefty price to get that footage. A reporter no doubt. The question was how did she manage to swipe that video? He viewed the precinct's cameras at least a dozen times. There was nothing on it to prove she was the thief. If Detective Lacher was the one that took it, she had to have been a freakin' magician. It was as though the damn thing had vanished in thin air. Now it was just a matter of time before the video became news for the world to see.

The rain had picked up, and the noise from the windshield wipers brought his mind back into focus, but still, that damn missing video would forever be in the back of his mind, frustrating the hell out of him.

He reached for the radio, turning it up, hoping it would clear his head. That's when he heard the news reporter talking about the *werewolf* caught on video.

"Damn it," Manuel muttered under his breath.

I guess the wolf's out of the bag now, so to speak, he thought. In fact, the more he listened, the more it became clear that the surveillance footage at the precinct of Jimmy Fratianno shifting into a rogue wolf had gone public. *Shit!*

One of the commentators on the radio station compared the disturbing video to the murders in the Salem Cemetery, speculating that this could all just be a hoax.

The idea of the man-wolf theory being fake was gaining favor by the minute. A female-voiced commentator presented her thoughts about the creature by saying the cemetery killer could be dressed up in a furred costume. There were even humorous discussions, and jokes about a possible Bigfoot sighting.

Manuel rolled his eyes as he continued to listen to the radio host's humorous speculations.

"In my opinion," the female speaker said, "the killer is using the ridiculous story of a real-life werewolf to draw attention away from his true identity."

"I agree," the other commentator stated. "The cemetery murderer is fabricating a story to cover up his identity and create a panic. The whole thing is nothing but a sick joke. I hope they catch this guy and put him behind bars for the rest of his life."

Thank God, Manuel thought as he arrived at the park. The setting sun had just peeked its way from behind the clouds as the storm moved out. Alongside the road were several police cars, and yellow tape blocked the entrance to the trails that led to the crime scene.

People didn't seem to be buying the story of a mythical beast creating a rampage in the city. There just wasn't enough physical evidence to support the wolf-man story. By what the broadcasters said on the radio, nobody thought the video was real. It was believed to be an elaborate, and well-planned-out device to generate a widespread panic, until a caller's voice came through the radio station.

"I saw the werewolf with my own two eyes," the caller stated. The seriousness of the man's voice was composed and self-assured.

"Are you saying you actually witnessed the creature?" the woman on the radio said.

"I was there when it crashed through the San Francisco Police Department's window," the caller replied.

The other commentator lightly chuckled. "Is that so? How do we know you're not just another person making this up, trying to draw attention?"

"Because," the caller said in a smug tone, "I'm a reporter for the Mercury News, and I've got it all on video."

Son of a bitch, Manuel cursed. "Damn reporters," he muttered and cut the engine. With his hands gripped around the steering wheel, he tilted his head forward and exhaled deeply. Just when the video was thought to be a fraud, some asshole reporter had to go and screw it all up.

As Manuel finally stepped out of his vehicle, Detective Perkins greeted him.

"Looks like we got another homicide, Detective," Perkins said grimly.

"Are you sure you're ready to come back to work?" Manuel asked his partner. "I can take care of things here if you need a few more days off."

"I'm good to go. Doc gave me a full release. How about you? How's that shoulder?"

"It still hurts like hell," Manuel grumbled. "But I'll be fine. Besides, I have too much shit going on with this case to lay around on my ass. I'm sure you feel the same." When Frank nodded, Manuel went on, "So, any luck finding the rest of Mr. Morgan's remains?"

"Nothing so far, but we've got several officers with K9s searching the trails. We're still waiting on the coroner to arrive. Until we get a positive ID on the victim, we can't be sure it's the same person that owns the car that was found."

Manuel sucked in a breath and made a show of squaring his shoulders. "What about the girl? Did anyone find out anything on her?"

"Detective Ratcliff located Ms. Flynn's next of kin. He said, according to her sister, she and Mr. Morgan lived together. Apparently, they were supposed to get married next month. We had a patrol car sent to their apartment this morning. So far, we haven't had any luck locating either one."

Manuel's shoulders sagged as if in defeat. "You think this has anything to do with the cemetery murders?"

Frank considered all possibilities. "I don't know. It could have been a bear," he said. "Or a cougar. It's not uncommon for them to be in this area of the woods. Either one could have dragged the remains back to its den."

"Or a human," Captain Hodge said as he walked up and stood next to Frank.

Frank looked at Hodge in disbelief. "Captain, you really believe a human did that? Going by what was left of the victim, whatever it was had to have been an animal."

"Come on, Captain," Manuel chimed in. "Surely you don't think a man could be responsible for something like this?"

"You know as well as I do madmen are known to have superhuman strength," Hodge said.

"Not like what I saw," Frank replied.

"There's one other possibility we haven't considered," Hodge said, his voice strong and clear. "It could be Jimmy Fratianno. We all have to admit what we witnessed at the station was no hoax. Although our fellow officers and the news think it was one, I know what I saw was real. What happened to Jimmy wasn't just a figment of my imagination," he continued. "You both saw it. I saw it. For crying out loud, we all saw Jimmy shift into..." He hesitated, letting out a deep breath. "...some kind of creature that looked like a damn wolf."

Manuel and Frank suddenly fell silent. Manuel knew if he tried to convince their captain or the precinct that a *real* werewolf was responsible for all the murders, he would end up diagnosed as insane and stripped of his badge. The only way to approach the killings was from the psychopath angle and see where that led.

"There has been a lot of strange things going on lately," Frank broke the silence, eyeing his partner with a worried look. "Hell, I don't know what to believe anymore." He shook his head. "Sometimes I feel like I've stepped into the *Bizarro World*. Nothing makes any damn sense."

"Are you saying you believe Jimmy Fratianno is responsible for all the murders?" Manuel's brow rose as he questioned Hodge. "What about the cemetery attacks? There is no possible way he could have done that. He was locked up behind bars."

Before Hodge could respond, a police officer interrupted and said, "Captain, the coroner just arrived. And we found some kind of animal prints not far from the crime scene."

Hodge turned to the officer and said, "What did they look like?"

The officer shook his head. "It's the damnedest thing, Captain. I've never seen anything like it. It looks to be some type of wolf prints but oddly shaped. Almost human-like, and they're extremely large."

"Shit," Hodge said under his breath. "Make sure you get some impressions, and keep this from the damn press."

When the officer nodded, Hodge looked to Manuel and Frank with a strained jaw. "Let's get this over with, Detectives."

As they moved toward the crime scene, Manuel regretfully told Captain Hodge and his partner about what he had heard on the radio station, not to mention what the reporter had stated.

"Damn reporters." Hodge bit the words out. "Did you get the reporter's name?"

Captain Hodge looked at Manuel, who shook his head. "No, but I know who the SOB is. He stopped me outside the precinct before all *hell* broke loose with Jimmy Fratianno. His name is Paul Reiss. He works for the Mercury News. The bastard tried to get information out of me about the cemetery attacks.”

“I want that damn video confiscated,” Hodge demanded, his throat working convulsively, his hands fisted at his sides.

“You want us to bring him in for questioning?” Detective Perkins asked.

Hodge kept his gaze stoically forward. “As soon as we’re done here, find out where Mr. Reiss resides. I want him picked up and brought in.”

With a nod, Frank said, “Captain, you know he’s not going to willingly turn over that video, right?”

“Yeah,” Hodge replied, exhaustion weighing his words. “One way or the other, I’m sure you two will figure something out.”

“Don’t worry, Cap,” Manuel spoke out. “Come hell or high water, we’re getting that video.”

Hodge huffed out a breath that hung between them for a second or two. “I’m counting on it, Detective.”

Chapter Thirty-Two

When a knock sounded at the door, Jena gulped in steadying breaths. Shortly after, a familiar voice called out, "Jena, are you there?"

Jena swallowed the ache in her throat. God, she wanted to break down and cry her eyes out. After she had welcomed the creature into the Covenant and weakened to the curse, the consequences of it were irreversible. It weighed her down with shame and guilt. She was to live the remainder of her life as a savage killer. According to the battle angels, she had to destroy the creature. It was the only way to control her bloodlust. Innocent lives depended on her. Although she tried to fight it, the thought of killing him was unbearable. It was a mystery, but for some strange reason, she was bound to him as if she was under a spell. The question in her head kept repeating itself like a broken record.

Do I have the strength to go through with it?

Tears brimmed at her eyelids, but she bit her lip to keep them at bay. She had to be strong and face what she had done. Confiding in Angie and confronting the Breedline Covenant was going to be the hardest thing she ever had to do.

Before Jena said a word, she looked over her shoulder at the three angels to gauge their reaction.

Cronus nodded in silence.

"What am I going to say to her?" Jena quietly asked. Her expression appeared as though she was begging for guidance.

"The truth," Helios whispered into her subconscious.

Jena responded with a halfhearted nod.

"Hang on, Angie," Jena finally said. She raised her voice as she started toward the door. "I'm coming."

After only a brief hesitation, Jena reached for the door and opened it. She seemed surprised to see her best friend's grinning face.

"Thank God you're here." Angie's teeth flashed in a wider smile. "I've got exciting news I can't wait to tell you."

Jena looked nervous. "Uh, okay," she muttered.

Angie noticed her troubled expression. "Hey girl, you okay?"

Jena's eyes widened a little. Then her gaze skated sideways to the winged trio waiting inside the room.

"Y-yeah," Jena stammered. "I've got something to tell you too."

Angie's mouth rounded in shock when she caught a glimpse of the three winged giants. They towered to the height of at least ten feet, and their arms were marked with odd symbols. Their enormous, black wings reminded her of the Archangels in the movie, *Legion*.

"What the *hell*?" Angie's words lashed like a whip.

"I can explain," Jena said as she stepped aside. "And don't worry. I promise, Angie, they are the *good* guys. They came here to help me."

Angie slowly peeked around Jena and nervously scanned the mysterious, yet handsome occupants of the room. "Who are you?" she boldly asked.

Cronus crossed the room to stand beside Jena and extended his hand. "My name is Cronus. We were sent by the Creator to help Jena."

A moment passed in silence while Angie stared wide-eyed at the dark-haired angel. In her mind, yellow lights flashed, warning her to proceed with caution. Authority radiated from the angel who seemed to be in charge, making him appear powerful and more dominant than the others. Attached to his waist he had a gold sword, similar to what a Roman gladiator would use. His presence was almost spellbinding.

Angie swallowed hard and nervously reached for his large hand. "Are you supposed to be angels?"

"Yes, Ms. Hawkridge." He lightly squeezed her hand. "We serve God, protecting heaven's gate."

She released his hand and muttered, "I can't believe I'm actually in the presence of real angels." Then she looked at him in question, cocking her head to the side. "Wait a minute. How did you know my name?"

"We're angels. We know just about everyone on earth."

Angie raised a brow. "Really?"

"Yes," Cronus replied, turning toward his comrade in arms. "These are my brothers, Icarus and Helios."

When Icarus nodded and stepped forward, Angie's jaw dropped.

"It's a pleasure to meet you," he murmured.

At the soft purr in his voice, her heart sped into a wild beat.

"Believe me." She batted her brows. "It's all *my* pleasure."

Damn, Angie thought as she ogled the gorgeous angel with a head full of luscious, blond hair. The thick, long strands tumbled around his massive shoulders and accentuated his handsome face. She could never tire of looking at him. Not only was he the most attractive male she had ever seen besides Bull, but his eyes also mesmerized her. The odd silver color in them shimmered like crystals. As she gazed into them, a lump grew in her throat and sweat sheened her forehead. Never in her wildest dreams would she ever imagine an angel to look like him.

Angie's eyes soon fixated on the other angel, who towered over Cronus and Icarus, as he came forward. When she looked up at him, his eyes sparkled like a pair of diamonds. His long, dark braids fell forward as he lowered his head in silence. He had an intimidating and remarkably muscular build that bulged beneath his dark skin tone. The tips of his magnificent wings were sharp as knives, and talons covered the tips of his hands and feet. When he lifted his chin, he spoke to Angie without moving his lips. It was as if he was speaking into her mind.

"I am called Helios." His voice was a deep baritone. *"Happy to make your acquaintance, Miss Angie."*

Angie gazed into Helios's bright eyes with a bewildered look on her face. "Did you just speak into my mind?"

He nodded in silence.

"Helios has a special gift," Cronus spoke out. "He is telepathic."

As Angie opened her mouth to speak, she flinched when someone came up behind her and placed a hand on her shoulder.

"I'm sorry, Angie," Tim said from directly behind her. "I didn't mean to startle you."

When Angie turned around, she was surprised to see Tim and the crowd of people waiting in the hallway. She also spotted a male with long, black hair standing next to Eve she did not recognize. The odd color of his eyes looked like flames of a fire, and he had an arrogant and conceited way about him. Whoever he was, it was obvious he and Eve were in some kind of a relationship going by the way they held hands.

"I'm guessing you already know about our guests," Angie finally replied to Tim, her eyes shifting back to the trio of winged giants. Then her eyes focused on her best friend. "They're here to help Jena."

Tim stepped forward with his eyes locked on the angel with the sword. "We never got the chance to thank you," he said as he extended his hand. "We would have never been able to defeat the Fury without your help. We are forever in your debt."

Cronus reached out and briefly shook hands with Tim. "You're welcome, Mr. Ross. Our priority is protecting heaven's gate and humanity."

Tim narrowed his eyes. "How did you know my name?"

Cronus smiled a little. "We have our ways."

Tim nodded, looking at Cronus in question. "Sebastian tells us the Fury is back on earth. Is it true they are no longer a threat?"

"They have taken an oath to protect all mankind," Cronus firmly stated. "In return for their service, they have been promised absolution."

Tessa stepped forward and stood next to Tim. "Can they be trusted?"

"They saved my life," Sebastian spoke out. When everyone turned to look in his direction, he continued to say, "If it wasn't for them, Lucifer would have killed me."

Cronus supported Sebastian's statement by saying, "He speaks the truth."

"I don't understand," Tessa said, focusing her eyes on Cronus. "If Sebastian was in the heavens, how could Lucifer get to him?"

"Sebastian was in a place called the In-between," Cronus explained. "It's the outer surrounding of heaven. All battle angels reside there to protect heaven's gate."

Jace moved in behind Tessa and said, "What are you protecting it from?"

"Demons," Cronus simply said.

Jace shrugged. "Demons?"

"We fight in battle with Satan's soldiers," Cronus told him. "He sends his chosen with the intention of destroying us."

"Is that possible?" Kyle chimed in for the first time.

"Right now we outnumber them," Icarus told him. "But if his soldiers continue to rise, we might have a problem."

It was all Jena could do not to spill her guts and get everything out. She opened her mouth and said, "I'm going to become..." Her words trailed off helplessly. She reached out and touched her best friend's hand. "Oh, Angie..."

Angie looked at her with concern. "Jena, what is it?"

Angie, I want to tell you the truth, but I'm afraid, she thought. *I'm afraid to let you down.*

"I'm going to become the creature." Jena could hardly get the words out. She had to tell her. She had to tell the Covenant. If she didn't tell them soon, she was going to explode. "I will hunt evil, kill them for their blood, and it will deplete Satan's soldiers."

The look on Angie's face appeared confused. "What are you talking about?"

"Angie, I..." Jena tried to choose her words carefully. "I gave in to the curse."

"Jena—"

"Please," Jena cut her off. "Let me explain to everyone." Her eyes roamed over the crowd that gathered in from the hallway. "I'm sorry. I wish I could take it all back." Tears rose up in the back of her throat. "I don't know why, and I know it sounds insane, but for some reason, I'm connected to the creature. It's like I'm in some kind of trance whenever he comes in contact with me."

The silence that followed was painful.

Cronus placed his hand on Jena's shoulder. "You are spellbound," he spoke softly. "You had no way of resisting him. It's part of the curse. I don't want you to blame yourself for his depravity and cunning trickery. Understand?"

In spite of feeling guilty, Jena managed a reluctant nod.

"So, if you're battle angels," Angie's tone was weary, "why can't you destroy the creature? Surely you can help Jena, can't you?"

"The only thing that can destroy this particular creature is one of its own," Cronus explained. "That means Jena must shift and bite the creature. If she is successful, her lust for human blood will not be for the innocent. She will only hunt evil beings. Jena will be eliminating dark souls before Satan can use them for soldiers."

"So what you're saying is," Jace blurted out, "Jena has no choice. She is going to become that damn *thing*, except she will only hunt down evil people. Sort of like the grim reaper."

For a second Cronus smiled at him, though it appeared to Jace that the look in the angel's eyes seemed dismal.

"Mr. Chamberlain," Cronus said, "the best way to answer your questions is yes. It's a way of serving justice, one that will serve a higher purpose, and our only hope at destroying the creature, saving Jena, and protecting our home."

"We need to gather the Covenant soon," Tim interjected. "And I want to speak with the Fury."

Cronus slightly bowed his head. "Gather your people. We will return tomorrow at dusk. We will bring our other two fellow soldiers, and the Fury." Then he added, "Should we take Sebastian back with us?"

"No," Tessa reluctantly said. "He can stay here."

Cronus nodded, and everyone looked toward Tessa, shocked by her statement, but kept their opinions to themselves.

"Thank you, Tessa," Sebastian said.

As Jace opened his mouth to protest, Tessa held up a hand to silence him before he got a word out. He let out an aggravated groan and flashed Sebastian a resentful glare.

Breaking the tension, Angie addressed Cronus with a question concerning her best friend. "What will happen if Jena doesn't destroy this creature?"

"She will live for eternity..." He exhaled a deep breath. "...killing innocent people."

On impulse, Angie reached out to Jena. "I'm here for you, Jena. I'll always be there for you."

As Jena took ahold of her hand, Angie tugged her into an embrace.

Jena buried her face into her best friend's hair. "Oh God, I'm so sorry," she whispered, trying not to cry. "Please forgive me, Angie."

It seemed like an eternity that they held each other. When Angie finally pulled away, she said, "You have nothing to be sorry for. It's not your fault, Jena. It was never your fault. Not any of it."

Chapter Thirty-Three

A nightmare woke Debi from her state of unconsciousness. As she opened her eyes, she discovered that someone had bound together her hands and feet. Debi struggled to move, but it was hopeless, the ropes were too tight. Exhaling a deep breath, she quickly surveyed her surroundings. The only light in the cold, damp room was from several flickering, long-stem candles. They formed a circle around her, illuminating the eerie darkness. Debi then realized she was on top of some kind of platform.

Oh God, please, she begged silently. *Please help me.*

Suddenly, blurred images flashed before her. She remembered the man—whose face contorted and twisted into something unholy—that had approached her. Then she recalled the terror she felt when his features were no longer human. It was at that moment she knew who the hideous creature was—the one who had savagely killed the man she was engaged to marry. Before she could open her mouth to scream, someone from behind had drugged her. Although she had no recollection at all who it was, the horrible memory of Chad was still fresh in her mind.

Debi could feel tears brimming in her eyes until they spilled over and flooded from the corners. Her mind thought back to the shocking and unspeakable condition of her fiancé's body: bloody, dismembered, and broken. She could still smell his already decaying flesh.

Her head was spinning. She tried to gather herself, tried to think, to calm her frantic breathing before she hyperventilated and passed out.

Trembling, she prayed for a miracle. "Please, God," she said barely above a whisper. "Please don't let me die…" Her words trailed off when she heard voices not far away.

"It's done," a voice she did not recognize said. "Everything is ready for Jena," he went on, his words curling off his tongue like dark silk.

"And the girl?"

Debi instantly recalled that particular voice. It was the same taunting and sinister voice she heard earlier, the one that lured her to Chad's body. He too spoke in a similar accent, pronouncing the words as though he was from the South.

What do they want with me? Debi fearfully thought. *And who is Jena?*

"She's prepared," the other man replied, "just as you instructed."

"Excellent. You've done well, as always."

"Have you ever known me to fail, brother?"

He leveled him a speculative look. His voice was smooth as velvet. "Of all my family, you've proven most faithful, little brother. Not once have you faltered. You've always looked after my best interests."

A frown settled across his brow as his eyes focused on the window directly behind his little brother. "In all the years," he went on, "do you ever think back on our human lives?"

His brother's laugh was humorless. "Why trudge up those memories? That was ages ago. I hardly recall those days."

A moment, almost mournful, hung between them. It wasn't long before the eldest of the two turned from the window and broke the silence. "Admit it, little brother. You remember more than you let on. Why do you always deny what you used to be? Is it that you're ashamed of the human life you once had?"

"What's in the past is no longer of importance to me," he replied. "Some things are better left forgotten."

"Well, unlike you, I can never forget some things." He cocked a brow. "My first love, Isabella. She always reminded me of a rose blossom. Delicate, and captivatingly beautiful to the eyes, yet forbidden to the touch. Just like the prickly-stemmed rose, Isabella too, had her own share of painful thorns."

His younger brother thought back. "I remember how much you loved her, and she you. Until..." he paused, his voice was gentle but firm, "she chose a different path."

He looked at his little brother with a deep and remorseful stare. "Yes," he murmured. "She betrayed me."

A heavy silence fell between them. He watched his older brother glance away, heard the weariness of his sigh.

"But now, you have another. You'll see, brother. Jena will prove to be a worthy bride."

"Yes, she will." Pausing, he added, "It would break my heart if she betrays me. Or even *thought* of betraying me as my Isabella did."

He watched as his brother's shoulders slumped, as his eyes took on a low-spirited gloom. And he felt that strong feeling of despair that always came when he spoke of Isabella. Her name brought up the past, and the memories that came with it. For a brief moment, his mind went back in time as if in a vivid dream.

* * *

Nearly two centuries ago, in the early 1800s, the world was a different place then. During the time living as a human, he and his older brother—whose ancestry derived from white, upper class—had everything handed to them on a silver platter. Their father owned a plantation in New Orleans and their mother inherited her family's fortune. With the combined wealth, they had a countryside mansion built, surrounded by acres of flourishing land. Their fortunate prosperity gave them many luxuries: imported furniture, expensive oil paintings, and vintage silk tapestries that decorated their home. While most of their peers lived in the middle class and poverty, their childhood lavished them in a wealthy lifestyle filled with Victorian fashion, fancy restaurants, and elaborate parties. Their mother would not settle for anything less. He and his family loved living this life. All except for his older brother. He hated those things. He was different from the rest of the family. The Catholic Church was what mattered to him. And that's where he met his beloved Isabella.

Isabella was breathtakingly beautiful. She had the fairest of skin, flawless like a porcelain doll. Her eyes were the color of the ocean, a pale blue with tiny specks of gold that glittered in the outer edges. Her honey-blonde hair hung in thick waves

257

past her small waist. Isabella was tall for a female, yet feminine and graceful. It wasn't unusual for a young, beautiful girl like Isabella to have several suitors, but it was obvious to everyone that her heart belonged to his brother.

The day his brother began courting Isabella, it was the year the nation had endured a widespread depression following the Panic of 1819 and the momentous issue of the extension of slavery into the territories. At the time, his older brother was in his twenties and already established in his father's flourishing business, regardless of the economy. He and Isabella courted for nearly three summers. His love for her seemed to have no end or limits. Soon after Isabella's eighteenth birthday, he went to her father to ask permission for her hand in marriage. The minute her father gave him his blessing, his brother—who was confident she would accept his marriage proposal—secretly arranged their wedding engagement with family and friends. Unfortunately, when he proposed to Isabella, she refused. A few weeks prior, she had decided on another path, vowing a life of celibacy. She made the choice to dedicate her life to the service of the Church and move to England where she would join a women's convent.

The devastating news destroyed his brother, nearly driving him to madness. He stopped attending church, refused to eat, and soon gave up on life itself. Overwhelmed with grief and despair, he abandoned his family and his love for God.

He briefly closed his eyes and remembered the day of his brother's death. It had been only a month after Isabella's rejection, and the worst day of his life. His brother's broken heart led him to take his own life. He left a note indicating his despondency. He could remember every detail as though he had a photographic memory.

My dearest Isabella,

Without you, I cannot take another breath. I can only live, either altogether with you or not at all. Yet you have made your choice. Please forgive me. I regret, the decision I must make.

Then another unforgettable memory—one that was irrevocable—flashed into his mind like it was yesterday. It was the day a dark and mysterious man dressed in a long, hooded cloak approached him the night before his brother's burial. He addressed himself as the Master and offered to return his brother Ashton back from the dead. He gave him a choice. In exchange for the gift of immortality, he must freely render his soul. Which meant he had to offer his brother's as well. What did it matter? Ash had committed suicide. His soul was already damned. Eternal damnation might be a hefty price, but for his big brother, he was willing to pay.

The memory of what he had done nearly broke him. If only he had known what would become of Ash, he would have never chosen to resurrect him. That dreadful night sealed his brother's fate and cursed him for eternity. Yes, they were to live forever, free from sickness and disease, but it was not worth the harrowing result. Unknowingly, Ash was to become something different... something diabolical and unholy.

He followed the Master's every detail. He instructed him to place his brother's corpse inside an aboveground tomb in the cemetery known as the "Cities of the Dead." It was imperative that he cover the body with sanctified soil before he sealed the coffin. Then, within three days, Ash would once again return to the living as promised.

He would never forget that third day. Everything about it would forever haunt his memory. The night had been relentlessly humid and muggy. As he stood outside the wrought iron gates that housed the dead, the full moon shining down from above gave him enough light to see by.

It wasn't long before he located his brother's crypt. As he approached the oblong house-like tomb, he reached out with a shaky hand and inserted a skeleton key to unlock the door. The rusty hinges creaked as he slowly pushed at the entrance. Although the brightness of the moon produced enough light to get him there, he prepared himself by bringing with him a lantern. The darkness instantly brightened as he aimed the light inside the crypt. He nervously hesitated for a moment before he crossed the threshold. The brightness from the portable light fell in all sorts of odd forms as he moved it around. The inside of the old structure was thick with dust, and in the corners were masses of spiders' webs. Oddly, he felt as though someone was following behind him. He continuously looked over his shoulder at every sound and every shadow, but there was no sign of anyone. His fear of the unknown led his imagination afar. Under different circumstances, if it were someone other than his brother, he would have abandoned the task at this point. Bringing Ash back to life gave him strength and a purpose to continue.

Finally, he came upon his brother's resting place and shined the light over the top of the long, narrow box. Straightaway he reached to open it, and as he lifted the wooden lid, he positioned the light so it would shine inside. But to his unforeseen revelation, the coffin was empty. Only the remnants of the holy soil remained.

It was certainly a surprise to find Ash's body missing, and it gave him a considerable shock. Then he wondered if all this had been just a ruse. His mind toyed with all the possible implications. Perhaps the cemetery's undertaker had taken his brother's body. He instantly became unnerved and angry with the one who addressed himself as the Master for taking him on such a deceitful journey. He was angry with himself for his gullibility.

As he closed the coffin lid, he heard the rustle of movement coming from behind like the sounds of heavy footsteps. He quickly spun around with the lantern in his hand and held it up.

What he saw brought him to his knees. His eyes rounded in sheer terror. *It cannot be*, he feverishly thought. *No...*

* * *

"Why do you always think back on that day?" his older brother said, bringing him back to focus.

He regarded him with a deep and compassionate stare. "How can I not?" he replied, keeping his voice low. "It will forever haunt me."

"Eternity is a long, long time, little brother. There's no sense in digging up old wounds, am I right?"

He conceded with a nod. "Yes, of course. You're right. It's just that..." He paused and shrugged. "I feel responsible for—"

"You are not to blame for anything," he said abruptly. "'Twas I who made the choice to end my own life. If not for you, I would be suffering in hell's eternal flame."

"But I..." he briefly paused, swallowing the bitter taste in his mouth. Mentioning that particular incident had been almost too much for him to bear. "I damned your soul."

"No, little brother." He shook his head. "You gave my life back. Why bother yourself with such things?" He shrugged. "You know my true feelings of this. I will be forever grateful to you."

"It's Jena," he told him. "She looks so much like *her*. I cannot help but remember the pain Isabella caused you. Thinking about it reminds me of—"

"Indeed she does," he quickly remarked. "Why do you think I chose her? At first, it was not clear why I felt so drawn to Jena that night in the cemetery. Then shortly, it finally came to me. Jena is a direct descendant of Isabella. That was the moment I knew she was the one. And this time, I will succeed." His mouth tilted into a sinful grin. "It's all a matter of... shall we say... selective breeding."

"How do you think Jena will feel when she discovers the truth?"

"The truth about her?" He cocked a brow. "Or Isabella?"

There was a moment of silence. Then he looked full into his big brother's dark eyes and said, "Both."

"Don't I always have a plan for everything?"

"Yes." He flashed a slight smile. "And more."

"Soon, very soon, all that Isabella had once promised and then denied me will finally be mine. I will have a bride, and then offspring to carry on my legacy. The name Ratcliff will live for centuries to come."

"And what of the battle angels? As of now, they are joining with the Breedline."

"I don't think you need to worry, little brother. They cannot destroy me."

"But Jena can."

"I am fully aware. And I am prepared." His tone was faintly bitter. "You, of all people, should know that, Nicolas."

He slightly bowed his head. "I do not doubt you, brother."

"Before Jena's arrival, I will need to feed once again." His eyes hazed over and a low growl trickled over his lips. "Whilst I'm gone, keep watch on the girl."

"Yes, brother," Nicolas obediently complied, glancing down in shame. "I will take care of everything."

"Of course you will." A smile played across his face the way Lucifer might have smiled moments before he fell from heaven. "You always do..." He seemed lost in thought for a few moments, then went on to say, "...take care of everything."

Nicolas watched miserably as his brother turned away and disappeared into the shadows of the dark and musky place that housed so much death. The images of all the innocent lives lost filled his head. His brother would have to die soon, for this might be his last chance to put an end to the curse.

Despite his disgust at the foul things his brother had done and his horror at what he was planning to do, deep down there was also a feeling of guilt and a strange sort of disloyalty. Betraying his own flesh and blood was going to break his heart.

He tried to think. Time was ticking. He had but a day to formulate a plan. Somehow, he had to find a way into the Breedline Covenant to confront Jena with the truth. He had to convince her to kill his brother. That would be the hardest part, for she was spellbound. Then, more importantly, he had to save the innocent girl his brother kept prisoner.

He paced back and forth, straining his brain to come up with a plan. Suddenly, he stopped and ran a hand through his hair. He looked puzzled for a moment then uttered a small gasp. "The journal."

Chapter Thirty-Four

After the battle angels exited the Covenant, promising to return tomorrow at dusk, everyone else turned in for the night except for Jena. She invited Angie to stay behind so they could talk. It had been a long and exhausting day. There were things Jena needed to say to her best friend, and hopefully, it wouldn't ruin the close friendship they shared. So far, after Jena spilled her guts in front of Angie and the Covenant, telling them about how she had weakened to the curse, not a single person looked down on her. In fact, everyone including the angels was nothing but supportive. They all had accepted what would become of her.

This was the first time in Jena's life, excluding Angie, that friends and family didn't judge her for her imperfections. Although her parents made her believe for years that she suffered with schizophrenia—after she told them of her special abilities to speak with the dead—she *now* knew God had given her this gift for a reason. She was born to give peace to the dead and their grieving families. That gave her a renewed purpose in life.

"Please sit," Jena said as she patted the seat next to her on the couch. "I have some things I need to tell you, Ang."

As Angie sat down, Jena fought back tears. She'd promised herself that she wouldn't break down, no matter how guilty she felt.

"Look, Jena," Angie said, noticing the tense look on her best friend's face. "You know I don't blame you for what's happened." She took hold of Jena's hand. "We don't have to talk about this if you don't want to."

Jena's eyes stared straight into hers, filled with so much raw emotion. "I have to talk about it. There's things that I…" she hesitated as her eyes misted with tears, though she made a gallant effort to hold them back. "Things I haven't told anyone, and you're the only one I can tell this to."

Angie went silent for a moment. Just thinking of what Jena had been through—and what worse things she had to endure—made her feel helpless. If there were a way to take her friend's place, she would do it in a heartbeat.

She leaned closer, and lightly squeezed Jena's hand. "It doesn't matter what it is, Jena. You can always tell me anything. Hell, you're like the closet thing I have to a sister. You know this will only stay between the two of us, right?"

Jena nodded and took a long, deep breath, struggling to get her emotions under control. She felt sad all of a sudden, and disappointed in herself. She'd welcomed the creature into her bed with wide-open arms and freely gave in to him. She instantly felt ashamed. Deep down, Jena knew she wasn't born evil, despite whatever she had to do in order to destroy the creature. However, after she completed the task the angels set her out to do, she would become something she despised—the same *thing* that killed Todd and Sophie. Once again, she was at the mercy of the memories of her weaknesses. *His alluring voice... his lips upon her throat... the taste of her own blood... their intertwined bodies moving together as though they were one...*

"Hey, girl." Angie's voice drew her firmly back again, forcing her memories away. "It's going to be okay. I'm here for you."

Jena attempted a smile, and then she choked out, "I slept with *him*."

Angie felt blindsided. She stared back at Jena speechless.

"I mean not the creature itself. He was in his human form, and he didn't force me," Jena went on. "I welcomed him. I wanted it."

"No, Jena." Angie's strained voice finally came out. "It's not your fault. He had you under some kind of spell."

"I should have known better. I was fully aware of what I was doing. I mean, when it happened, it was like a dream, but at the same time, I was kind of—"

"Hypnotized?" Angie said, cutting Jena off.

"It was more like some kind of connection with him." Jena paused, as if thinking. "I know it sounds insane, but even when he first came to me in the hospital, there was something familiar about him. Like somehow I've met him before. Perhaps in another life."

Angie shrugged. "Maybe." She seemed to accept this without surprise. "Anything is possible. Did this *man-beast-werewolf thing* happen to mention its name?"

Jena frowned. "Man-beast-werewolf thing?"

"Well?" Angie cocked a brow. "What would you call it?"

"I don't know?" Jena heaved a deep breath. "He didn't say. But you make it sound so—"

"Terrifying?" Angie uttered suddenly.

Jena hesitated as she took in the concerned expression in her friend's eyes. "You're right. I should be terrified, or even repulsed by him. For heaven's sake, he killed Todd and Sophie. But..." She shook her head. "I'm not."

"Whoever *he* is," Angie continued, "it's obvious he wants to control you, and I'll be damned if I'm going to let that happen."

Jena shook her head again. She couldn't bear the thought of another person she cared about becoming the creature's next victim.

"Angie, I don't want you getting involved. It would kill me if anything happened to you."

"Listen to me, Jena McCain." Her tone was stern. "Like it or not, I'm in this with you. Besides, I might be able to help you fight this thing."

Jena studied her friend's face with a look of confusion. "But how?"

"Well..." Angie sounded resigned. "It kind of happened unexpected. Last night..." she hesitated with a slight grin on her face, "Bull and I hooked up."

Jena stiffened for a second, and then blurted, "Are you serious?"

Angie winked and gave Jena a solemn nod.

"That's a good thing, right?" Jena asked.

"Oh, yeah." Angie batted her brows. "It's definitely good."

"So, are you saying what I think you're saying? That you got your—"

"Breedline wolf," Angie finished Jena's sentence. "Yes, and that means I can help you fight this thing."

"No, Angie." Jena let out a weary sigh. "I can't let you do that. Besides, you cannot kill him. You heard what the angels said. I'm the only one that can destroy the creature."

Angie rolled her eyes and continued to argue, "I'm helping, and that's final. So don't try to change my mind. I'm not taking no for an answer."

Jena looked at Angie in total frustration. "Let's agree to sleep on it." She shut her eyes for a second, then opened them and yawned. "We can talk about it tomorrow."

"Okay, okay," Angie groaned as she got to her feet. "We'll talk in the morning."

As Angie started for the door, Jena stood up and said, "Ang, can I ask you a personal question?"

"Jena, you know you can ask me anything. We've always been an open book."

"What was it like? I mean, how did it feel to shift into a wolf?"

"It was the best thing I've ever experienced, aside from the wonderful and multiple orgasms Bull gave me." Memories of that night made Angie bite on her bottom lip. "I feel like a teenager all over again. It's like I've been reborn."

Jena smiled at her. "That sounds wonderful." She briefly closed her eyes, envisioning the image of her own transformation. The creature she had shifted into was hideous and terrifying. It was definitely *not* a wonderful experience. More like a nightmare.

Then Jena looked her friend square in the eyes and asked, "What did your Breedline wolf look like?"

"Well, you've seen those *Twilight* movies, right?"

When Jena nodded, Angie said, "The Breedline wolves are bigger."

Jena's eyes rounded. "No way," she spouted. "They're like the size of horses."

"Yeah," Angie replied. "That's why we have to keep our species from the human world. Can you imagine the hysteria we would cause if we were to show ourselves?"

"I'm sure it would," Jena said, and then she added, "I wish I shifted into a beautiful Breedline wolf." Tears suddenly came to her eyes. "The *thing...*" She hesitated for a second and released a heavy sigh. "I change into… it's the most terrifying thing imaginable, Angie. I have seen myself as the creature." She shook her head. "It's just awful."

Angie placed her hand on Jena's shoulder and lightly squeezed. "It's going to be okay, Jena. I don't care what you look like. I will always see you as my best friend. Nothing will ever change that."

Jena wiped her eyes with her hand. "Thanks, Ang."

"Can I ask *you* something?" Angie said, narrowing her eyes.

Jena nodded. "Of course."

"What does *he* look like? And I'm talking about his human form."

"He's beautiful," Jena simply said. "He has an eighteenth-century Gothic aura about him: long dark hair, beautiful complexion, and his lips…" Then Jena laughed a little. "It's funny. His features are similar to the actor that portrayed Vlad the Impaler in that movie, *Dracula Untold*." Then she let out a long sigh. "Go figure?"

"Are you talking about Luke Evans?"

When Jena nodded, Angie lifted her brows. "Damn, girl. I can see why he has you so spellbound."

Jena smirked. "Now you know why it's so hard to reject him. He has such a strong hold on me. Anyway," she went on, "let's turn in for the night. I'm exhausted."

Before Angie walked out, she turned to Jena and said, "Remember, you hold all the power, Jena. And I think the creature knows it. Keep that in mind."

Jena nodded and said, "I think it's great about you and Bull." She smiled a little. "I'm happy for you, Ang."

"Thanks, Jena. I'll see you in the morning."

As soon the door closed, Jena headed straight for the bathroom and propped herself wearily against the sink. Angie's words echoed over, and over in her head.

You hold all the power, Jena.

Angie had sounded so sure of her, but Jena doubted herself, and her strength.

"What a nightmare," she whispered, looking into the mirror at her own reflection.

Still shaken by all the previous events, one thing in particular weighed heavily on her mind. She had to do the unthinkable. She had to kill *him.*

Jena's heart twisted in agony just thinking about it. *Could I actually go through with it?* she silently said to herself. *If so, how?*

Suddenly, the light above the mirror flicked once, and then went out. A shiver went through her, bringing her thoughts back to focus.

Jena looked away from the mirror and turned to the bathroom door. The dark seemed to swallow her whole. *What?* It didn't make any sense. She was sure she had left the door open. Her heart began to pound, filling her ears with panic. She leaned back against the porcelain sink and tried desperately to get a grip on reality.

Maybe I forgot that I closed it. Pull yourself together, girl, and just go check the light switch.

As Jena blindly made her way to the door, the illumination shining underneath barely gave her enough light to see by. She ran her hand along the wall, searching aimlessly for the light switch. Somehow, it had mysteriously switched off. *But how?* When she flipped it on, nothing happened. Determined to stay calm, she reached for the door and tried the knob. It wouldn't turn. She pulled at the door, but it did no good. *Has someone locked me inside?*

In spite of the situation, Jena tried to remain calm. *Think, Jena,* she thought, trying to reason with herself. *There has to be a good explanation. The door must be stuck. It doesn't lock from the outside.*

Out of nowhere, a blast of prickly, cold air washed over her. Then, a voice came to her, like a gentle whisper.

"Jena..."

She stiffened at the sound of the voice. Although it had a familiar southern drawl, Jena realized it was not *him.*

She built up the courage and called out, "Who's there?"

There was no answer, only silence.

Swallowing the lump in her throat, Jena listened through the stillness. All of a sudden, the creak of the floorboards made her flinch. It was coming from the other side of the door. It sounded like footsteps.

She should be terrified, especially after finding herself locked in a dark room. Sure, she felt a little shaken and bewildered. *But not terrified.*

Instead, a rush of excitement kicked in with such force that she felt a smile tug at the corners of her mouth. As she inhaled a deep breath, she caught the scent of a man's cologne that enveloped her senses. It was a wonderfully manly scent of sandalwood, citrus, and something with its own unique essence. Then, to her surprise, something slid underneath the door.

As Jena looked down, she noticed a book. She could tell that it was unique although she only had the light from the small space below the door. The leather binding on the book appeared brittle and cracked with age.

She stood over it for several more moments, hesitating to pick it up. Slowly, she knelt down to get a closer look. As she peered down at the tattered ledger that was covered in dust, she chewed at her bottom lip, wondering who had left it, and why? Obviously, whoever it was had gone now. For some reason, Jena sensed that the book had something to do with *him.*

With a trembling hand, she reached for it. At the very moment she took it in her grasp, the lights suddenly came on, and the door made a noise as it slightly inched open.

Jena ignored the fact that she'd been stuck in a pitch-black room, so dark she could barely see her hand in front of her face, and made herself comfortable on the floor. She found herself completely enchanted by this peculiar book.

The gold, engraved letters on the outside were hard to make out, but it appeared to be someone's name. It was a journal, or some sort of logbook, she finally realized.

Smoothing her hand over the front, Jena wiped away most of the dust until she was able to read the name. It apparently belonged to a Nicolas J. Ratcliff.

Carefully, she opened it. The regal handwriting inside seemed to be written with a quill, and some of the ink was a little faded. Whoever this Nicolas was, he couldn't possibly still be alive, going by the date at the top of the page. The first official record of events dated back in 1819. Then she wondered. Who had been this Nicolas Ratcliff, and what had become of him? What secrets did the journal hold? Jena felt as though she was strangely drawn to it and found she couldn't go to bed until her curiosity was put to rest. Maybe this Mr. Ratcliff had some kind of connection to the man that held her spellbound... to the creature she had to destroy.

Desperate for answers, Jena began to read.

September 26, 1819—I must confess that I have never written down a single word in this journal, but today I find myself in a state of uncertainty. For my moral conscience will not allow me to keep silent any longer. It soothes me to express myself here, if only on paper. It is like professing to one's self his darkest secrets and forbidden desires.

I, Nicolas Jacob Ratcliff, regret what I must declare. I write this so that perhaps my damned soul will someday regain redemption. This is the record of what I have chosen, and the repercussions of my sins.

It all started in the summer of 1817, the day my brother, Ashton Christopher Ratcliff, met his beloved, Isabella Rose Westfield. That day forever changed his life and mine.

I couldn't blame Ash for falling deeply in love with her. Isabella's beauty was breathtaking and somehow hypnotizing. Even in a crowd, her presence was compelling. Isabella radiated an aura of purity and innocence that was intoxicating. The way she moved, the way she talked, the way she smelled, it all created a powerful temptation.

In spite of the fact that she was taller than most of the young girls her age, she carried herself with elegance and grace. Her long, thick hair tumbled past her shoulders in curls that she always kept pulled back in a stylish arrangement. Her pale blue irises were the color of the ocean, a trait inherited from her father along with her honey-blonde hair.

Isabella turned the heads of nearly all the eligible bachelors in New Orleans. Many of them were reputable and young, around Ash's age. I, too, found myself captivated by her beauty, but it didn't take long for Isabella to become fascinated by my brother's witty and charismatic charm. She had a way of looking at Ash with those amazing sapphire eyes, leaving him to believe he was the only one for her, and nothing could stand between them.

Ash was taller than my father and I, and more broad-shouldered, with sinewy musculature that lent well to the current fashion of snug tailoring in breeches and coats. Although we were three years apart, we had very similarities in our features. We both had ink-black hair like our mother. Ash kept his tied at the nape with a simple leather strap, and I used the finest silk money could buy. His dark eyes were sharp, piercing with a drive for success and fulfillment. I had my father's amethyst eyes. Not only did Ash inherit our family's good looks, he was also brilliant. In his early twenties, he had already established a career in our father's cotton business. Ash was a respectable and honorable man, whom I dearly admired. He had a gentle soul, integrity, and a kind heart, all the attributes I wished I had. Wealth had no value to him. What profits he did gain he gave mostly to the church and to those in need. Where I indulged in wealth and materialistic things, Ash lived a modest lifestyle. Although he had many good qualities, his devotion to the Catholic Church was what won Isabella's heart.

Our family lived a lavish and rich lifestyle, but still, we were decent people. Unlike Ash, however, we were not as faithful to the church and we took value in the almighty dollar. I suppose no one is without imperfections. No matter our good intentions and sincerity, we all have sinful ways.

At the beginning of the courtship, my mother became suspicious of Isabella's true intentions, worried she was marrying my brother for the family's fortune. She felt Ash was choosing far beneath himself and disagreed with the mismatch. To speak truthfully, Isabella was more than worthy of my brother. Ash considered himself the one marrying down. Although she did not come from money, Isabella's family was highly respected in the community. Her father ministered a small, reserved congregation in Louisiana, and her mother dedicated her spare time as a missionary. When they met Ash, they treated him, along with myself, like part of their family.

My brother ignored our mother's distaste and courted Isabella for nearly three summers before he asked her father for her hand in marriage. At the tender age of sixteen, it was imperative that the courtship remained supervised. Isabella's father forbade her to marry until she reached an appropriate age.

Seemingly odd, I was the one that her father chose as their chaperon. Of course, I agreed. I would do anything for my brother. Granted that we were opposite when it came to our lifestyle, Ash and I were considerably close. I accompanied them to every party, and to every social function. At times, on summer evenings, I stayed a fair distance while they took leisure walks in the park and picnicked by the river. Perhaps a stolen kiss or two, Ash honored her father's wishes and behaved like a true gentleman. Even though it took time away from my personal life, I didn't mind. I enjoyed seeing Ash so full of life and lucky in love. Besides, I grew a fondness for Isabella. It seemed she adored my brother and treated me as though I was part of her family already. There was no doubt in my mind that Izzy, a pet name my brother chose for Isabella, would someday agree to be his wife. If anyone deserved happiness, it was those two.

To this day, I can still remember how excited Ash became as Isabella's eighteenth birthday drew near. Alas, his beloved Isabella would soon become his blushing bride. Unfortunately, the happiest day of his life turned for the worst.

A few weeks prior to Ash's proposal, Isabella completely took the wind out of his sails, including my own. Instead of marriage, she chose another path, vowing a life of celibacy. She refused his hand in marriage to embrace her religion. Isabella decided to move to England and dedicate her life to a women's convent.

At first, Ash didn't believe her. He thought it was merely her nerves getting the best of her, or perhaps a lack of maturity. He begged her to sleep on it. That night, my brother and I prayed. As soon as the sun rose the next day, Ash felt certain she would come to reason and agree to be his wife. Although Isabella agreed to sleep on it, she did not change her mind. Her final decision broke my brother's heart. Ash had offered Isabella the best of both worlds—a respectable Christian husband and the passion of a man who would do anything to earn her love—and he believed he could make her happy. How foolish he'd been.

The devastating news destroyed Ash, driving him to madness. I tried everything I could to help him, but nothing would ease his pain, not even the strong bond we shared as siblings. It wasn't long after Isabella's rejection that my brother isolated himself from everyone. He even refused to obtain nourishment. Ash had always been an intensely physical man, to this broken, frail, and decrepit person that I barely recognized. So overcome with grief, he soon abandoned our father's business, and our family, his faith, and then finally life itself.

The night my brother took his own life, I begged God for mercy. I, too, wanted to die.

As Jena finished the last paragraph, she felt she could no longer continue to read any further. It was as though she could feel Nicolas's loss like it was her own. Then she wondered what he had meant when he said his soul was damned. Her curiosity got the better of her, and she vowed to find out as soon as she awoke the next morning.

She carefully closed the journal, wondering why she felt so overwhelmed for this stranger. As Jena brought the tattered leather-bound to her chest, she held it close to her heart and whispered, "I'm so sorry, Nicolas."

Chapter Thirty-Five

The next morning, as soon as Jena opened her eyes, she couldn't wait to read more of Nicolas's journal. As she reached toward the nightstand and withdrew it from the dresser drawer, her heart raced with anticipation. It almost felt as though she'd known him somehow. Although his story pained her so, she found herself enchanted by this stranger's touching memoir. She opened it up and continued to read.

September 27, 1819—I begin to fear as I write in this journal that Ash will someday find it, although I must continue to record what has become of my brother, for he is no longer human, nor am I.

Goosebumps rose on Jena's skin. Strangely, she could see an image as it slowly revealed itself, but only in her mind. It was a man's face. A handsome man with mesmerizing lavender eyes, the electrifying pull of them seemingly hypnotic. He oddly looked to be from another era of time, resembling a style from the eighteenth century. His regal features were both soft and masculine. He had his long, dark hair tied back with a blue silk ribbon. His flawless, pale skin appeared as though it had never seen the sun. There was a sense of heartache about him and a restless energy in his eyes that brought on an overwhelming sadness to her. It was at that moment, as this man captivated her in a way she could not understand, that she realized the journal had something to do with the age-old creature and her curse. Desperate for answers, she continued to the next paragraph.

After the death of my brother, I found myself grief-stricken and barely able to prepare the ghastly formalities and preparations for his funeral. My family had absolved themselves of such duties, leaving the burden to weigh on my shoulders. Due to Ash's act of blasphemy, they renounced his name, and the church denied him a Christian ceremony. Left with no other choice, I had to search for a place to bury my brother. My family would not allow Ash near our family's burial plot.

I wrote to Isabella, who had already taken to England, of my brother's death.

As Jena turned the page, she found a letter. It was a returned letter from Nicolas, addressed to Isabella Westfield. She was curious to why Isabella sent it back to Nicolas. Maybe there was a reason and Nicolas would explain later in the journal, Jena thought as she carefully removed the letter from the envelope.

Dearest Isabella,

I hope this letter finds you well. It is of my deepest regret to bid you this dreadful news. For I wish it were anything but what has transpired.

I am writing to inform you that my brother, Ashton Christopher Ratcliff, of his own accord, passed away on 29 July 1819. I have enclosed a final letter from Ash addressed to you. I do not suppose there are words to express the sorrow that weighs heavy on my heart. After your departure, Ash did not take well to your absence. For many days, his state of mind drifted toward despair. Unfortunately, he could not recover. If only to ease your sorrow, Ash loved you to the end.

Yours faithfully,

Nicolas J. Ratcliff

Out of nowhere, Jena brought her head up and looked forward. She suddenly had an unexplainable urge. Placing the letter back into the envelope, she set the journal down on the bed and got up. Then she took a seat at the easel Angie had given her as a gift. As she stared at the blank canvas, an image came to mind. Using a small brush, she dipped it into her paint palette, mixing the colors, and began with the figure right away. Her strokes were slow as she made an outline of a face. Soon she began to define the features. Gradually, the face took on the form of a young woman. She recognized the face, but it didn't make any sense. It was then she realized who the woman was in her painting. It was of herself, although somewhat different. "How odd," she whispered. Her painting appeared vintage, as if she had painted herself in another era of time, similar to Nicolas's generation.

Releasing a sigh, she put the brush down and moved to her feet. Jena was eager to absorb herself into Nicolas's story once again. As she slipped back into bed, she reached for the journal. Before she began to read, she noticed there seemed to be several pages missing, as though, for some specific reason, someone had torn them out. *How strange,* Jena thought. Regardless, she continued to read.

The night before I would say my final farewell, I went to bed as usual, feeling overcome with sorrow and despair, but after hours of staring at the ceiling, I finally fell asleep.

As I lay in bed, something alarming roused me from a deep slumber. I sensed a presence looking down on me. My eyes rounded in fear when I opened them. For a moment, I doubted if it were real or just a dream. The room was the same, unchanged in any way since I fell asleep. I could see the brilliance of the moonlight shining through the thin drapery covering the windows. It was then I began to rub my eyes to see if I were truly awake. It felt like a nightmare to me, and I expected that I should suddenly awake and find myself alone in my bed, but my eyes were not to be deceived. I was indeed awake but found that I could not move. My body felt as though it was frozen in place. I could barely manage the effort to breathe.

I was not alone.

It appeared to be a man standing above me. A tall, older man dressed in a black hooded robe. He loomed over me in a manner that made me fear for my life. Strands of long, white hair flowed from the inside of his large, loose cowl and past his wide shoulders. As he lowered himself closer, his ab-normal and unearthly features rendered me speechless. His ghostly complexion was almost translucent, and his eyes were as black as coal. It looked to be the angel of death coming to claim my soul.

When the hooded stranger reached out his hand, I quickly shut my eyes and shuddered in terror. The instant he placed his palm against my arm, it was cold as ice, more like the hand of the dead than the living.

I was afraid to raise my eyelids but peeked out from the corner of my eye and saw perfectly as he bowed in a courtly way. I remember his words all too clearly as he said, "I've come to ease your soul."

His intriguing words brought my head around and my eyes to meet his pale-skinned face.

My mouth fell open as a stutter escaped, "H-how?"

When he removed his hand from my arm, he then extended it out to me. "Take my hand, Nicolas," he said, "so that I may show you."

Although peculiarly sharp white teeth protruded over his lips when he spoke, his soothing and spellbinding voice seemed to have dissipated all my fears. Then, I wondered, how did this ghostly visitor know my name? As I debated my decision, I noticed his nails were long and filed to sharp points. Who was this stranger, I feverishly asked myself, and what did he really want? I found that I could no longer hold my tongue and asked, "Who are you?"

His lips took on a cruel curve. "I am... the Master."

"Why are you here?" I hesitated to ask, but my emotions were on edge, and I refused to continue to cower at the face that would frighten most men.

He stepped closer, narrowing his haunting eyes on me that seemed to be almost red when they contrasted with the pale, yellow moon. "I have the power to bring your brother back to the living."

A weighted pause fell between us as I deliberated over the meaning of his words. "But how," said I, "is it possible to bring back the dead? Tell me, I beg you!"

The Master smiled, and his long, sharp teeth peeked out from beneath his lips. "Take hold, Nicolas," he murmured, bringing his hand closer. "The answers you seek are just within my grasp."

As he awaited my decision, inviting me to join hands, somehow his soulless eyes spoke to me as though they were daring me to seek what I desperately wanted. I remained silent, staring at him in anticipation. It was with some *weakness in my heart that I finally reached out and took hold of his icy-cold hand.*

Then his mind meshed with my own, relaying things that were impossible and unimaginable. In that instant, an agreement exchanged between our minds and swept through me as quick as lightning.

While looking at my face attentively, the Master said in a soft whisper, "You are, and will forever be... the immortal."

I instantly became weak and feverish, but it faded as quickly as it came. I realized at that moment what was transpiring. I was dying. From then on, my body grew stronger and I experienced things that I cannot put into words. It was as if I had been reborn, looking at everything through a new set of eyes, eyes that could see beyond the human eyes I once possessed. It was as though all my senses awakened for the first time.

Then the Master went on to explain in detail of how I was to resurrect Ashton. His instructions were chilling and seemingly unforbidden, but I later followed them with perfect precision.

If only I'd known what was to become of my brother, I would have never brought him back from the dead. Gifted with eternal life and heightened perceptions were what I sought for my brother and me, although Ash was entirely something else, something derived from hell itself.

A knock startled Jena. Her eyes averted from the journal as she focused them on the bedroom door. Then a familiar voice called out to her, "Jena, it's Angie. You coming down for breakfast?"

"Yeah, give me a few minutes," Jena replied as she quickly hid Nicolas's journal, tucking it beneath the bedsheets. "Go on ahead. I'll meet you downstairs in fifteen minutes."

"Okay," Angie said. "No hurry, girl. I'll see you then."

As Jena hurriedly got dressed, she debated whether to tell Angie about the journal. While her brain scrambled to make a decision, the answer soon became obvious to her. She had to tell someone about it, and her best friend was someone she could trust without a doubt.

Fifteen or so minutes later, as Jena neared the kitchen, she could hear chatter coming from inside. When she walked in, she was surprised to see the room filled to capacity. Even though the kitchen was spacious, with a table big enough to seat more than thirty people, the room seemed crowded, but there was a peaceful and soothing atmosphere to it all. The truth was, she felt welcome here, although she barely knew anyone except for her best friend.

"Hey, girl," Angie said, waving her over. "I saved you a seat."

As Jena sat down next to her, Tessa set a plate in front of her.

"Help yourself, Jena," Tessa said, supporting little Jem over her right hip. "I think there's a combination of just about everything." She lightly chuckled. "The guys got up early and cooked for us."

"Thank you," Jena said as she looked over the platters of food. Everything smelled delicious even though she wasn't very hungry.

"You're wel—" Tessa stopped short as Jax let out a high-pitched squeal and slipped out of his high chair. He took off, balancing himself on teeter-tottering legs.

Tessa sighed. "Having twin boys is not easy. Soon, I'm going to have to get a pair of running shoes just to be able to keep up with them."

Jumping to attention, Jace scooped him up into his arms. "Come here, you little rascal," he said, tickling his belly. Jax giggled and buried his little face in Daddy's long hair.

Jena watched as Tessa went over to them with little Jem in her arms and reached out to Jax, who in turn reached out to her with his tiny hand. His other one stayed with his daddy. It was as though the four of them were a united little family. The thought made Jena smile.

While Jena filled her plate, she listened to everyone at the table as they laughed and engaged in conversation. When Jena settled back in her chair and began to eat, she noticed Bull—who was sitting on the opposite side of Angie—lean in and whisper something in her ear. Whatever he'd said must have been private, going by Angie's reaction. She had that look on her face, the look you get when the person you care about says something that makes you feel a certain way. At that moment, Jena knew her friend was deeply head over heels for that man. And it was obvious Bull felt the same for her.

"What are you grinning about?" Angie asked, noticing Jena staring at her and Bull.

Jena turned away, pretending to focus on her plate. "Oh nothing," she said around a little chuckle.

"Uh-huh," Angie remarked as she raised a brow. Then she leaned close to Jena and whispered, "If you only knew, girl. If you only knew."

Jena's smile broadened as she turned to Angie and said quietly, "After breakfast, come up to my room. I want details, plus I've got something interesting I need to show you."

Angie looked at Jena with an inquisitive expression. "Something interesting, huh?" she kept her voice low. "Well, now you have my curiosity all stirred up. It's nothing serious, is it?"

Jena shrugged. "Nothing bad has happened, but it's definitely interesting," she whispered to her. "I wanted to share this with you before anyone else."

Angie nodded. "No problem. Whenever you're done girl, just say the word."

After everyone finished eating, Jena and Angie helped clear the table. Moments later, they thanked all the men for the meal and headed upstairs to Jena's room. As they went inside, Angie closed the door and said, "Okay, I'm dying to know. What's this *interesting* thing you wanted to show me?"

"It's a secret journal," Jena said, reaching into the nightstand to retrieve the old leather book and handled it as though it was something breakable.

"A secret journal?"

Jena gave Angie a tense smile as she gingerly extended the journal out to her. "It belongs to a Nicolas Ratcliff."

Angie took the journal from Jena and asked, "Where did you get it?"

"The thing is," Jena said slowly, "I don't know where it came from."

Angie stared at the book in her hand and then focused her eyes back on Jena with a puzzled look on her face. "What do you mean you don't know where it came from? Then how did you end up with it?"

"Last night someone came into my room while I was in the bathroom and slipped it under the door."

"Someone was in your room?" Angie's eyes rounded. "Shit, Jena. Why didn't you tell me sooner?" Her tone was faintly chiding. "It could have been the creature. What were you thinking?"

Jena stood there looking regretful. For the last few weeks, she'd been grief-stricken over everything that had happened since the night of the cemetery attack, and her recent weaknesses. She had tried over and over to erase all the horrible details and images inside her head. Just thinking about it brought her close to the edge of insanity. Once again, she wished she could go back in time.

"I'm sorry, Ang." Jena's shrug was apologetic. "I didn't feel like I was in any danger, and I'm sure it wasn't the creature."

Angie sighed. "You are totally unbelievable, girl."

Jena shut her eyes for a second, then opened them again, her expression guilt-ridden. "You're right. I should have told you sooner."

"You're damn right you should have," Angie shot back. "From now on, no more secrets okay?"

Jena nodded. "I think the journal is linked to the creature."

"How do you know?" Angie queried. "Did the journal mention anything about it?"

"I've only read a few of Nicolas's recordings, but I did find out he is the creature's brother. Nicolas seems to be telling the story of how the curse began. This dates back to the 1800s."

"But that's impossible." Angie shook her head, startled by Jena's findings. "If he is the one that came into your room and left the journal, how can he still be alive? And how in the hell did he get past the Covenant's security?"

"I'm not sure how he managed to get past them undetected," Jena said, shrugging her shoulders. "Maybe he has some kind of supernatural powers. I know one thing. Nicolas and his brother…" Jena paused for a second. She could feel a lump forming at the back of her throat. Saying the creature's real name created a pins-and-needles reaction. Swallowing hard, she said, "Ashton… the creature's real name is Ashton… and they are both immortal."

"Immortal?" Angie looked at Jena in bewilderment. "How?"

"In 1817, Nicolas's brother fell in love with a young girl named Isabella. Her father, who was a minister of a small Catholic church, would not allow her to be married until she turned eighteen. Three years later, when she became of age, Ashton asked her father for her hand in marriage. After Isabella's father gave him permission, Ashton proposed to her. Although, a few weeks prior, she decided to move to England to join a women's convent and turned down his proposal. As Nicolas tells the story," Jena continued on, "his brother couldn't get over Isabella's refusal to become his wife and later killed himself. The day before Nicolas buried Ashton, something evil came to him that night. He called himself the Master and offered to bring his brother back from the dead."

Intrigued by what Jena was telling her, Angie said, "Well, did he do it?"

"Going by what I have read so far, he did. That is how his brother Ashton became the creature. I guess the deal Nicolas made with this evil being had a hefty price."

"He sold their souls?"

Jena slightly nodded. "I think so."

"Maybe this journal can help you, Jena. If indeed this Nicolas Ratcliff was the one that came into your room, there might be a reason why he wants you to read it."

"I think Nicolas wants my help," Jena said.

"To do what?"

"Destroy the creature."

"But wouldn't that be killing his own brother?"

"Nicolas feels responsible for what Ashton has become," Jena explained. "I don't think he ever intended to bring harm to anyone. He was just grieving over his brother's death. In order to stop all the killing, he knows something has to be done. Nicolas wants to set Ashton free, and if death is the outcome, I believe he'll accept that." Jena exhaled and went on, "And there's something else that's been bothering me. Something strange."

"What do you mean strange?"

"For some reason, I feel like I know Nicolas," Jena told her. "I get this strange feeling that I've met him before. I can actually feel his pain when he describes his brother's death. It's like I have these weird emotions I can't explain."

"Like what kind of emotions? Are you talking about the same you feel for the creature?"

"It's hard to describe," Jena said. "It's a different feeling, like a strange closeness. As I read his journal, it's almost as if I can feel his heartache."

"Maybe it has something to do with the binding spell his brother has on you."

"I don't know. Maybe." Jena stared at the journal that was in Angie's hand, seemingly distracted by what secrets it held and somehow connected to its owner. "I need to find out more."

"So, what are you waiting for?" Angie prompted. "You need to get reading, girl. The battle angels will be back at dusk."

"Yeah, I guess you're right. Time is ticking. So, what about you and Bull?" Jena asked, changing the subject. "How's that going?"

Angie couldn't help but crack a little smile. "Let's just say everything is heading in the right direction. We'll talk details another time. Right now, your situation is more important."

Sighing heavily, Jena said, "Should I tell the Covenant about the journal?"

"Don't worry about that." Angie offered the journal back to Jena. "I'll take care of it while you get back to reading. Hopefully, there's something in there that will be useful."

As Jena took the journal from Angie, she reached out to hug her. "Thanks, Ang. Thanks for always having my back."

"I'll always be here for you. And remember," Angie said, embracing Jena. "You hold all the power, Jena. You're the only thing this creature wants, and you're the only one who can destroy it."

Chapter Thirty-Six

As Detective Manuel Sanchez and his partner, Detective Frank Perkins, arrived at the observation room, they came upon a uniformed officer who stood guard outside the closed door.

On the other side of the glass they could see Paul Reiss, the reporter from the Mercury News, pacing inside the small interview room. By the look on his face, it was obvious he wasn't too thrilled about his current situation.

The officer shook his head and said, "How did you manage to get this jerk to come down to the station?"

"We didn't," Manuel replied. "We cuffed him and dragged his ass here."

"He's been asking for his attorney," the officer said. "About every five minutes."

Manuel looked at the officer with a smirk on his face and said, "He'll get his phone call, right after I get some answers."

"Do you want me to go in with you?" Frank asked.

"Not at first. Watch from here," Manuel told him. "I'll motion to you when I need you."

"I get it." Frank's brow rose. "Good cop, bad cop?"

With a nod, Manuel opened the door to the interview room and stepped inside. As soon as Paul saw him, he stopped pacing and pointed his finger at the detective.

"You're a fucking piece of work, Detective," Paul spat. "Dragging me here for no good reason and refusing to let me contact my attorney. I have rights. I'll have your badge over this. You're lucky if I don't sue the whole damn police department."

Manuel did not have the time nor the patience for Paul's tantrum. "Sit the fuck down," he said through gritted teeth as he took hold of the reporter's shoulder with an iron grip and shoved him into a chair. The force caused Paul's glasses to slide down his nose.

He quickly reached up to adjust them. "What's your problem?" he snapped, taken aback by Manuel's aggressive behavior.

Manuel tried to push his rage down a notch, but he *really* needed to get his hands on that video. "Look, Mr. Reiss, I don't have time to play your games." He huffed out a breath that hung between them for a second or two. "You're *going* to turn over that video." His brows furrowed. "We can do things the easy way, or the hard way. It's your choice."

Paul's expression hardened. "I don't have to give you shit. That video is the property of the Mercury News."

Cool your jets, Manuel tried to talk himself down before he shoved the reporter's head through the wall. "That video is evidence," he said, his voice a little calmer. Then he reached inside the pocket of his jacket and leaned in closer. "I've got a warrant to seize that video," he said as he retrieved a piece of paper and held it in front of the reporter's face. "If you'd cooperated when my partner and I came by your apartment, we could have saved all this trouble in the first place."

Paul peered at the warrant through a pair of thick lenses and then focused his eyes back on Manuel. "I don't..." He exhaled a deep breath, "have it anymore."

"What do you mean you don't have it anymore?" Manuel asked roughly, his patience wearing thin. "Where in the hell is it?"

"One of your guys has it."

Manuel straightened and stuffed the warrant back into his pocket. "What are you talking about?"

"A cop from this precinct," Paul told him. "He offered me five grand, so I took the money. Everyone's gotta make a living, right?"

"How do you know he's a cop?" Manuel grilled the reporter. "Did he give you his name?"

Paul shook his head. "He said he was a cop but wished to remain anonymous. I didn't even get a look at this guy. Besides, I didn't care about his identity. I just wanted the money. We had an arrangement for the exchange."

"What kind of arrangement?" Manuel demanded.

"The guy had me drop off the video at a cemetery. The very one where those attacks occurred."

Manuel narrowed his eyes. "Are you talking about the Salem Cemetery?"

When Paul nodded, Manuel said, "What about the money? How did you make the trade-off?"

"In a mausoleum," said Paul. "And there was something strange about the drop-off location."

"What do you mean *strange*?"

"It was at the place where Carla Rosi's parents put an empty casket," Paul said grimly. "You know…" He looked at Manuel unsettled. "…the body of the dead girl they found in that open grave. The one that had been missing for years. The same grave your men found that girl who claimed she was bitten by a werewolf."

"Yeah, yeah," Manuel grumbled. "I know the one you're talking about."

"So, do you think the video is somehow connected to the murders, and this cop?" Paul quizzed Manuel, the reporter in him coming out. "You think the cop is the killer?"

"It doesn't matter what the hell I think," Manuel shot back. "Just like I told you before. This case is none of your damn business."

"Oh come on, Detective," Paul said in a whiny voice. "For crying out loud, give me something to go on. I couldn't get that cop to tell me a damn thing."

Manuel leaned forward and got in the reporter's face. "I'll give you something all right," he ground out. "How does a jail cell sound?"

"What?" Paul's eyes rounded. "You don't have the right to arrest me."

"Don't I?" Manuel smirked. "You illegally obtained money in exchange for crucial evidence to a case." He jabbed a finger at the reporter's chest. "I can get you for extortion. Under federal and state laws, it carries a prison sentence up to twenty years."

Paul stiffened in his chair. "Now wait one damn minute," he argued. "I know something or another about the law. You refused my rights to an attorney, and you failed to give me my Miranda rights. Everything that I've said isn't legally binding."

"You still refused to turn over evidence," Manuel said, managing to keep his temper.

"What evidence?" Paul shrugged. "I don't know what you're talking about."

He grabbed the front of Paul's pinstriped Oxford shirt and yanked him to his feet. Then he slammed him against the wall so hard the reporter's glasses bounced off his face and crashed to the floor.

Manuel put his face so close to the reporter's they could have kissed. "Don't give me that shit," he said, more loudly than he had intended. "I heard you on the damn radio bragging about the video, dumbass. How did you think I knew about it in the first place?" He gritted his teeth. "It won't be difficult to get that recording from the radio station. That's all the evidence I need to lock your ass up."

Paul blew out a deep breath. "Alright, alright," he said. His face suddenly flushed, and sweat beaded his forehead. "What the hell do you want from me?"

"You're going to do something for me," said Manuel, keeping his hand fisted in Paul's shirt. "You're going to draw attention to that dirty cop."

"Isn't that considered extortion?"

Manuel slammed him again. A painful groan echoed through the room. "Tell you what, Mr. Reiss. If you work with me, you might actually walk out of here. Otherwise, I'm going to enjoy putting you in a cell with a bunch of gangbangers. And I bet you'd be pretty popular there. Nice white boy like you. Do you understand these rights as I've stated them?"

"Shit," Paul muttered under his breath. As fear kicked in, he seemed to consider the detective's deal for a moment. With a slight nod, he stammered, "I... if I agree, won't that be breaking the law?"

"Nope," Manuel said. "Not if you're doing it without payment. You're going to agree to do this because it's the civil thing to do."

"Okay," Paul finally said, releasing a heavy sigh. "I'll do whatever you want. Just don't put me in jail."

"Smart decision," Manuel replied as he released his grip and watched the reporter square his shoulders and rearrange his rumpled shirt. "Hang tight for a minute while I get my partner. I'll be back to discuss our agreement and go over the paperwork. I'd hate not to follow *proper* protocol."

As Manuel stepped out of the interview room and shut the door behind him, his partner said, "Whatever happened with the good cop scenario?"

"The bad cop seems to be more effective," he told Frank.

Frank rolled his eyes. "Did you get Mr. Reiss to agree to cough up that video?"

Manuel shook his head. "He sold it."

"You've got to be kidding me," Frank replied, and then tacked on, "Did he say who he sold it to?"

"Apparently he sold it to one of our finest here at this precinct, but Mr. Reiss didn't get a make on the guy. And there's more," Manuel went on. "The drop-off location was in the mausoleum where Carla Rosi's parents placed that empty coffin."

"Holy shit," Frank bit out. "You think this cop might have something to do with the murders?"

"You sound like that reporter," Manuel replied. "He asked the very same question."

"Well?" Frank shrugged. "Do you think there's a connection?"

"Could be. I'm definitely not throwing the theory out the door."

"So what's the plan now?" Frank asked.

"During Mr. Reiss's interview..." Manuel paused with a sinister grin on his face. "...I suddenly got an epiphany."

Frank crossed his arms and looked at Manuel with an inquisitive stare. "Is that so? Please, do tell." His voice expressed a hint of dry humor. "The suspense is killing me."

"Since one of our fellow officers seems to be so interested in that video, I thought we'd let him know there's another one, although you and I both know there isn't."

Frank cocked a brow. "And how are we going to do that?"

"We'll put the reporter back on the radio," Manuel said. "He can go on the air and brag about having more footage of our *mystery* werewolf. Maybe it will captivate our guy's attention to contact Mr. Reiss with another offer. If he does, we'll stake out the exchange location."

"So how did you get Mr. Reiss to cooperate?"

"I was *very* persuasive," Manuel bluntly remarked. "We just need to have him sign a waiver acknowledging he understands and agrees to go along with our plan and wear a wire."

"You should notify the Covenant," Frank suggested. "They're going to want to know about that video. And before you have Mr. Reiss sign any agreement, you better run this by the Captain first. You know how he gets when we go ahead and do shit without checking with him first."

Manuel nodded. "Yeah." He raised a brow. "Believe me, I know all too well."

The sound of Manuel's phone going off abruptly halted their conversation. "Hang on," he said as he dug his cell phone out of his back pocket. When he looked at the screen, he recognized the caller and glanced up at Frank. "I guess I won't need to make that call to the Covenant after all. It's Tim Ross."

When Frank nodded, Manuel swiped to answer and put the phone up to his ear. "This is Detective Sanchez."

After a few moments of silence, Frank noticed that Manuel's facial expression grew tense.

"Don't let anyone else touch it," Manuel finally said. "If we're lucky, we might be able to get some prints. Detective Perkins and I will be there shortly."

As he ended the call, Frank said, "What's going on?"

"Apparently someone got past security at the Covenant," he replied. "They left a journal in Ms. McCain's room. And going by the name on the outside, it belongs to a Nicolas Ratcliff."

Frank's eyes rounded. "Surely it's not our Nicolas Ratcliff."

"Who knows," Manuel said, shrugging his shoulders. "It's hard to believe, but it's quite the coincidence, wouldn't you say? You have to wonder. Nicolas has always seemed odd."

"Yeah, I get that about him." Frank nodded in agreement. "Don't get me wrong. He's one hell of a detective, and I like the guy, but it seems like he doesn't belong in our time. I never paid much attention to it until now. I just thought it was his Southern upbringing."

"Well," Manuel let out a long sigh, "if it is the very same Nicolas we know here at the precinct, he's linked to the creature."

"How so?"

"According to that journal," Manuel briefly paused with his brow raised, "he's the creature's brother."

"Shit," Frank said under his breath. "This can't be the same guy. We've known Detective Ratcliff for at least fifteen years."

Manuel sighed. "I know, but after everything we've come across in the last year, anything is possible. And think about it. The reporter did say he sold that video to one of our guys here at this precinct. And the only few people that had access to it was us, Captain Hodge, Detective Lacher, and Detective Ratcliff."

Frank shook his head in disbelief. "Yeah, it makes sense. But why would Nicolas want that tape? It isn't connected to the creature. That was Jimmy Fratianno."

"That's a good question," Manuel said. "Before we confront him, let's see if we can get some prints off that journal. And then we'll go from there."

"The way things are going, we may not need our reporter's help after all," Frank mentioned.

"Yeah," said Manuel. "I can't say I hate the idea. Mr. Reiss seems to be more trouble than he's worth."

Chapter Thirty-Seven

Anxious to continue reading Nicolas's last recorded events, Jena settled comfortably back into her bed and opened the journal. Turning to the page where she left off, Jena began to read, hoping it would reveal the answers to all the questions that plagued her mind.

September 28, 1819—I will never forget the first time I laid eyes upon my brother after he had risen from the dead. It was as though I had stepped into my worst of nightmares, although I knew all too well that my eyes did not deceive me.

After following the Master's instructions with careful exactness, I awaited what seemed to be the longest three days of my life. I found myself to be joyful at the thought of Ashton alive and breathing once again, yet fretful of the unknown. Once he awoke, would he be angered and resentful by my decision to bring him back to the living, or welcome what I had chosen with open arms?

As instructed, I placed my brother's corpse inside an above-ground tomb in the cemetery of the "Cities of the Dead," and covered him with sanctified soil before I sealed his coffin. I was to wait three days and then return to find Ash, once again, among the living. That is what I believed to be, but surprisingly, on that third day, as I opened his coffin, I found it empty. My mind contemplated the possible implications. The first thought that came to mind was that perhaps Ash had already risen and somehow escaped the confined tomb. Then my thoughts went to the cemetery's undertaker. Would he have taken Ashton's body? Out of nowhere, something else occurred to me. Could it be that all this had been a cruel scheme just to gain my soul? The thought of being misled angered me to no end. The torment of false hopes burned deep within me, but soon my unpleasant emotion shifted from rage to fear.

What I saw next, peering inside the crypt, brought me to my knees. The moment I saw him—an unGodly creature combined with Ash's features and that of a wolfish beast—I knew what I had done. In that instant, I could feel my new life crumbling before me. As I looked upon what used to be my handsome brother, the brother I adored and loved with all my heart, I wanted to die. I silently begged for God's forgiveness. How could I be responsible for such? Was I evil? Could I restore the depravity that I had created?

I remember my words all too clearly. "Forgive me, brother, for I have damned our souls."

His glowing eyes just stared at me for a moment, and then my brother, the beastly creature, spoke to me. "No, little brother." His voice seemed rough, but still I recognized it was Ashton. "You freed my soul. You gave me a new beginning." His hideous mouth seemingly formed a wolfish grin, exposing rows of sharp teeth. "If not for you, I would be burning in hell's eternal flames."

I was shocked at his declaration. My brother was amazingly calm in his newfound transformation. It was then I feverishly wondered if Ash was to be stuck in this ghastly form for the remainder of his life. If so, what kind of life would this serve?

With all the puzzling questions whirling inside my head, I found that I would surely lose what sanity I had left if I did not seek the answers.

"I make no judgments upon you, brother. But please, tell me," I asked, praying my words would not offend him. "Are you to be trapped in this beastly form for eternity?"

"No," he answered, moving closer. "I am still the brother you grew up to know, only better now."

"But how?" I said to him suddenly.

"Don't you feel it, little brother?" He held out his clawed hands and flexed his long, hairy fingers as though he held some kind of magic within them. "These hands, strong hands, wield the power of life and death."

Hearing his words, there was no question in my mind that Ashton was now a killer. I could not bear this truth. My agony was unbearable. I closed my eyes, and in my pain, I silently asked God, praying he would have pity, could I take back what I had done?

As I waited for God's answer, if only the slightest suggestion, I heard a voice whisper beside me. "Set yourself free, little brother. Let all the pain go."

When I opened my eyes again, Ash stood facing me. Not the beast, but my brother, a smile on his human face. "You are not evil," he whispered as he took hold of my hand. "We are immortal. The world is at our feet. Do not turn away from it. You must embrace it to the fullest."

I nodded at Ash as he nodded at me. It was at that moment I knew there was no turning back. It felt as though the world had gone mad, and I along with it. For I now know the truth about my poor brother.

It was three months after Ash's death when Isabella planned to return from England to pay her respects. After I had sent her the dreadful news, I had no idea Ash would return from the dead, although she quickly returned a letter in response.

Jena became curious as she turned the fragile page and discovered another envelope. As she read the outside, she realized it was a letter from Isabella addressed to Nicolas. Carefully, she reached inside and retrieved the delicate piece of paper. As soon as she unfolded it, she began to read.

My dearest Nicolas,

After receiving your letter of this dreadful news, I find myself utterly distraught and overcome with grief. I have asked my Mother Superior for a leave of absence to pay my respects, but due to my recent vow of stability, I cannot take leave for three months. I promise as soon as permitted I will return home with haste.

I hope my prayers find you, dear Nicolas, some comfort.

Dear Father of all,

Give us the strength to surpass this unfortunate day. I pray you bring comfort to Ashton Christopher Ratcliff, and for all who loved him. Grant Ashton your power of forgiveness and shield him from suffering, dear Lord.

May his soul rest in eternal peace. In Jesus Christ's name, Amen.

With my deepest sympathy,

Sister Isabella R. Westfield

Reading Nicolas's recollection of his brother's curse took Jena on an emotional roller coaster, but she felt she must go on. There had to be a reason why Nicolas left the journal in her possession and the letter from Isabella. Something in his recorded events held important information, and she would not stop until she found it.

I kept Isabella's letter dear to my heart, and secret from my brother, praying he would not discover her plans to visit. Aside from Isabella's decision to dedicate her life to the Amesbury Abbey in England, she still loved my brother.

During this journey into my new life, I have discovered immortality has its many pleasures and all the boredom and unhappiness that comes with it. It's as though my days and nights swirl together like a never-ending nightmare.

As time passes, I must soon say good-bye to this place I call home, leaving family and friends behind, for I am forever ageless. My youthfulness has already brought forth suspicion among others.

The days after discovering that Ash was once again among the living, I found that prayer was my only salvation to this evil I had invoked. After witnessing what Ash had become, and all the savagery that followed, I finally came to terms that the brother I once knew no longer existed. Instead, a brutal and dark-hearted monster now inhabited his body. Although there is nothing that I can do to stop it, I continue to pray that someday this hellish curse will find an end.

My brother used his cunning new skills to lure in his victims. He was as cultured as he was cruel. As I have regretfully witnessed, most of them were utterly vicious and ended in the most brutal ways. Some days I cannot help but despise Ash for what he is, and other days I find myself enduring the inevitable. For my brother was the only companion I had in this dismal and lonely immortal life.

Human blood was what he craved. Ash needed it to survive. The blood served him in many ways. It gave him the ability to shift from his human form and into the creature at will. He had the power to transform himself into various nocturnal animals and take on forms of a fog-like substance, a shadow, or a cloud of smoke. Not only was he cursed to be this evil thing, he could pass it on to others from a single bite, but Ash always made sure no one survived, consuming them almost whole. He sought out his victims carefully, making sure they were not free of guilt or sin. They were mostly murderers, rapists, and those who committed the worst of crimes, until one day, something inside him changed. It destroyed what good remained in my brother.

Jena now realized that Ashton was not reborn the monster she thought him to be, nothing like the killer he is today. It became clearer as she read more of Nicolas's words that his brother only preyed upon evil, not the innocent. It was at that moment she wondered what had changed Ashton. She prayed there would be something in Nicolas's recordings that explained why his brother turned so dark.

Nearly three months later, in late December, Isabella kept her promise and returned home. She was to contact me as soon as she arrived, but instead, she went to where she thought was Ash's final resting place... to the cemetery of the "Cities of the Dead."

As long as I've known Isabella, I knew she would decide to go alone. Giving her privacy, I kept a close distance in the cemetery and waited for her arrival. It seemed like a respectful thing to do.

It was nearly dusk when she arrived at the eerie place that held row after row of above-ground tombs. Unbeknown to Isabella, there was nobody buried as she approached the oblong, house-like crypt—there hadn't been one to bury due to my careless actions. Ash had already returned from the dead.

The expression on Isabella's face looked exactly how I felt: broken on the inside. Before she went in, she took a halting breath and trailed her fingers across the marker on the door with the inscription of Ash's full name, the date he was born, and of his death, and one sentence at the bottom: In loving memory.

When Isabella reached for the door to open my brother's tomb, the sound of a high-pitched howl drew her attention. As she turned to look, something came out of the darkness, traveling in a blur at the speed of lightning.

It was at that moment I knew Ash was aware of Isabella's plans to visit, and that he too was here.

I hurried to warn her, but it was too late. As I watched my brother approach her, the look on Isabella's face started as shock, but shifted quickly to utter disbelief. Then she fell to her knees and cried out, "Dear God. It cannot be."

He dropped to his knees beside her. "Izzy, it's me, Ash," he spoke to her softly. "It's really me."

Isabella stared at him wide-eyed, like a frightened animal trapped in a cage. "No," she gasped. "You're not real. Ash is dead."

When he reached out to her, she flinched in horror. "Please," she sobbed. "Whatever you are, please..." She turned to look away. "Leave me be."

As I watched my brother move to his feet, the devastation in his eyes was painful to see.

"Isabella, I—"

She covered her eyes. "Please, go away!"

I will never forget the look on his face. I have witnessed it before. It was the look of a broken man, the same broken man who had taken his own life not so long ago.

He stared down at her, just stood there staring like his heart had shattered into a million pieces.

I wanted to run to him, to comfort him, to ease his broken heart, but deep down I knew there was nothing I could do. It was too late. Just like before, the damage had already sealed his fate. It was as if my brother had died all over again.

After that day, I never heard from Isabella again. For many months, I perpetually wrote to her, but she returned all my letters. When a year had passed and still no word, I respectfully discontinued my efforts. I can only pray that Isabella would someday find it in her heart to forgive me.

On that same distressing incident, the day Ash confronted Isabella, he disappeared as though he had mysteriously vanished from the face of the earth.

By Nicolas's descriptions of how Ashton took Isabella's rejection, it was clear to Jena why he had changed. He was broken once again. It was obvious there was no turning back now. Although it was painful to read, it was imperative that she finish Nicolas's story.

February 2, 1830—I am worried. I have not heard from Ashton in years. My great fear is that he hates me, for I am responsible for the curse upon his head, and his broken heart. I pray that he will return and somehow find it in him to forgive me. I will be in endless torment until then.

During my brother's absence, I discovered that I have a strange ability. I can make myself invisible to those around me. I wonder what other unknown skills I might possess. The thought captivates my mind and frightens me all the same. Although I never fall ill or seem to age, I am desperate to find my way living as an immortal. As time passed, I wanted to be of service to others instead of always concerned with my own personal profit, or pleasure.

June 4, 1834—I found my true calling. I joined the New Orleans police force. It was during the time that the notorious murderer Marie Delphine LaLaurie, more commonly known as Madame LaLaurie, fled New Orleans after her residence caught fire. When the authorities and fire marshals got there, they found a seventy-year-old woman, the cook, chained to the stove by her ankle in an attempt to commit suicide in fear of punishment by Madame LaLaurie. During an investigation, there were findings of LaLaurie's involvement in the torture and murder of several of her own slaves.

The Pittsfield Sun newspaper wrote several weeks after the evacuation of LaLaurie's slave quarters. Police discovered seven slaves horribly mutilated. The lead headline proclaimed "SEVEN SLAVES MUTILATED IN LALAURIE'S MANSION." The article described in great detail the dismemberment of Madame LaLaurie's bond servants. Two things struck the writer of the article as peculiar. One was the brutality of their deaths. They found the victims suspended with rope at the neck, with their limbs stretched and torn from one extremity to the other, and the decomposing bodies imprisoned for some months. What was more puzzling about all this was the fact that the other slaves in the household, including Madame LaLaurie's husband, physician Leonard Louis Nicolas LaLaurie and their two daughters, kept quiet. Perhaps they were afraid to report this to the police in fear of Madame LaLaurie.

Later, they discovered bodies of other victims buried in the grounds of the LaLauries' mansion, including a child. Madame LaLaurie escaped authorities and took refuge in Paris.

March 1, 1842—The circumstances of Madame La-Laurie's death were unclear. Stories traveled that she had died in France in a boar-hunting accident, although it was no boar that killed Madame LaLaurie. My brother was the beast that ended her miserable life. That was when Ash finally returned from his long departure. At first, I was overjoyed to see my brother after all these years until I witnessed the worst of his darkness.

It was during the opening of the enormous and extravagant St. Charles Theatre, also referred to as "The Temple of the Drama," where I found peace and tranquility in the midst of all my despair. This was the place I could escape to and pretend to live somewhat of a normal life.

Inside, the auditorium featured 4,000 seats with a spectacular chandelier made of crystal prisms illuminated by 176 gas jets. The theatre attracted the biggest theatrical stars in the country and later became a center of amusements for all New Orleans.

December 13, 1842—A coffin factory behind the theatre caught fire, burning it to the ground. I remember that tragic night as though it was yesterday, but unfortunately it was no accident. My brother was responsible for the fire that burned New Orleans' beloved St. Charles Theatre and the brutal deaths of several innocent people. The terrible incident was just the beginning of his killing crusade. That same year, less than a month apart, police found twenty women, their bodies mutilated and half eaten. The families of the victims hired detectives to bring the person responsible to justice, but their investigations and weeks of searching proved fruitless. The police conjectured a possible pack of rabid wolves were responsible for the attacks, but they never found any evidence to prove their theory.

In the weeks following the brutal slayings, there were no further incidents of attacks. It was not until the next year that police reported two people missing. A couple of backpackers from out of town visiting relatives had gone camping at the Mississippi River trails for a few days. When they hadn't returned in over a week, a search was initiated, with dreadful findings. The bodies of the missing persons had been torn to pieces and half eaten. Although the killings remained a mystery, I had no doubt all the victims and my brother were connected.

Not long after that, the body count continued to stack. It soon launched an organized manhunt that later involved myself. I was put in charge of the investigation, although I knew all along who was responsible for all the savage murders. I had no choice but to become something I despised in order to protect my brother. I had an obligation. I had to be accountable for my actions. I was the one to blame for the evil that possessed Ashton's body, so I covered up any evidence that might lead back to him. Each time, I prayed for God's forgiveness.

As Jena finished reading, this, however, was not the last entry in Nicolas's journal. One more page waited to be uncovered. It was apparent he loved his brother but was desperate to put an end to all the killing. When she turned to the last page, it was as though a different person had written it. The handwriting was shaky like Nicolas had written in a hurry, and the date was current. It was the same day he had placed this journal in her possession.

October 1, 2019—Time is running out, and I have not much time, for my brother will return soon. Something horrible has happened that, out of guilt, I dare utter only in this journal. Ash has once killed again, and this time he has acted beyond reason. I fear this may be my last chance at stopping him.

Dear Ms. Jena McCain,

I am sorry to be the bearer of this dreadful burden that I must lay rest upon your feet. As you read this, by now, you are aware of my and Ashton's history. It was important that you have this knowledge, for I have no choice but to plead for your help. You are the only one that can put an end to all this madness. An innocent life is at stake, and we have not much time to save her. After you read this, please meet me as soon as you can. I promise, as God as my witness, I mean you no harm. Tell no one, and come to the Salem Cemetery at dusk.

Yours truly,

Nicolas J. Ratcliff

It all suddenly became clear to her. There was no hidden mystery to solve, no secret knowledge to uncover, and no way to remove the curse. Nicolas had brought the journal to her because he wanted her help. He was begging for it. This was his way of asking her to kill Ashton. Jena knew she had no choice. She had to do this. The question was, how was she going to get past the Covenant's security?

A knock at the door startled Jena. As she averted her eyes from the journal, a familiar voice called out, "Jena... it's Tim Ross. There's something important we need to talk about."

Jena lowered her eyes and stared at the journal one last time. *I have to do this,* she fretfully thought. *I'm the only one that can help Nicolas and finally put his brother's curse to rest.*

Before she answered the door, she tore the last page from Nicolas's journal and quickly hid it under the mattress.

Chapter Thirty-Eight

As Debi strained through the unbearable silence that nearly drove her to madness, she heard a door open. She closed her eyes and drew in a slow, deep breath, praying someone was here to rescue her.

When the sound of footsteps moved closer, her eyes opened wide and her heart began to pound as if it was going to beat right out of her chest. Her imagination quickly gave way to horror. *Is it the monster?* she thought, trembling violently.

With tears in her voice, she said, "Please… don't hurt me."

"Shhh… I'm not going to harm you," a voice that she recognized from earlier said, and the same person that brought her sustenance and was kind enough to help relieve her bladder each day that she'd been kept captive. It seemed he watched over her, although he kept his identity hidden by placing a blindfold over her eyes. Then she felt a hand lightly press down on her shoulder. "I'm going to help you, but you must remain patient." His voice sounded kind, but she couldn't see his face. "I promise I will return soon and set you free."

Debi was breathless and shaking, her eyes looking nervously from side to side. *Who was he?* She was desperate to see the stranger, but the ropes that bound her to the platform she was on kept her confined on her back and her movement restricted.

"Please," she pleaded, struggling against the restraints. "I can tell you're not a bad person. Please, don't leave me here."

She felt fingers stroking her hair. "Trust me," the stranger softly explained. "I will come back for you."

"W-what's…" Debi's mind raced feverishly. "What's your name?"

The stranger did not answer. Instead, he removed his hand from her hair and walked away. As the door quietly closed, there was nothing now. Only silence.

After Nicolas left Debi alone in the room, he sat locked in indecision. Should he release the girl now, in fear of his brother's return and that he would hurt her, or go along with his plan to wait for Jena? It was imperative that he continue with his original plan so as not to rouse Ash's suspicion. One thing was clear: he must make sure the girl remained unharmed. He'd promised her.

* * *

It was approaching midday and *he* was eager to have Jena wrapped in his arms once again. It seemed as though it had been forever that he'd held her. Soon, she would be his for eternity.

His plans were to lure Jena back to the cemetery, to the place where it all began, and present her with a gift. The young girl he held captive in the mausoleum was to be Jena's first kill. Oh, and how glorious it would be to witness. It would be the final step of her transition. Although, before he went to her, he would need to ensure his strength with the flesh and blood of an innocent victim.

* * *

"I can't believe we're actually here," Micah said, whirling around in a circle, admiring the redwood forest and all the beauty it held. "Look at all the timber." She waved her arms in the air. "They're magnificent. I bet if they could speak, they'd have some great stories to tell. Think about all the history they've seen."

"Talking trees?" Krista smirked, rolling her eyes. "Really, Micah?"

Micah shot her sister a disparaging look. "Oh, come on, Krista. Can't you at least pretend like you're enjoying yourself? You used to love nature. What happened to that fun-loving person I grew up with?"

"She got married, and then divorced... twice," Krista grumbled. "Not to mention my recent broken engagement." She furrowed her brows. "My life isn't all rainbows and unicorns, like yours. I practically had to jump through hoops to get time off for this. Not all of us have the luxury to do

302

whatever we want at any given time. You're lucky Pete takes care of you, Micah. I'd kill to have a husband like yours. It's been tough for me the last few years after Robert ditched me and the kids to be with a younger woman. Being a single parent isn't exactly what I planned for my future. Between my full-time job and juggling my kiddos, I barely have free time to sleep much less enjoy a day off."

Micah let out a long sigh. "I know, I know." She placed her hand on Krista's shoulder and lightly squeezed. "That's why I brought you here. I thought it would be good for you." Her voice softened, "Life is too short, Krista. You need to spend more time for yourself and stop stressing so much."

Krista's lips formed a half-smile. "Yeah, you're right. I'm sorry, sis. I promise not to be such a downer and try to enjoy myself. Besides, how can anyone be in a blue mood around you?" She laughed a little. "You're like a ray of sunshine."

Micah pulled her into a hug. "I knew you'd come around." When she pulled back, she said, "Admit it. This place is like a slice of heaven, isn't it?"

"Sure," Krista said reproachfully and swatted herself on the shoulder. "I'll tell myself that tonight while I'm itching from all these mosquito bites."

They both laughed, and then Micah reached for her sister's hand. "Come on, girl." She tugged at her. "Let's go hiking."

* * *

Hours later, *he* stood somewhere in the redwood forest that went on for miles under a cloudy sky, waiting there until the change came on. Not far into the woodland, as the wind started to pick up, he caught a whiff of human flesh. It was a good scent as he inhaled it deep into his nostrils. He then realized it was the distinctive smell of females. The perfumed fragrance mixed with sweet-smelling skin instantly brought forth his transformation. The hunger rose in him, and the instinct to kill whoever crossed his path took control.

All of a sudden, he felt a heated rippling sensation growing beneath his skin. As his frame began to stretch and pull, the material of his shirt split down the middle of his expanding chest, and his pants ripped at the seams, exposing bulging, muscly thighs. In a matter of seconds, dark hair began to emerge from all over, covering every inch of his skin. He could feel his face reshaping and his mouth contorting into a long, beastly muzzle. His teeth tugged at the roots until sharp-pointed canines filled his mouth. He watched as his fingers lengthened with claws emerging from the tips and his shoes shredded by his enormous wolfish feet. As he ripped away the remnants of his shirt from his shoulders, his entire body expanded and hardened, growing stronger and stronger, readying himself to devour his prey.

As he began to track them, a sharp snap of a twig spun him around. Every muscle was taut with anticipation and readiness. As he lurked on the perimeter of the trees and undergrowth, a howl emerged in the near distance that sounded as though it had come from something big. Then, to his surprise, a chorus of howls suddenly arose, seemingly moving closer in his direction.

He held his stance and waited, flexing his powerful thighs. Then before his glittering eyes, out of the deep shadows came four giant, hulking, rogue wolves. At that moment, he then realized they too were hunting. However, it wasn't humans they were after—perhaps deer or some other pathetic weak animal. He, on the other hand, was on the prowl for human flesh, and this time, nothing would stand in his way.

As they caught sight of him, he made himself so still they grew bolder and crept forward on all fours. Pinpointing the largest one, he sprang in the air with one great leap as if he'd been launched from a catapult and slashed his razor-sharp claws into the rogue's hide. It yelped and spun away. The other three turned to defend their furry companion, snapping at him with jaws full of lethal, sharp-pointed teeth. They appeared to him as nothing more than a pack of snarling dogs.

He released a deep gargling roar, snapping back, daring them to engage in battle. But before the furry trio closed in, the sound of voices drew near, stopping them cold in their tracks. In fear of being exposed, they tucked tail and bolted away.

In spite of his rivals' retreat, *he* kept his feet planted firmly, readying himself for the kill.

As they suddenly came upon him, their eyes rounded in sheer terror. Then screams erupted and echoed through the colossal of thick timber. In a heated rage, he sank his claws into one of his victims, slashing her carotid artery, unleashing a crimson geyser. The sharp scent of blood ignited his thirst and heightened his senses. When the other girl turned to flee, he snared her by the hair and yanked her head back, snapping her neck easily as if it were merely a twig. In a split second, both girls were dead. Their flesh and blood were his now.

His hunger was undeniable, but there was no time to waste, no time to savor the feast, for he yearned to be with Jena.

He wished that she could be with him, embracing the new life he had given her, a world filled with wonders beyond what the human eyes could see. Before he claimed what belonged to him, he had unfinished business with his brother to tend to.

* * *

Apollyon sat in an oversized chair next to Yelena while she rested in bed. With their son cradled in his arms, he simply watched as baby Tobias slept, content that all seemed well with his beloved and their child.

After the big scare he'd just been through, worried he'd lose Yelena in childbirth, he should have felt on top of the world now that she and the baby were doing fine. But the nightmare wasn't over. He still had a task to do. At dusk, he would be leaving with his sisters and the battle angels to meet with the Breedline Covenant. They were to prepare for battle against the creature God had tasked them to help destroy.

Although he hated the thought that if things took a turn for the worse, this could be the last time he had with his family.

"Apollyon?"

He turned to see his mother peeking around the door as if she was waiting for his approval to enter the room.

He nodded and silently motioned her in.

As she moved inside, she whispered, "I don't mean to disturb either of you. I just wanted to make sure Yelena and the baby were all right."

"They're doing fine," he said in a hushed voice. "Yelena's resting, and your grandson seems very content."

Sonya put her hand on Apollyon's shoulder and squeezed lightly. "He's beautiful," she murmured, peering down at the baby. "I'm so proud of you, and Yelena."

Apollyon reached up to cover her hand where it lay on his shoulder. "Thank you, mother."

They kept silent for a moment, watching as Tobias slept soundly. Then Apollyon looked over at Yelena, noticing the peaceful look on her face.

"I love her, dearly. I want to spend the rest of my life with her."

Sonya smiled. "And she loves you too. Both of you have a bright future ahead. You have a family of your own now. Everything will work out just fine."

Doubt crowded Apollyon's mind. "I pray that—"

"Pray what?" Sonya asked as her brows tensed with worry.

Apollyon sighed. "That you're right. I can't bear the thought of leaving them behind."

"Before you worry yourself over something that may not happen, have faith, son. I know you will watch your son grow up to be a man."

As he looked up at her, he shook his head. "You need to realize that I may not. This is going to be… risky. If I do not complete my task, I cannot return."

Her expression showed compassion as she stared down at him. "I know, son. And there's something you need to understand. Love comes with sacrifices. You will do what is right and come back to your family. I promise."

"I love you, mother," he simply said.

She leaned down and kissed his cheek. "I love you too, son." Then she reached down and gently caressed Tobias's dark curls. "I do have to admit I never expected you would ever provide me with a grandchild. Although I'm grateful you did. He's as precious to me as you are."

The corner of Apollyon's mouth lifted. "I'm blessed to have you as a mother, and the grandmother of my son."

Sonya patted his cheek and cast one last look at her grandson. Then she looked toward the bed at Yelena and said, "Tell Yelena when she wakes, if there's anything she needs for her not to hesitate to ask."

He nodded. "I will."

After a final pat to his cheek, Sonya quietly left the room, praying she was right about her son. She couldn't bear the thought of losing him again.

Chapter Thirty-Nine

Before Jena answered the door, she briefly closed her eyes and drew a deep breath. If she was going to help Nicolas, she had to come up with a way to get past the Covenant's security. She only had until dusk, and time was quickly ticking away.

"I'm coming," she called out.

When Jena rose from the bed, the journal slid from her lap and landed next to her pillow. She took another deep breath as she reached for the bedroom door. As soon as she opened it, she saw Tim Ross standing in the hallway with Tessa alongside him. She knew from the expression on their faces they already knew about Nicolas's journal. At least Angie gave her enough time to finish reading it before she alerted the Covenant.

"I take it you're here about the journal," Jena said, her eyes going from Tim to Tessa and back again.

Tessa nodded and Tim said, "Jena, there's a good possibility we may be able to identify the person who left it in your possession. Detective Sanchez and Detective Perkins are waiting downstairs. They want to check the journal for prints."

"But..." Jena's voice faded helplessly as she looked at them confused. "H-how is that possible?"

"The detectives believe they may know who the journal belongs to," Tessa explained. "It might be someone from the police department. They have substantial evidence that might prove their theory. All they need is the journal. If they can find fingerprints that match, they'll know for sure."

Jena stood there, slightly taken aback. Her mind couldn't seem to process what she'd just been told or what she should do. It seemed as if she had let everyone down. Because of her, Todd and Sophie were dead. Now, Nicolas depended on her, and time felt as though it was getting away from her. She only had a few hours until dusk. How was she going to get past security to help him? To make matters worse, it was most likely that the creature was still killing innocent people. *I have the power to stop all this... to end all the senseless and savage brutality. Everyone is counting on me.*

"Jena," Tim said patiently, "where's the journal?"

His voice brought her back to focus. She slowly turned toward the bed and looked at the fragile logbook lying next to her pillow. "It's..." Jena swallowed hard, seemingly disappointed with the decision to give up Nicolas's memoir. "It's on the bed. I'll get it for you."

A second later, she retrieved the journal from the bed and offered it to Tim. As he held out a plastic bag for her to drop it into, Jena said, "Will you please let me know what the detectives find?"

"Of course," Tessa said, touching her lightly on the shoulder. "Angie told us you feel somehow connected to this person's journal. I know this must be difficult for you. You've been through more than enough already, but it's important that we gather as much information as we can before the angels arrive."

When Jena nodded an understanding, Tessa went on to say, "I promise, Jena, if we hear anything, you'll be the first one to know."

Jena then gave her a half-hearted smile. "Thank you, Tessa."

As the door closed behind Jena, she leaned against it with her arms crossed and closed her eyes. She felt uneasy about giving up Nicolas's journal. It was as though a piece of her was gone. It made her think of all the pain Nicolas had endured for so many years. Now that he had finally found a way to end his brother's curse, had it been all for nothing if she couldn't get to him? Then she wondered if she should wait for the battle angels. Their plan was to help her destroy the creature, but Nicolas had asked her to come alone.

Jena opened her eyes and blinked away tears. As she looked across the room at the mirror above the dresser, she stared at herself for a long moment, not liking what she saw. It was the image of someone... weak. And she would be damned if she continued to remain this way.

She wanted to scream, but she found the courage to remain strong. Whatever it took, she had to keep it together. There was no time to lose it now, and nothing worthwhile came easy, she thought. She wasn't going to wait around here a moment longer. She had to figure something out, and fast.

"Time to suck it up and deal," she said in a quiet, determined voice.

Despite her circumstances, she finally managed to keep a level head. *Think, Jena,* she silently told herself, trying to come up with a solution. *How in the hell am I going to get out of here?*

Out of nowhere, she heard a faint whisper as if it was coming from a distant place.

"Jena... my beloved, Jena. Come to me."

In an instant, Jena knew who it was. She had a sudden "awareness" that *he* was close. As she turned around and looked to the balcony, expecting to see him, there was nothing but the sun dipping below the horizon.

Jena found herself breathless and shaking, staring at the sky as it darkened, resisting the urge to run to the bathroom and lock herself inside. It was then she remembered what had happened in this room, and how he managed to lure her onto the balcony, and how he had seduced her. Guilt crashed down on her. She had welcomed him inside this very room, and into her bed. Every place he'd touched her had stirred all those hidden desires and temptations she kept locked away— *excitement... pleasure... lust...*

Please, God, she silently prayed. *Help me resist him.*

Yet even as her self-control remained intact, Jena's eyes were fixed forward, focused on the sliding glass doors that led to the balcony, and to *him*.

A sweat suddenly broke out all over her body. Every inch of her skin was getting warmer and warmer by the second. Jena could feel the blood draining from her face and her heart racing. As the nerves in her hands and feet prickled like static electricity, she forced herself to take several slow breaths.

Then the skin on her arms began to itch and tingle as though something was crawling beneath the surface, searching for a way out. As Jena looked down at her hands, dark hairs sprouted like wildfire and her fingernails grew into razor-sharp points. When she reached up to touch her face, she felt it contorting and reshaping as if it had a will of its own.

"No," she said, begging the transformation to go away. Her tone grew heavy, deeper than her own normal voice. "Please, not now."

Jena felt herself expanding and lengthening until the clothes she was wearing tore free from her body. In a matter of seconds, dark, thick fur poured out of her skin and down her shoulders, covering her entire body. When she looked down at her chest, her eyes rounded in amazement. Sleek fur extended over her breasts, completely concealing her nipples. Peering further down, she watched as hairy clawed feet pushed out of her tennis shoes.

It was at that moment a feeling of euphoria surged through every cell in Jena's body. And this time... it felt *good*. It made her want to go out into the night, to run and seek out things she had yet to experience in this new body.

As the change completely took hold, an urge to howl rose in the back of Jena's throat, but she swallowed, forcing it down. It wasn't long before another intense craving broke loose. Her throat felt as dry as sandpaper and a gnawing sensation grew in the pit of her gut. The desire for blood burned deep in her veins. The hunger was almost unbearable. It was sickening to her, yet somehow tantalizing. Yearning for the taste called out to her in a strange way. And it terrified her.

I must resist, she urged, pleading with herself. *I have to stay focused.*

Although Jena's bloodthirsty instincts screamed inside, she was determined not to give in to the curse. More importantly, she had to do whatever she could to get out of the Covenant and go to Nicolas before it was too late.

Slowly, she made her way to the sliding glass door and reached out to pull the curtain back that was partially blocking her view. Tugging it aside, she could see the entire backside of the Covenant. Trees, shrubbery, and various assortments of flowerbeds landscaped the grounds, which would work perfectly as camouflage. Scanning the area below, her eyes caught sight of a humongous swimming pool and an outdoor patio practically big enough for an entire village. When her eyes averted from the large body of water, she noticed a small building next to the gated entrance and two men inside. It looked to be the Covenant's security, going by all the cameras mounted above the door and windows. That's when the hairs on her nape started to rise, worried she wouldn't make it past the guards without being seen. It was definitely going to be challenging. The minute they figured out that she flew the coop, they'd alert the Covenant.

"I can do this," she whispered, trying to convince herself.

As soon as she pushed open the balcony door and stepped out, she felt the coolness of the light breeze against her newfound transformation. It drew her further out, driving her willpower to continue. When she inhaled the night air, all her senses came alive and drove her onward. Using all the courage she could muster, she looked over the edge of the balcony to gauge the distance. From her viewpoint, it looked to be twenty feet or so. Exhaling a deep breath, she dropped to the ground with one giant leap and surprisingly landed with ease. In an instant, as she sprang forward, she could hear heavy footsteps in hot pursuit.

A man's voice from behind shouted, "Hey, you there, stop!" Then there was the sound of a radio crackling to life as the second man said, "I need backup, now!"

With her eyes locked on the wrought-iron gate, Jena kept running, praying that she'd escape before whatever backup arrived. Her mind raced, not knowing if the guards were gaining on her or if they had tranquilizer guns. Jena was too determined to make her escape to look back, but half-expected they would catch up to her any second.

As Jena neared the gate, adrenaline shot through her, giving her the strength she needed to pick up the pace. Never in her life had she run this fast. With lightning speed, she hurdled high into the air and cleared the fence without difficulty. When her feet hit the ground, she had a one-track mind—it was to get to Nicolas before the curse completely consumed her. Time was running thin, and her lust for blood had reached its limits.

Please God, she pleaded silently. *Get me to Nicolas before it's too late.*

* * *

Angie's lips turned down into a grimace when she overheard the guards reporting to Tim of Jena going AWOL. To make matters worse, Jena had turned. It was then she decided to search her room. Maybe Jena left something behind that would give her a clue to where she was going.

When Angie got close to Jena's room, she found Tessa standing outside the door as she was about to reach to open it.

Tessa turned as Angie dashed over and said, "We must be thinking alike."

"You think we'll find something that will tell us where she went?" Tessa asked her.

Angie let out a deep breath. "I sure as *hell* hope so. It's not like Jena to take off like this."

Tessa brought her wrist up to check her watch, noticing the time. "It's almost dusk," she said, opening the door. "Come on." She nodded, motioning Angie inside. "We don't have much time. The angels will be here soon."

They searched the bedroom, praying they'd find something, anything that would give them an idea as to why Jena shifted into her creature and took off, or where she might have gone.

"Hang on," Angie said, tugging at a piece of paper hidden under the mattress. Remembering back when she was a teenager, knowing where Jena had always hidden things from her parents, it drew her there to look. "I think I found something."

As Angie unfolded it, Tessa moved next to her and said, "What is it?"

"It looks like a page from that journal," Angie told her.

Moments later, as they read over the contents, they instantly knew where Jena was going: to the Salem Cemetery.

Chapter Forty

It wasn't long before an anxious group of Breedline filled the Covenant's library as they gathered for a sit-down. Tim stood at the head of the table next to where Tessa sat as they surveyed the other occupants of the room. Everyone's nerves seemed frayed and on edge. The tension was so thick you could practically cut it with a knife.

Roman and his team, consisting of Lawrence, Bull, Justice, and Lena, sat close to one another in utter silence waiting for the battle angels to arrive. Under normal circumstances, when Roman had to face unusual situations involving emotional stress, he had the ability to remain calm and steady. Between dealing with the creature, and Jena taking off as she did, and knowing Lailah was about to arrive with the other angels, his nerves were just about shot.

Detective Manuel Sanchez and his partner, Frank Perkins sat in the chairs across the table from Tessa, looking nervous as hell. Sitting at a table surrounded by people who had the ability to shift into wolves as big, or bigger, than horses, and some gifted with supernatural powers, wasn't something you normally dealt with on a daily basis. It was definitely intimidating at the least, not to mention the fact that in a matter of minutes, they were about to be face-to-face with real live angels. And one of them was Manuel's sister, who had been murdered over forty years ago by the same creature they were after.

Then there were the regular Breedline crew: Jace, Jem, Kyle, Casey, Drakon, and Alexander. And Tessa's brother Steven, the newest member in the Covenant. They too were uncertain of the turn of events they were all about to face. You didn't have to be a psychic to know what was on the minds of every single person in the room. It was obvious they dreaded revealing the news of Jena's disappearance to the battle angels.

While the other females in the Covenant attended to the children upstairs, the room mostly bristled with testosterone overload. The silence was heavy until Eve and Sebastian entered the room.

"Please, have a seat," Tim said, breaking the stillness.

Sebastian and Eve moved toward the empty chairs at the opposite end of Tessa, far away from Jace. As soon as they sat down, Jace glared at Sebastian with a look that said without words he wanted to choke the life out of him. At the sound of Tessa's voice, he looked away and refocused his attention on her.

"As you all know, we are gathered here to meet with the angels," Tessa said. "But before they arrive, I want to bring to your attention some unfortunate news." Before she continued, she discreetly cleared her throat and scooted her chair closer to the table. "Jena has shifted into her creature and somehow got past security."

"What?" Jace blurted as he turned to look in Tim's direction. His temper was already on edge with Sebastian in the room, and the news of Jena irritated him further. "For crying out loud," he grumbled. "How in the hell did she get past the guards?"

Tim shook his head. "I should have made sure she was guarded twenty-four seven," he said tightly.

"That's on me, Tim," Drakon hesitantly said. "I'm the one in charge of security. It was my responsibility. I should have been better prepared for something like this."

"It's not your fault, Drakon," Tessa told him. "It's no one's fault. There was nothing anyone could have done to stop her."

"So what now?" Jem asked. "What are we going to do?"

Tessa shrugged. "I'm not sure what we can do. We'll have to rely on the angels for guidance. But so far, this is what we know." She glanced at the two detectives. "Going by what Detective Sanchez and Detective Perkins has recently discovered, it's evident that someone from the police department has been in contact with Jena. He somehow left a journal in her room. His name is Nicolas Ratcliff," she went on to explain. "According to what is written in the journal, Mr. Ratcliff, or rather, Detective Ratcliff, is the creature's brother."

While everyone stared at Tessa in stunned silence, Drakon asked, "Does this Nicolas mention anything in the journal about what he wants?"

"He is desperate to put an end to his brother's curse," Tessa replied. "Apparently he's the one responsible for all this."

"How so?" Alexander spoke for the first time.

"From all the information we've gathered from Nicolas's journal," Tessa said as she began to unfold all the details. "Nicolas and his brother Ashton have been alive since the eighteenth century."

Frank's jaw dropped, and the look on Manuel's face was an expression of sheer astonishment.

"Damn," Manuel gritted out. "I can't believe he managed to live a double life for all those years. Sure, he seemed a little different, but hell, who isn't nowadays? As long as you do your damn job, and he did his well, it doesn't make a shit to me what you do off duty as long as you walk the straight and narrow. But this?" He shook his head. "I can't wrap my brain around it. We've worked with Nicolas for fifteen years or so, and I had no clue he was hiding anything, especially something like this."

"Yeah," Frank chimed in, "he completely pulled the wool over my eyes. I can say this... Detective Ratcliff would have made one *hell* of an actor."

"I guess I was right after all," Manuel pointed out. "I knew I saw someone else in that car the day my sister was murdered. I swear..." He heaved a deep breath. "If Nicolas had anything to do with her death..."

"I'm just as shocked over all this as you are, Detectives," Tessa said as Manuel's voice trailed off. "We're all taken aback by what's transpired, but I don't think Nicolas had anything to do with your sister's death."

Manuel cocked a brow. "How do you know?"

"So far, from what all I've discovered in his journal, it appears he's been searching for a way to end the curse. Over a decade ago, Nicolas's older brother took his own life. This is how it all started by what Nicolas tells in his memoir. Apparently, his suicide was over a young woman he fell in love with while he was human. Her name was Isabella. And I believe she is somehow linked to Jena.”

“Are you saying you think she’s a descendant of Isabella?” Manuel asked.

“Yes, I do,” Tessa replied. “By the way Nicolas describes Isabella, she sounds similar to Jena.”

“What else did you find out?” Jace cut in conversation, anxious to hear more details.

“After their courtship of nearly three years,” Tessa continued, “Ashton asked for Isabella’s hand in marriage. And remember, this was during the eighteenth century, so long courtships were typical in that era, especially if the girl was underage, and Isabella was only sixteen at the time. Unfortunately, before he proposed, Isabella decided to move to England to devote her life to a women’s convent. Ashton did not take the news well. He eventually took his own life. To make a long story short, Ashton’s family, who owned a prosperous cotton business in New Orleans, disowned him due to his act of blasphemy, and the church would not allow him a Christian burial. They left the burden on Nicolas. Of course, Nicolas was completely grief-stricken over his brother’s suicide and was beside himself over his family’s refusal to grant him permission to bury Ashton in their family’s burial space. Nicolas stated in the journal that he had a close sibling bond with his brother growing up, which caused him to grasp at anything to keep Ashton from eternal damnation. That’s when something evil came to him the night before his brother was to be laid to rest. In Nicolas’s own records, he spoke of someone who referred himself as the Master, promising him immortality and that he could bring Ashton back from the dead.”

“I take it immortality came with a hefty price,” Manuel commented.

Tessa nodded in agreement. “Yes, it did. He sold their souls, but he did not know that his brother would come back as something evil.”

Manuel leaned forward and stated, “So, Nicolas had no idea his brother would be cursed?”

"No," Tessa replied. "He was tricked. At first, Ashton wasn't what he is now," she went on to say. "He only killed corrupt individuals, something similar to what the angels told Jena she would become if she destroyed the creature."

"What made this Ashton character change?" Jace asked.

"After Ashton was resurrected, he went to Isabella. Of course, her terrified reaction didn't go over so well. She refused to have anything to do with him. Being rejected a second time sent Ashton over the edge. From what Nicolas wrote, his brother was never the same, and became a cold-hearted killer."

Jace shook his head. "Damn. That sucks."

"So now you all can understand why Nicolas left Jena the journal," Tessa pointed out. "He knows she's the only one that can end Ashton's curse and destroy the creature."

"Is that where she went?" Manuel queried. "To help Nicolas?"

Tessa nodded. "Nicolas asked her to meet him alone at the Salem Cemetery. He also mentioned a girl his brother is keeping captive. He didn't say what the girl's name was, but he did plead for Jena to help him save her. I think this girl is meant to be Jena's first kill."

"That girl could be the missing person at the crime scene we got called to just a few days ago," Frank commented as the others in the room looked at Tessa, completely shocked by what she had told them.

"The one from the Presidio National Park?" Tessa queried.

Frank nodded. "Her name is Debi Flynn. And we still haven't found the rest of Mr. Morgan's remains."

"I saw this on the news, but they didn't release any names," Tessa stated. "Was Mr. Morgan someone related to her?"

"By what Ms. Flynn's sister said, he was her fiancé."

A feeling of sadness took hold of Tessa, her expression turning mournful. "I'm sorry to hear that," she said, releasing a heavy sigh. "And you could be right, Detective. This could be the same girl. Hopefully, something can be done to save her before it's too late."

"But what about the battle angels?" Eve spoke out. "Why didn't Jena wait for them?"

"I don't know, Eve," Tessa reluctantly said.

While everyone engaged in the discussion, Bull suddenly noticed someone very important to him was missing. He rose from his chair and said, "I'm sorry to interrupt, but where's Angie? Shouldn't she be here?"

Shit! Tessa thought as her eyes roamed over the occupants sitting at the table, realizing Angie was nowhere in sight. Before she could utter a single word, a deep voice laced in a Scottish accent caught her off guard.

"Pardon me, Ms. Tessa. Ye hae visitors."

When everyone turned to look, Bruce Carmichael, a Breedline guard, had his head peeked inside the doorway.

"Please," Tessa said, nodding an approval. "Show them in."

As Bruce opened the door, Cronus, Icarus, and Helios came in first.

Every person in the room stared at them in complete silence. Although they had witnessed the glorious battle angels beforehand, their presence alone would make the most courageous of any man or woman weak in the knees. It was as if they were larger than life itself.

The instant Tessa rose to her feet, the sound of several chairs scooting across the floor broke the silence. Everyone, except for Bull, who had already risen from his chair, was now standing like soldiers at attention.

Roman shifted from one foot to the other as he nervously waited for Lailah to make her appearance. His gut instincts had told him she was here the minute Bruce popped his head in the door and announced they had visitors.

A moment later, as she walked into the room, he damn near swallowed his tongue. Lailah was as breathtaking as the first time Roman had laid eyes on her. She looked like a Greek goddess. The long strands of her hair hung in crimson ringlets, giving her a fierce but feminine look that almost made him groan. Her lashes were long, accentuating her green eyes that sparkled like emeralds. Around her waist, she wore a golden sword that shimmered as it caught the light.

Before Roman caught her eye, Lailah focused on her brother, Manuel. His face beamed when she nodded at him with a slight grin on her youthful face.

Meanwhile, as Roman's eyes ventured to Lailah's long, toned legs, he wiped at his mouth to make sure there was no drool. When he focused back on her lovely face, she smiled at him.

Roman averted his eyes from the redheaded beauty as another angel with bleached spiked hair walked into the room and stood beside her. He reminded Roman of an English rock musician from the '80s. For some odd reason, the song *"Rebel Yell"* came to mind.

Instantly, a feeling of uneasiness swept through the room as a trio of unearthly beings crowded in behind the angels. As they moved next to Lailah and the other angel with spiked hair, everyone at the table focused on the tall male with a scar marring his left eye. His vertical, split pupils reflected light like a cat's as he surveyed the room. Looking into his cruel stare was like looking into the face of a vampire and an assassin all rolled up into one big package... or the devil himself.

As Tessa looked into Apollyon's cold, golden gaze, she felt the hairs on her neck stand. She noticed the silver ring he wore, remembering it from Zeke Rizzo's description not long ago. She wondered what the signet on the ring symbolized. It protruded when he tightened his hand into a fist. Then he sneered at her, revealing one of his fangs, and it transformed his face. He looked more savage, wolf-like. For a moment, she was speechless, shocked by his dark and dominating presence. Then, her eyes took in the two females that stood by his side. Electra was the one with a muscular build and born with the power to conduct electricity within her body, using it as a weapon. Her fraternal twin sister, Callisto, was feminine and had used her beauty in the previous months to lure in her victims. She was born with the ability to create a shield that was so powerful no other weapon could penetrate its indestructible force field. During their past altercations, not even Jem's powers were strong enough to break through it.

By what Tessa remembered about the Fury, all three were siblings, created in a lab by an evil scientist for the sole purpose of destroying the Breedline species and dominating the human race for the sole purpose of food. Born with the genetics of a Breedline, an Adalwolf, a succubus, and the abilities of a powerful Wicca, their lust for human blood was unstoppable until the battle angels came to earth and rendered them powerless. According to the angels, God had released them from their bloodlust and promised them absolution if they helped destroy the creature. In order for them to remain on earth, they had to take an oath to help the Breedline protect the human race from the dark forces.

As Tessa's thoughts came back to focus, she motioned them over. "Please, make yourself comfortable. We have some rather unfortunate news that has suddenly come to our attention. It's about Jena." She let out a deep breath and went on, "She's gone missing, and we're almost positive she's going to the Salem Cemetery to help the creature's brother."

Chapter Forty-One

While everyone else in the Covenant gathered for a meeting, Angie had alternative plans. She was going after Jena.

Beyond the Covenant's boundaries, at least fifty yards away, Angie stopped in the middle of a large area surrounded by a dense growth of trees and underbrush. This would provide enough camouflage, she thought, knowing she had to shift into her Breedline wolf. It was a risk she had to take to help her best friend, but also imperative that she stay hidden.

The Breedline were not ordinary wolves, nor human, but a supernatural combination of the two, genetically more powerful and invincible than either one. However, if they were to be exposed, it would put them in danger, and they already had enough to deal with as it was.

As Angie looked up at the star-filled sky, she found herself captivated by the brilliance of the full moon, although it had no effect on her transformation. Somewhere out there, she could hear the muffled sounds of small animals as they foraged throughout the forest and the whistling of tree branches rising with the wind. The noises coming from all around seemed to amplify within seconds. When she inhaled a deep breath, her senses came alive. All the scents of the night instantly filled her nostrils with a tantalizing aroma. The distinctive scent of pine needles and evergreens enhanced the night air, creating goosebumps that coated her skin.

Suddenly, she felt the prickle of tiny hairs erupting from every pore as they began to cover the surface of her entire body. When she quickly started to remove her clothes, the hair was thickening and growing almost like it had a mind of its own. The instant she kicked off her shoes and slid out of her jeans, she fell to her knees and doubled over. With her eyes closed, she took several deep breaths, realizing the impending changes were rising fast. Her muscles underneath her skin rippled and her limbs stretched as if from some unseen force. When the transition completely took over, she did not feel pain, but since this was just her second experience shifting into her Breedline wolf, the unstoppable changes caught her by surprise.

When Angie opened her eyes and looked down, she found herself standing on all fours. Her hands were now enormous paws, and she could see her hind feet were no longer human, but instead those of a wolf. She saw that her skin was no longer visible, completely hidden beneath thick brown fur. It was amazing how fast it grew. Every particle of her body electrified with an overwhelming sensation. At that moment, she knew instinctively what to do. Time was of the essence. While Angie's mind focused on one thing, to get to the Salem Cemetery before it was too late, the wooded path that led her there would provide enough coverage to keep her hidden from prying eyes. Every muscle in her body sang with ever-increasing strength. She had never felt so compelled, so driven. It was as though she'd been reborn with a newfound purpose. The impulse and desire to howl rose in her, although she clenched the muscles in her powerful jaws and kept it at bay. With the full power of her hind legs, she sprang forward and darted through the woods, running at such speed the trees blurred as she passed by them.

* * *

As Jena finally made her way into the Salem Cemetery, she walked among the rows of ornate headstones that marked all the gravesites. It seemed different than she remembered. The time she'd been here before, in her human form, she never noticed the twin statues of angels perched over the wrought-iron gate's entrance. It was as though they were watching over all the dead. She could tell the years of exposure had slowly aged them by all the cracks and bits of chipped stone.

While she searched for the mausoleum, the same one which housed Carla's empty coffin, a memory flashed through her mind: she and Angie sharing a heart-to-heart talk, and the seriousness of her best friend's voice. "You're the only thing this creature wants," Angie had told her, "and you're the only one who can destroy it."

Do I have the strength to kill him? Jena thought, second-guessing herself. *Please God,* she silently prayed, *give me strength.*

With all the courage she could muster, she continued onward. Jena didn't make it far before a whispering voice called out to her.

"The night is ours, Jena," his alluring voice traveled in an echo. "Come, my beloved... share it with me."

Jena stopped in her tracks and whirled around, her eyes darting over the dark and desolate graveyard. Although she couldn't see anyone, she could feel *his* presence near, and she could sense his eyes upon her... watching... waiting.

Her first instinct was to flee, but she fought it with all her strength. She had to do this. Everyone depended on her. Ashton wasn't going away no matter how hard she wished it.

"Aren't you going to show yourself," she called out in a guttural voice, turning in a slow, deliberate circle.

She stood still and waited with uncertainty. After a few minutes had passed of what seemed to last for eternity, she became impatient and said, "Ashton, I'm waiting." Her eyes widened, the silence rubbing her nerves raw. "Show yourself."

The rustle of footsteps moving closer, coming from the dark shadows, caught her attention. As she turned to look, her heart leapt into her throat at the sight of a pair of amber eyes that glowed. They stared at her from a face that was all too familiar.

His features were that of a man and a wolf, covered in black matted fur and a muzzle for a mouth that made her cringe because Jena knew that she looked the same. It was the only similarity between them, other than their lust for human blood. While her humanity remained intact, he was nothing but a black pit of darkness.

"Tell me," he demanded as he came forward. There was a hint of aggravation and resentment in his tone. "Did you really think I wouldn't find out about your and Nicolas's plans?"

For an endless moment, Jena stood frozen in place like a stone statue, staring at him until the sound of approaching footsteps made her look away.

Out of the darkness came a huge, hulking wolf.

Jena involuntarily gasped and stepped back. The ferocious animal was dark brown and as big as a horse, if not bigger. It had its eyes pinned on Ashton's beastly form, glaring at him with a baleful stare.

Jena watched the four-legged canine with amazed disbelief as it took a few steps closer, moving with feline grace, and lowered its head. With its lips drawn back, it snarled at Ashton with a mouth full of razor-sharp teeth.

As Jena turned to look at Ashton, his eyes met hers, and they were furious. He was fuming with so much fury that she could hear a low, rumbling growl in the back of his throat.

At first, Jena had thought his anger targeted toward her, but then he looked away and spoke to the enormous animal. Ashton seemed to weigh each word before he spoke it. "Heed… my… warning… dog." His upper lip curled back over his teeth. "Leave now while you have a chance."

The mysterious wolfish creature went silent for a moment, its eyes flickering between the two until finally they zeroed in on Ashton. Then abruptly, it leaned forward with its teeth gritted and growled low in its throat as if it was preparing to attack.

Ashton narrowed his eyes in a final warning with his clawed hands wound into tight fists. Then he crouched into a fight stance and released a wild growl as though daring the unwelcome animal to make a move.

Suddenly, Jena remembered Angie's description of her Breedline wolf. Without a doubt, she then realized what it was, and for some reason, it appeared as though it was trying to protect her. But who was the person beneath the mystical wolf? Surely, whoever it was knew she was the only one that held the power to destroy the creature. As she pondered the Breedline's identity, and how it knew to come here, the answer to her questions instantly rang clear.

No, Jena thought. *Please, God, no…*

At the sound of something pawing at the ground, Jena quickly averted her eyes from Ashton and refocused them on the giant wolf. It looked ready to spring forward.

"Please, Angie," she pleaded, praying that her best friend would come to reason. "Don't do this."

For a split second, the enormous Breedline wolf took its eyes off Ashton and glanced in Jena's direction. It looked at her in a strange way. She could see that there was a conflicting confusion in the wolf's eyes. During that short blink in time, everything seemed to move in slow motion. It was as if the wolf was trying to relay some kind of message to Jena.

In that moment, Ashton used it to his advantage and lunged at the wolf with his claws reaching out in front of him.

Before Jena could react, or even jump in between them, Ashton had her friend on the ground. Time seemed to stand still as the creature and the Breedline wolf tore at one another. Then the sickening sounds of flesh tearing and bones cracking nearly brought Jena to her knees.

"No..." she yelled, her deep voice traveling through the cemetery in a distant echo.

As Jena brought her clawed hands close to her face, they were trembling. The curse was giving her more than heightened senses and a lust for blood. An unleashed anger... a murderous rage...

She felt stronger now. More courageous. Enough to *save* Angie. All of her conflicting emotions and fears melted away, replaced with the task to destroy him and preserve innocent lives.

* * *

There was a tense conversation, mostly between Tessa, Tim, the Fury, and the battle angels as they discussed the current situation dealing with Jena. As everyone else took their seats and listened in hushed silence, Bull's thoughts had drifted to Angie, worried that she'd taken off after Jena. He couldn't believe she would have done something this foolish as to go by herself. He couldn't stop thinking of the worst. Then, out of nowhere, a prickle of unease snaked down his spine, and he knew it had something to do with Angie. The bond they shared told him without a doubt she was in trouble, or worse. He could sense it within every fiber of his body.

When Lena glanced over at Bull, she knew something was wrong going by the grim expression on his face. She'd recognize that look anywhere. Each time they were assigned to a mission, either one that involved a rescue or a takedown, he'd always bottle up his emotions on the inside, but on the outside, it was obvious his nerves were stretched thin.

"Brother," she said, keeping her voice low. "What's wrong?"

"It's Angie," he mouthed. "Something's not right."

Lena got out of her chair and bent low next to Bull. "What's not right, brother?" She continued to keep her voice down.

Justice noticed something was off as he shifted in his seat and looked at Bull, whose face turned as white as a sheet in two seconds flat. His breaths seemed to be coming out in short gasps.

"Talk to us, buddy," Justice said, as he leaned in close to Bull, straining to hear everything he had to say.

"Angie went after Jena," he said, fear nearly choking him. "And she's hurt... bad."

"Oh shit," Justice declared, raising his voice. "How bad?"

Everyone at the table, including the battle angels and the Fury, immediately turned their full attention to Justice's outburst, looking at him oddly.

Annoyed by the interruption, Tim eyed Justice sharply. "What's going on?"

Bull sucked in a deep breath. "Angie went after Jena," he said grimly. "I have this strong feeling that she's been hurt. I can't..." He shook his head. "I can't lose her."

Cronus walked over and put his giant hand on Bull's shoulder. "You aren't going to lose her."

Bull lifted his chin and looked squarely at Cronus. "How can you be sure?"

"It's not her time," he simply said.

Bull turned to the others knowing that Angie's fate now rested in the hands of his supernatural companions. "We have to go after her."

Lena rested her hand over Bull's and then looked up at Cronus. "Please tell me you have a plan."

Cronus nodded. "We're going to the Salem Cemetery."

"And kill whatever the hell gets in our way," Apollyon added.

Jace abruptly pounded his fist on top of the table. "I second that," he said, his eyes going from Apollyon to his fraternal twin sisters and back again. "Before we go kick some ass, I've got one question that's been driving me crazy."

Tessa glared into Jace's stubborn blue eyes and grumbled. "Come on, Jace. This is not the time."

"Now hang on a minute," he said, and there was a sort of bitter humor in his voice. "I think I deserve to know. The three of them did try to kill us once."

"Okay, Jace," Tessa said, releasing a heavy sigh. "Go ahead, but make it fast."

"Answer me one thing." Jace pointed to the signet ring on Apollyon's hand. "What's up with that symbol? I've noticed all three of you have one," he said, averting his eyes from Apollyon and focusing them on Callisto's necklace and then to Electra's bracelet, noticing all three pieces of jewelry had the same particular shape of a trefoil knot. "What does it mean? Is that where you get your powers from?"

Apollyon smirked. "We were born with our powers," he said, looking down at the ring on his hand. Then, as he looked back up, his hard expression softened a little. "They were gifts from our mother. While our biological father kept her prisoner, they were the only things he allowed her to give us. The symbol represents the Holy Trinity of the Father, the Son, and the Holy Spirit." Then he went on to say, "My mother has always had a strong Christian faith."

"Well, hell," Jace huffed out, shrugging. "Okay, then. I guess that answers my question." He rubbed his hands together in anticipation. "So, let's go kick some ass." He wiggled his eyebrows. "I call first dibs."

"You may go in first," Cronus said to Jace. "Your Beast, along with everyone else, has the strength to fight the creature. You will all serve as a distraction. Jena is the only one who has the power to destroy it."

"What about all of you?" Tessa asked, her eyes going from Cronus to the other four angels and back again. "Aren't you going to help us fight this creature?"

Cronus looked at Tessa wearily. "Our Creator sent us here to help Jena, although we are also here for another reason. There is something *evil* coming, and we are chosen to destroy *it*."

Chapter Forty-Two

Without further delay, Jena moved in quickly and knocked Ashton off the Breedline wolf with a powerful swipe of her clawed hand. He struck the ground with a blinding force and rolled along the gravesites, the impact smashing several concrete headstones into bits and pieces.

Throughout all his immortal years, the creature had never faced anyone or anything that had come close to his power and strength. Tonight, Jena had vowed, that would all change.

Angie watched, in her Breedline form, as Jena went after the creature. She had to help, but when she struggled to stand on all fours, she was still too weak from the injuries inflicted by the creature's sharp claws to be of much help. Blood was seeping from her thick hide, and there were gaping wounds in a few places—although she could feel the beginnings of the Breedline healing doing its work.

When Jena came upon the creature, she stopped in her tracks as he slowly took to his feet. Covered in flakes of dirt, he was bleeding from his shoulder and other places on his torso where Angie's wolf had used her teeth. As Jena prepared herself to fight against him, she knew it was time to wipe the creature's evil existence from the earth. She *had* to succeed. Innocent lives, including Nicolas, depended on her.

Then, before her eyes, his body began to reshape, and spasms of pain contorted his face as though something inside of him was clawing its way out. Within seconds, the creature stood in front of her in his human form, wearing only the torn remnants of his pants.

A look of self-assurance came over his face as he said, "You kill me, and Nicolas dies."

Jena shook her head, realizing Ashton was trying to confuse her, but she remained strong and pushed his words aside. "You're lying," she said through gritted teeth.

Ashton's voice was calm, but his eyes blazed. "It's true, my beloved."

Jena growled and took a single step forward. "Don't call me that! I am *not* your beloved!" The words came out of Jena's mouth before she could stop them. It was as though she had no control over what she was saying. "Your powers—they no longer have a hold on me."

Ashton was looking at her, stunned, his mouth open. Jena imagined that no one had ever spoken to him like that.

"No, it cannot be," he uttered, warily stepping back. Then an expression of disappointment showed in his eyes. It was only there for a moment before it shifted into something harsh and resentful. "I am *your* creator." His voice became angry. "You. Will. Obey. Me."

His words took her by surprise and she found that her power of resistance began to fade. "N-no," she muttered as her body suddenly began to shrink. It was as if the impending changes took on a will of their own. No matter how hard she fought it, her body continued to transform itself. She could feel every pore in her skin absorbing all the hair that had blanketed her body until her creature was no more and she was just a human again.

Naked and exposed, Jena quickly wrapped her arms around herself. "Why did you do this to me?" she demanded. "Why did you *curse* me?"

Ashton's lips twisted slightly, although it was not a smile, more like a conceited smug. "Don't you see, Jena," he said, his words mocking. "You are my true beloved. My blood flows through your veins, and so does my dearest Isabella's."

Jena thought back to the words in Nicolas's journal as he told the story of Isabella Westfield and how she broke Ashton's heart, not only once, but twice, and what her rejections had done to him. So far, she couldn't figure out how Isabella was linked to her. She was almost positive there was no one by the name of Westfield on either side of her parents' ancestry.

"I don't understand," she said, her eyes brimming with tears. "What does that have to do with me?"

"Not only are you a descendant of Isabella," he began to explain, "you have the blood of my Master in you. You were not born entirely human, nor just the creature I created. You are something extraordinary, something entirely other. A

Necromancer," he said with a calculated grin. "How else did you think it was possible for you to speak with the dead?"

Jena's heart sank. "B-but, God gave me that gift," she said, her expression hopeless. "The angels said—"

"They lied," he interjected with an acidic flash of bitterness. "Your true *father* gave you this special gift, and I'm not talking about the one up above." He made a show of mockery by rolling his eyes.

"My father?" Jena looked at him in question. "What are you saying?"

"Your parents kept a secret from you," he told her. "They are not your biological family. You were adopted."

Jena opened her mouth and then closed it again, until finally, she built up the courage to speak. "Who is..." she said, choosing her words carefully, "my real father?"

Ashton stood there silent for a moment, his eyes shining in the moonlight. He seemed hesitant to give her an answer, the stillness unraveling Jena's already stretched nerves. Then he simply said, "Lucifer."

Jena drew in a breath, and for a moment, everything went dizzy. Ashton's words seemed so convincing, and yet—

"No," she said breathlessly. The ground beneath Jena began to sway, tipping from one side to the other. Her legs trembled, and her body shook with the horror of his revelation. It all seemed like a nightmare, trapping her in a state of torment and misery.

With her arms wrapped around herself, she dropped to her knees and let out a scream that sounded like shattering glass.

Ashton crossed the short distance to where Jena was and knelt down with his hand out. "Come, my beloved. Let me take the pain away."

When she looked up at him, tears streamed down her face like from an endless river.

"Take my hand," he said softly, "and share this precious moment with me. Together, our powers will be limitless. We will start a new race. It will be a powerful race that will dominate the human species and destroy all supernatural beings on earth."

Her lips quivered. "Y-you want me to give you... *children?*"

Now he was grinning. "Yes, my beloved. You will provide me a strong bloodline."

"No, she's not," said a voice, laced with a southern accent.

Startled, Ashton straightened and spun around on the balls of his feet, preparing to meet a familiar face. Although he recognized the voice, there was no one there.

"Where are you?" Ashton called out as his eyes darted over the dark and fog-covered graveyard. "Show yourself..." He paused and snarled his upper lip. "...little brother."

Out of nowhere, a faint outline of a ghostly image appeared behind Jena. When it fully took on a corporeal shape, the figure leaned over Jena and draped a long shawl around her, blanketing her bareness. The moment she felt hands on her shoulders, blurred memories came rushing up in a torrent flood—memories of a man embracing a woman, touching her face intimately and softly, although she couldn't make out their features.

As Jena flinched and looked up, she was shell-shocked for a moment. The handsome face that stood above her took her by surprise. He looked at her as if some realization had dawned on him. Then, a strange sense of familiarity hung between them as though they had met before—perhaps many years ago in another life. She could definitely see the resemblance between him and Ashton. They had the same square jaw, an ageless pale complexion, and ink-black hair that fell past their shoulders.

Jena's face flushed, the color high in her cheeks, and Nicolas wondered if it was the vulnerability of her nakedness, or something else.

She took a breath and exhaled slowly. "Nicolas?" she murmured, pulling at the shawl so that it covered more of her exposed skin.

He gave her a comforting smile that seemingly eased her in some way, but his eyes looked tensed with worry.

As he opened his mouth to speak, a growling voice cut him off. "Why have you been keeping all these secrets from me, Nicolas?"

He lifted his head to meet Ashton's menacing stare, realizing his brother was aware of the journal and his ability to vanish and reappear at will. "I'm sorry, Ash," Nicolas said, his hands clenched at his sides and his eyes filled with regret. "I had no other choice. I can't continue to let you do this."

"You had no other choice?" Ashton drawled. "Tell me, little brother..." He raised an eyebrow. "How long have you been planning all this..." He hissed out a breath through his teeth. "...betrayal?"

Nicolas looked at him grimly. "That day you disappeared," he told him, "after you confronted Isabella at the cemetery. When you returned, you were never the same."

Ashton gasped as if his brother had sucker-punched him and took an involuntary step back. "So, this is your plan?" He looked at Nicolas, his dark eyes shooting daggers. "To have my beloved do your dirty work?"

"It's the only way..." He slowly shook his head. "...and it's the right thing to do."

"If she destroys me..." He grinned, his fangs shining like ivory pins. "...your life will end as well."

Nicolas nodded. "Whatever it takes to stop all this madness."

Ashton threw his head back and laughed. The short, sharp bark sent chills through Jena's veins.

"By now, you should know, Nicolas. Jena will *not* kill me." He paused and narrowed his eyes at her. "She's powerless in my presence."

A look of distress passed over Jena's face. As if in anguish, she lowered her head and closed her eyes. She did not know if what all Ashton had said were entirely true. Was she indeed the daughter of Lucifer, born a Necromancer, and still under Ashton's spell? Her heart wanted to believe in what the angels had told her.

As silence fell between them, the only sounds that Jena heard were the trees blowing in the wind and her own blood pounding in her ears. *Think Jena, think,* she feverishly thought. *How can I possibly defeat something that has such a strong hold on me?* Jena wanted desperately to grab ahold of her inner strength and bring forth her creature once again.

But struggling against Ashton's binding spell was like struggling to breathe underwater.

Jena took a deep breath, opened her eyes and looked up at Nicolas.

"You hold all the power, Jena." She heard Nicolas—or was it Angie's voice—whisper into her mind. She realized now what Angie had meant by her words. Jena had become a part of the Breedline family, and they had become hers. If she did not destroy the creature, she would lose them all. At that moment, something inside of her sparked with valor. Then she looked forward, her eyes glaring viciously at Ashton. "I hold all the power," she said, her voice demanding and seemingly full of confidence.

His eyes widened as if her words threatened him in some way, or was it that he was worried the spell had been broken.

"That is not possible," he said with a clear smirk in his voice. "Not possible—"

Before anyone could get another word out, the sound of heavy footsteps moving at a high speed caught their attention. As they turned to look, Ashton was blindsided by something monstrous moving at the full speed of a freight train.

As hundreds of pounds of raging fury drove Ashton to the ground, it was then that Jena realized who it was. She quickly got to her feet and screamed, "Angie, no!"

Before Jena rushed forward, Nicolas instantly reached out and held her back. "No, Jena," he warned her. And when she responded by trying to pull away, he looked at her intently and added, "Please, Jena."

The time it took Angie's wolf to tackle Ashton, his transformation was already taking place. The power surge within him only took a matter of seconds, and he was the creature once more. Then, in a frenzy of snarling sounds, the battle between the Breedline wolf and the creature began again.

Jena looked up at Nicolas, her eyes wide and glassy with tears. "She's my best friend. I've got to do something," she said, her voice pleading. "He'll kill her."

Nicolas stared down at Jena, his eyes expressing concern. He gently grasped her hand and spoke to her in a soft voice, "Use your curse, Jena. Bring forth the creature within you."

It was hard to hear him over all the vicious sounds coming from the enormous creatures. They were biting and ripping at one another, destroying anything that got in their path.

Nicolas raised his voice, and lightly squeezed her hand, "You can do this, Jena. It's the only way."

Ashton had never fought a creature this big, this he determined as they scuffled and grappled on the damp ground among all the dead. Again, and again, he raked his sharp claws into the enormous wolf, maddening the four-legged animal, and then tearing into its thick layer of hide with all the strength he had in his powerful jaws.

Although Ashton seemed to be overpowering Angie's wolf, she would not give up the fight. With lightning reflexes, she used her body as a battering ram and pummeled into Ashton's side, knocking him completely off balance. He crashed into a nearby gravestone, crumbling it to pieces before hitting the ground hard.

Seizing the opportunity, the wolf crouched low and launched off the ground using its powerful hind legs. As it leaped into the air, Ashton braced himself against the ground and kicked at the Breedline with all his strength. The mighty blow instantly sent Angie's wolf in reverse. With a yelp, she crashed to the ground and tumbled out of control.

I have to help her, Jena thought. She struggled to bring forth the change, but no matter how hard she tried, nothing happened. Ashton's binding spell was too strong. Jena felt helpless as she stood back and watched her best friend fight a losing battle. At that thought, her heart seemed to shrink inside her chest. It was then she wondered, could Breedline wolves die, or was it only silver that could kill them? If only she had made an effort to find out, had asked Angie.

Ashton allowed the wolf no time to recover. He quickly got to his feet and pounced on the fallen enemy. It roared in pain and recoiled as Ashton began to use his razor-sharp claws to rip at the animal's backside.

No! Please, no, Jena despairingly thought as she stood in horror, focused on the awful images transpiring right before her very eyes. She watched helplessly as Ashton repeatedly sliced his claws across her best friend's hide with a ruthless vengeance.

"Stop it!" Jena shouted at Ashton. "You're killing her!"

The murderous creature, on the other hand, was not at all fazed. Dripping in blood, he ignored Jena's outbursts and took hold of the wolf's throat. With a firm grip, he squeezed with all his strength.

Jena prayed, despite everything, Ashton would show leniency, if only the smallest, and have mercy on Angie.

Chapter Forty-Three

When a distinctive scent mingled with the wind, it took Ashton by surprise. It was a scent like no other. The musky odor mixed with the smell of a wet dog infuriated him to no end. He snarled deep in his throat, sensing something big approaching from behind.

The light of the full moon cast its enormous reflection on a headstone ahead. The shadow of the dark figure was nothing he had ever encountered before. *What the hell?* There was much he still didn't know about the secret world of the Breedline, but he knew whatever had come here wasn't of their kind. It was something else. Something much more lethal... more powerful.

In the midst of his fury, he loosened his grip and released the Breedline wolf. The time it took him to look, something with sharp claws had grabbed him roughly by the scruff of the neck and lifted him off the ground.

Ashton was shocked as he dangled in midair by the shear strength of the *thing* that had ahold of him. He barely caught a glimpse of the shaggy beast, its pelt as white as snow, before he found himself sailing across the graveyard, tossed like a flimsy, rag doll.

Just as he was about to slam into a nearby crypt, the same one that held Debi captive, he instantly vanished, leaving nothing behind but a cloud of smoke.

Angered by Ashton's clever maneuver, the monstrous, white-haired beast reared back on his hind legs and let loose a deafening roar.

It felt like time stood still as Jena stared in bewilderment, wondering if her eyes were deceiving her. She could not take them off the malevolent beast standing only a few feet away. It stood on two legs, towering to the height of at least seven feet, covered with thick white fur, and the thing was visibly pissed. It was then she remembered what Angie had told her about Jace Chamberlain. He was the good-looking blond who was married to Tessa and had the twin brother—known as the Chosen Son—that could create a firebomb out of the palm of his hand. Although Jace was born a Breedline, he was also like her, something entirely other, and rage was its catalyst, invoking his internal beast.

A sense of relief took hold as Jena averted her eyes from Jace's beast and searched the shadows for Ashton to reappear. After a few seconds had passed, she suddenly came back to focus. Without thinking, Jena rushed to Angie's side to see to her injures. The moment she reached out, a hand grasped her arm, claws piercing her bare skin. She gasped and whirled around to find herself facing Ashton's venomous stare. She tried to pull free, but his grip was too strong.

"You *will* come with me," Ashton demanded.

Instinctively, Jace's beast dropped into a defensive stance, raising his razor-sharp claws, preparing to lunge forward. Before he could make a move, Nicolas shot over with incredible speed, so fast he was nearly a blur, and stood behind what was once his loving brother.

With a watchful eye, the beast hung back and remained on guard.

"You'll have to go through me first."

At the sound of Nicolas's voice, Ashton released his hold on Jena and spun around. "That," he said in a tone that dripped with scorn, "can be arranged, little brother."

Nicolas stood firm as Ashton lashed out, reaching for his throat. Everything to Nicolas seemed to be moving in slow motion—the tips of his brother's sharp claws aiming toward his jugular, and the snarling look on his wolfish face. It all mingled with Jena's desperate screams.

A distant memory from long ago suddenly flashed before Nicolas's eyes: Isabella, falling to her knees at the sight of Ashton standing before her resurrected, and the horrified look on her face. In that split second, his hand automatically came up and grasped his brother's wrist, squeezing it with an iron grip.

Disbelief passed over Ashton's hellish face, and he looked decidedly less sure of himself than he had before. Then his eyes went dark with rage, but his voice was numb. "How could you betray your own blood?"

Tormented by his brother's bitter words, mixed emotions warred within Nicolas's chest. Although he could not deny that Ashton had savagely murdered for many years, taking the lives of countless innocent people, and yet, he could not be at fault for what he had become. He himself was responsible for Ashton's fate.

Nicolas stared in sorrow at his cursed brother, wrestling with his own conscience. "Please forgive me, brother."

"You're no brother of mine," he viciously said, his face stern and unforgiving as he unexpectedly exploded into action. He jerked his arm back, violently snapping Nicolas forward and slammed his head into his face.

Jena screamed as Nicolas staggered on his feet and crumbled to his knees. Ashton lunged at him, claws out, and Nicolas went down hard, his head cracking against a gravestone, rendering him unconscious. Taking full advantage, Ashton slashed into Nicolas with a flurry of violent blows.

"No!" Jena helplessly cried out.

Still in his beast form, Jace sprang forward without hesitation. His roar offered Ashton only an instant's warning before he even knew what hit him. With a single swipe of his arm, the beast delivered a powerful blow that sent Ashton tumbling backward. He disappeared in a cloud of dust as he smashed straight through the wall of a stone crypt.

In the silence that followed, Jena searched anxiously for Ashton, but he was nowhere in sight. She hesitated, but only for a moment, and rushed over to Nicolas. When she knelt down, blood trickled from the corner of his mouth. *Please, no,* she dreadfully thought, smoothing a long strand of his hair back. *You can't die.*

"Please, Nicolas," Jena said aloud, wiping at the blood on his face. "Don't leave—"

Without warning, a dark winged figure dropped from the sky. The sound of it landing startled Jena, compelling her to look up. Her eyes rounded as his bat-like wings unsheathed to their fullest and then snapped together as they tucked behind his back.

His terrifying appearance would have brought Jena to her knees if she'd been standing. He had an aura of authority about him, radiating power of dominance over others. *Was this devilish creature friend or foe?* she thought, watching nervously as he came forward.

A sudden flicker of hope swept through Jena when she noticed the winged visitor exchanging a look of understanding with Jace's beast. If they had any misgivings about being in the presence of one another, she found no trace of it so far.

"Speak your name," he said, scowling at her.

Although she tried to remain calm, her trembling voice betrayed her. "J-Jena. Jena McCain."

He blinked in surprise at the name. "Are you the one who is cursed?"

Jena gaped up at him, seemingly uncertain how to respond. For all she knew, the bat-like creature standing before her was here to kill her. She shifted uneasily on her knees and scooted closer to Nicolas's body. "Are you here..." She paused, swallowing the knot that had formed in the back of her throat. "...to kill me?"

He regarded her with a skeptic stare. Then he arched a brow and said, "My name is Apollyon. *We* have come to help you kill the creature who has cursed you."

"We?" Jena asked, looking at Apollyon, confused.

Just then, two women came out of the darkness and moved to stand on opposite sides of Apollyon. The one on his right had the physique of a bodybuilder, and although it was nighttime, she wore a pair of dark sunglasses. The line of her square jaw was set hard in the dim light. Her intimidating expression reminded Jena of a contract killer. She then wondered if the woman was an assassin by day and a dominatrix by night, going by all the black leather she had on and the silver whip attached to her hip. The other woman seemed the opposite. She was feminine looking with long legs and had a conspicuously dark, mysterious presence about her. She almost seemed conceited by the way she stood and the smug expression on her face.

Apollyon glanced to his right and said, "This is my sister, Electra."

She acknowledged Jena with a slight nod.

As he started to introduce the long-legged woman on his left, she stepped forward and said, "Cut the chit-chat, brother. Let us get on with it." She flipped her long hair back and smirked at Jena. "My name is Callisto," she said, cocking a brow. "So, where is *this* creature?"

Jena shook her head, and before she could answer, Ashton suddenly appeared like a ghost out of thin air. "Come and kill me if you think you can," he growled, glaring at Apollyon and his fraternal twin sisters. Then, he glanced about the cemetery at Angie's injured wolf and Jace's beast. "You'll have to do better than the dogs you sent."

"Stop this madness!" a female voice demanded.

Ashton cut his eyes to the sound of the familiar voice. Striding from out of the shadows, with her dark wings tucked behind her back and her expression fierce, was the redheaded battle angel gifted with holy fire. Next to her, Drakon stared at Ashton behind a pair of dark sunglasses, and Kyle, who had a lit cigarette between his lips, cracked his knuckles. On the other side of Drakon stood Alexander with his lips formed into a straight line and his hands fisted at his sides.

"I command you," the angel raised her voice, "surrender now!"

"Lailah," Ashton said in a measured tone, narrowing his eyes as more precarious-looking strangers came forward and stood by the winged redhead. "Have you come to witness everyone's death?"

"Only yours," Lailah shot back, reaching for the glimmering sword she had sheathed alongside her waist.

A boiling rage poured over Ashton as he cruelly kicked at Nicolas's unconscious body. "And what of my dear, little brother?"

Instantly, Jena positioned herself over Nicolas, trying to shield him from further harm. "You're nothing but a coward," she said, looking up at Ashton with hatred in her eyes. "How could you do this to him? He's done nothing but protect you his whole life."

Ashton raked his eyes down at Jena, cold and callously. "You," he said with disgust in his voice, "have *feelings* for him, don't you?"

For a moment, his words created a feeling of confusion and uncertainty within her. *Could it be?* Jena thought, closing her eyes. *Could there be some kind of hidden feelings between me and Nicolas?*

It was then an image suddenly came to her—a vision. As Jena blinked her eyes open, a memory from somewhere deep in her subconscious flashed inside her mind, fading out everything surrounding her...

All Jena could see were yellow wildflowers. It was as if she had materialized in the middle of a field, surrounded by a sea of what looked to be butterweeds. As she scanned the area, she looked for anything that might give her a hint of familiarity. For some strange reason, an odd shimmer went through Jena, the kind that made her wonder whether this was a memory from a long time ago, or perhaps from a dream. Nevertheless, she felt as though she had been here before.

Out of nowhere, the sound of approaching voices caught her attention. When she turned to look, not far away she could see a man dressed in a long gray coat with puffed sleeves, knee breeches, tall riding boots, and a woman who wore a dress of brilliant pink silk and matching gloves. They reminded her of a prince and a princess out of a fairy-tale book.

Jena watched like a distant observer as they moved closer. The wind was slightly blowing and had ruffled the man's ink-black hair as the pair crossed the brightly colored meadow. By the way they glanced fondly at one another and held hands, it was apparent they were a couple.

As the two looked her way, Jena froze, but to her relief, they appeared to gaze past her. Although she could see them, it was evident they could not see her. How strange, Jena thought. It wasn't until they were a few feet away that she recognized their faces. Jena caught her breath. It was Nicolas, to her surprise, and a young woman that resembled the girl in her painting... identical to herself, except she looked to be from another era of time. Which meant it could only be one person: Isabella Westfield.

Jena stood completely baffled by what she saw. It didn't make any sense. There were no records in Nicolas's journal of him and Isabella having a relationship. However, this perhaps explained the reason for all the missing pages.

Refocusing her attention ahead, Jena could see the uncanny similarities between her and Isabella, the features they shared: long blonde hair, their height and frame, the pale blue color of their eyes. Looking at Isabella was like staring into a mirror at herself.

For the longest moment, Nicolas and Isabella both stood face to face with their hands joined as if they were preparing to embrace.

As Isabella released Nicolas's hands, Jena heard her say, "Although my heart cannot deny my true feelings, I cannot bear to continue this betrayal." She broke eye contact with Nicolas and lowered her head, but not before Jena saw the pain in her eyes. "It would destroy Ashton if he discovered the truth."

Nicolas instantly grasped ahold of her hand, his expression overcome with distress. "Please, Isabella."

She lifted her teary gaze. "You and I both know this is wrong," she said, shaking her head. "God will surely punish us."

Nicolas's violet eyes bored into Isabella's pale-blue gaze. It made him seem more vulnerable, and his eyes, too, were unguarded, open like a door.

Then, as Jena painfully observed, he placed their joined hands over his heart as though it was a piece of glass in fear of shattering. "Punish us for what, Isabella?" he asked. "For falling in love?"

Isabella leaned into Nicolas with tears rolling down her cheeks. "For allowing it to go this far."

Jena's heart caught in her throat as Nicolas leaned in further and rested his forehead against Isabella's. "I wouldn't take any of it back for the world. The only thing I regret is..." He swallowed back tears. "...that I didn't meet you first."

"I know, I know," she whispered. "If only..."

"No matter what happens," he whispered back. "I will always love you, Izzy."

"And I you, Nicolas."

In spite of Nicolas's and Isabella's outward appearance of calm, it was obvious their hearts were breaking. And her heart too, along with her state of mind, felt broken. It was then Jena knew why Isabella decided to dedicate herself to a women's convent in England, vowing a life of celibacy. Although she loved both Nicolas and Ashton, she could not carry the burden of hurting either one. Regardless of the grief of having to say good-bye, Nicolas loved Isabella enough to let her go. Unfortunately, no matter the choices, the outcome was still the same.

As Nicolas and Isabella quickly embraced, something took hold of Jena's throat.

And then Jena was abruptly back to the present, returning to the cemetery... where Nicolas remained unconscious, and Ashton held her by the throat, squeezing with a death grip.

Jena struggled to breathe, much less remain conscious. In her peripheral view, she saw a blurry image of someone moving closer. "Please, Ashton," a voice she recognized said from the vision she had. "For God's sake, I beg you. Please don't do this."

Distracted, Ashton released Jena and instantly looked at the voice he recalled from a long time ago.

Jena took a deep, gasping breath and saw Isabella standing close to the redheaded angel, easily recognizable by the remarkable resemblance in her vision and her pink silk dress.

"Izzy?" Ashton muttered. His eyes rounded in stunned disbelief. "But how—?" he began, but before he could say more, the snap of a whip interceded as it hurled forward at lightning speed. It carried with it a sizzling bolt of electricity that crackled through the air, end over end, and struck his chest like a blazing torch. As it burned and scorched his hide, black smoke rose from his body as if he was burning from the inside out.

Ashton howled—howled and writhed as everyone watched him transform into a vapor-like fog. In an instant, he disappeared.

Surprised, Jena turned to look at the woman dressed in leather, who held a whip that sizzled with smoke, and then at the bat-like creature standing beside her who raised an eyebrow and said, "Nice throw, sister."

The corners of Electra's lips curled up. It wasn't a pleasant grin, more like a satisfied smirk. She turned away from Apollyon to look at Callisto. For a moment, the two sisters stared at each other in silent understanding.

It was then Jena wondered what they had in mind by the calculating look on their faces. Suddenly, she felt a chill at the pit of her stomach just as something flashed next to the redheaded angel. Jena turned to look. Standing behind the angel was Isabella, and she was glowing, light blazing all around her. Jena watched as her body stretched and elongated. It was as if she was shifting into someone else. Glancing around, Jena saw that everyone else—seemingly oblivious to what was transpiring—had their eyes focused on where Ashton had previously stood, as though they were expecting him to reappear. When Jena averted her eyes and refocused them on Isabella, wings instantly burst from her back—massive black wings, similar to the battle angels. Then, to Jena's surprise, Isabella's image vanished and a male angel with bleached, spiked hair magically took her place. Jena looked startled for a moment and then came to realize the angel must have the ability to shapeshift, using her visions of Isabella to trick Ashton. The angel's quick thinking had saved her life.

The sound of heavy footsteps made Jena tear her gaze from the angel and peer past him. As three giant shadows slowly came into view, a feeling of relief washed over Jena in waves, realizing the remaining battle angels had arrived. When Cronus, Icarus, and Helios crowded in next to the other male angel and Lailah, a tall man with long black hair, who she remembered as Sebastian, stood alongside them. The golden orbs of his eyes glowed with a harsh acidic light. With his brows pinched together, he appeared more sinister than the last time she saw him, almost equivalent to Apollyon's savage disposition.

Jena was about to look away when a deep voice took her by surprise.

"Fear not, Jena," Helios spoke into her mind. *"We are here to help you."*

She looked up then and met her eyes with his. His diamond eyes bored into hers with confidence, and for some reason, it gave her hope.

Chapter Forty-Four

Meanwhile, Ashton's ghostly apparition shot upward and tried to escape, but to his dismay, he found himself trapped in some sort of force field even though there was nothing visibly solid surrounding him. Within seconds, he started to shift back into a solid form.

Jena turned just as a shadowed outline of a monstrous figure began to take shape.

"What in the hell," Ashton gritted his teeth, "is this?"

With a stone-cold expression, Electra drew back her fierce weapon and positioned it back on her hip, while her sister Callisto looked visibly amused by Ashton's unsettling reaction. The force field, after all, had been her doing. Although this time, the creature was defenseless when her shield surrounded him.

Apollyon raised an eyebrow in Callisto and Electra's direction. "Hasn't anyone ever told you?" He averted his eyes from his sisters and focused them on Ashton. "Never piss off a woman who can kick your ass," he said mockingly. "Much less two," he tacked on.

Ashton shot Apollyon a murderous glare. "Shut your foul mouth," he growled, exposing rows of sharp teeth, "before I *rip* your tongue from your *fucking* head."

As Jena watched, nestled under the shawl and huddled closely to Nicolas, she half-expected the bat-like creature, who called himself Apollyon, to make some sharp-witted comment in response, but he simply looked at Ashton coolly and remained silent.

It wasn't until Roman and Bull stepped from the shadows and saw Angie's wolf lying on the ground, motionless and bloodied, that Bull's panic-stricken voice broke the silence. *"Noooo!"*

"Bull—" Roman started, but Bull was already running toward his beloved, fearing the worst. As he neared her, a crackling noise thundered through the air and the ground under his feet began to tremble. He reeled back, surprise blooming across his face, as the earth abruptly broke open and exploded with light. The cemetery that housed the dead suddenly lit up with flames, rising in colors of gold and red.

Bull looked from the fiery pit to Angie's unconscious wolf, to the battle angels. The air was thick with smoke, and the smell of fire was choking. Then he coughed and coughed again. "Someone," he finally said, shielding his face from the burning flames, "do something—"

And there it came, crawling out like a demon rising from the deepest pits of hell. As it dug its clawed hands into the ground, lifting itself up, the enormous creature was definitely not human. It had five heads, all of them shaped like a serpent: golden vertical slit-pupiled eyes that glowed against its blood-red scales, wings like a dragon, and jaws filled with dagger-sharp teeth.

A wolfish grin played across Ashton's face. "Master," he hissed, and raised his powerful wolf arms, his claws reaching for the sky almost as if he was reaching for the *thing* that had risen from below, pleading for its help.

One of the reptilian creatures leaned close to Bull and roared in his ear. The sound sent a jolt of adrenaline through his body—and along with it, rage. He gritted his teeth and tried to stand, but his legs buckled under him. He struggled on his hands and knees, trying to pull himself closer to Angie's wolf, but the thick smoke and heat radiating from the flames were too much.

"Benjamin!" Lena cried out to her brother, her heart twisting inside her chest as she and Justice rushed to his side.

Everything after that seemed to happen in slow motion. Jena turned, her eyes searching the graveyard desperately for Lailah and the other battle angels. She couldn't see them through all the smoke, but she heard growling, and then several pairs of glowing eyes suddenly flickered in the darkness. She scrambled closer on her hands and knees, trying to get a better view, but she could make out only the flash of weapons that looked to be swords and the dark shapes of enormous wolves along with another dark outline of what seemed to be an enormous feline of some sort.

Jena turned to scramble back only to find Ashton waiting for her, in his human form, standing next to his brother's motionless body. He bitterly smiled down at Jena, who was too shocked to do anything but stare up at him.

"I'm going to ask you one more time," he said, offering her his hand. His voice was harsh, impatient. "Join me, my beloved."

The shrieking noises coming from the five-headed serpent caused Jena to flinch and look away. There was a scream, and among the smoke and burning flames, she could see three dark figures that looked to be a woman and two men, standing before the demonic creature. It snorted plumes of smoke and hissed at them like a cobra, readying itself to strike in unison. Jena took a deep, shuddering breath and tore her eyes away from the horror. For a moment, everything seemed to hang in suspension. Then her attention focused back to Ashton, her eyes darkening as they met his gaze. As she stared into his haunted eyes, she remembered the intimate night they had shared. Images, more than thoughts, were rushing through Jena's mind, terrible and disturbing images of the next morning, of the monstrous creature she'd become, of the repulsive face looking back at her in the mirror. It was like a distant dream, like something that had happened to someone else and not her. Then her mind came back to focus. Somehow, Ashton managed to seduce her then, but now, she was determined not to give in to him a second time.

"No." She shook her head, crawling back slowly. "I refuse to be the monster you have become."

His face twisted into a mask of rage and his eyes blazed with a wave of painful anger. It was then that Jena braced herself, noticing his impending changes were rising fast. She watched in silence, pleading to God to stop it, as his features began to contort and elongate until he was entirely unrecognizable. Jena was amazed at how quickly his transition took over. Thick black hair pushed out of every inch of his bare skin and trailed down his broad shoulders. In a matter of seconds, it covered him completely.

With her eyes fixed on his hideous face, Jena felt her chest tighten. Ashton looked very angry. Angry enough to kill her. The vicious expression on his face was enough to impel Jena to her feet.

The moment she stood, she heard him growl deep in his throat, and then his clawed hand was on her arm, gripping painfully, forcing her forward.

Jena took a shaking breath. "Please, don't do this," she pleaded, straining against his strong hold, but her resistance only infuriated him further. He jerked her arm with such force her feet went out from under her. Jena fell to her knees, agony shooting through her as the skin tore from the bits of gravel and the uneven ground below.

"Get up," he growled.

Painfully Jena turned her head, searching for help, but she couldn't see past all the smoked-filled darkness. Her head jerked back when something sharp dug into her skin and wrapped tightly around her ankle. Jena cringed but didn't scream, biting her lip to keep it at bay. In sheer panic, she clawed at the ground as Ashton dragged her from behind.

"Let her go," a stern voice said, seemingly close by.

Ashton froze in his tracks but kept a firm grip on Jena. He looked away from her and to the unfamiliar voice.

"Let her go?" Ashton said, squinting his shrewd luminous eyes, searching for the stranger among the thick cloud of smoke. "Who dares to tell me..." He let out a deep-throated cackle. "...what to do? And more to the point, whoever you are, what do you mean to do about it? Surely, by now, it would seem obvious that none of your *kind* can kill me."

A tall blond, who Jena recognized as Jace's twin brother—the one who Angie described as the Chosen Son—emerged from the veil of smoke as though he came out of nowhere. Behind him were huge wolves, perhaps as many as ten, a giant black panther, and Jace's beast. They paced back and forth, growling and snarling.

"Maybe we cannot kill you," Jem said as he stepped forward, his palm crackling with light. "But sometimes there are far worse things than death."

Jena watched in amazement at what looked to be a bolt of lightning shooting straight out of the palm of Jem's hand. As it made contact with Ashton's chest, he instantly howled and clutched at his charred and scorched hide.

Among his piercing howls, Jena could hear the sounds of wings flapping. Crouched on the ground, she looked to the dark sky and a sense of relief suddenly took hold. Flying above—so close she could feel a soothing current of air breeze against her face—were the glorious battle angels, equipped with swords, preparing to fight against the five-headed serpent. Then she heard them shouting.

"Attack!" Cronus called out, leading his comrades in arms into battle.

With lightning speed, Icarus swung his sharp-edged weapon as one of the serpents snapped its head forward, slicing clean through its thick-scaled skin. The monstrous head struck the ground and blood spurted like an acidic red fountain.

The remainder of the reptilian creatures simultaneously let loose a hellish shriek as though they felt the death of the fifth companion.

Seething with anger and unbearable agony, Ashton fell to his knees, grieving over the foreseen death of his Master. A look of despair flashed across his face by the tragedy of his loss, but it passed quickly, and unbridled fury reawakened inside him.

"Now!" Cronus yelled, louder this time. *We can do this*, he thought silently, rearing back his sword, getting ready to slay his enemy. *God created us for this, to protect the innocent from evil, and we will not fail him.* As he swung his mighty sword that was as long as his forearm, Helios, Lailah, and Frigg followed suit. All at once, they decapitated the snake-like heads in the flash of light, and at the same time it released Jena's binding spell. Now, their task was almost complete.

At first, nothing happened. Then Jena's breathing suddenly became deeper and more guttural. It was at that moment she gasped in relief, realizing the spell had been broken and she was changing quickly now. Already, straining muscles rippled beneath Jena's skin, while coarse black hairs sprouted from every pore and began to cover the vulnerability of her nakedness. The shape of her face twisted and stretched until her human features were no more. Jena felt herself expanding as if her skin could no longer contain its human form. Her inner creature throbbed with power and a lust for blood—the blood of the monster who had created her.

Ashton's eyes widened in alarm as he grasped what was transpiring. He slowly rose to his feet and backed away, wary of Jena's creature. "No," he uttered in stunned disbelief. Then his voice became angry, "This cannot be!"

Jem and his allies stood back and watched as Jena released a predator's growl and moved into an upright position, her body rising and rising until she towered to the height of at least six feet or more.

For the first time in over two hundred years, Ashton took a step backward in fear of his life.

"Remember, Jena," Ashton said, looking at her desperately, continuing to slowly back away, getting closer to the opening in the ground. "If you kill me, Nicolas dies."

Jena was fully aware that Ashton was trying to dissuade her, but she ignored his statement and kept her focus. Although she now had the instincts of a killer, an important part of her still remained intact, something Ashton had lost a long time ago—his humanity.

"I hold all the power," Jena simply said.

Baring her teeth, she lunged forward and struck Ashton with a flash of fangs and claws, driving him backward. Time seemed to slow as they fell over the edge of the pit below and disappeared into what looked to be Satan's dark abyss. The haunting sound of a mournful howl went on and on, fading into a distant echo.

Chapter Forty-Five

When everyone rushed to the edge and looked into the pit, it was too far down and dark to tell if Jena was dead or alive. With her ears flattened to her head, Angie's Breedline wolf whimpered as she peered into the huge opening, praying Jena survived the fall. Bull stood next to her, overjoyed that his beloved was alive and regretful that her best friend's fate hung in limbo.

As if it was instinctive for him to do, Apollyon expanded his wings, and before he stepped off the edge and plunged into the dark hole, Electra called out, "Brother, no!"

A moment beyond that, as the others watched in stunned silence, Apollyon was gone, disappearing into the darkness below. Electra's heart pounded when she lost sight of him completely. In the back of her mind, she was shocked that her brother had thrown himself into the pit without a second thought, unaware of what dangers lay beneath, to risk his life for a stranger. Her eyes closed on a shuddering, deep breath, fearing she'd lost him forever.

Then Electra's eyelids lifted slowly and her gaze riveted to her sister Callisto, who paced with restless energy, worried that their brother would not return.

"Electra..." Cronus set his hand on her shoulder.

The warm weight of his hand brought her head up. As Electra looked upon the giant-winged angel, the optimistic expression in his gray eyes gave her hope.

"Have faith," Cronus told her. "Your brother is iron-willed."

"Not to mention," Frigg chimed in, "stubborn as a damn mule."

Callisto stopped pacing and glared at the battle angels. "Why are you just standing around?" Although her voice didn't rise, the firmness and urgency in it were unmistakable. "You're angels for fuck's sake. Can't you do something to save them?"

"We cannot intervene," Lailah said to Callisto. "Your brother must save Jena. It's God's will."

"Oh, fuck G—"

"Look..." Roman cut Callisto off before she could finish her derogatory statement. "I think I see someone." His words were uttered in a tone so guttural it took Callisto a moment to figure out what he'd said. Roman had shifted into his Adalwolf, which changed the pitch of his voice.

Electra sank to her knees beside Callisto, who was looking over the edge of the opening, her eyes frantically searching for Apollyon. Electra reached out, wanting to comfort her sister, but her hand froze midway when Apollyon miraculously appeared. With the agility and strength of his enormous bat-like wings, he rose above the ground like the angel of death. He had ahold of Jena, who was now in her human form, limp and naked.

"Apollyon..." Callisto wiped at her eyes as tears fell from the corners. "Thank God!"

"Ohhh," Frigg said with a smirk, rolling his eyes, "now she thanks *Him*."

The instant Apollyon's feet touched down, he crouched low and gently lowered Jena to the ground. He looked to everyone that crowded close and said, "She took a hard fall, but she's alive."

Bull quickly shrugged off his T-shirt and bent down next to Jena. As he positioned it over her head, he carefully drew each arm through the sleeves and tugged it all the way past her hips so that it covered most of her exposed skin. The XXL tee fit more like a dress on Jena than it did a shirt.

When Angie's wolf nudged Bull's arm and whimpered, he soothed her state of mind by smoothing his hand between her lupine ears. "Don't worry, sweetheart," he whispered softly. "Jena is going to be just fine."

"What about the creature?" Jem asked, looking at Apollyon as he rose to his feet. "Is it dead?"

"I don't know." Apollyon regretfully shrugged. "It was gone when I found Jena."

"Jena was successful," Cronus said, drawing their attention. "The creature is destroyed."

"What in the hell was that *thing* that came out of the ground?" Roman asked, now in his human form.

"A demon Hydra from hell," Icarus pointed out. "It was summoned by Lucifer."

"How was it connected to the creature?"

"Lucifer created the creature," Icarus told Roman. "All of his dark creations are bound to him. Destroying it was the only way to sever the connection between the creature and Jena. We were brought to earth by our Creator for this task."

"So, all this time, you knew it was coming?"

Icarus nodded. "Yes, Roman. We were prepared for the Hydra."

"How are we going to explain all this..." Roman pointed to all destruction and chaos in the cemetery. "...to everyone else?"

"It's already taken care of," Cronus replied. "Everything you and I can see is not visible to the human eye, although we have made a few exceptions," he pointed out as Detective Manuel Sanchez and his partner, Detective Frank Perkins, rushed over.

"What in the Sam Hill happened here?" Manuel said, looking at the huge crater in the ground and the decapitated Hydra. "And please tell me that *thing* is dead."

Cronus placed his hand on Manuel's shoulder. "Don't worry, Detective. It's dead."

Frank shook his head and asked, "How are we going to get rid of it before..." His voice trailed off just as the Hydra's remains began to turn to ashes.

"Okay, that explains my question," Frank said, "but how are you going to explain that damn hole in the ground?"

"Calm down, Detective," Frigg replied, smirking at Frank. "We're angels for crying out loud. I'm sure we can handle it."

Cronus cleared his throat, glaring at Frigg with a disapproving look. "I understand that you and your partner found the girl in the crypt," he said to Frank, changing the subject.

Frank nodded. "Ms. Debi Flynn is alive and safe. Lawrence and Tessa just left with her," he explained. "We figured it would be best, considering the circumstances, to avoid a hospital, so they took her to the Covenant instead. I know she'll be in good hands with Dr. Helen Carrington."

"I agree," Cronus replied. "We'll see that her memory of anything supernatural is erased."

"What about the creature's brother, Nicolas?" Jem asked as he averted his eyes from the angels and looked to where Nicolas lay. Jem stood motionless, surprised at what he saw, and so was everyone else, especially the two detectives.

Manuel shook his head slowly, from side to side. "What the..." He sucked in a breath.

Lailah was cradling Nicolas in her arms, her giant wings wrapped around his limp body, and she was glowing.

Jem turned to Cronus, but before he could get a word out, Manuel said, "What is my sister... doing?"

There was a long, long silence. "Lailah is..." Cronus hesitated, and then finally said, "giving up her immortality to give Nicolas life."

Manuel looked as if he'd been slapped. "What?" His voice rose. "Why?"

Cronus took a quick, shallow breath. "It's what she's chosen, and our Creator has granted her a mortal life."

As the other angels gathered around, Manuel could see the beginning of sorrow in their eyes as well as Cronus's. It was as if they were losing someone close to them.

"Why would she choose this?" Frank asked.

"To be with the Adalwolf," Frigg said, narrowing his pale blue eyes at Roman.

Jem widened his eyes at the bleached, spiked-haired angel. "Are you saying she wants to be with..." He paused to look at someone he'd only known for a short while, but still considered him part of the Breedline family. "Roman?" he finally said, his eyes darting away from Roman—who appeared frozen in place—and back to Frigg.

Frigg nodded, focusing on Jem. "They've bonded." He sighed, gazing away from Jem to where Lailah was healing Nicolas.

While everyone stood back in silence, witnessing life emerging from death's door, Nicolas—still in a state of unconsciousness—heard a familiar voice, whispering in his ear like a distant echo.

"Nicolas... Nicolas. Open your eyes, little brother."

"Ashton?" Nicolas said, swallowing hard. "Is that you?"

"Yes, brother." Ashton put his fingers under Nicolas's chin, tilting it up slightly. "Open your eyes so you may see me."

Nicolas slowly lifted his lids and glanced up wearily to see Ashton kneeling next to him, staring down at him with tears in his eyes. He looked different. All the evidence of evil and darkness that used to mar his face seemed to be gone. Now, light and purity shone as bright as day.

"Where's Jena?" Nicolas said, his eyes wide, filled with fear.

"Shhh," Ashton soothed, lowering his hand. "Jena is fine."

"But what of you?" Nicolas asked, his eyes searching over his brother's face. "The curse..."

Ashton smiled. "Jena set me free."

Nicolas frowned. "Are we..." He hesitated, and finally uttered the word he dreaded, "dead?"

"Listen to me, little brother," Ashton murmured. "Your soul has been returned. This is a second chance for you to have a good life."

"But how?" Nicolas slowly shook his head. "I damned our souls."

"God granted you this gift."

"Why?" Nicolas sighed. "I've done nothing to deserve it."

"Because, little brother, you have love in your heart."

"And you?"

"I am going to another place," Ashton explained. "A place where I can do good. Although I must leave this world, I will always be with you, little brother." He placed his hand over Nicolas's heart. "I will be here, always."

Nicolas bit at his trembling lip, forcing his tears back. "I'm sorry, Ash. I'm sorry for everything."

"You have nothing to be sorry for. Not for anything. I took the coward's way out when Isabella left me. I had a good life, a loving family, and a wonderful, devoted brother. I'm sorry I let you down, Nicolas."

"B-but, I'm the one who let you down. I betrayed you, Ash. Isabella and I—"

"I know," Ashton quickly cut him off. "And it's okay, little brother. I forgive you."

"I don't know if I can bear to live my life without you, Ash. Please, tell me how I can take all this back. There has to be some way. Please..."

"No, little brother. We have no choice. There is no other way. But if there is one thing perhaps I could ask of you?"

"Anything," Nicolas simply said.

"I want you to be happy. I want you to fall in love and have a family."

"Do I even deserve such a thing?"

Ashton nodded. "Yes, little brother. You deserve a life filled with happiness. Besides, Jena will need you. What I have done to her..." He paused for a moment, regretting the horrible things he had done to Jena and all the innocent lives he'd taken. "She deserves someone like you."

"She may not want anything to do with me after all this."

Ashton smiled again. "I think you'd be surprised. After all, she is your destiny."

Nicolas smiled back, and at that moment, childhood memories of long ago flashed inside his head. He remembered the two of them as children, running through their father's cotton field, playing in mud puddles after a spring rain, hours of swimming in the creek during hot summer days, staying up all night talking and laughing. He would never forget those memories.

Tears rolled down his cheeks. "I love you, Ash."

"And I love you, little brother."

They stayed looking at one another for a moment, and then Ashton's face began to fade, until finally, he was gone.

Go in peace, brother, Nicolas thought, closing his eyes.

"Nicolas." He heard a voice, a woman's soft voice. "Nicolas... can you hear me?"

As Nicolas opened his eyes, a beautiful, young woman was staring down at him, smiling. She had long, red hair and bright, emerald-green eyes. Her features looked youthful and there was a kindness in her smile.

Nicolas slightly tilted his head in question. "Who *are* you?"

"My name is... Lailah."

"Where's Jena?" he asked, pulling himself in an upright position. "Is she okay?"

"She'll be just fine," Lailah said, placing her hand over his. "Jena released your brother's curse."

"Thank God." Nicolas sagged in relief and lowered his head. "It was real. I really spoke to Ashton." He sat up straighter and looked up at Lailah. "He's in a better place, isn't he?"

Lailah nodded. "Your brother will take my place," she told him. "He will help protect heaven's gate."

"After all the damage I've caused, why did God give me a second chance?" he asked, staring at Lailah with a look of confusion.

"God's love is unconditional," she told him. "He can see the love within your soul." She smiled again. "Besides, Jena will need you. And you'll need her."

"I would love that more than anything, but..." He shook his head. "...how do you know she'll have anything to do with me?"

Tilting her head to the side, Lailah raised a brow. "I have a feeling... She's pretty fond of you already."

Nicolas smiled at her soothing words.

Then she felt a warm hand on her shoulder and heard a familiar voice that said, "Lailah..."

As Lailah turned to look over her shoulder, she had never felt so happy. Tears streamed down her cheeks as she looked up to see her brother standing above her.

"Manuel," she gasped.

When she rose to her feet, Manuel reached out and tugged her into his arms. "I can't believe it," he whispered next to her ear. "Is this real, or have I lost my ever-loving mind?"

"It's real," she told him. "And I'm back for good this time."

As Manuel pulled from their embrace, he looked at her from head to toe and back up again. "It's really you, isn't it?" When she nodded, he said, "Sis, you have no idea how much I've prayed. I never gave up hope."

She wiped at her eyes. "I know, little brother. I heard all your prayers. I'm so proud of you."

The corners of Manuel's mouth curled up. "Little brother?" He smirked. "Hell, I'm an old man now. You still look like my seventeen-year-old sister. You haven't aged one bit."

Lailah giggled. "Yeah, being an angel comes with perks. Although I may look seventeen, I'm still four years older than you."

"Like I said, you haven't changed a bit." Manuel hugged her again. "I love you, sis."

"I love you too, Manuel," Lailah said, and then her eyes caught sight of another person she was happy to see. The joy and relief in her eyes were crushing.

"Roman?"

He looked at her shell-shocked. "Wow. Y-you're... h-human," Roman muttered.

When Manuel released Lailah, she said, "Well, not exactly." She smiled at Roman. "Technically, I'm no longer a battle angel, but I still carry the genetics of a Breedline."

"T-that's unbelievable," Roman said, stumbling over his words. "I-I mean... that's fantastic."

As Lailah slowly moved closer to Roman, she reached out with her hand. Without hesitation, he slipped his hand in hers and squeezed. *My beloved*, he silently thought, his expression content as she nestled against his side.

Manuel eyed Roman with uncertainty, and Roman stared back, his dark eyes steely with resolve.

"Just remember, Roman," said Manuel, placing a hand on his holster that held a Colt .45. "Accordance with the laws of California, I can shoot whoever I perceive is the bad guy."

Roman cocked a brow. "Good to know, Detective." He chortled lightly. "Message received."

That brought chuckles from the others, but they all stared at Manuel, and then at the new couple with complete respect in their eyes.

A glimmer of a smile lit Manuel's face. "Looks like we're starting on good terms so far."

Roman pulled Lailah tight against him. She smiled and looked up as his arms came tighter around her.

"I do have one question," she said, keeping her voice low.

Roman shrugged. "Oh?"

"You do want to be with me, right?"

"Hell yes," he shot back. "I wouldn't have it any other way. I want you more than anything, Lailah. You're mine." He batted his brows. "All mine. Are you okay with that?"

She stared at him for a moment, devotion shining in her eyes. "Oh, I think I can live with that."

For once, Roman thought, things seemed to be moving in the right direction. To him, having Lailah here was as close to heaven as it got. The very thing he'd prayed so hard for when he'd thought it wasn't possible or even imaginable—a chance at love. True love.

Chapter Forty-Six

Six months later...

Steven was about to wear a path in the floor, pacing back and forth outside of Abbey's hospital room. He was going to go crazy. Around midnight, Abbey had gone into labor. When he got her to the hospital, the baby had repositioned its bottom toward the birth canal instead of the head. While doctors attempted to try to turn the baby, Abbey had a seizure. When intravenous medication did not stop it, her physicians decided to deliver the baby by C-section, which meant Abbey had to be put under sedation due to another uncontrollable circumstance. Abbey was a Lupa, and if she got upset or out of control, things could take a turn for the worse if she shifted. Not just for her, but for everyone else.

With the exception of a few members, most of the Breedline Covenant sat in the waiting room, looking at Steven with concern.

Lawrence and Tara were one of the couples not present. They had recently taken off to Maui for their honeymoon. After realizing they were destined to be together, they couldn't wait to start their life together. Skipping the traditional ceremony, they decided on a courthouse wedding.

Although Tessa agreed to allow Sebastian Crow to reside in the Covenant's guesthouse with Eve to raise their twin boys, they thought it best to keep a low profile and stay home, considering the fact that Jace still wasn't too thrilled over Tessa's decision.

After the battle angels made sure the Salem Cemetery looked as it did before Lucifer's five-headed Hydra split through the earth, they said their final good-byes to Lailah and flew back to the In-Between to guard heaven's gate.

Since Apollyon, Callisto, and Electra helped the Breedline battle the creature, God granted them absolution and allowed the supernatural trio to remain on earth.

Now that Lailah was no longer a battle angel and God had granted her a mortal life, Roman had taken her on a little adventure. Losing her human life at such a young age, he wanted her to experience some of the things she'd missed out on. A trip to the Rocky Mountains was first on their list.

Bull had left with Angie two weeks ago for a romantic, long getaway, and they decided to invite Nicolas and Jena to go with them, considering the two of them seemed to be getting close. All four of them were due for some downtime, especially Jena.

Detective Manuel Sanchez and his partner, Detective Frank Perkins, were relieved to finally solve the mystery behind all the savage murders in the city, thanks to Jena McCain. Now that the wolf was out of the bag, so to speak, and God had forgiven Nicolas Ratcliff, the two detectives agreed to keep his identity a secret and put the past behind them. Besides, crime never stood still, and they needed Nicolas's help protecting the innocents from the dark forces that lurked in the shadows. After all, he was immortal and one helluva detective.

Tessa was sitting across from her brother, holding Jem and Mia's baby. Three months prior, Mia had given birth to the most adorable and healthy little girl, Eva Alexandria Chamberlain, although everyone called her Evie. They named her after Mia's twin sister, Eve, and Jem and Jace's biological father, Alexander. She had her mother's bright crimson eyes and her father's blond hair. Evie was a perfect addition to the Breedline family. Tim and Angel's daughter, Natalie, along with the other children in the Covenant, adored having a new playmate.

When Tessa noticed the panicked look in her brother's eyes, she stood and handed the baby back to Mia and went over to Steven.

He stopped to look at the clock on the wall. "What in the hell is taking so long?" Steven grumbled. "Why won't they let me in there?"

Tessa touched his arm. "Everything is going to be fine, Steven. It's not uncommon for mothers to be sedated during a Cesarean section. In Abbey's case, I'm sure it's also a safety precaution, considering she's a Lupa."

Steven let out a long breath. "I know, I know. It's just—"

"Abbey is in good hands," Tessa said in a quiet voice. "Helen is an excellent physician, and Cassie is one of the best neonatal nurse practitioners in the city. I'm sure they will let you know something as soon as they can."

Jace came over and placed his hand on Steven's shoulder. "Listen, man, if it makes you feel any better, I know what you're going through. I've been in your shoes once before. But don't worry. If things start to take a turn for the worse, you can just heal her like you did before, right?"

Tessa gritted her teeth and looked at him wide-eyed. "You're not making the situation any better, Jace."

"Hey, look on the bright side," Jace said, patting Steven on the shoulder. "At least Abbey's not having twins."

Tessa shot Jace another look that said, without words, to keep his mouth shut.

"Okay, okay," Jace muttered, throwing his hands up in defeat. "Sorry. I was just trying to show some sympathy for the poor guy."

Seconds later, Kenneth walked into the waiting room and shot his daughter a worried look. Then his gaze rested on his son, who looked like he'd been to hell and back.

"Abbey is going to be fine, son," Kenneth said, placing both hands comfortingly on Steven's shoulders. "She's one tough young lady, and this is a cakewalk to her." He squeezed Steven's shoulders reassuringly before he lowered his hands. "Son, you must have faith. Abbey has been through far worse than childbirth."

He nodded. "You're right, Dad, but it's just that I don't want her going through this alone. I wanted to be there when our baby is born."

Steven turned when he felt the weight of a large hand on his arm. When he saw Drakon standing next to him, he tilted his head up and looked into the eyes of a mountain of a man.

"Don't worry, buddy," Drakon said. "My Cassie will take excellent care of your girl."

"I know. Thanks, Drakon."

Suddenly, the door to Abbey's room opened, and they all looked to Cassie as she stepped out. "Congratulations, Steven. You have a beautiful and healthy baby boy."

Steven swallowed, his Adam's apple visibly bobbing up and down in his throat. "How's Abbey?"

"She's doing just fine." Cassie smiled and Steven heaved out a sigh of relief. "If you'd like, you can come in to see her and meet your son."

The biggest grin lit up Steven's face as everyone gathered around to congratulate him.

Drakon gave him a pat on the back. "Congrats, buddy."

Tessa wrapped her arm around him and whispered close to his ear, "Congratulations, Steven. I'm so happy for you and Abbey."

Steven tugged Tessa snugly against him. "Thanks, sis."

Cassie held the door open for Steven as he moved past her and ducked into Abbey's room. His heart skipped a beat and his eyes shone with unshed tears when he got his first look at Abbey sitting up in the bed, holding their baby.

As she turned toward him, her face melted with a glow of love. "Come meet our son."

Steven pulled a chair close to Abbey's bed and sat down. He took her hand and curled his fingers around hers. "Oh, my God, he's... perfect," he said, reaching out with his other hand to touch his son, but it shook so badly he had to stop midway in an effort to control the wave of emotion soaring through his entire body. When his hand finally calmed, he gently smoothed it over his son's dark hair. It was so fine, so delicate, and soft to the touch.

The baby cooed and leaned into the warmth of his hand.

Steven moved forward and pressed his lips to his son's forehead. "I love you, Jonah," he whispered. "And I love your mama, too."

Abbey exhaled, absorbing the sound of Steven saying their son's name for the first time. Jonah was her father's name, and she was glad they had chosen it.

"And I love his daddy," she whispered back.

He looked up to see Abbey smiling, her face edged with exhaustion, but it also radiated with happiness. He moved closer to her and kissed her softly on the lips.

When he pulled away, she stared up into his teary green eyes and said, "Would you like to hold your son?"

Steven nodded, struggling to keep his emotions in. When he reached out to pick up the baby, a single fat tear dropped from his left eye, and then another fell from his right. He blinked them away and gently scooped the small bundle into his arms. Jonah settled instantly in his father's hold. As Steven cradled their son, tucking him in close, his chest swelled with renewed purpose. Reality had just kicked in. He was a father. Then the word made his head tilt slightly. *Father.* That was something he'd never had until only recently. Then he wondered if he possessed the parental instincts to be a good father.

As Steven sat there holding his son for the first time, he thought back to the rough period in his and Abbey's lives. He'd never forget the day Dr. Hans Autenburg—the ruthless German scientist who stole him from his mother and Abbey from her family for the sole purpose of experimentation—and locked them together in a cell. They were just five years old. She was like a feral animal trapped in a cage. As they grew up, they fell in love. After years of relentless torture, they found a way to escape, but unfortunately, they ended up separated for years. Now, here they were, happily together again experiencing a miracle—the birth of their first child.

Abbey had shown a lot of courage and trust. Starting her life over after what she went through took a lot of bravery and guts. Not only was Abbey his beloved, but she had also saved him from hell, and now, she was the mother of his child. God, he loved this woman.

He looked up at her, and when he saw Abbey staring at him with admiration in her gaze, his mouth twitched into a half-smile. "Thank you, sweetheart."

She slowly shook her head. "For what, honey?"

"For making me the happiest man on earth."

Abbey smiled. "I love you so much, Steven."

"And I love you, Mary Abigail," he murmured, using her birth name.

"Can you keep a secret?" she said.

"Of course."

"Cassie is pregnant."

Steven's eyes rounded. "Drakon's Cassie?"

"Yep."

His eyes softened. "That's great. Does he know?"

Abbey grinned and shook her head. "Not yet. That's why it's a secret."

"Oh." He cocked a brow. "Mum's the word. Although, when Drakon gets the news, I'm sure he'll be thrilled to know he's going to be a father. I sure as hell was."

The baby squirmed in Steven's grasp and let out a little whining demand.

"I think he wants something only his mother can provide," Steven said, shifting the baby in his arms as he rose to his feet.

"Come here, little Jonah," she said, reaching out for the baby.

As Steven made the handoff, he leaned down and kissed Abbey, his lips lingering on hers for a moment.

Jonah let out a happy coo when his mother cradled him against her breast, already acknowledging he was about to be fed.

"He definitely knows what's good," Steven said around a light chuckle.

Abbey's eyebrows lifted. "He takes after his father."

"You got that right," he shot back.

As Steven eased back into the chair, taking in the most beautiful sight, his beloved nourishing their child, he wanted to lock this image into his memory forever. He would thank God every day for giving him a second chance at a happy family. He knew Abbey still fought her demons from the past, as he did, but they'd get there. As long as they had each other, they could conquer anything. True love could do amazing things.

To be continued...

Will you still want her, after her rage?

Do you have the balls, to unlock her cage?

Careful I tell you, a monster indeed...

A Viking she seeks, but a wolf she will need.

One that will howl, at the moon as she does.

A dog that will bite, but embrace how she loves...

—N.R. Shepherd

Thank you, dear friend.

Reference for terms and cast of characters

BREEDLINE – A species of humans that have the ability to change from human form into wolf form if they are born an identical twin. They are not like the old legend of the Lycanthropy myth. The Breedline species can shift into their wolf at will. The moon has no power over them. They do not pass their ability to other humans. Although they live among humans, their species is secret. In wolf form, they have super-strength, speed, and heightened senses. Compared to humans, Breedlines have tremendous advantages when it comes to health. Their bodies heal fast and are not subject to illness or diseases. The only thing that slows their healing process is silver. It is their kryptonite. Besides old age, a silver bullet to the brain is the only way to kill a Breedline.

All male Breedlines change into their first wolf at the age of eighteen. Female Breedlines do not go through the change until they make love to their Breedline bonded mate.

BREEDLINE TWINS – They have a strong, unbreakable bond from birth. Born with telepathic abilities, they have the power to sense their twin's emotions or injuries. In some cases, the bond between twins is so strong they cannot live without the other.

BREEDLINE BONDING – The male Breedline spends his life searching for their bonded mate. When two Breedline species experience a bond, they instantly feel a simultaneous, desirable attraction. The bond is for life. It is possible for them to have more than one mate in their lifespan.

BELOVED – A word used by a Breedline to express the bond to their mate.

DOUBLE BONDED – In some cases, male Breedline twins bond with the same female.

BREEDLINE COVENANT – The Breedline species must live within the boundaries of their Covenant. There is one in every state. A council governs its laws and oversees the species population.

THE BREEDLINE QUEEN – A Breedline queen is born once every one hundred years. Her massive stature, black fur, and red eyes are the queen's trademarks. Her alpha wolf has twice the strength, speed, and size of any Breedline. She rules over all the Breedline Covenants. She is their absolute law.

TRUE LAW – All Breedline Covenants have a book of laws. If disobeyed, they must face the Breedline council. Punishment for taking another life out of revenge, or evil—other than protecting their life and the life of another—they will instantly shift into a rogue wolf for life and shunned by the Breedline Covenants.

ROGUE WOLF – A Breedline wolf who has killed with the intent of evil. They can never shift back into their human form.

RED (BLOOD) MOON – During this time, all Breedline species have a strong desire to create offspring. This is a time when Breedline females are more fertile for the conception of twins.

CHIANG-SHIH DEMON (Kiang shi, a.k.a. Ramael Arminius) – An ancient demon that can inhabit the body of a Breedline fetus or during a Breedline's death. It continues to take the soul over the natural lifespan of a child or the deceased Breedline. When the demon possesses a fetus, it breaks the bonding and telepathic abilities with its twin. If the demon possesses a deceased Breedline's body, it must do so before the soul passes on. If the soul is not intact, the body will soon die. The demon's sole purpose is to seek world domination.

THE BEAST – It is the second-born son of the Chiang-Shih demon. When provoked into a rage, he will shift into the Beast instead of the Breedline wolf. The Beast is also known as the Great White due to his white fur and enormous, two-footed stature. One bite from the Beast has enough venom to kill the Chiang-Shih demon, leaving the soul of the person the demon possessed unharmed.

SHADOW WALKER (a.k.a. Shadow Figure, or Black Mass) – When a Breedline species dies and their soul continues to roam the earth as a shadow of themselves—a ghost—because they have unfinished business before their death.

ZADKIEL (Tzadqiel, a.k.a. "Righteousness of God") – The archangel of freedom, benevolence, and mercy, and the patron angel of all who forgives. The Breedline species considers Zadkiel the Angel of Mercy.

SUCCUBUS (a.k.a. Creepers) – A succubus feeds off the blood of a Breedline species. They are skilled with hypnotic abilities and capable of using their beautiful features to influence the thoughts of the Breedline species and humans.

HALF-BREED – A species born with the genes from both a Breedline and a succubus. They can bond with either species. Although they cannot shift into a wolf, they need blood from a Breedline to survive.

WICCA (or Wise One) – According to the Breedline species, a Wicca is the Goddess of magic, witchcraft, the night, the moon, ghosts, and necromancy. They can do white magic (good) or dark (evil).

GUARDIANS (a.k.a. Spirits of the Forest) – They originated during the Middle Ages with the purpose of protecting the Breedline from the destruction of any creation of a dark Wicca. They can stay invisible, with the power to move through any barrier and over any distance instantly.

THERIOMORPH – They are born with the genes of a Breedline, but do not shift into a wolf. They shapeshift into an enormous black panther. They possess powers of mind manipulation and random visions of the future. They must use the drug dopamine to suppress their urges. Their eye color shifts into a bright lavender when their Theriomorph nature takes over. In some cases, the Breedline see them as a threat to their species.

ADALWOLF – A species that has the power to shift from their human form into a beautiful creature, twice the size, resembling half man and half wolf. Born with super-strength, they can move from one place to another in supernatural speed. Their eyes take on the appearance of two shimmering diamonds. With the power to regenerate their own cells, an Adalwolf will stop aging at thirty. The moon has no power over them, and they are immune to silver. They can bond with any species.

LUPA (she-wolf) – The ancestors descended from the old legend of the lycanthrope, but the moon has no power over them. The species only affects female offspring. A lupa is a dangerous creature which shapeshifts into a therianthropic hybrid wolf-like creature.

Jace Chamberlain (a.k.a. the Beast) – He is a Breedline species who later discovers he was born with a curse of the Beast, inherited by the Chiang-Shih demon. His bonded mate is Tessa Fairchild. He's an IT engineer and the lead singer and plays acoustic guitar in the band Chaos.

Jem Chamberlain (a.k.a. the Chosen Son) – He is a Breedline species and Jace's identical twin brother. He carries the gene of the Chiang-Shih demon, which gives him the power to create a portal and a force of electrical energy used as a weapon—and other powers he discovers later. His bonded mate is Mia Blackwood. He's an IT engineer and the drummer in the band Chaos.

Tessa Fairchild (a.k.a. the Breedline Queen) – She was born into the human world and later discovers she's a Breedline. Abandoned by her parents, and raised by her aunt and uncle, Tessa has no knowledge of being born a twin. After she meets Jace, they become bonded mates. During her first change into her Breedline wolf, she shifts into the new Breedline queen. She is an inspiring artist.

Jax and Jem Chamberlain – Jace and Tessa's identical twin boys. Both have inherited the Breedline genes.

Dr. John and Sarah Chamberlain – They are Jace, Jem, and Cassie's adoptive human parents. They are physicians in a children's unit, donating their time to the emergency center.

Chester and Amelia Ewan – They are called Guardians— a species originated during the Middle Ages—with the purpose of protecting the Breedline from the destruction of any creation made by a dark Wiccan.

Katlyn Gray – She is a Breedline and Jace and Jem's biological mother.

Jackson Gray – He is Jace and Jem's biological uncle— Katlyn Gray's older brother. Although he carries the gene of the Breedline, he does not shift into a wolf. He's a medical supply pilot.

Mia Blackwood – She is a half-breed and Jem's bonded mate. Abandoned at birth and raised in human foster care, she later finds her identical twin sister, Eve.

Eve – She is a half-breed, and Sebastian's bonded mate.

Sebastian Crow – He is a half-breed and Eve's bonded mate. He has the power to summon a portal.

Arius and Tidus – They are Sebastian and Eve's identical twin boys. Both have inherited their parents' genetics of a half-breed. Arius carries the mark of the Chiang-Shih demon with the power to create a portal and the ability to heal others.

Alexander Crest – He is a Breedline species, Jace and Jem's biological father. He is bonded to Dr. Helen Carrington.

Tim Ross – He is a Breedline species and the council head of the California Covenant.

Angel – She is a half-breed and Tim's bonded mate.

Natalie – She is a half-breed and Tim and Angel's daughter.

Kyle Jones – He is a Breedline species that resides in the California Covenant. Celina Baldolf is his bonded mate. He's a mechanic and plays bass in the rock band Chaos.

Casey Barton – He is a Theriomorph and lives in the California Covenant. He is a clothing model and plays backup bass and keyboards in the band Chaos.

Dr. Helen Carrington – She is a Breedline species and a physician at the California Bates Hospital for both Breedlines and humans. She later bonds to Alexander Crest.

Drakon Hexus – He is a Breedline species and bonded to Cassie Chamberlain.

Cassie Chamberlain – Adopted at age two by Jace and Jem's adoptive parents after her mother abandons her. Later, she discovers she is a Breedline species and bonds with the handsome Drakon Hexus. She is a nurse practitioner, specializing in the neonatal intensive care unit.

Celina Baldolf – She is a Breedline species with the power of a Wiccan, but only practices white witchcraft. Her twin sister, Taliah—a dark Wicca—murdered their parents when they were twelve years old. Dr. Helen Carrington is their aunt, and Kyle Jones is Celina's Breedline bonded mate. She is an editor for a local publishing company.

Steven Pasquale (a.k.a. Steven Craven) – He inherited the genes of a Breedline and an Adalwolf. He is Tessa Fairchild's fraternal twin and is Abigail Winthrop's bonded mate.

Abbey (a.k.a. Abigail Winthrop) – She inherited the genetics of a Lupa from her mother and is bonded with Steven Craven.

Dr. Kenneth Craven – He is a Breedline and an orthopedic surgeon at the San Francisco General Hospital. He is Steven Craven and Tessa Fairchild's father.

Lisa Wellington (a.k.a. Lilith) – She is a Breedline with the gift to heal. She is Steven Craven and Tessa Fairchild's biological mother.

Lila Demont – She is a Breedline, born into a wealthy, prestigious family. She is a lab technician and assists Dr. Helen Carrington with the cure to the Breedline aging process. She later bonds with Casey Barton.

Victor Demont – He is a Breedline and Lila's father. He is a retired council member of the Pennsylvania Breedline Covenant.

Raphael (a.k.a. Buddy the cat) - He is the Angel of healing who secretly disguises himself as a black cat who resides in the Breedline Covenant as their pet. He guards the children in the Covenant.

Nathan Gage (a.k.a. Nate) – He is a Breedline and the owner of several upscale night clubs in the largest metropolitan areas of Northern California.

Zeke Rizzo – He is a Breedline, born with a curse of a sin-eater, and the owner of the Cat Club. He is bonded with Anna Saeni.

Yelena Smirnov – A full-blooded succubus from Russia. She is bonded with Apollyon.

Anna Saeni – She was born with the genetics of a Breedline from her father's side, who died when Anna was a baby, but she does not shift into a wolf. She is like a sister to Sebastian Crow and bonded with Zeke Rizzo.

Roman Kincaid – He is an Adalwolf trained in military tactics, hired as a special breed of warriors from Brazil. Hired as a bodyguard for Valkin Steele—a billionaire funding a group of unethical scientist's research—he later learns of Steele's underground sex-trafficking and illegal drug and weapons trade and informs the Breedline Covenant. He also forms a team of Breedline soldiers who work for a private Special Ops group contracted by the military for missions that no one else can or will do to help put an end to Valkin Steele's corrupt organization. He resides in the California Breedline Covenant along with team members, Lawrence, Bull, Justice, and Lena.

Lawrence Colbert – A Breedline council member of the New Jersey Covenant, trained in military tactics and as a medic who worked alongside Roman Kincaid, the Special Ops team, and the Breedline Covenant to help take down Valkin Steele.

Lena – She is a Breedline, highly trained in survival skills, martial arts, and anything dealing with weapons, hand-to-hand combat, and hired by Roman Kincaid to help take down Valkin Steele. She oddly resembles the character Xena the Warrior Princess from the '80s television series. She is also Bull's little sister and is bonded to Justice.

Bull (a.k.a. Benjamin Allen Calvero) - He is a Breedline, highly trained and an expert in a variety of military tactics, who is part of Roman Kincaid's team. He gets his nickname because of his size.

Justice – He is a Breedline who is part of Roman Kincaid's team. He's highly trained in military tactics, an expert with explosives, hand-to-hand combat, sniper training and is a pilot. He is bonded to Lena.

Detective Manuel Sanchez – He is a homicide detective at the San Francisco Police Department who late discovers he carries the Breedline genetics. His partner is Detective Frank Perkins. His sister is Lailah.

Detective Frank Perkins - He is Manuel Sanchez's partner and discovers the secret world of the Breedline. Born as a human, Frank pledges his loyalty to the Breedline. Fighting alongside his partner, they take an oath to help the Breedline protect the world from corruption and unknown creatures that prey on the innocent.

Captain James Hodge – Unaware of the Breedline species, he is Detective Manuel Sanchez's and Detective Frank Perkins' superior at the San Francisco, California Police Department.

The Fury – Three fraternal twins—Apollyon, Electra, and Callisto—created by an evil German scientist named Dr. Hans Autenburg. Using his own DNA, he mixed it with the genetics of a Breedline, an Adalwolf, and a powerful Wiccan.

Battle angels – Their one purpose for existence is to serve the Creator in the war against demons and evil havoc on earth. The battle angels are unlike any of the Creator's angels. The indigenous battle angels, on average, stand ten feet tall, although a few tower to the height of twelve feet with a more muscular build. Tattooed with unique warrior markings, the black-winged warriors are suited with armor typical of ancient heroes, and they wield a type of sword associated with a long-gone empire. They are the bravest of angels, who consider only the importance of their mission, and are perfectly willing to give their life in the service of righteousness. Gifted with special powers, they fight against the dark side. They are particularly fond of the human race and consider themselves humanity's special protectors.

Cronus – He is a loyal and devoted warrior in charge of God's battle angels. He wields the power of the sword of truth and has the ability to use his body as a shield. His mission is to protect the heavens and all God's creations.

Lailah – She is a battle angel gifted with holy fire used to trap or immobilize demons and other evil supernatural beings, rather than killing them outright. Forty-one years ago, in her human life at age seventeen, she was savagely murdered. Although her killer got away with the crime, her younger brother, Detective Manuel Sanchez, promises to dedicate his life trying to solve the murder.

Helios – He is a battle angel and a descendant of an African king. When God brought him into the group, he converted Helios' body into a lethal weapon. The tips of his feathers are sharp as knives, and he has talons capable of shredding through skin and bone. Although he was born without vocal cords, he can communicate using his mind.

Icarus – He is a gorgeous battle angel gifted with the power of telekinesis. He can influence, manipulate, and move matter using his mind.

Frigg – He is one of God's originals, serving as a battle angel for more than a century. With a personality bigger than life, a bit of an attitude, and a love for rock-n-roll, cheeseburgers, and classic black-and-white movies, he oddly resembles the singer, Billy Idol of the '80s punk rock band, sporting the same trademark bleached spiked hair and English accent. He has the unique power of shapeshifting. He can transform and reshape himself into any living thing.

About the Author

Shana Congrove has always had a passion for fantasy, romance, and the supernatural world, and her idea of heaven is creating new adventures for her Breedline characters. In 2019, Shana ranked the second novelist in FanStory.com, where she enjoys sharing her stories and receiving helpful feedback from readers and other talented authors. She also loves to interact with new readers on Instagram and Facebook/A Novel of the Breedline Series.

Take a sneak peek into the sixth Novel of the Breedline series, THE CURSE... coming soon!

Chapter One

While he sipped on his brandy, he looked around the bar, taking in all the half-naked bodies gyrating on the dance floor to Marilyn Manson. The Cat Club was packed tonight, full of freaks and wannabes, dressed in a ghastly fashion between gothic black leather, tight mini-skirts and ripped jeans. To him, they all appeared as rejects or outcasts who did not fit in with normal society.

But then, he wondered, what was considered *normal*? If indeed, there were a checklist, he definitely would not fit into those categories. No, he was something else. Something dark, sinister... cruel. Going by the diagnosis of his childhood psychologist, he suffered from a chronic mental disorder with violent tendencies, an inability to love, and a lack of remorse or guilt. At age thirteen, he showed all the traits of a psychopath. Dismembering stray cats was the beginning of his vile and sadistic behavior.

Although, it wasn't like he had the best upbringing. His father was an abusive drunk, and his mother felt trapped, fearing if she left him, he would track her down and kill her. He'd witnessed firsthand all the threats and abuse his mother endured. As he dredged up those painful memories, his body responded to the remembered horror of his mother's battered and bruised body. His heart ached just thinking about it. He brought his hand up and touched the center of his chest. He would never forget that one horrific day. The worst day of his life. It was a cold and rainy Saturday afternoon. He was only five years old at the time, but he remembered that tragic incident like it was yesterday. His mother was late coming home after a run to the liquor store to appease his father's addiction. By the time she arrived, he was already in a drunken stupor. In a fit of rage, he repeatedly kicked and beat her. No matter how much he pleaded and begged his father to stop, the bastard continued his brutality. Before his father beat his mother unconscious, she dragged herself over to him and reached out. She could barely open her swollen eyes. She said one last thing before he watched the light in her eyes dim and then go out.

"*Don't ever forget... Mommy will always love you.*"

He could still hear himself calling out to her over and over again.

That was the day his life changed forever, and when he shot his father. As he thought back on that day, he was surprised at that young age he was capable of firing his father's 9mm semiautomatic pistol. Although it didn't kill him, he had meant for it to.

When the neighbors heard the blast from the gun, they called the police. As they arrived, he still had it in his hand and aimed at his father. He would never forget the female officer that arrived at the scene. She had dark skin, braided hair, and big brown, caring eyes. He kept her face and the sound of her voice embedded in his memory.

"*Put the gun down, honey.*" Her voice had been soft and comforting like his mother's. "*I know you didn't mean to hurt anyone. We're here to help you.*"

"*He hurt my mommy,*" I remember hearing myself tell the officer. "*I won't let him hurt her no more.*"

"*I know,*" the officer soothed, her expression softening with understanding. "*What's your name, honey?*"

"*Joseph,*" I answered, looking at the officer with troubled blue eyes that seemed to carry a lifetime of violence and pain behind them.

"*Okay, listen to me, Joseph. My name is Officer Katie, and I'm here to help you. Do you understand?*"

When I nodded an understanding, she continued to say, "*I promise I won't let anyone hurt your mother, but I need you to do something for me.*" She knelt down and held out her hand. "*Please, Joseph. Please give me the gun.*"

"*I can't,*" I told her. "*He'll kill her.*"

Back then, he wasn't the cold and calculating person he was today. He was just a scared little boy trying to protect his mother. It took almost thirty minutes, but finally, Officer Katie coaxed him into giving her the gun. Then, he remembered watching as the paramedics loaded his mother into the ambulance and drove away.

The next day, she suffered from an aneurysm, caused by all the blunt force and died in the hospital. Immediately following her death, the police arrested his father. Charged with aggravated assault in the first degree, the judge sentenced him to twenty years in prison. During his father's trial and with no other living relatives, he'd been placed in foster care. Spending most of his childhood in the system wasn't exactly any better than what he had at home. He'd gone through ten foster families before he was carted off in a straitjacket—due to his psychopathic behavior—and put into a mental institution where he spent most of his adolescent years.

Twenty-one years later, here he was, rehabilitated and back in the real world. During the years he'd spent in the mental hospital, he quickly mastered the skills of manipulation. He said all the right words and all the things his therapists wanted to hear. For good behavior and therapeutic reasons, they allowed him to take online college courses of which were funded by the government. The day the institute finally discharged him, believing he'd been cured, it wasn't long before he landed a job as a freelance journalist at the San Francisco Chronicle. For the first year, despite the fact that he'd been released, it was mandatory to check in with his therapist on a weekly basis.

Soon after, he discovered his father's whereabouts. A year prior, after doing his time, dear ol' dad was now living as a civilian. His father should have killed him when he had the chance, or better yet, made his mother abort him before he was ever born. No amount of therapy, drugs, or shock treatment could cure what he was. If you were unlucky enough to be one of his victims, the monsters in your worst nightmares would be nothing compared to what his father had created. At least in a dream, you always woke up.

Growing up in an abusive household was just something he learned to cope with. No matter how hard he wished it, he couldn't change the hand that had been dealt. He couldn't stop himself from wishing things were different, though. That maybe he could have been born into a *normal* family.

His mind took him back to that day, to the memories of when his father took his last gurgling breath. He'd sliced his throat so deep, it nearly severed his head. There was so much blood. He was gratified to watch his father's life drain in a pool of crimson red. He had been planning to kill him the day a social worker delivered the dreadful news of his mother's death. At that moment, it was as if something evil—a dark, soulless entity—clawed its way inside of him and inhabited his body. It was the day he heard the voice whisper in his head. It introduced itself as the *Shadow* and spoke to him in a way that was both soothing and malicious. Although he was just a child, the Shadow gave him courage, taught him things, helped him survive, and kept his mind focused for all those years. Focused on one thing. To *kill*.

While he reminisced of the past, and before his imagination got the best of him, someone caught his eye. Across the crowded dance floor, a young girl with long blonde hair, dressed in a pink strapless top and a pair of tight jeans stood by the bar observing all the social misfits.

He leaned back in his chair and simply watched her. The short distance that separated them, he studied every detail, every curve. Regardless of the high-heeled boots she wore, she couldn't have been any taller than five-foot-two, and no older than twenty-five. The smoothness and flawless lines on her sun-kissed skin gave her a youthful glow. She had that girl next door look to her. Pretty, but not overly attractive. She looked out of place like she didn't belong here. He noticed the way she chewed at her bottom lip and the swell of her breasts as she took each breath. And she appeared to be alone.

"She's perrrrfect," the Shadow whispered to him in a soft purr. *"We need her."* Its voice remained calm and collective, but also insistent. *"Pick her, Joseph."*

Joseph briefly closed his eyes and drew in a wavering breath. The Shadow was his driving force to take lives, always in his head, always picking out their next victim. It was like having an evil twin inside your head twenty-four-seven.

Sometimes it was exhausting. *God,* he thought, *how in the hell have I made it all these years without going mad?*

"Well, you are clinically insane," the Shadow answered. *"Admit it, Joseph. You need me. You're weak without me."*

In a flash, he recalled the day the Shadow gave him the courage to go back to his parents' home one last time, to avenge his mother. God, he could still remember how his father begged for his pathetic life. But mostly, he looked back on the memory of watching the house go up in flames with his father's body burning inside. As he savored that moment, he felt reborn.

Yes, Joseph silently agreed. *I need you, Shadow.* He would kill if the Shadow asked it of him. Slaughter anyone without thought or hesitation. Besides, everyone eventually dies. He just sped the process up a little. And then, he smiled, his eyes growing hooded as his gaze lingered on the girl's lips. But to his surprise, she wandered off, probably heading for the ladies' room. His smile disappeared.

"Don't let her get away," the Shadow urged. *"Follow her, Joseph!"*

Joseph tossed back the rest of his drink, swallowing it whole. The minute he rose from his chair, a waitress wearing a bustier made of leather and lace, a studded choker that resembled a dog collar, skin-tight leopard pants, and four-inch heels came up to his table, working her hips as if they were double-jointed.

She swirled her tongue over her black-coated lips and said, "How 'bout another round, sweetheart?"

For a brief, lapsing moment, the Shadow's voice came back to him. *"Hurry, Joseph! The girl is leaving the bar!"*

Joseph quickly reached into the front pocket of his jeans and dug out a twenty-dollar bill. "No thanks," he said, placing the money on the table. "I was just leaving."

On her way out of the bar, the blonde-haired girl swiped her phone and initiated a call. After a few rings, it went straight to voicemail.

"Dammit, Kevin," she cursed under her breath, and ended the call. This had been the fourth time her boyfriend was a no-show, and this time she'd make damn sure it was his last. He was a total loser with a fat trust fund. And to make matters worse, he'd made plans with her later tonight for a *supposedly* romantic Valentine's dinner.

It was already after midnight, and she should probably call for an Uber, but her apartment building was only five blocks away. Besides, she was pissed and the walk might do some good.

As she walked along, she noticed some of the businesses were hopping. Other than the Cat Club, there was Dino's bar and grill, JJ's Smoke Shop, and a hole-in-the-wall pool hall further down the main strip. Across the street was a tattoo parlor, an adult/lingerie shop, a Mexican restaurant, a pizza place where you can make your own pies and a little burger joint around the corner. Above the Cat Club, there were loft rentals that suited the local bartenders and servers. Most of the places seemed safe enough, especially for a female all by her lonesome at this hour. Although, there were a couple of places she didn't care for. Ziggy's pool hall had been one of them. It mostly brought in a rougher crowd that usually involved the police before closing time. She knew this because her cousin Rodney was the manager. The Cat Club had been the other place she disliked. If it weren't for Kevin saying he'd meet her there, she would have never stepped foot in that particular bar in the first place. The clientele that hung out there easily stereotyped as members of the Vampire-Goth subculture, and not exactly her type. With a passion to help others and currently employed as an assistance program counselor for substance abuse, she stuck out like a sore thumb.

When she rounded the corner and walked past Biggy's Burgers, she got an uneasy feeling in the pit of her gut like someone was following her. As she turned to look, she saw that no one was there. She exhaled a sigh of relief when a noisy crowd of people suddenly walked out of the burger joint. With her nerves still intact, she hurried across the street toward Sunset. By the time she got on Richmond, she noticed it was unusually quiet. The street looked deserted, but her apartment complex was just a few more blocks away.

A thick fog hung in the air, but the streetlights overhead and the headlights from an occasional passing car made the visibility tolerable. She slowed when leering whistles caught her attention.

Don't look back, her inner voice warned her. *Keep your eyes forward and stay focused on getting home.*

Ignoring the obnoxious catcalls, she rolled her eyes and kept moving.

Then, to her surprise, two men hurriedly crossed the street and jogged up to her from behind. Quickly, she reached into her purse, searching for the Taser her uncle—who was a detective at the San Francisco Police Department—had given her a few months ago. It had been a gift for her birthday along with a container of pepper spray.

"What's a pretty girl like you doing out at this hour all alone?" the tall one said as he came up alongside her, his eyes trailing down her body and then back up again.

Her eyes rounded in fear but she kept them focused ahead, preparing to defend herself by any means if he made a move.

"Damn girl," the other guy said, his beady eyes focused on her hips. "You're fine as hell."

Not far down the street, Joseph stopped in his tracks when he caught sight of the two men ogling the blonde-haired girl he'd spotted in the bar. It appeared as though they were taunting her, and maybe contemplating on assaulting her.

With his hands fisted at his sides, Joseph stood back and watched as the tall guy circled her.

"How 'bout we give you a lift?" he asked, winking at his bug-eyed buddy. "Seriously, it's no trouble. Our car is just across the street." He held up his hands in question. "Whaddaya say, sweetheart?"

She ignored him and picked up her pace. *Where in the hell is that damn Taser?* Her hand continued to fumble aimlessly inside of her purse. Then, a knot formed at the back of her throat. It was at that moment she remembered she'd left the damn thing in her gym bag and the pepper spray at home. *Shit!*

"We are not going to just stand back," the Shadow said, *"and do nothing. She belongs to us."*

"It's too risky," Joseph said in a hushed voice. "Besides, there's two of them."

"But there's two of us," the Shadow pointed out.

"I don't know." Joseph furrowed his brows, contemplating the idea. "One of them could have a gun."

"Pussy!"

Desperate to drown out the Shadow's derogatory remark, Joseph closed his eyes and let out a deep breath.

Just as the girl was about to step onto a crosswalk, the tall creep grabbed her from behind.

Joseph's lids flipped back open at the sound of a high-pitched scream. The taller guy had his arms wrapped around the girl's waist and was dragging her backward. Although, she was putting up one hell of a fight, kicking and punching.

He managed to get her in a choke hold and roared in her ear, "Shut the fuck up, bitch!"

She choked as his arm tightened around her neck making it nearly impossible for her to breathe. He smelled like sweaty pits and a dirty ashtray. She felt her stomach churn as he dragged her off the sidewalk and to a dark alley. The other beady-eyed creep followed them as they took her deeper into the shadows. They pushed her up against a brick wall of a vacant building. The tall, foul-smelling guy held her in place by the throat while the beady-eyed guy pinned her wrists over her head with one hand and pressed them against the rough exterior of the building. As soon as the stinky one slipped his free hand underneath her blouse, she screamed. He slapped her hard, splitting her lip open.

"You scream one more time," the tall guy muttered, his breath filling her nose, reeking of cigarettes and alcohol, "and my buddy here will cut you."

When the guy with bulging eyes put a knife to her throat, she felt the sharp edge of the cold steel as it slightly pierced her skin.

"Are you going to keep that mouth of yours shut?"

She slowly nodded, averting her tear-stained eyes from the man that held a knife to her throat and to the one who stunk like he hadn't bathed in days.

"Good girl," the tall guy said as he leaned in and drew his tongue over her cheek. "Mmm," he purred deep in his throat. "You taste sweet."

She cringed and held back her gag reflex.

The other guy chuckled and lowered the blade. "I bet the rest of her tastes even sweeter."

"Stop wasting time, Joseph," the Shadow demanded. *"Kill them and take the girl."*

As though something had taken control of his body, Joseph's expression took the shape of a stone-cold killer. His handsome face twisted into a snarl, and he began to breathe in a strange rhythm. It was almost as if two people were inhaling and exhaling at the same time. Suddenly, he stopped blinking and the teal blue color along with the whites of his eyes turned as black as coal.

Before Joseph started forward, an outpouring of guttural sounds exploded from the thick veil of fog. It sounded like the growls coming from a wild animal or a rabid dog. Then, out of nowhere, something *big* moved at the speed of a blur and tackled the tall guy, knocking him off the girl and onto the ground.

Joseph's jaw dropped. "What the—" He could not believe what was transpiring right before his very eyes. How was this even possible?

No matter, he thought. Despite the nightmarish spectacle, Joseph refused to cower. Besides, he had the *Shadow* to give him strength and he did not frighten easily. Instead, he took a couple of steps back and hid in the shadows, watching in stunned disbelief as an enormous wolfish creature with dark matted fur tore at the man's throat in a snarling frenzy. The man's bloodcurdling screams lasted only a few seconds before he went still.

Paralyzed with fear, the girl screamed into the palm of her hand and fell to her knees.

It was a *werewolf* of some sort, Joseph realized, recalling the eerie stories he'd read from the institute's library. It was said that the immortal creatures had been once human until they'd been bitten and infected with the virus.

He couldn't believe what his eyes were telling him. The stories were *real.*

While the savage creature ripped and feasted on the man's flesh, the other girl's attacker turned to flee. As he ran, believing he could actually get away, something heavy with the speed of a moving train hit him from behind. As he toppled to the ground, he felt the weight of the ravenous creature on top of him, pinning him down.

"Please..." the beady-eyed guy called out, "...help—"

His call for help was cut off by the blunt force inflicted by the creature as it crushed the guy's skull. Blood coursed from every orifice of his face, pooling on the ground beneath him. His body twitched and convulsed, then finally went limp.

Throwing back its head, the wolfish fiend let out a thunderous roar.

With a bolt of adrenaline, the girl got to her feet and ran, her screams filling the alleyway.

To Joseph's surprise, the creature did not chase after her. Although it seemed inconceivable, he could have sworn that it was somehow here to protect her. *But why,* he wondered.

"What are you waiting for, Joseph?" the Shadow said, sounding impatient. *"Go after the girl."*